Praise for Stable Mates

'A great treat for readers who love their books jam-packed
with sexy men and horses.'
Bestselling author Fiona Walker

'Fans of Fiona Walker will love this book.'
ThatThingSheReads

'A delightful romp stuffed with fun, frolics and romance.'
BestChickLit

'Stable Mates is up there with Riders and Rivals.'
Comet Babes Books

'Move over Mr Grey, the Tippermere boys are in town!
Highly recommended.'
Brook Cottage Books

'A seductive fascinating novel. Mucking out the horses just
got sexy!'
Chicks That Read

ZARA STONELEY

I live in deepest Cheshire surrounded by horses, dogs, cats and amazing countryside. When I'm not visiting wine bars, artisan markets or admiring the scenery in sexy high heels or green wellies, I can be found in flip flops on the beach in Barcelona, or more likely sampling the tapas!

I write hot romance and bonkbusters. My most recent releases, 'Stable Mates' and 'Country Affairs', are fun romps through the Cheshire countryside and combine some of my greatest loves – horses, dogs, hot men and strong women (and not forgetting champagne and fast cars)!

Country Affairs

ZARA STONELEY

Harper*Impulse* an imprint of
HarperCollins*Publishers* Ltd
1 London Bridge Street
London SE1 9GF

www.harpercollins.co.uk

A Paperback Original 2015

First published in Great Britain in ebook format by Harper*Impulse* 2015

Cover images © Shutterstock.com

Zara Stoneley asserts the moral right
to be identified as the author of this work

A catalogue record for this book is
available from the British Library

ISBN: 9780008122829

This novel is entirely a work of fiction.
The names, characters and incidents portrayed in it are
the work of the author's imagination. Any resemblance to
actual persons, living or dead, events or localities is
entirely coincidental.

Automatically produced by Atomik ePublisher from Easypress

To Paul

Tippermere

Welcome to tranquil Tippermere, set deep in the Cheshire country-side. Home to Lords and Ladies, horsemen and farmers.

Set on the highest hill, keeping a close eye on the village and its inhabit-ants, lies Tipping House Estate. In pride of place is the grand Elizabethan style mansion, sweeping down in front of her are immaculate gardens, well-kept parkland and rolling acres that spread as far as the eye can see.

Follow the stream down to the flat below, and nestling between copses and lakes, you find Folly Lake Manor and the sprawling grounds of the bustling Equestrian Centre. The country lane in front wends its way between high hedges to the village green, the church and two village pubs. Then fans out into tributaries, follow them further and you find a small eventing yard, a scattering of country cottages and rambling working farms.

Take the road north eastwards, travel on a few short miles and soon the elegant village of Kitterly Heath unfolds before you - a village whose origins were recorded in the Domesday Book. At one end of the ancient high street a solid 14th Century church stands sentry, with an imposing school at the other, and all around sprawl the mansions old and new that house the rich and famous...

The Residents of Tippermere

Charlotte 'Lottie' Brinkley – *disorganised but loveable daughter of Billy. In line to inherit the Tipping House Estate and become the next Lady Stanthorpe.*

Rory Steel – *devilishly daring and sexy three day eventer, owner of a small eventing yard in Tippermere. Lottie's boyfriend.*

Tilly – *head of the terrier trio that accompany Rory everywhere.*

Todd Mitchell – *Lottie's ex. Australian surfer who abandoned her on the beach in Barcelona.*

William 'Billy' Brinkley - *Lottie's father. Former superstar show jumper, based at Folly Lake Equestrian Centre.*

Victoria 'Tiggy' Stafford – *wife of Billy. As friendly, shaggy and eternally optimistic as a spaniel.*

Lady Elizabeth Stanthorpe – *owner of Tipping House estate, lover of strong G&T's. Meddler and mischief maker. Lottie's gran, Dominic's mother.*

Bertie & Holmes – *Elizabeth's black Labradors.*

Philippa 'Pip' Keelan – *headline hunting journalist. Trim, sophisticated and slightly scary. Staunch supporter and ally of Lady Elizabeth.*

Mick O'Neal – *expert farrier, Irish charmer, dangerously attractive. Living with Pip.*

Dominic Stanthorpe - *dressage rider extraordinaire. Uncle to Lottie, son of Elizabeth, slightly bemused and frustrated by both. Husband to Amanda.*

Amanda Stanthorpe – *elegant and understated, delicate and demure. Owner of Folly Lake Manor and Equestrian Centre.*

Tom Strachan - *sexy ex-underwear model and single dad to Tab.*

Tabatha 'Tab' Strachan – *teenage daughter of Tom. Horse mad, smitten by Rory, but suitably unimpressed by most other things.*

David Simcock - *England goalkeeper, resident of the neighbouring Kitterly Heath.*

Sam – *partner of David. Lover of dogs, diamonds and designer delights.*

Chapter 1

Adrenalin rushes were one thing, but this was a step too far Todd Mitchell decided, as his mount, Merlin, charged between the ornate gates, his tail high with excitement.

Hanging on for dear life, he inadvertently dug his heels in hard, and with a squeal of delight half a ton of horseflesh took it as a red light to go faster, speeding at what had to be a life-threatening pace towards the stone fountain that somebody had inconveniently placed down the home straight of Folly Lake Manor some twenty years previously.

Coming to Tippermere to talk to Lottie was admirable, Todd told himself, as he hauled ineffectually on the reins. However, riding heroically to her rescue might not be such a good idea, particularly as his one and only experience in a saddle had involved a donkey and a beach.

'Christ almighty, are you trying to bleeding kill me?' Spotting the very large and very solid-looking ornate angel, which stood guard on the edge of the water feature, Todd grimaced and wondered if he had time to bail out. Wings spread like scimitars, she smiled smugly at him and he knew he was seconds away from a grisly death by decapitation or a good dunking. He shut his eyes.

The horse swerved alarmingly, nearly unseating him, the sharp point of an angel wing tugged at his left shoulder and as the smell

5

of freshly mown grass hit his nostrils he realised two things: he was alive and they'd changed course. With a relieved whoop and a grin Todd dared to look again.

As dinner-plate-sized hooves sent clods of earth in all directions, distant chatter floated across the air to them and the cob's large ears flickered. For a second his pace slowed and his rider shifted into a more secure position on his broad back. Then hearing familiar voices, and anticipating mints and carrots, Merlin stretched his neck and picking up speed again he thundered across the immaculate lawns that stretched before the imposing house, his mane and tail flying out behind him.

Todd ducked to avoid being garrotted by the colourful bunting that marked the entrance to a cordoned-off area and then realised he was being carried down the red carpet towards bride and groom at a completely inappropriate speed. 'Struth! Where are the anchors on this thing?'

It was the last thing that came out of his Aussie mouth before the horse took matters into his own hands and ground to a halt, expertly veering left at the last minute towards an attractive and to what he no doubt suspected was an edible flower arrangement.

Force of momentum kept Todd on his original trajectory and he would have landed in the Very Reverend Waterson's lap if a quick-thinking Rory hadn't dragged the shocked minister out of harm's way.

Tranquil was the word most often used to describe the village of Tippermere, and Folly Lake Manor was one of its most serene corners. Usually. And today's wedding, despite the celebrity status of the groom, had been planned as a quiet, family affair.

The assembled wedding guests, gathered on the lawns in front of a large marquee, watched open-mouthed as Todd rolled like an expert and got to his feet, brushing himself down as he went.

He straightened, six foot of muscle in jeans and open-necked shirt, topped by a shock of sun-bleached hair and a mud-spattered face and flashed his best grin at his shocked audience before spinning round to locate the man he'd been heading for.

'Mate.' He tipped a hand in the direction of his hat, which he'd actually lost a good few hundreds yard back along the way, then looked past the speechless vicar to the bemused bride and groom.

'Hell,' he took a step closer, 'if you'll pardon the language, Rev, but I never thought you wanted a bloody father figure, Lottie.'

Todd stared hard at the slightly tubby figure, who had been having his cravat straightened by a flustered Lottie, and shook his head. He'd decided quite rashly that it was his job to save her from whatever kind of matrimonial harmony she thought she was heading for, but it had occurred to him on the way over that he might have made a mistake (although once the horse had started to gallop, changing his mind hadn't been an option). Standing here now, seeing her husband-to-be, he just knew he was doing the right thing. Whatever the man had to offer, Lottie deserved better. And younger. And preferably with more hair. 'No way, Lots. Come on, hold your horses! You can't be serious about marrying a guy like him?' He raised his eyebrows and looked at the girl he'd shared a summer of love and lust with, then glanced back at the man beside her. 'No offence, mate, but I bloody object, or whatever it is you're supposed to say.'

Charlotte 'Lottie' Brinkley let go of the silk cravat, which she'd been clutching a little too firmly.

'I can't be serious? Father figure?' She put her hands on her hips. 'He IS my bloody father, you great...' Oaf? Moron? Most unwelcome uninvited guest in the universe?

Of all the people that could have turned up at the wedding, the one person who had not been on the horizon (in an actual or metaphorical sense), as far as Lottie was concerned, was Todd. Her ex. As in very ex. As in the very last person she ever expected, or wanted, to see again. Todd was supposed to be riding the waves on the other side of the world, which was just fine by her. 'And it's you who should be holding your horse.' She nodded in the direction of Merlin, who, sensing freedom, was heading straight for the refreshment tent. 'Horses are not like surf boards you know. You can't just dump them.'

Todd ignored the instruction, not quite realising the trail of destruction the large horse could cause when he set his mind to it. 'Father? Isn't there a law against that?'

'Object to what? What bloody law? Who the—' Billy Brinkley, Olympic-medal-winning show jumper, and the 'bloody father', raised an eyebrow and looked at the tall, blond man who had just spectacularly interrupted his wedding.

He'd been about to add a particularly strong swear word, but out of the corner of his eye had seen the vicar, who was turning a whiter shade of pale, and toned it down. 'Hell' didn't seem an appropriate word either, in the circumstances.

'I'm not marrying him, you idiot.' Lottie, tried to resist the smile that was tugging at her insides, but she knew any minute now she'd lose the battle.

'So who the hell are you marrying?' Todd looked puzzled. Which made it even funnier.

'Do you know this Australian chap, Charlotte darling? I must say I can understand now why you haven't rushed to marry Rory.' Lottie groaned and covered her face with her hands as Lady Elizabeth Stanthorpe's imperious tone carried clearly over the by-now murmuring guests. Explaining this to her father was one thing, but to her aristocratic grandmother? 'I can imagine he's very impressive without his clothes on. Reminds me of a gardener we once had.'

A chuckle spread through the guests like a Mexican wave.

'I couldn't give a monkeys what he looks like without clothes on. We're supposed to be holding a bloody wedding ceremony. Mine! If he's not got an invite he can shove off.' Billy, determined to regain control, but used to the chaos that seemed to follow his daughter around, folded his arms and stared at Lottie. 'Well, has he?'

Lottie didn't hear. Oh God, if Todd had to reappear in her life, why did he have to choose right now? Right now was her father's wedding day and everybody in Tippermere was there. And all of their family. And, of course, Rory Steel, top eventer – the man who warmed her bed and her heart. And who, after rescuing the vicar from Merlin's hooves, had stood by quietly watching.

This morning, as she'd pinned up the bunting and straightened the chairs in the early- morning sunshine, she'd actually known for the first time that everything would work out fine. Mick, farrier and friend, had been right; when she'd returned to Tippermere her feet had brought her back to where her heart was. Here, with Rory, with her family, friends and the wonderful estate that one day would be her responsibility. She loved it and she finally knew with all her heart where she belonged. And she knew she could do this; inherit Tipping House and make her family proud of her.

She knew that she could never, ever be like her autocratic, to-the-manor-born, gran, and she was fairly sure she would never live up to the promise of her elegant mother, Alexa. But she would do it her way, and do the very best she could for the place that she truly loved.

Lottie had long ago concluded that she had inherited the happy-go-lucky side of her mother, but her looks and organisational abilities were all down to her father's side of the family. Not that most of the residents of Tippermere would have agreed with her disparaging view. Lottie may not have been the whirlwind force of nature her mother, Alexa, had been, but she was kinder, gentler and her beauty shone through just as brightly. With her big green eyes, long legs, shapely body and honest, open face Lottie was as beguiling as her mother had been wild, impulsive and elusive. The mischievous, but strangely vulnerable, Alexa had enchanted all, and Billy had feared what her future as Lady of the Manor would have done to her. But Lottie, with her father's stubborn, down-to-earth

9

streak was different. Billy knew that his daughter could do this, and as each day passed he'd seen the growing certainty in her. The confidence. And he saw the same love for the place shine from her eyes as it had from her mother's. There was no doubt in his mind that his scatty daughter was the true heir of Tipping House and that the Stanthorpe determination ran deep in her veins. He could also see the same glint of determination as she looked at the man standing in front of her.

Lottie glared at Todd, who she hadn't seen since he'd been marched off a Barcelona beach and out of her life. It might not have actually been that long ago, but it seemed to have happened in a different lifetime now. Like some crazy adventure that had happened to somebody else, before she'd realised what really mattered to her. This place and these people, not some footloose and fancy-free Australian, who just wanted to share a beer and a laugh.

She shot a warning glance at Elizabeth, her grandmother, which she knew wouldn't help at all, tried not to let Billy catch her eye as she just knew that was asking for trouble, then glanced anxiously over at Rory.

It looked like a massive penny had just dropped with a horrendous clang. He frowned, his hands tightening into fists at his sides and took a step forward.

It was just at this moment that a panting Tabatha arrived, slightly pink in the face, and made a grab for her horse just as he made his way into the marquee.

When her ex-model father Tom Strachan had made the decision to retire to the countryside, dragging his reluctant teenage daughter with him, Tab had been distraught. He had ruined her life.

Despite the fact that she was going through a goth phase, she'd envisaged a future of bright city lights, nightclubs and fashion ahead. Not a life of being stuck in the sticks to stagnate with old farmers and smelly sheep.

Discovering that several of her equestrian heroes lived on the doorstep had slightly mollified Tab, and being allowed to groom for Billy (who had superstar status, but let's face it, was a bit over the hill) and Rory (who was the sexiest eventer on the planet, but still insisted on hanging out with the far from glamorous Lottie, unfortunately) had almost been enough to make her break out of her teenage sulk. She'd grudgingly (but not openly) admitted that Tippermere might be an okay type of place.

But when the amazingly attractive and very out of place stranger had arrived on the yard at Folly Lake Equestrian Centre an hour earlier, just as she was untacking Merlin, she decided there might be a God after all. He was gorgeous, he was fit, fun and with an accent to die for.

So when he'd vaulted on to the horse's back, asked for directions to the wedding and set off across the field towards the manor, she was too busy staring to tell him that Merlin bareback might be a death wish. But he probably wouldn't have cared. He was amazing. She was awestruck. She was finally going to get a shag.

Tab, who now had a firm grip on her horse, edged back closer to the proceedings, sensing that Todd's no doubt dramatic entrance was only the start. Merlin, less entranced, tugged, nearly pulling her arm out of its socket. 'Okay, okay.' She passed him one of the mints she kept in her pocket for emergencies. No way was she going yet – things looked far too interesting here.

A red-faced Lottie was staring at Todd as if she knew the blond sex god intimately. Which was bloody typical, thought Tab, and would normally have annoyed her more, except she couldn't see how she could lose. Lottie had Rory, which left Todd free for her (and she could still feel the smacker of a kiss he'd given her before leaping onto Merlin – which had to mean something). But if it turned out that there really had been something going on between Lottie and Todd, then surely Rory would be keen to take advantage of her shoulder to cry on?

She helped herself to one of the mints and passed another one on to Merlin, who was nudging her shoulder impatiently.

'Well, if it isn't Todd the tosser himself.' Tab grimaced, it sounded as though Pip (who'd emerged from the wedding crowd with folded arms) knew him as well.

Tab stared at the immaculately turned-out journalist with her perfect blond bob. The older girl oozed a kind of professional polish and city know-how, and Tab still hadn't quite decided if she admired her, envied her or liked her. She'd hated Pip at the start. The way she'd zoomed in on her father, Tom, then had bedded him had been so predictable, so bloody boring. But then they'd actually become kind of buddies when she'd shown her the ropes at Rory's yard. And now it turned out even *she* knew the Australian sex god. Although that figured; Pip knew everybody and everything. And had tried them out between the sheets probably – the 'everybody' not the 'everything'.

Great, Tab frowned, somebody interesting turns up and she was the only one who hadn't slept with him. Which was the story of her life at the moment. One day they'd stop treating her as Tom's kid and realise she actually wanted to ride more than bloody horses.

'Todd.' Rory's voice broke into her thoughts, and from the sound of it he didn't actually know him, it was more a statement of intent, possibly murderous, which could make things interesting but could completely screw up her plans. On no account was Rory going to be allowed to kill him, or hound him out of Tippermere. Not yet, please God! Tab, who had resolutely refused to even pretend to pray since the day she'd been born, decided that if this worked out she would make up for it.

'Watcha mate.' Todd, oblivious to the danger, grinned in Rory's direction and was obviously impressed with the mark he'd left on his audience. He winked at Pip. 'Long time no see. Didn't recognise you with your clothes on.'

'Don't you "watcha mate" me,' Rory was probably the only one who missed the murmur that was spreading through the crowd.

'You're the waste of space that dumped Lottie on that Spanish beach, aren't you? Well?'

Lottie squirmed as the heat rushed into her face.

'Well, to be fair, I wouldn't exactly say "dumped", mate.' Some of the bravado left his voice as he registered the look on Rory's face. 'It was just one of those things.'

'I'll show you what's fair, come here, you Aussie git.'

As Rory lunged, Todd decided not to come or hang about. He made a dash for it, straight towards the by-now bored Merlin, who had a half-eaten red gladioli hanging from his mouth. Making a split-second decision that he was sure he'd regret later, Todd vaulted on to the startled horses back before he, or Tab, had time to object.

Rory glanced around, his face set, spotted the quad bike at the side of the marquee and made a dash for it.

'Jeez, fella, what is your problem?' Not waiting for an answer, Todd dug his heels in and grabbed a handful of mane as Merlin plunged forwards. The horse rocketed back across the lawn, happily obliging his rider, with Rory in hot pursuit, waving a fist and yelling what everybody took to be obscenities.

'Think they'll be back?' Pip grinned, this was turning out to be far more entertaining than she could have possibly imagined. And bringing a photographer along with her had definitely been a worthwhile investment. She could picture the newspaper headlines now.

Lottie Brinkley shut her eyes and a new image of Todd swam into her vision. Todd the last time she'd seen him – his bronzed body naked apart from a pair of swimming trunks, his impressive six-pack nicely oiled and the promise of a good night in shining from his eyes.

Until the dream had been demolished by a bevy of Spanish policeman all dressed in black, who'd surrounded them and waved a warrant.

Chapter 2

Apart from the humiliation of having to watch her lover being marched across the sand away from her, what had really bothered Lottie on the beach that day was that she hadn't even been wearing a decent bikini.

It was one thing Gran bringing her up with the belief that one should always wear decent knickers, just in case one was run over, but whoever warned you that your beachwear should be up to the scrutiny of a half a dozen very sexy members of the Spanish Mossos?

If it hadn't been for her new best buddy, Pip, who had helped her cram everything into her rucksack, booked emergency plane tickets and escorted her all the way back to Tippermere, Lottie wasn't sure what would have happened next in her life.

Meeting journalist Pip Keelan in Barcelona had been a godsend. She was all the things Lottie wasn't – organised and logical in everything, including her love life. The fact that she'd then actually decided to hang around and adopt Lottie's home village as her own, and then proceeded to bring her own brand of fun and mayhem to Tippermere life was a source of constant amazement.

It seemed that for Pip country life was the perfect antidote to the city living that had started to turn stale, and the fit men were a bonus. And the fact that she was semi shacked-up with the fittest farrier for miles appeared to suit her fine.

'He is so, so fit. How come you know so many hot men, Lot's?' Tabatha's wistful tone brought Lottie back to the present and she glanced at the teenager, who was gazing longingly after her rapidly disappearing horse and the careering quad bike. Then her gaze fixed on Rory, who was alternating between waving his fist and frantically grabbing at the handlebars as he rocketed off course.

'I'm not sure this lawn will ever be the same again.' Amanda Stanthorpe, owner of all she surveyed, joined them, but seemed more preoccupied with what had been an immaculate expanse of green, than the cause of the destruction.

Agreeing to host the wedding at Folly Lake Manor had seemed the neighbourly thing to do, even if she did like everything neat and tidy. But Amanda did truly love the people she'd met in Tippermere and Kitterly Heath, and this had seemed the perfect way to thank them for everything they'd done for her.

After the death of her billionaire husband, Marcus, they had made her feel part of the community and, in fact, had made her feel worth something again. From the loveable Lottie and daredevil Rory to the scheming Elizabeth. From the unprincipled Pip and the brooding Mick, to the gruff Billy and charming Tiggy, and from the perfectly handsome Tom to his outwardly difficult, but inwardly, sweet daughter, Tab, they were all like the family she wished she'd had.

Even the glamorous, but warm-hearted and generous Sam and her charming footballer husband had supported her.

And, of course, there was dear, reserved and very proper Dominic. Her husband. She loved them all, but she loved him most of all.

And there was the crux of the matter, the main reason for hosting the wedding. It was a generous gesture of goodwill from Dominic, her husband, towards Billy Brinkley, the groom. Mending fences, building bridges.

Dominic and Billy had been childhood friends, but affection had turned to hatred after Alexandra, Lottie's mother, had died in a tragic accident. Both men had outwardly blamed each other, but inwardly carried a burden of guilt for something that neither was actually responsible for. And it had taken Lottie and her grand-mother, Lady Elizabeth, to unravel the puzzle and make them see sense. Make them see that neither was to blame for the death of Alexa – Dominic's sister, Billy's wife, Lottie's mother. Force them to acknowledge that hate and disapproval wouldn't bring her back.

Amanda sighed as all of a sudden the city girl in her, who she'd hoped had been quashed down, rose up in anguish. She loved Lottie, truly adored her, but the girl seemed doomed to a life of chaos and untidy disorder. And cavorting on horses was just not what she'd expected at this wedding, well at any wedding. Much as she'd tried to involve herself in equestrian life and appreciate the beauty of the massive animals, surely horses belonged in fields?

'Are we getting on with this bloody ceremony? I need a beer.' Billy's blunt tones rang out into the shocked silence.

'Sorry, Dad.' Lottie gnawed on her bottom lip anxiously. It was very heroic of Rory to go after Todd like this. In fact, it was one of the most romantic things he'd ever done, but what if he caught him? 'Er – doesn't Rory have the wedding rings, though?'

Billy ruffled his hand through his hair and winked at his bemused bride, Tiggy, who was waiting as patiently as the spaniel that was sitting beside her, a red ribbon tied to its collar in honour of the occasion. 'You can always rely on our Lottie to make sure the occasion is a bit different, can't you? Come on, love, let's just get on with it, shall we? The lad will be back soon enough.'

'But he's your best man.' Lottie could easily see the day she'd so carefully planned (well the day she'd done her best to sort out, and which Pip, Sam and Amanda had tactfully prompted her about when she'd forgotten things), ending up in a state of chaos. Everybody was looking at her expectantly, as the man she loved disappeared into the distance in hot pursuit of her bigamist ex.

She didn't know whether to be pleased that Rory seemed intent on upholding her honour and wreaking revenge on her behalf, or upset that at her first event as Lady of the Manor to be (or should that be Lady in Waiting?) he'd abandoned his duties as best man and disappeared in pursuit of a horse. Going after them wasn't an option, was it?

'I think I'll go after my horse and, er, check everybody is okay.' Tab observed, but nobody was listening.

'He'll be back in time for the beer, love. Never known Rory to miss a party. Right oh.' Billy rubbed his hands together and nodded at the vicar, who after a little hesitation decided to carry on where he'd left off. Lottie glanced back in the direction of the Equestrian Centre, which was where Merlin (irrespective of any rider intentions) was heading, then turned her attention back to her father. She was, after all, supposed to be responsible for arranging his marriage to the scatty Tiggy Stafford. And up until this point in the ceremony it had been going reasonably well, considering.

Organisation wasn't her strong point, unless it involved horses and getting ready for a competition. That she could handle brilliantly, but managing events was different altogether, and it was so easy to get distracted. But she'd done this because she knew she had to. Discovering that she was the rightful heir to Tipping House Estate, not Uncle Dominic as she'd always assumed, had been a bit of a shock. Well, it had been a major shock.

It had all seemed a bit unreal, until Dom and Amanda had married, and he'd had less time for his caretaking duties. She had to get ready to take over the reins, he'd said (repeatedly, in his stern looking-down-his-aristocratic-nose way). To be fair, he'd spent an awful lot of time encouraging and helping her and she wanted to take over. She really did. She was far too independent to be on a lead rein and even before Lady Stanthorpe had dropped the bombshell, she'd known she belonged here. This place was part of her, she loved every shabby inch of it, and she really thought that Uncle Dominic was being a bit too much of a fussy mother hen. So she'd been determined to prove to him, and to herself, that she was more than capable of being Lady of the Manor. Of organising stuff. And organising her father's wedding had seemed a perfect opportunity. And once Uncle Dom saw how brilliant she was, maybe he'd stop looking over her shoulder and trust her.

She sighed. Well, that had been the plan. And it had been going splendidly. Until Todd had arrived. A few months ago she might actually have been pleased to see him, but things were different now. She was different – her life had moved on.

'Certainly. Right, I er…' The Very Reverend Waterson straightened his dog collar and cleared his throat, waiting for the guests to settle. 'Ah, yes, we were, hmm...'

Lottie stared at the vicar. He actually seemed to be enjoying himself, which was a first. Maybe becoming a Very Reverend, as opposed to a Reverend, had cheered him up. Promotion was good for everybody, she supposed, even if you were never actually going to get the top job in his line of work.

'If any of you can show just cause why they may not be lawfully wed, speak now or else forever hold your peace.' He smiled. Paused. 'I charge you both, here in the pre—'

'I do.' Tiggy spoke for the first time, her soft voice singing out into the near silence with an unusual clarity. 'Oops, I mean, I can.' She giggled. 'Show just thingy. Cause. I can show just cause why we can't be, er, lawfully wed.'

For the second time that day there was a gasp of horror. Lottie looked in alarm at her father and tried to ignore the wicked delight on her grandmother, Elizabeth's, face.

'What? But. You can't. I. Why?' Lottie ran out of words. How could the bride have an objection? She wasn't that up on weddings, but she had a damned good idea that any objections were supposed to come from the guests not the bride or groom. And she'd always thought Tiggy was so nice and harmless. 'Dad?' She made a grab for his arm, not quite sure what she was going to do next.

Billy guffawed, which wasn't right. 'She can't, because she's already married.'

All eyes swivelled from Billy to Tiggy and back again, as Lottie's hands flew to her mouth. It was her worst nightmare.

'Oh my God. Not her as well.'

Chapter 3

Lottie was on her second glass of bubbly and feeling slightly disorientated by the time Billy had finished the speeches, filling in for his AWOL best man, Rory, last seen riding his mechanical charger into the distance.

So far the day hadn't gone to plan at all, she thought, as she gazed across the lawn towards Folly Lake Equestrian Centre, home to her father and his new bride.

She had been totally confused when Tiggy had dropped her bombshell, mainly because they both looked happy, and surely you were supposed to be devastated (or at least seriously upset) if it turns out your future forever person was on the verge of becoming a bigamist? She certainly had been when she'd found out that Todd had two weddings but no divorces to his name. I mean, she hadn't exactly been planning on marrying him herself, but it was still the type of news that came as a bit of a shock.

So, it had been a toss-up. Did she burst into tears because she'd gone to all this bloody trouble organising this wonderful day for nothing? Did she have a 'life is so unfair' tantrum? Or did she follow Rory and Todd's example and do a runner?

She'd opened her mouth, but nothing had come out. Which was when Billy had put a gentle hand on her shoulder. 'To me. She's already married to me, Lottie. Sorry love,' he didn't look that sorry, in fact he looked very pleased with himself, 'but we got married last month when we were away. Didn't want to hang around any longer and, er,' he gave her an apologetic look, 'we didn't know if you'd pull this off. So, it's like a blessing, isn't it Rev?' He'd glanced at the vicar who nodded and smiled with, Lottie thought, a certain un-reverential smugness.

The fact that even the bloody vicar was in on it seemed so unfair, thought Lottie, why was she always the last to know everything?

But her Dad had looked so pleased with himself it was hard to be ratty with him, and he'd even given her a brief bear hug, which was almost unheard of. 'And it's a bloody good excuse for a party as well, of course. Right then, let's get this wound up and get on the razz.' He'd hugged Tiggy in close and there was a collective gasp of relief and outbreak of laughter from the crowd, who'd agreed that this topped even the best of the Brinkley's previous disorganised events.

And talking of bigamists, which for a brief moment it had looked like her new step-mother had been in danger of becoming, Todd had almost slipped Lottie's mind. 'Do you think he's okay, Pip?'

Pip, who was in the process of grabbing a bottle of bubbly from a passing waiter, topped up their glasses, resisted the man's attempts to reclaim the bottle, and followed the line of Lottie's gaze. It wasn't hard to see where Todd and Merlin had been, and Rory had followed. 'Who, the beach bum?'

'No, Rory, silly.'

'I wouldn't like to say who's the fittest. Who do you reckon has the most stamina?' Pip raised an eyebrow and Lottie hoped she hadn't gone the shade of beetroot she normally did when asked questions like that.

'Rory, of course.'

'Of course.'

'You never were very keen on Todd, were you?'

'I didn't need to be, he had it covered.'

'That's a bit mean. He was quite nice, really, until…'

'Lottie that man spent more time looking in the mirror than both of us put together when we were in Barcelona. Hey, look. Is that them coming back?'

'Crumbs, I'm drunker than I thought. I knew I should have eaten something, but I was frightened I'd bust out of my dress.' Lottie squinted, and when that didn't help she tried covering one eye, but she was definitely seeing double, or triple. There were only two men (two was good, they hadn't killed each other) and one girl (that had to be Tab), but several…

'Why've they brought all those horses?' Pip said the words Lottie hadn't dared, in case she actually was imagining it.

'Thank heavens for that.'

'What do you mean, "thank heavens for that"? You don't bring horses to wedding receptions. Amanda was upset enough with just the one. She'll have a pink fit if she sees this lot.'

'I thought I was seeing things.' Lottie giggled with relief. 'I didn't mean thank heavens for all the horses.'

'Charlotte, what on earth is Rupert doing now?'

The giggles froze in her throat when she realised her gran was breathing down her neck. Lady Elizabeth Stanthorpe had sneaked up in her usual manner and was now peering across the lawn at the rapidly approaching group. 'And who is that fellow with him and young Tabatha? He doesn't look like a groom. The man hasn't got a clue what he's doing. Terrible hands and just look at that seat! Looks like he's about to come off the horse.'

Lottie sighed. For some reason of her own Elizabeth insisted on calling Rory by anything but his actual name, usually to his face. She was pretty sure her gran was actually fond of Rory (just as she was fond of Billy, who had married her late daughter and given her her only grandchild, Lottie), but for some reason she seemed determined not to acknowledge the fact. And Rory, just like Billy before him, refused to rise to the bait. Maybe it was some weird kind of test.

'That's the Australian.' Pip supplied helpfully, and Elizabeth grunted and looked again.

'I thought William told him to shove off?'

'I do love the way you say that.' Pip grinned. 'Shove orff.'

'I wish he had.' Lottie muttered, wondering why on earth they'd all come back.

Rory and his entourage came to a halt several feet away, and this time Todd wobbled but he didn't fall off.

'How's it going, Lots?' All grins. The man she never thought she'd see again. She peered more closely. She'd expected to see at least some signs of a fight or a minor scuffle, or at the very least like Rory had told him off.

'Who exactly is that man, Charlotte?'

Lottie brushed the feathers, once jaunty but now drooping sadly from Elizabeth's hat, out of her face.

'That man,' Pip was enjoying herself, 'is Todd, and he's the reason Lottie came home.'

'Well, at least he has some uses.' Elizabeth sniffed dismissively and turned her attentions to Rory. 'And what are you up to Richard?'

'We decided to have a competition. Like a duel but without the death.'

'A duel?' Elizabeth had really perked up now, thought Lottie, unlike the feathers.

Rory shrugged and grinned. 'Well not exactly a duel. We just thought this party needed livening up, and old Todd here is game.'

Lottie looked at 'old Todd' and back to Rory. She didn't like the sound of this at all. Well, it was good that they didn't actually seem at loggerheads. In fact Rory seemed to have ditched the idea of protecting her honour, which she had to admit miffed her slightly. 'Not a duel? You don't want to kill him then?'

'Kill him?'

23

'I thought that's why you were chasing him.'

'Oh that. Well, I ran out of petrol and he fell off and we couldn't be arsed to kill each other.' He slid off his horse, landing at her feet and gave her a smacker of a kiss, which mollified her a little bit. 'He explained everything, darling.'

'He did?'

'He's sorry, it was just a bit of a cock-up. I think I might have overreacted a bit when I chased him.' He grinned sheepishly. 'Thought he wanted to whisk you away, but he only came to apologise.'

'A cock-up?' Lottie stared. She wasn't sure if it was good that Rory and Todd had decided they were buddies, or bad that she was the last one to get the explanation, as per normal. And the apology. She looked at Todd.

'He's spot on, Lots. I mean, I didn't exactly have time to say goodbye or anything before they bundled me on the plane, did I? But it was all a misunderstanding, mate.'

'The horses Robert?' Elizabeth tapped her foot impatiently and looked disapprovingly at Todd, who wisely shut up.

'Tippermere against the rest of the world. Once I've had a drink, that is.' He nodded in Todd's direction. 'And you better have one too. Looks like we've some catching up to do.'

'Whatever you say, mate. How do I get off this thing?'

It was at this point that Lottie realised the wedding was at a turning point, and there was absolutely nothing she could do about it. Or about getting an explanation from Todd.

Her father, Billy, Uncle Dom and several of the other guests had already been drawn by the sight of the horses and the competitive spirit was kicking in faster than the alcoholic kind.

'It's you,' Rory nodded towards Billy, 'me and Dom against him,' Todd got a look, 'Mick and' he looked round, searching the expectant faces for a suitable outsider.

'And me.' Tabatha, who had spent most of the afternoon chasing after the elusive Todd and Merlin finally spotted her chance. 'Don't you dare say I can't.'

Rory chuckled. 'If Todd's happy with you, then it's fine by me.' Todd looked more than happy. In fact, the look on his face was one Lottie remembered well.

'But you can't.'

Tab scowled and Lottie hastily qualified the statement. 'None of you can. I mean, I mean…'

'Now, now Charlotte. No harm in a bit of fun.' Elizabeth had a twinkle in her eye and stiffness in her backbone that Lottie hadn't seen in a while.

'But, they're going to…' She wasn't exactly sure what they were going to do, but if it involved horses and teams it wasn't the type of thing you normally saw at a wedding reception. Lottie looked around wildly for inspiration. 'Amanda won't like it.'

She glanced out of the corner of her eye at her Uncle Dominic. It was what Dom thought about it all that she was more bothered about. She had been determined to impress him today, and not with her horsemanship skills.

They'd agreed that she would take the day-to-day management of the Tipping House Estate off his hands, so that he could spend more time with Amanda, and so that when the day came for her grandmother to step down (although it was a bit like waiting for the Queen to abdicate), she'd be ready to become the next Lady Stanthorpe.

The list of 'things that needed taking care of' was a bit like an Ikea catalogue: very large, very varied and very difficult to prioritise, but with the help of Dom she'd drawn up a plan of attack. And raising money to repair the roof was item number one. Mainly because, as Dom pointed out, if the roof gave way then the list would get considerably longer. And she really didn't want that.

Her father's wedding would showcase her organisational skills. Well, that had been the plan. And Rory was about to wreck it.

'Nonsense, Amanda's up for it.' He gave her a hug.

'And we have to get up early.' She really had wanted to get up with a clear head so that she could go through the accounts her uncle had given her, and prove that not only was she an organisational whizz, but that she was the image of efficiency. And then he'd stop fussing and leave her to it.

And Rory had promised to do whatever was needed to help her out. In fact she had been hoping that he'd help her with one of the horses before breakfast, which he'd enjoy. Then he'd hardly notice when they moved onto looking at accounts, which he hated. Rory was the type of man who shoved bills in drawers and then conveniently forgot about them. Unless they were related to horse feed, of course.

With the wedding plans and all the little jobs she seemed to have taken on at Tipping House she had found it harder and harder to find time to ride with Rory. And she missed it.

'Right,' he smacked her bum, 'that's settled, let's get the party started.'

'But Rory, we do need to get up in the morn—' It wasn't that she didn't want a bit of fun, it was just that when Rory had one of his ideas it never ended in an early night and sobriety.

'This is going to be a wedding to remember, darling.' He kissed the tip of her nose. 'You've done a brilliant job.' His lips moved down to her mouth. 'Have I told you how gorgeous you look in that tight dress? I can't wait to rip it off. Right, back in a bit.'

Seeing Todd again had been a nasty shock to Lottie's system. One of the trickier aspects was that she couldn't remember for the life of her exactly what she'd told Rory about the brief hiatus in their relationship, when she'd set off on her world tour to discover herself. And instead discovered Todd. Which had been quite a nice distraction until the police had turned up, of course.

'Get me another drink, Charlotte dear, and do stop looking like a wet weekend. It's your father's wedding day, well his party, at least. And there's no point in moping over that man. I'm not surprised he abandoned you, you're not exactly his type, are you?'

Lottie took the empty glass that Elizabeth was pressing into her hand without thinking. 'He's very pretty, but totally irresponsible, I'd say from the look of him.' She stared totally unselfconsciously at Todd. 'How many wives did the man have?'

'I don't know. Why don't you ask him, Gran?'

'I might do that. Somebody needs to stop him pawing young Tabatha. No idea of how to behave. No wonder the Spanish deported him.'

Lottie decided not to point out the obvious, that it was actually Tab who was doing the pawing, and that she was plenty old enough to look after herself these days.

'Chop, chop dear. And do make sure it's a double gin, or shall I ask Roger to get it?'

'You know very well his name's Rory.'

Rory was oblivious to the conversation. After tethering the horses to the pegs that held the marquee in place (which seemed a bit of a dodgy idea to Lottie), he was getting down to the serious business of planning the competition (on the previously pristine white tablecloth) and drinking. Which left Lottie with the job of getting another drink for her gran and wondering what the hell Todd was doing in Cheshire, well even in the UK, at all. Obviously they didn't have long prison sentences for bigamy, well not long enough, or he'd just charmed his way out early.

***

Billy Brinkley was used to competing at the Olympia Horse Show, which always took place indoors and was guaranteed to be big, noisy and involve fancy dress and night-time events. And so were his horses. At the sight of strobing disco lights (somebody's vain attempt to keep the party on track) his favourite bay stallion pricked his ears and got ready to party.

Perched bareback on top of his horse, still in his wedding finery (but minus the top hat), Billy couldn't believe his luck. Despite being determined to make an honest woman of Victoria 'Tiggy' Stafford, the word 'wedding' had initially made his hands clammier than they'd ever been when he'd been about to represent his country at the Olympic Games. But Tiggy knew him so well and her suggestion to quietly marry in advance with the minimum of fuss so they could enjoy the occasion, followed by this unexpected competition, made it the perfect day. He winked at Tiggy, who he really did adore, then glanced back at Rory, gathering his reins up as he did so. 'Keep the flowers on my right, champagne bottles to the left, eh?'

Rory gave the thumbs-up then grinned as his chestnut mare, Flash, who stoically refused to mature and settle, but retained the spirit she'd shown as a yearling, reacted in her normal aghast manner when a rider waved their hands about unexpectedly. She kicked out backwards, her heels narrowly missing the top tier of the wedding cake, before throwing in a buck and squeal for good measure. Todd visibly paled beneath his perma-tan. In fact, from where Lottie was standing he looking more a translucent shade of green than brown.

'Here.' Tab passed him a bottle of whiskey, her fingers touching his for a second longer than was actually necessary, as far as Lottie could tell.

The course that Rory had designed was interesting, to say the least. It involved jumping over several tables still laden with glasses and plates, before exiting the marque and re-entering it at the back. The horse and rider then had to clear a row of chairs and a table, followed by the final hurdle, which was the stand that now held the one remaining layer of wedding cake. A swift left turn then took the rider along the front of the bar, where the challenge was to grab a champagne bottle and take a swig before exiting the marquee for the final time.

Rory had insisted that Todd ride Merlin, as they'd bonded. And to be fair, he was the only horse that the poor man had a chance of sticking on.

'Go Billy.' Rory waved a piece of the bunting, which acted as a starting flag. Flash half-reared as the scrap of cloth whizzed past her eye, and then went swiftly into reverse and nearly cannoned into the solid bulk that was Merlin, who was unperturbed and looking around lazily for something to eat.

Billy went, the stallion flying into canter from a standing start like the old pro he was. They nearly took Elizabeth's hat off when they cornered a bit too sharply, getting dangerously close to the guests, who'd wisely abandoned the main tables. Amanda covered her eyes and the wedding cake trembled alarmingly, but it was a clear round for Tippermere.

Bending down, Billy grabbed the grinning Tiggy, who screamed as he swung her onto the horse behind him.

Tab giggled and forgot her gothness for a second, and the fact she had a short skirt on. 'I'm next, aren't I? Rory, am I next?' Getting no answer from Rory, who was preoccupied trying to control Flash, who had gone into a spin, she turned to Mick, who, true to form, had no such problems with his own horse, which was standing patiently behind him, as though jumping wedding cakes in a marquee was an everyday occurrence.

'You are, treasure. Go show these Tippermereians what proper riding is.'

'Will you hold Merlin for me? He's totally ignoring Todd.'

'Anything for you, my darling.' Lottie watched as Mick O'Neal reached out with his spare hand, the other holding a large chunk of wedding cake, to take over the horse-holding duties.

If she hadn't known better, she would have said Rory's farrier had been avoiding her lately, but that was just her being stupid. He was busy and he was seeing Pip, and she was happy for both of them. But it had seemed quiet since he'd moved out of their yard and into Pip's cottage. She did miss the chats they used to have, and his dark, slightly brooding, presence that simultaneously excited and unnerved her a little. And the calm way he assured her she could do anything, and the way he watched her with those dark eyes…

Well, thinking about it, it was probably good that he wasn't around as much these days. Being excited by a strange man, well a man who wasn't Rory, wasn't right at all.

Lottie supressed a sigh. She had loved riding out with him, he made her feel supremely safe and gave her a confidence she'd never felt before. With Mick by her side she'd felt like she could do anything: ride any horse, jump any jump, which was too weird for words as she hardly knew the man.

It was probably just because he was good with horses and she admired him. He was calm and steady – that was all. The fact that his Irish brogue gave her goose bumps, and when he took his shirt off to work she couldn't resist a peek, was beside the point.

He caught her eye, but didn't wink as she expected, just stared with those searching eyes that seemed to see far too much. Lottie felt the heat rush to her cheeks; the last thing she needed was a man who could read her jumbled-up mind.

Luckily a shout of encouragement from Todd to Tabatha broke the spell and Merlin, thinking he was missing out on something, stamped on Mick's foot. Mick swore, dropped his cake and Lottie forgot all about his mind-reading abilities and giggled.

Ignoring all offers of a leg-up, Tab leapt from one of the tables onto the back of one of Billy's quieter mounts and, gathering up the reins, took off at a canter, her skirt flying up and treating the audience to the sight of some alarmingly pink knickers.

'I thought she always dressed head to foot in black?' Pip nudged Lottie, who by now had given up all pretence of trying to organise anyone or anything. Now that it was obvious she had no say in the matter, her only regret was that her figure-hugging dress would have needed a severe modification before she'd be able to climb on a horse, and her thighs just weren't up to the type of scrutiny they'd get if she went for the split-to-the-waist look. Unless she had a couple more bottles of champagne first, by which stage she wouldn't care if she even had any thighs, well-padded or not.

'I used to wear knickers like that.'

'And now you don't bother at all?' Rory, horse in tow, slapped her bum before kissing her neck in a way that was guaranteed to make her wriggle.

Tab, meanwhile, had narrowly missed one of the main poles in the marquee, which had made the whole place shake alarmingly, and decided to take a short cut along the back of the DJ and his equipment rather than exiting the tent. Mr Music Man (as his equipment stated) lurched forwards, his hands clutching at the nearest thing he could find, which happened to be his laptop, abruptly replacing the current smoochie track with some heavy rock.

As the bass kicked in, Tabatha's horse plunged forwards, took off too late to clear the row of chairs and skidded to a halt in front of the disapproving Dom.

Lottie's Uncle Dominic, who was more used to the controlled environment of a dressage arena and conducted his life in the same measured and precise way as he rode, gave a wry smile. He had standards, ones that Lottie often felt she fell woefully short of, and a natural aristocratic air that she knew she would never get close to. However much she practised in front of the mirror. Tab, however, not being a family member and having no reputation to live up to, just thought he was slightly stuffy but a bit of a softy. She grinned.

'Amateurs.' Dom shook his head and gave the horse an encouraging slap on the rear as Tab regrouped and aimed her mount at the final hurdle. As she did a victory lap around the tent there were a few shouts for her knickers, but even in her elated state it was a step too far for the hormonally challenged but inexperienced Tab, who elected to keep her bottom covered.

The next competitor, Dom, rather let the side down by riding in an efficient and completely controlled manner, as though he was out for a rather boring afternoon hack. Impressive though the riding was, it fell woefully short of the wow factor that the audience had come to expect from the other competitors. He did, though, earn an enthusiastic round of applause from the love of his life, Amanda, who had been keeping her distance from the excited horses. She got so carried away that she ran up to give him a chaste kiss as he dismounted, rapidly retreating when the horse struck one impatient hoof on the floor.

And then it was Mick's turn. Mick was a true horseman in the way that only an Irishman, born and bred, can be. He understood his horses, knew how to cajole the best from any animal in a way that was a million miles from the flamboyance of most of the other Tippermere residents.

But today was not a good day.

Ever since Todd's unexpected arrival and the resulting look of shock on Lottie's face, Mick had been unsettled. And, as a man of few words, he'd found a bottle of whiskey to be a better partner than the eagle-eyed Pip, who he knew would spot his agitation and interrogate him.

It wasn't that it was any of his concern – Lottie was very much Rory's and in Pip he'd found a woman who was as undemanding emotionally as she was demanding in bed. He'd accepted the way things were, but the appearance of the man he knew had caused the sweet Lottie a great deal of distress bothered him. And he knew it bothered him more than it should. So he'd withdrawn. Which all meant that when he vaulted onto the horse's back, his mind wasn't fully on the job. Horses liked Mick, and now this one was confused by the light hands that had suddenly become heavy. It shook its head in warning, expecting reassurance and Mick suddenly realised he couldn't give it. 'Sorry old fella.' The horse, sensing a difference in his rider, decided to step up to the mark. The round was careful, the gelding who was still young enough to be headstrong, ignored the temptation to be flamboyant and strong picking his way around, and coming to a gentle halt at the makeshift bar so that Mick could reach for the champagne. He gave the horse a rueful pat on the neck. 'I think we'll skip the bubbly this time, fella.'

On the far side of the marquee, Lottie frowned. Mick might not be a top competition rider like most of the others, but there was something wrong. He could settle and take care of any horse he rode, but this time it had looked as if the horse was taking care of him.

The holler took her attention back to Rory, who was back in the saddle and hanging on to Flash as though he expected the usual fireworks. Which the horse complied with, destroying the flower arrangement on the first table and landing a hoof in the wedding cake as her finale. A shower of icing coated all those standing near as the mare skidded to a marzipan-induced halt in front of Todd.

'Your turn, mate.' Rory waved his by-now empty bottle in Todd's direction. 'And I've lowered the cake jump to give you a chance.'

'That is so unfair. He's not going to make it round the course, you know he can't ride.' Tab was hanging on to Merlin's head looking as if she was afraid her sweeties were about to be taken away. Which they probably were. It would be just her luck to find the man of her dreams, only for him to be hospitalised before she even got a snog.

'Unfair?' Rory's eyes narrowed. 'He's not some kind of cissy. You're up for it, aren't you Todd?'

'Well it's not fair on me.' Tab realised what she'd said too late and turned the colour of her knickers.

'You?' Rory looked confused. 'What's it got to do with—'

'Lottie, you don't want him to do it, do you?'

Lottie, who hadn't really disapproved of the whole event, just Rory's involvement in it, hesitated. 'I don't mind, honest.'

'But he'll fall off, and you don't want him to get hurt, do you? Please, Lottie.'

'Well, I, well no.' Lottie knew as she said it that she didn't. Todd was the kind of guy you could actually split up with and still like. Once you'd got over his method of splitting up, not to mention his unexpected reappearance. It was the last bit that had shook her up, but it was surprising how much a few drinks could change the way things looked. And in fact she quite liked the new assertive Rory who had emerged. She still thought Todd's apology had been pretty half-hearted, well, pretty much non-existent, in fact, and she would have been quite happy never to see him again. But he obviously hadn't known what he was agreeing to when he'd cooked up this plan with Rory.

'Relax, it's cool.' Todd grinned, then turned his attentions to the worried Tab. 'Do I get your pink knickers if I make it round?' Tab blushed again, but a shade lighter than the lingerie under discussion this time. 'Can't be that bloody difficult after all, can it? Bet I can get round in record time and have a drink on the way. Pass us the bubbly, mate.'

He didn't get a drink on the way, or get round in record time. Tab letting go of the bridle was a mistake. Merlin took one look at the course and his sensible, lazy cob brain decided it all looked too much like hard work. Freed of Tab's firm hand, he did what all good ponies do – and headed for his hay net. Which unfortunately was half a mile due southeast, back at the equestrian centre stables. 'Blimey. What the hell do you feed this thing on?' Todd, who thought he was fit after a lifetime of mornings in the gym and afternoons on the surf, pulled two-handed on one rein to no avail as the horse swerved past official jump number one and headed out of the marquee. Merlin wasn't a surf board. He kept his course, his neck resolutely set, totally ignoring his riders ineffectual attempts to influence matters. One of the pink balloons that festooned the marquee caught in his tail as he veered to avoid the diving Tab, then he set off at a resolute trot, the balloon bobbing gently behind as they made their way across the lawns along a route he now knew so well.

'Had I better go and get him?' Tab looked hopefully from Rory to Lottie.

***

Lottie went barefoot, carrying her high heels in one hand, as she and Rory made their way down the drive towards the equestrian centre, the string of horses ambling behind them. She had been planning on talking to Rory about Tipping House Estate, about their future, about how she thought that one day soon they needed to move into the House. But as she glanced out of the corner of her eye at him she didn't want to spoil the moment. It was too perfect. He was just so damned handsome, in his sharp white shirt, sleeves rolled up and collar open, his bowtie still somehow dangling untied around his neck. He caught her looking and grinned. Warm, uncomplicated. The only man she'd ever wanted.

On a warm night like tonight all they needed to do was throw new haynets in and check water buckets. As she pushed the last door firmly shut and breathed in the sweet smell of horse, Rory's warm hands settled on her waist, his breath against her neck.

She shivered.

'So,' Rory stroked a finger lazily down her back, taking the zip with it. 'How did Todd know where to find you?'

Which was a question that had been on Lottie's lips since he'd careered back into her life several hours earlier, along with the more important question, why?

But as she turned to face Rory her gaze lingered on a copse of moonlit trees that lay to the east. Nestled behind them was Tipping House Estate, where a far more pressing problem than Todd lay.

'Hey, forget Todd.' Warm lips traced a path along her jawbone, his teeth teased at her lower lip.

'I already have.'

And as her dress slipped from her shoulders, pooling at her feet in the deserted stable yard she decided all the questions could wait for another day. She gazed up at the inky-black sky, spattered with diamond studs, the moon casting a ghostly glow over the buildings and finally forgot all about all her worries as Rory eased her thighs apart and headed for his final victory of the day.

Chapter 4

'Morning, babe.'

Lottie, who was concentrating on the mobile phone in her hand as she walked down the stairs, was caught completely unawares by the deep male voice and simultaneously dropped the phone and lost her footing.

The mobile, which luckily was slim and light, shot out of her hands and hit one of the terriers, which was patiently waiting for her at the bottom of the stairs, squarely on the rump. With a surprised yelp the dog sprang to its feet, shot up the narrow stairs and completed the job of sending the still half-asleep Charlotte flying.

She landed face first in the crotch of the male in question.

Which was so not where she wanted to be – and opening her mouth to say so could have been seriously misconstrued.

For a moment she froze, not quite sure what to do next. Hoping she hadn't been noticed was not an option. Nose-deep in a man's unmentionables was also not an option. Especially when those private parts were not attached to her boyfriend.

'And there was I thinking you didn't care any more.' He chuckled.

As she couldn't decide where it was safe to put her hands to lever herself up, she settled for slithering to the floor, which was pretty undignified, but safe. Well safe-ish.

Tilly, the head terrier, relieved to see she was still alive, leapt on her thigh with a delighted whimper and proceeded to give her a reassuring kiss, which did nothing at all to help the situation.

Being caught in her Minnie Mouse PJ's and bare feet was one thing, still having her bed hair and bad breath was another. Crouching on the floor with dog slobber on her face lowered her to altogether new depths. Low even for her.

'Want one? Or had you got something tastier in mind?'

She looked up into the grinning face of Todd Mitchell, who was waving a bacon sandwich in her direction, and clearly had lots of things in mind - none of them remotely connected to bacon.

Todd in the kitchen eating breakfast was so not how her day was supposed to start.

'Some knees-up you had last night. Your folk certainly know how to party.'

Lottie did her best to piece together the rest of the evening after Todd's unscheduled departure, and failed miserably. There was a rather fuzzy memory of spin-the-bottle that probably shouldn't be thought about too deeply, followed by an award-winning performance from Rory in the stable yard. She probably still had straw in her hair, just to finish off the sophisticated look. And she had a vague recollection of Uncle Dom insisting they had to talk. Whether they had or not was a different matter.

'You okay, Lots?'

'What are you doing here?' She took in the smell of coffee and tried to decide if actually drinking some would make her feel worse or better.

'Brekkie.' He waved the sandwich in the air again briefly before taking a large bite. She watched him chew. Mesmerised. 'Tab brought me over and told me to wait here while she did her horse business.' It was definitely good when he spoke with his mouth full, made him far less attractive. 'Good type that Rory, when you get to know him. Makes a mean bacon sarnie.'

Lottie looked at him suspiciously, wondering what kind of male bonding could have possibly taken place over a pan of crispy bacon and when nothing came to mind she rescued her beeping mobile from the dog's basket before it got chewed up. Uncle Dom, it seemed, had been busy this morning, texting and calling her, which was a bit weird. For him a phone was a functional item to be used only when necessary. Maybe somebody had died. Or she'd done something exceptionally outrageous at the wedding. Or, more likely, forgotten to do something she'd promised.

Had they put all the horses away or had they left some on his front lawn? She was tempted to put the mobile back in Tilly's basket and hope the terrier ate the evidence.

'I didn't mean what are you doing in my kitchen? I meant what are you doing in the country?'

'Oh, I get you now.'

'So you're not in prison then?' The faint note of optimism was probably just a little bit mean.

'Let out early for good behaviour.' He winked.

Laid-back could be good, but it could also be annoying at times. Todd must be the only man on the planet who didn't think being dragged off a beach by the police was an issue, and who could shrug off imprisonment. Did nothing ever get under his skin?

She'd been to hell and back wondering what was going to happen to him, what it was all about. And it didn't even bother him a teeny weeny bit. It looked as though he'd just ridden the wave and come to carry on where they'd left off. Except he couldn't. No way was she ever going to trust a man like Todd again, and anyway she'd moved on. Or, more accurately, moved back – to the life she used to have, except this time it was better. Now she knew Rory loved her. And she felt needed; by him, by her family and by the massive, beautiful estate that plucked at her heartstrings.

But even with the hangover from hell, she couldn't stay sore at anybody for long. Not even Todd.

'Going to give me a hug, kiss and make up?'

That was pushing it too far, though. Time to change the subject. 'Don't you think she's too young for you?'

'Who?'

'Tabatha.'

'Tabatha?'

'The one with the pink knickers, remember?'

He raised an eyebrow. 'Ah, no chance of forgetting those pink knickers. Bit young for me to what?' And grinned. 'Seriously,' and for a second the smile did disappear, 'I am sorry, and I never actually was in prison, you know. We just forgot to post that final divorce thingy, what do you call it? Absolute, decree absolute. Why you Brits have to complicate everything beats me. All that bloody legal stuff.' She watched as he took another healthy bite out of his sandwich. 'And would you credit it? My second bloody marriage was never legal.' He laughed: a loud, healthy laugh that reminded Lottie that her head hurt. In a kind of throbbing, pounding way. 'These beach weddings on remote islands have hidden benefits. Paperwork's a shambles.' He grinned and displayed a set of perfect white teeth. 'So hey presto! No probs and here I am.'

Not that she saw 'here I am' as 'no probs', which took her neatly back to the 'why are you here?' question.

'I was sorry about the whole beach thing,' he was giving her his earnest look, 'I was looking forward to that paella.'

'It wasn't the paella that was the problem. It was the police.'

'The police?' He looked blank. 'They didn't bother you, did they?'

'Not apart from surrounding us on the beach and then dragging you off it.'

'To be fair, they didn't drag, hun.'

'But they were there. They arrested you. I was sunbathing. I was in a bikini, and,' she paused at the critical bit, 'it wasn't even my best one.' Humiliation had not been the word for it. It was like that nightmare of arriving at a party in fancy dress only to find out that the event was actually black tie. Well, that was one of her nightmares, along with the one when she sat down for dinner and then realised she was naked. She probably should talk to somebody about her weird dreams. Or maybe not.

Todd looked confused. Obviously, getting arrested on the beach was just a normal occurrence for him, and what else would you be wearing on a beach? 'Anyhow, all in the past now. Thought I'd come and see what your neck of the woods looked like. No,' he held up a hand to stop the words she wasn't going to say, 'no worries about putting me up. Got it all sorted.'

Putting him up? Was the man mad? He had to go. Soon, now, immediately.

All Lottie wanted to do was bang her head on the wall, or just curl up on the floor, shut her eyes and try to blank him out.

'So you didn't actually come here to find me and say sorry?'

'Well, I am sorry, babe, honest. I know it was all kind of unexpected, and it was me who persuaded you to head to Spain.' He shrugged, ever nonchalant, but she could see in those deep-blue eyes that he actually was at least a tiny bit bothered. 'And it worked out better for you in the end, didn't it?' He gestured round the kitchen. 'You were getting bored of beach life weren't you? Couldn't wait to get back to all this, eh?'

'That's beside the point. It was a shock. But you're right, I am happy to be home.' She paused. 'I'm fine, so you'll be, er, moving on now you've got that off your chest?'

He shrugged. 'Thought I might hang around for a bit and explore your neighbourhood.'

'You can't.' That did sound mean. 'I mean why? I mean shouldn't you be surfing or something?'

'A change is as good as a rest, isn't that what they say?'

'You don't need a rest, Todd. You surf and you lie on beaches and er…' She racked her brains for some valid reason that didn't sound like 'I'm far too busy to babysit you', and drew a blank. 'You'll be bored, you don't like horses and…' He couldn't stay, he really couldn't. She had meetings with Dom and roofs to mend (literally) and horses to look after and her inheritance to, well, inherit. 'I'm very busy.' She finished lamely.

'No bother. I've sorted digs. You won't even know I'm here.'

Todd had known, better than Lottie, that their time together had a very limited span. And he knew that for both of them it had just been a good dose of sunshine and harmless fun. It would have just been better if it had ended differently. At an airport, with a farewell kiss before they boarded different planes. In normal circumstances they would never have met, but they had. And it was his fault, of his making – as was the abrupt and unconventional ending to it all.

He should have just left it at that, given it up as a bad job and gone back to his normal life. But he couldn't. What ever happened to riding the waves, having a few tinnies and a lot of belly laughs? When the hell had he grown up and developed a conscience? Well, the honest answer to that one was probably when he realised that blood really is thicker than water.

The knock on the door made them both jump guiltily, along with the three terriers, who all hit the floor running and scrambled for pole position, hurtling towards the door like cannonballs, yapping at each other and the as-yet unseen visitor. Lottie had long since learned that you let the dogs get to the door first, unless you wanted bruised shins and burst eardrums. Her early habit of jumping to her feet when the doorbell or phone rang had long since departed after a few catastrophic collisions that had taught her just how unstoppable a terrier in full flight was. It was safer to fall off a bucking horse than be swept along by a pack of rampaging Jack Russell terriers.

The whirlwind of brown and white fur went into reverse as the door swung open to reveal a neatly dressed Pip, sleek blond hair in a neat ponytail, clothes that suggested she wasn't about to get stuck into mucking-out duties. She was waving a copy of the *Daily Mail*.

'You have just got to see this—' She stopped dead on seeing Todd, then shoved the paper in his direction with a smirk. 'This picture of our surfer dude.'

Lottie got to the paper before Todd did and spread it out on the pine kitchen table. It was the perfect homage to a Thelwell cartoon. The barrel bodied Merlin was flying (along with the bright-pink balloon that was attached to his tail), the terrified Todd clinging to his mane, long legs stuck out in a futile attempt to put the brakes on.

'Oh and Dom said he needed to track you down, Lottie. Where've you been all morning? I've been trying to call you.'

Todd was frowning as he stabbed a finger at *Wizard of Oz?* 'Hey, what's with the funny headline?'

Which meant Lottie didn't need to explain she'd spent the best part of the morning in bed, and it also meant she didn't have to wonder why Dom was so determined to track her down.

'Merlin, the horse is called Merlin, you know as in King Arthur?'

'Oh, right.' He obviously didn't know.

'Wizard as in Merlin, Oz as in Australian?' Pip shook her head and gave up the explanations as a lost cause when she saw his blank expression. 'You even got in the *Manchester Evening News*, which normally doesn't do horse stuff.'

'Didn't know the press were invited to the party.' He held the paper at arm's length, unsure whether to be pleased at what had to be a spectacular entrance to English country living or disappointed with the pink balloon, which really wasn't his style. 'Anyhow, what's with all the fuss? You never seen a stranger in this neck of the woods before?'

'Nothing quite like you, no.' Pip suddenly relented and smiled. 'I'm the press.' She might have forsaken the daily grind of a journalist's life in London, but writing was her life and Pip had found that working as a freelance in Cheshire was remarkably lucrative, given the fact that the place was awash with scandals and celebrities.

Tippermere might appear tranquil, but underneath the surface lurked secrets begging to be uncovered. And as for nearby Kitterly Heath, you didn't even have to delve under the surface. In a place where footballers brushed shoulders with rock legends and film stars it was more a case of picking which stories to publish and which to ignore. And Todd's abrupt entrance at the wedding had been an unexpected bonus.

'Oh yeah.' Todd looked at her speculatively, the more relaxed Pip had caught him unawares. He'd forgotten all about the slightly jaded chief reporter version of Pip that he'd first met in Barcelona. All that seemed a long time ago. 'I thought you did fashion shows and red-carpet events, not country weddings and horsey stuff.'

Pip ignored him. 'And Billy is a celebrity around here, well not just here, everywhere. You know, Olympic medals and all that jazz.'

'So if he's the celeb, why've they got my face on the front page?'

'Well it isn't exactly your face.' Lottie said reasonably, taking another close look at the photo, which wasn't quite as blurred now she'd got used to daylight. 'You can actually see more of your bum than anything.' She giggled and had a closer look.

'Your arse is the one on the front page because you're funnier. Billy can ride a horse and they've got fed up of running his bonking pictures.' Lottie flinched, aware that Pip wasn't intentionally being hurtful. 'But a picture like that is one in a million.' Pip tried not to look too smug, but she was pleased. She'd just known it would be worth shelling out to get Bob the photographer there, and he'd earned every penny of the three bottles of wine bribe it had taken to persuade her editor to send him.

'Not sure how to take that, mate.'

'I'd just go with the flow if I was you.' Lottie, who had decided to risk the coffee, sat down and cradled a large mug of it in her hands. 'You're a novelty, they've got loads of pictures of Dad playing the fool. And Wizard of Oz isn't a bad headline, he got Bronco Billy.' She sighed. Even now she hated those headlines that had followed her around at school.

'Really?' He paused and stared at her. 'What was that about

then? Does he do rodeo riding as well?'

'No, you don't want to know. Honestly.'

'I hardly knew you at all, did I?' And it was true, thought Todd. The Lottie he'd met in Australia, the Lottie he'd taken to Barcelona with him had just been a fun-loving girl looking for a good time. He knew nothing about Tippermere, her family, her real life, apart from the brief comments about horses, boredom and being taken for granted. Okay, he had known she came from the countryside, and he did know her dad was big in the horse world. Oh yeah, and he'd had an inkling about the whole gentry thing. But it didn't seem to have anything to do with the girl he'd briefly known. He'd just seen flip flops and fun. And, well, a great deal of booze and her glorious body.

Yesterday had been a bit of an eye-opener seeing her surrounded by men who might look out of place amongst body boarders, but seemed more than in control on the back of a horse. Which was one experiment he wasn't going to repeat in the near future. Talk about chafing! His hand automatically went to his crotch.

And boy could they drink. Even the old girl she'd called gran had been knocking them back. In five hours he reckoned he'd seen more of Lottie (in the fully clothed sense) than he had in five weeks on a beach. And it suited her. He was seeing her in a whole new, and very appealing, light. Which was not how his mind was supposed to be thinking.

'Think I'll go and find Tab, then, shall I?' Sensing he was on the road to screwing up again if he wasn't careful, Todd was up out of his chair as he swilled down the last of his sandwich with a gulp of tea. 'Nearly forgot. That posh dude was after you. Something about her ladyship. Catch you later, babe.'

Pip stared at the newspaper headlines. 'Is he for real?'

'Well, I was hoping that last night was a nightmare, or you'd slipped me some hallucinogenic drugs.' Lottie slumped into the comfy chair next to the Aga and let Tilly cuddle up next to her. She stroked the dog's muscled-up little body. 'I can't still be dreaming, though. I wouldn't have a hangover like this, would I?'

'No dream. Do you think Tab is going to give him a lift to the airport?'

Lottie gnawed the side of her fingernail with a worried expression on her face. 'He said somebody was putting him up, said he was hanging around for a bit.' She groaned. 'She can't be taking him back to her place, can she?'

'You're kidding. Can you imagine Tom's face if his little girl arrives home with a man like Todd, well any man, really? And he adores you, so all you'd have to do was say the word and Todd would be out.'

'I suppose so.' Lottie hugged the little dog closer and carried on worrying.

'Does it bother you, him being here?'

'It's not that. I mean I don't know exactly what he said to Rory, but he doesn't mind. And it's weird, but it just seems like it was years ago, and it was fun, but...' She shrugged, then grinned. 'I've got Rory now.' Then the smile faded as she remembered. 'And I haven't got time to look after him or anything, and I don't really know why he's here, to be honest.'

'Mm. Maybe he's bored? But look on the bright side, I'm sure somebody would be happy to take him off your hands.'

'What am I supposed to do? I can't just ignore him, and he doesn't know anybody else.' She paused, as she suddenly realised that he did know somebody else.

Pip caught the look and laughed nervously. 'Oh, no.'

'But you know I promised Uncle Dom I'd take on the running of the Estate, and I said I'd move into Tipping House soon,' she glanced nervously at the door. This was something she still hadn't managed to discuss with Rory properly. She had mentioned it, more than once, but they hadn't exactly set a date. She'd thought that after the hugely successful wedding had taken place would be an ideal time, but it hadn't been quite gone as planned. Either the wedding or the chat, given that Todd had stormed into the ceremony, and Rory had decided to liven up the proceedings that came after. If he'd only be serious just for one moment it would be so helpful.

'Tell me you're not serious, please Lottie.'

'Well, er I was being serious. Is that a problem? I mean, you know him, and all you need to do is—'

'No way.'

'He'll soon get bored and you can put him on a plane?'

Pip laughed at the note of optimism in Lottie's voice. 'Lottie, you know I love you, but you know me and Todd never really hit it off.'

'Will you at least think about it? Can you imagine what Uncle Dom would say if he found out about Barcelona and Todd getting arrested?'

'I think he might already know.' Pip's tone was dry.

'Gran thinks it's entertaining, but you know what Dom is like, he can be so...'

'Stuffy?'

'Particular. He'll think I'm not being serious enough. And have you any idea what he wants? He's acting weird, phoning me even more than normal, and this morning he actually sent me a text. An actual text.'

'No idea.' Pip stared at Lottie, and squashed her original intention for coming. She'd wanted to talk to somebody and Lottie had seemed the ideal person. But suddenly she wasn't sure. She wasn't the type to unburden herself and if she was going to she had to be sure it was the right person, right time, right place. She was the stable one, Lottie was the scatty one. She was the one who never let relationships get to her. Lottie was the one who had ex-boyfriends who left her in the lurch only to reappear months later. And Lottie was the one who would soon be inheriting a mansion complete with a leaking roof and mountainous debts. The one who needed good friends she could rely on.

But the niggles that Pip had squashed the first time she'd

stripped herself bare in front of Mick had come back with a vengeance. And each day they were getting harder to ignore.

'Are you okay?' Lottie was frowning.

'I don't think he loves me.' It was out before she could stop it. So much for right time, right person.

Lottie jerked upright from her slouch, letting go of the dog abruptly, her mouth dropping open as the little dog landed on the floor and started to run around in circles after her tail, barking. 'You don't mean—'

'Any chance of a cup of—'

'Go away.' The two girls shouted out in perfect unison and Rory, one foot hovering over the threshold of his own home, beat a hasty retreat, taking the dogs with him.

'Oh blimey.' Lottie was mortified. She'd never shouted at Rory before, let alone at the same time as Pip, which had made it pretty forceful. 'I better go and explain, hang on, don't go away.' And she was across the kitchen and out of the door, still barefoot, before Pip could speak. 'You won't will you? I won't be a sec, honest. Stay, stay there.'

Pip sighed, wondering why she'd ever thought a quiet heart to heart was possible in such a chaotic place. She studied the photos on the wall opposite. Rory on the back of one of his favourite horses took pride of place, being presented with a cup by Princess Anne. He looked dashing and fun, tawny eyes dancing, pure joy spread across his open features, even in the face of royalty. And even the royal in question was entranced.

Why couldn't life be more bloody straightforward?

Pip made a sudden decision. Elizabeth was the one she should be talking to.

She had just got out of the front door when Rory appeared, coming in the opposite direction, Lottie clinging on to him and squealing.

'He said he'd give me a piggy back across the gravel, it's a bugger in bare feet.' She was red-faced, which had to have more to do with where Rory's hands were than it had to do with sore feet. 'You're not going are you? Oh please don't. Oh Pip, I thought, but you had…'

'I'll catch up with you later, urgent call.' It was only as she pulled out of the yard on her bright pink Vespa, nearly mowing down a jogging passer-by, that she remembered she'd promised to get Lottie to call Dom. Oh well, she had mentioned it, not that Lottie would remember, and she'd remind her again later. After she'd worked out just why her normally organised life had suddenly become an emotional whirlwind. And what she was going to do about it. About Mick.

***

'You have to be the hardest person in Tippermere to get hold of, what have you been doing, Charlotte?'

Lottie who had finally given in and answered her phone (mainly because it wouldn't stop ringing and the dogs steadfastly refused to eat it) stopped the examination of her feet, rubbed at the last bit of gravel and gave a worried sigh. 'I've been here, Uncle Dom.' She was only half listening as she watched one of the horses gallop enthusiastically around the paddock, kicking his heels in the air. A youngster, she really did need to work this morning even if she didn't manage anything else.

'Well, I asked that Australian chap to pass on a message if he saw you, and I asked Philippa, who is about the most reliable of your friends.'

Registering his tone, she picked up a pile of three-day eventing entry forms from the nearest chair, dropped them on the table and sat down. On the TV they always told people to sit down when there was bad news coming.

'Charlotte, we have to talk. I've put this off as long as I can, but it can't wait any longer. I'm coming to see you now, and don't you dare disappear again.'

Chapter 5

'Amanda is expecting.'

'Expecting what?' Lottie only had a fraction of her attention on her Uncle Dominic, partly because the two-year-old horse on the other end of the lunge rope had a way of knowing exactly when you weren't concentrating, and partly because she had absolutely no idea why Dom was there and suspected she was about to get a telling off for something. And she was following the strategy of pretending he wasn't there in the hope he'd forget and go away.

She loved Dom, but she didn't love the disapproving looks or the lectures when she didn't quite come up to his very high standards. Which was quite often.

'Charlotte, are you listening?'

'Of course.' She glanced his way, and the stern look and folded arms meant he wasn't going to forget, or go away. The black horse, which someone had imaginatively named Badger due to the broad white stripe down his nose, gave an experimental pull on the other end of the rope.

'She is expecting a baby.'

'What?' She spun around to face him properly, inadvertently flicking the lunge whip as she went so that it caught the youngster on his nicely rounded rump. The horse gave a squeal of what could have been evil intent, or glee, and did the type of fly buck that was more often seen at a rodeo.

Dom watched in silence as Badger followed through by putting his head between his knees and arching his back in an even more impressive one, and his one thought, before the animal charged forward, was that the horse had incredible athletic potential. A loop of rein was dragged through Lottie's hand, catching the lunge whip on its way, which narrowly missed her head before she fully came to her senses and took a firmer grip, desperately trying to keep her footing in the middle of the circle as the horse tore around at a dizzying pace.

'Hey up, Dom, what are you doing here?' Rory arrived just as Dom was trying to decide whether to step in and rescue his only niece before she was accidentally garrotted, or corkscrewed into the ground, or whether he should trust in her ability to slow the horse down. As Tilly the terrier tore into the arena, desperate to join in the fun, dodging hooves and curses, he decided that if he didn't do something within the next ten seconds man (well woman) or dog was going to die.

But, just as Dominic vaulted over the wall, the horse miraculously slowed to a trot, dropping its head in a show of subservience. Lottie laughed and finally managed to pick up the lunge whip.

'Wow, did you see that power? He could demolish a cross-country course.'

'That's what I bought him for darling.' Rory sounded satisfied.

'He nearly demolished you.' Dom's tone was dry as he climbed back out of the arena. The master of control, he was never quite sure whether to be in awe of, or despair of, the totally chaotic girl, who somehow carried some of the same genes as him. 'And I couldn't see the power the speed he was going.'

'He's only a b—' Lottie was about to say baby, then it hit her. The word that had caused the explosion in the first place. She walked up to the horse, holding it firmly at its head, the other hand patting the strong neck, and stared at Dom. 'Amanda is, you are, you're both…'

'Expecting. Yes.'

'A baby?' Just to be sure.

'Woohoo. Didn't know you had it in you, Dom. Congratulations!' Rory gave Dom a manly slap on the back and nearly launched him back over into the arena again. 'It is yours, I take it?' Dom arched an eyebrow, stared down his aristocratic nose and refrained from comment.

'Amanda's pregnant?' Lottie wanted to make doubly sure.

'Isn't that what I said, Charlotte?'

It was, but she was still trying to get her head around the statement, which was damned tricky considering she saw Dom as: A – too stuffy and pernickety to have a baby (or even sex for that matter) and B – too old. After all he *was* her uncle.

'But…'

'And I need to talk to you about your gran and Tipping House. Charlotte, I do appreciate that you've started to take on some of the responsibility, but I'm afraid we really do need to speed the process along.'

'Speed it along?' Lottie, who by now had forgotten all about the horse, got a smart reminder when it gave her hand a sharp nip.

'It's your inheritance, and although I know I said I'd carry on helping until you were ready, the ball is now in your court.' He shrugged, looked apologetic. 'I'm going to have to support Amanda, which means I need to be in her home, our home, at Folly Lake Manor. And,' he leaned forward in a way she didn't like at all, and sighed, 'unfortunately Mother has been ill, which rather brings things to a head. She needs assurance that you're in control and she doesn't need to have any concerns about the estate and everything it entails.'

'Ill? Gran isn't ill, she was at the wedding, and –'

'She hides it very well, but she's getting too old for all the worry, whatever she says.' The small frown he couldn't hide worried Lottie. 'The doctors say she's had a small stroke, and the best way to help is for us to take the pressure off.'

'I will, I will. I can go and help her, visit more, spend time up there, can't we Rory?' Lottie had wild, and totally impractical, thoughts about making soup and taking dictation, neither of which she'd ever done in her life, while Rory did manly thing like standing at the fireplace and supplying Elizabeth with perfect G&T's.

'It's not about spending time with her, Charlotte. It's about money.'

'But you've already told me about the money. I've got a plan and we're seeing the bank manager, and I—'

Dom sighed. 'What we've discussed is just the tip of the iceberg. That estate needs managing, it needs a cash injection—'

'I know, I've thought about how to raise money and—'

He held up a hand to stop her words. 'A serious amount of money, Charlotte. What we've talked about is the substantial sum needed for the essential repairs, that have been left for far too long, but there are also the huge day-to-day running costs as well as actually overseeing it all.' His tone softened. 'I've tried to break you in gently, but the bank manager had been running out of patience, and we really need to appease him. I think you're the person that has to do it.' Dom patted the horse, which had taken advantage of the situation and pulled away from the confused Lottie. 'You are the next Lady of Tipping House, my darling girl, and we need you to become that Lady now, whether you're ready or not. Come up and see your grandmother later and we'll talk.' He paused and looked at the horse again. 'Nice-looking animal, needs some discipline, though.' And he was off, before Lottie had time to ask him about babies, or her gran, or what he meant by a 'small stroke'.

She looked at Rory. 'I can't manage the whole estate, can I?'

'Of course you can, gorgeous. If that shower of relatives of yours can, then it must be a piece of piss.'

'Stuff and nonsense.'

'No, it's not.' Dominic straightened the painting above the mantelpiece and wondered just how many years attempting to prolong his mother's life would knock off his own. 'Doctor's orders and you know it, Mother.'

He loved his mother, every irascible inch of her, and the idea of her not being around was unthinkable. When Elizabeth died it would change not only his life, but the life of everybody in Tippermere. But handling her retirement would be like handling an uncut colt who knew you were just about to cut off the very part of his anatomy he held most dear. Separating her from her responsibilities would be like castration, if that was not too crude a way of putting it. Although the thought of what she might say if she could read his mind did lighten his mood slightly.

'And what does that young whipper-snapper know? If I did everything the doctors told me I'd have been pushing up daisies for the past twenty years, just like your father. Gin is good for one. And do stop fiddling, dear.'

Dom stopped and resisted the urge to pour himself a stiff brandy. Tipping House Estate had been his home all his life, and he had at one stage wondered how he would feel when it came to letting go, handing the beautiful estate over to the care of its true heir, or more accurately, heiress, his niece, Lottie. But he now felt only a strange relief, along with guilt that he felt that way. Meeting Amanda had been his saving grace. She'd coaxed a caring side out of him that he never knew he possessed and now she was his priority. Along with his unborn child.

'Thank heavens for that. Finally somebody who will talk some sense.' Elizabeth's backbone visibly straightened as Pip, with a wink in Dom's direction, waltzed into the room. 'Pour me a drink Philippa, and you,' Elizabeth glared at her son, Dominic, 'can take the dogs out for some exercise if you want to be useful.' Bertie, the portly Labrador, picked precisely that moment to wander into the drawing room, a very fat but very dead rabbit hanging from his soft mouth.

Pip grimaced. Dead things, especially in the house, were something she could never quite get used to. She might have grown up surrounded by fields, but that was a Welsh mining village, where very little moved and very little died apart from the elderly residents.

She wrinkled her nose and sloshed a generous measure of gin into the nearest tumbler. Dom frowned and raised an eyebrow.

'It's for me. I need a drink.'

Dom wasn't convinced. He'd asked Philippa along to the discussion because he knew his mother liked her. They had an unexpected affinity, which he could only put down to a shared interest in mischief-making, and maybe loneliness. They were of a type: fiercely independent, smart and undemonstrative. Elizabeth had never been one for shows of affection, but Dominic knew that beneath the surface she was as kind and caring as they came. But she wasn't about to lay herself bare to anybody.

He sometimes wondered about his parents' relationship, if his mother had ever truly opened up, even to his father. And he hoped very much that he was different. That he could share everything with Amanda, the woman he'd never expected to find. But his upbringing and genes meant it didn't come naturally. But, there again, unburdening oneself and breaking down wasn't always a good thing.

He studied Pip, who was sipping her gin with a look of mischief on her fine features. He didn't trust them together, but he would use any means at his disposal to aid his attempt to get his mother to hand over the reins to her granddaughter. Going on as they had been was no longer an option. He was spending far too much time meeting with the new bank manager, who didn't have any of the understanding of the old one, who had helped manage their money for years. He couldn't explain the situation to Elizabeth and risk damaging her health even further. He'd been told to avoid stressing her. Although, he had a sneaking suspicion that she knew exactly how dire the situation was, and had decided to ignore it. Something Lottie was very good at.

Although Lottie's most recent attempt at organising an event, her father's wedding, had not exactly been a success in the conventional sense, he was still convinced that she had to start to shoulder much more of the responsibility, had to prepare to be Lady of the Manor. And hopefully work out how to save it in the process.

And, although it made him feel very selfish, Amanda needed him. He'd never, until he met his wife, had anybody really need him. But he had now, and he wasn't going to let her down. His caretaking duties had to come to an end sooner or later, and as Charlotte showed no inclination to get married and follow the path of inheritance, she could at least start to assume responsibility. It was all going to be hers one day soon, and sooner if she didn't help him find a way to get the bank off their backs.

Pip opened her blue eyes wider, a hint of a smile wrinkling the corners. 'Well, you said Elizabeth wasn't allowed.'

'She isn't. But I don't expect that will stop the two of you.'

'I am not dead yet, you know, unlike that animal Bertie's got. Where on earth did you get that from, you naughty animal? Do get Cook to hang it in the kitchen, Dominic. And Philippa, come and sit down.' Elizabeth patted the seat next to her. 'The pair of you can stop talking about me as though I'm not here. I'm beginning to sympathise with that Mark Twain fellow, who was presumed in his grave before his time, even if he was American. I take it we're all gathered, so you can persuade me it's time to take a back seat?'

Dom looked at his mother and wished, not for the first time, that she wasn't so shrewd, just a nice old lady in her dotage. 'Yes.' He sighed, prepared for the fight.

'Well about time too. Why you haven't got Charlotte sorted

57

before now is beyond me. The girl is more than ready.'

'What do you mean, sorted?' Lottie chose just that moment to arrive, swiftly removing the rabbit from Bertie's jaws and dangling it out of his reach as she looked from Elizabeth to Dom and back again.

'You need to organise things, dear. Now get rid of that carcass and pour us all a stiff drink. Your Uncle Dominic spends all his time trying to hide bank statements from me, but he appears to have forgotten that you need to feed and water the living.'

Dom opened his mouth to respond, then wondered why he was bothering and shut it again.

There was something wrong if Elizabeth was being compliant. She must be up to something, which probably involved getting her hands on a large gin and tonic.

Lottie wondered whether she could just shove the dead animal under the table, then decided to give it to Dom instead, before eyeing up the drinks suspiciously.

'That's Philippa's G&T. Come on now, before we all expire. And pour your uncle a brandy. He's looking a bit peaky.' Lottie picked up the bottle and was staring at the assortment of chipped cut glass, trying to decide how much brandy was a good measure, when Dom returned from his disposal duties.

'Let me.' He took the bottle and ignored his mother's gimlet stare. Intending to take charge was one thing, but he now had a horrible feeling that his plans were about to be hijacked, and pouring drinks might well be the most useful contribution he could make.

'Now Charlotte, I'm sure Dominic will show you all the boring bank statements later, and those awful spreadsheet things. Damned confusing if you ask me, when all you need is a bottom line.' The clearing of Dom's throat was audible.

'He's already shown me some.'

'Yes, well, I'm sure he has, dear, but he hides a lot of them, thinks I'm losing my marbles.' She looked at Dom as though challenging him to comment, which he wisely didn't. 'We are in a bit of a mess, but nothing that you can't deal with, I'm sure. When I took this place on things needed doing, but we muddled through and so shall you, dear. All you need to know is that I'm not having the general public tramping through the place and sticking that nasty chewing gum everywhere, so you can scotch that plan. When I'm dead and buried you may do as you wish, but as I am far from it,' she shot Dom another glance, 'I do want you to maintain standards. But I will not interfere.' There was a splutter from the direction of her son. 'And I don't want the grounds destroyed. None of those yuppie hunting and fishing events. Just raise some money, dear,' she had one eye fixed on Lottie and the other on Dominic and the bottle of gin, which he was being far too careful with, 'young people do it all the time these day for charity, so if long-haired pop people like that Bob Dildo can raise a million or so, then why can't you? He doesn't even look particularly attractive. Dirt under his fingernails, I imagine.'

'Do you mean Bob Dylan?'

'Whatever you say, dear.'

'Isn't he all religious, or something, these days?' Lottie was confused.

'Charlotte.' Dom decided things were going off-piste. 'Can we concentrate?'

'But, Bob Dylan?'

'Bob Geldof.' Intervened Pip with a grin, already enjoying herself.

'Oh.' Lottie paused. That made slightly more sense. 'Isn't he Sir Bob now?'

'He certainly is not.' Elizabeth looked at the bottle of gin pointedly. 'He has a KBE and let that be enough.'

'You knew all along it was him and not Bob Dylan, didn't you?'

'Charlotte, darling,' Elizabeth as was her norm, didn't deign to answer the question. 'At the moment you do not appear able to raise a round of drinks, let alone money.'

'But I can't organise big events like that.' Lottie thought her point had been proved by the wedding, which was fairly small-scale. 'Uncle Dom is so much better at being organised.'

Dom, who was trying to decide if it was worth attempting to fob Elizabeth off with pure tonic, concluded that doing so might shorten his lifespan considerably and instead settled for pouring a very small, but very strong, one.

'Dominic might well be, he's had lots of practice. All you have to do is oversee things. It's the ideas that are the important part. And you are perfectly capable. William's wedding may have been slightly unconventional, but it was a success.'

'But nobody had to pay.' Lottie felt herself shrivel inside when she thought about her father's wedding and just how much the event had cost. It wasn't just the flowers (most of which had been eaten by the horses), but the general destruction that came when a marquee and trestle tables were used for show-jumping practice. And an awful lot of champagne had been drunk after most of the guests had gone. And the poor Mr Music Man had been a quivering wreck, so she'd sent him home, clutching his laptop, with double his normal fee and a bottle or two to calm his nerves.

If it hadn't been for the fact that the venue, Amanda and Dominic's home, had come for free, the whole event would have cost Billy more than he'd paid out for his latest show jumper. She'd also been driven to showering the caterers with gifts, in the hope that they wouldn't refuse to come anywhere near Tippermere ever again.

'Do a little gymkhana at your father's place for practice, dear, the pony club is always up for a bit of support.'

'No.' Dom and Lottie spoke together. Both horrified at the thought of chaos that could ensue if dozens of pony-mad children on spirited mounts had the run of the grounds.

'You'll think of something. Right, let's have that drink. I feel much better already.'

'How about a dog show?' Pip, who had taken the role of observer, decided it was time to chip in. Elizabeth looked at her as though she had grown an extra head.

'You know, start small.'

'Have you ever heard the expression "going to the dogs" Philippa?'

Pip laughed.

'I'm not convinced that inviting every dog owner in the county to bring their animals to defecate on the premises will raise enough money to fix the roof.'

Dom grimaced. So she did know about the roof.

'I was just thinking of how Lottie can improve her organisational skills. Okay, if you don't want people traipsing in and out every day, and you want a big fundraiser, how about a pop concert?' Pip grasped on Elizabeth's earlier comment, knowing it would be harder for her to dismiss it. 'Not that Bob Dildo, or even Sir Bob, will come.'

Dom rolled his eyes heavenwards.

'I saw that, Dominic.' Pip was not in awe of Dom in the same way that Lottie was. In fact, she was rarely in awe of anyone. 'You know, party-in-the-park type thing. If it's good enough for royalty, then….'

'Royalty did not exactly have everybody in the front garden.'

'For the Diamond Jubilee it was Party at the Palace.' Pip finished triumphantly. 'As in Buckingham Palace.' Just in case anybody wasn't following.

'Well, you may do it at my funeral, dear, but not before.'

'It would make a lot of money.' Lottie gazed thoughtfully at Dom, who was looking his most stern.

'Charlotte you had enough problems trying to control your father's wedding guests. How on earth are you going to co-ordinate a pop concert?'

'Well, there won't be any horses, for one. And Prince Harry did it.'

'True.' Pip was almost buzzing with anticipation. 'And if he managed, I'm sure you could.' She grinned encouragingly. 'He's nearly as daft as you are.'

'Well,' Elizabeth drained her glass and put it on the table with a clatter before levering herself out of the chair. 'As we've all agreed that Charlotte does need to step up to the plate, I don't think you need me here interfering, do you? I could always move out to the Lodge for some peace and quiet, which I am beginning to think I will need.'

'You can't do that.' Lottie looked horrified, and Dom thought his mother was now going a step too far in her bid to show indifference. She was definitely up to something.

'Nonsense mother.' His tone was mild, but she shot him an assessing look.

'Jolly good! As long as we're all in agreement. And I did notice how small that drink was, Dominic. Right, I am going to rest my eyes. This weather is very drying. Come on, boys.' And she was off, the dogs' claws click-clacking on the polished wood as they followed closely behind.

'I think Prince Harry had considerably more help than you will get.' Dom drained the last dregs of the brandy and sat down. 'And he also has more contacts in the music industry.'

'I have lots of contacts.' Pip looked a bit disgruntled.

'And we have a long-term problem here. One injection of cash isn't enough.'

'We could make it an annual event?' Lottie sounded more hopeful than confident. 'Like Glastonbury?'

'I think you need something big to put you on the map, and then you need to capitalise on it. You know, let people visit, or something.' Pip poured herself another drink.

'Which is something mother has steadfastly refused to do, speaking of which I better check that she's okay.'

'But you never check…' Lottie stared at Dom, her heart suddenly a lump in her chest. 'Is there something you haven't told me? She isn't really ill is she?'

'Would she have said yes to you getting involved otherwise?' His voice was soft and he put a gentle hand on her shoulder, then headed off towards the stairs, tossing an 'I won't be long' over his shoulder as he went. Which made the lump in her chest move up to her throat. There couldn't be anything wrong with Gran, there just couldn't. She was the one person who was never ill and never let anything stop her doing anything. Wasn't she?

Chapter 6

'Isn't it something all girls want?'

Pip was only half listening to Sam, who had been waiting on her doorstep when she got home. Well, more precisely, waiting in her soft-top car with a dreamy look on her face. When Pip had glanced over her shoulder she'd been horrified to see that Sam was flicking through baby pictures on her mobile phone.

The news that Elizabeth was ill worried her. It was easy to forget just how old Lottie's gran was as she meddled in the villagers lives, supped her gin and tonics and strode out in her Hunter wellingtons and Barbour jacket. Pip couldn't imagine her not being around and nor, she imagined, could Lottie.

'Sorry, what did you say? God, it stinks in here!' There were many good things about living with Mick, the farrier, but one enormous negative. The smell. Of horses and burnt hoof. And open windows didn't seem to solve the problem. And then there was, of course, the whole maybe-he-didn't-love-her thing.

'Are you okay, babe? You seem bothered.'

'Bothered and bewildered.'

Sam stared, confused.

'I've just come from Tipping House. I don't think Elizabeth is very well.'

'Oh no, not her Ladyship. You two get on so well, don't you?' Sam wrapped her arms around Pip in a spontaneous hug. 'Although she is quite old, I suppose, but the Queen Mum went on for years, didn't she? And Lady S is, like, related to her, isn't she? I'm sure she's got wonderful gene things. She's not in hospital or anything is she?'

'No, she's not in hospital, but she's only got the Queen's genes several times removed. I guess I just forget she's an old lady. She doesn't seem like one.'

'She's a card, bless her.'

'And Lottie is going to have to start behaving like a Lady.' Lottie worried her as well. She'd been her normal scatty self when Elizabeth was there, but after her gran and uncle had left the room Pip had seen a glimpse of the woman her best friend was maturing into. Whatever Lottie thought, the Stanthorpe genes were obvious, the determination to succeed and do her duty impossible to ignore. Which was great, except she still seemed to be worried about the whole Todd situation and had asked again if Pip couldn't at least keep an eye on him. And how did she get out of that one without seeming totally unhelpful and selfish? Assuring Lottie that they'd sort something out didn't somehow seem enough.

'Wow, that is so exciting, isn't it? Lottie a real Lady.' Sam clapped her hands together. 'Does she get to hold tea parties on the lawn and wear a tiara?'

'No, Sam. She gets to climb up and repair the roof if she can't work out where to get the money from.'

'Really? Does she know how?'

'Nope.' Pip raised a grin from somewhere, staying serious was impossible with Sam around. 'Sorry, what were you saying before?'

'Oh, I said wouldn't you like one, babe? You know, a little mini-me. It would be so amazing.'

Pip, who was accustomed to hearing Sam talk about hair extensions and facelifts, hoped she'd misunderstood the question. 'One what?'

'You know, a baby. Doesn't every girl really want one?'

She wasn't sure now which was worse, worrying about Elizabeth and Lottie, or this conversation. 'Sam, I don't even want a dog, let alone a baby.' She stared at the glamorous Sam and wondered what on earth it was that triggered baby lust in a woman after she'd been with the same man for any length of time. Personally, she was more interested in a different type of lust, which was pretty incompatible with babies, as far as she could see. And she'd thought Samantha Simcock would be the same. After all, if a girl is married to the seriously ripped England goalkeeper, lives in a mansion and has access to as many designer clothes as her heart desires, why on earth would she want to swap them for dirty nappies and middle-of- the-night feeds? 'You're not telling me you…?'

Sam shrugged, which Pip took as a bad sign. And even though it was only four o'clock in the afternoon, she decided it was probably time to open the wine.

'Your boobs will sag.' She passed Sam a glass and hoped that the alcohol would help the conversation take off in a more sensible direction.

'Ah, that's no problem, babe. You can always have them done, you know – implants. A lot of men love them all pert and it shows you still care about them, doesn't it? And you can have them any size you want.' She grinned. 'That's what all the girls do, you know, after they've weaned the babbies off them, that is. They won't do them straight away, of course.'

'Urgh, I don't want to hear.' Pip put her hands over her ears and tried not to think what Mick's reaction would be if she landed him with a baby and a new pair of boobs. 'And you'll get bags under your eyes from lack of sleep. Implants won't help with those.'

'Oh bags are just so easy to fix, babe. I know one girl who had a job lot, you know –boobs and a bit of lipo on her thighs as well as having her eye bags sorted. I'm sure she got a really good deal for having the lot done all at once.' She looked at Pip with an earnest expression. 'You shouldn't let a bit of sagging stop you.'

'I'm not, believe me. When you've had as many brothers and

sisters as I have, not to mention a load of cousins. then it puts you off bum-wiping for life.'

'You can't mean that. I want lots.' Sam had a dreamy look in her eye. 'Davey would like a whole football team. And I could always get a nanny or au-pair or something. He'd love that too.' She winked.

'Does he know how much that'll cost in nappies as well as plastic surgery?' Pip had a sudden vision of Sam's gorgeous body being lifted, sucked and tucked in all directions as daddy David drilled them into becoming mini-me goal keepers. Not that many people would object to a few David clones.

'And you'd need a bigger Jacuzzi.'

Sam ignored her, too taken with the fantasy world she was busy creating in her head. 'Oh, babe, can you imagine having a little girl to take shopping? Just think about all the gorg stuff you can buy. You can get all the same stuff for kids now as for yourself, you know. Even, like, mini Barbours from when they are really teeny tiny. And' she was warming to the subject, 'the girls could have cute ponies and join in with the jumping that everyone does here. They just look so good in white pants and those black jackets, don't they? Have you seen Jordan when she does that dressage stuff like Dom does? She looks cool, and so glam too with her hair up and that red lipstick. Somebody told me she had to have her boobs reduced so she could ride properly. That can't possibly be true, can it?' She paused, obviously considering that dressage might not be the ideal pursuit for her as-yet unconceived offspring. 'I mean, I can see that it might make it more difficult to jump, but that stuff is just on a flat bit, isn't it?'

'I haven't the foggiest, although you don't see many big-boobed riders do you? Not professional ones anyway. There's lots on the hunting field.' Pip paused, aware she was being drawn into the ridiculous conversation.

'Maybe she was scared they'd pop if she fell off?' Sam gave a hearty laugh and opened her big blue eyes wide in mock horror.

In her brief time with Lottie and the Tippermere crew, Pip had seen a fair few falls – some of them quite spectacular (and most of them arse over tit, as Billy liked to point out), but she could never remember seeing any breast implants explode. Never. It would have made a lasting memory and the easiest piece of journalism she'd ever done in her life. 'I thought they were supposed to be robust. Anyway it's probably better to fall on your boobs than your nose. Although I suppose you could get a nose job.' The sarcasm was lost on Sam.

'You can get anything fixed now, babe. I know some really good people. Them days of black eyes and having to hide away for weeks have gone. Davey said that Jose's fiancée had her boobs done for the World Cup and was on the beach by the time they'd played their first match.'

'I thought she was just his girlfriend.' Pip was faintly miffed that not only had she somehow missed out on the news that the England football manager had got engaged without her knowledge, but that she still hadn't managed to get an interview with him. When Sam and her footballing husband, David, had moved into Kitterly Heath she'd had plans to grab some headlines of her own, but somehow her eye had drifted off the ball once she'd moved in with Mick. And she hadn't realised quite how much until now.

'Oh she went all out for the World Cup and he was so pissed after they won it that he proposed. She would have been gutted if he hadn't after having her nails and her tits done specially.'

It was at that point, when she really felt that the conversation was getting out of control and taking on a life of its own, that there was a loud rap on the door, followed by an unnecessarily long ring on the buzzer. 'Here, pour us another glass while I see who that is.' Hopefully sanity would have returned by the time she did.

***

'Now aren't you a sight for sore eyes. Thought I was never going to find this place. Going to invite me in?'

Pip stared at the hunk standing on her doorstep and her heart plummeted straight to her boots. Todd. As far as she was concerned, the only solution to the Todd problem was to put him on a plane, not look after him. And now he was on her doorstep. With, she noticed in alarm, a rucksack. A big rucksack.

In Barcelona she'd never really got to know him that well, but she did know that he was a complete heel for dumping Lottie like he had. And if he'd come back and said sorry, like Lottie had said, then that was fine. But that was it.

'I'm hallucinating.' She was pretty sure that when Lottie had made the suggestion that she babysit Todd, she had not said yes. She had not even said maybe. Either time. She had definitely said no and changed the subject. 'You're not here and this is not happening. I thought you'd be on a plane by now.' Pip clamped her mouth and the door shut simultaneously. Except that an oversized boot got there first. 'You've done that before, I bet. Used to having doors slammed in your face, are you? Now move your bloody foot out of my doorway.' She pushed harder, but he didn't budge. Just grinned. 'Just like you've done other things before.' She didn't add the 'like get married before you get divorced' bit, because she didn't need to.

'Ah come on, be a sport, give us a chance. I didn't have you down as a tight arse. Thought you'd be pleased to see me again.'

'Piss off, Todd. I don't want to see you again, and neither does Lottie. She's just too nice to tell you where to go.' And they really didn't need him right now, she could have added, when Lottie was settled with Rory and a line had been drawn under what had always had the potential to be a disastrous relationship. And Lottie had far more important and serious things to think about. Like raise mega amounts of money. 'You've seen her and apologised.' He grinned. 'So you can go back Down-Under now before you cause any more problems.'

'How do you know I haven't changed?'

'How do I know a dog's got bollocks?'

He looked confused for a second. 'Take a look under its tail?'

'Exactly! And with you I don't even need to look. Still got yours?'

'You betcha, babe.'

'Well, we don't want to see them here. And leave Tab alone, she's a kid.'

'You're not still sore about the whole getting-arrested-on-the-beach thing are you?'

'Yes.' She tried kicking her side of the door, in the hope it would hurt. But he didn't even have the manners to flinch. 'You just have no idea the state you left Lottie in, have you?'

'You mean it really didn't go down at all well?'

'That's one way of putting it.'

'She seemed okay about seeing me, all things considered. We had quite a chat and she was cool.'

'Are you stupid? It went down like a lead balloon. She's just being polite. Though God knows why.' Maybe if she put her shoulder to it, it would help, she thought, still wrestling with the door.

'Come on, mate, it's not like I murdered anyone, now, is it? Be reasonable. I'm pretty damned sure Lottie is totally cool about it now. You saw for yourself at her old man's wedding.'

'Well, I'm not cool about it, totally or otherwise.' I could be the one doing the murdering right now, thought Pip, wondering how the hell Lottie had ever fallen for the blond beach bum who was currently loitering on her Cheshire doorstep. Well, apart from the obvious, like the baby blue eyes, wicked grin and muscles. But he was a complication too far. Yesterday had been entertaining, today he was outstaying his welcome.

'Anyway, weren't you deported or put in prison, or something?'

'Out early, for good behaviour.' He saw the frown deepen. 'Kidding, honest! I got off. No charges.'

'How can you get off? You got married but forgot you were supposed to be single first.'

'Didn't Lottie tell you? Like I explained everything to her, the marriage was never, like, legal or whatever, no paperwork. So I did only get married once. Good eh?'

'Brilliant. Only you could call a wedding that wasn't legalised a stroke of luck. So was that the first one or the second? Or are there more we haven't heard about yet?'

'Oh the second, babe. Don't think the first wanted to divorce me really, which you can understand, can't you?' He winked. 'That's why she didn't make it absolute. But it's done now, just been to the courts to sort it.' He didn't look remotely bothered. 'That's one of the reasons I came over to the UK.'

'And you honestly think I want to talk to you? Even if Lottie is daft enough to forgive you, I'm not. You hurt her, Todd, don't you get that? She's my friend and if you think you're getting another chance, dream on.' He'd already found Lottie, gate-crashed the wedding and made himself a local celebrity. Wasn't that enough for anybody? Tippermere was a small place. If anybody saw him here then she'd be the talk of the village as well. Murder was sounding more inviting by the second.

'Me and Lots were only fooling, nothing serious.' Which was the conclusion Pip had come to in the end, once Lottie had stopped crying, but she wasn't about to admit that to Todd. 'I reckon she was pleased to see me again.'

'It doesn't matter what you were doing – you were fucking married and you just abandoned her.'

'Well, to be fair, I didn't have much choice about leaving her.'

'You could have sent a message, anything.'

'Ah, stop nit-picking.' He shrugged. 'Come for a drink if you're not going to ask me in. I need to talk to you.'

'To me?' Pip sighed inwardly. 'Lottie didn't tell you to come here, did she?'

He looked confused. 'Lottie? Why would Lots send me over?'

Pip was actually feeling nosy and increasingly guilty that she hadn't offered to help Lottie out. And she was feeling a bit miffed, as she'd been abandoned by Mick once again as he'd put a horse higher up in his list of priorities than her, which was why Sam had popped in. Except she hadn't bargained on the baby and cosmetic surgery talk.

Lottie had tried to warn her about the whole men-and-horses thing when it had started to look serious with Mick. Told her she'd need to understand, but she still wasn't convinced she wanted to. She'd bought into a relationship with Mick, not a stable full of horses. Yes, she wanted some independence and wanted them to do stuff on their own, but she loved him. And she wanted him to ditch the horses at weekends so they could do something different for a change. Together.

She was beginning to understand why Lottie had fled abroad, and into Todd's bed. It did have a certain appeal.

Her last image of Todd, prior to his unexpected arrival in Tippermere, was in Barcelona jogging across the beach with his surf board. She'd left him and Lottie to soak up the rays while she'd gone off exploring the stylish bars and boutiques in the nearby El Born district. And, much later, after a good shopping trip and a couple of glasses of wine, she'd been shocked to find Lottie in tears. It had taken quite a while to make sense of her friend's hysterical outpourings, but from what Pip could gather he was being escorted to the airport and onto a plane bound for Australia. And now he was here. The other side of the world. And nobody was quite sure why. If she let him in she might find out.

'I suppose you can come in, but don't put your rucksack down.'

He grinned. 'Fair dinkums.'

'Don't dinkums me, you dingo.' And with that she was engulfed in the type of man hug that amounted to borderline asphyxiation.

When Todd had arrived in Cheshire his plan had been quite simple. Find Lottie, apologise for the fiasco on the beach, and ask if she could put him up for a while so he could sort out some family business. But things had gone wrong from the start. The whole wedding thing had knocked him off his stride. He'd got completely the wrong end of the stick when Tab had gone on about ancient men and 'Lottie's wedding' and had decided on impulse that as he owed Lottie one, and he did really want her to be happy, he had to get in his 'don't' bit before she got in her 'I do'.

All things considered, things has worked out quite well in the end, though. But he couldn't ask her for a bed for the night. She and Rory, who had cropped up in more than one conversation in Barcelona, were obviously a serious item and he had a fair idea (thick- skinned though he knew he could be) that he'd outstayed his welcome.

He grinned. This solution could be perfect, though, once he won Pip round. Even if, with Tabatha's directions, he'd spent the best part of an hour getting lost down the lanes before finally realising that the cottage he'd driven past three times was in fact the right place. England might be cute and quaint, he decided, but it was a hell of a lot easier finding a shack in the middle of the bush than locating someone in this village.

And one step further into the cottage convinced him it had been more than worth it. Perched on a bar stool, large glass of white wine in hand was the most glamorous woman he'd seen since landing at Manchester airport.

'This is Todd.' Sam and Todd exchanged admiring glances, which was worrying, given his track record, though at least it might stop the 'lifting and tucking' and nappies conversation for a bit.

Sam beamed. 'Wow, I've heard all about you. Did Tab really let you ride that horse of hers?'

'Well I guess to be fair, I didn't really ask.' He moved in closer and winked. 'I was on it before she had a chance to say no.'

'You were with Lottie in Barcelona weren't you? That is just so romantic, just spending time chilling and not worrying about anything. When we go away it's always to these places with your own chef and hairdresser and stuff. It must be cool not having any of that. When I was a kid we went camping, but my mum didn't like the mud, and then when me and Dave first went out we went to Cornwall with these big caravans, you know before he got the contract, so I suppose it was a bit like that?' She topped up the wine glasses. 'The only time I've been to Barcelona is when Dave was playing and they arranged for this coach to take us to all the sights while the boys were training, then to this really posh tapas bar with these amazing cocktails where the stuff was like in smoke and froth, but it's not the same as just sitting on the beach is it?'

Pip, seeing the look on Todd's face sensed interesting times ahead. 'Sam is married to David Simcock, the goal keeper.' He didn't look put off. 'The England goalkeeper.' Not that Sam would ever be interested in a beach bum with a penchant for bigamy. 'Todd is a surfer, who's married to lots of people.'

They ignored her, Todd plonking himself on the bar stool next to Sam and ditching the rucksack, which sat like an unwelcome guest in the corner.

'Cool. So you go all over the world with him, then?'

'A bit, but I like it here. I didn't at first, did I Pip? Cos I didn't know anybody, but Pip has been lovely and we got a dog.'

'And she's thinking of getting a baby next. Well, lots of them.'

'Getting? Like Brangelina? All different colours? Good on you.'

Pip sat back and decided to watch this one out.

'No, silly.' Sam giggled, glad that somebody was actually interested. 'I want to have them myself. Davey loves kids. So where are you staying then, with Pip?'

'No, he's not.' She tried to avoid looking at the scruffy rucksack.

'Well actually,' Todd shifted in his seat and grinned, 'I am. Rory introduced me to your man Mick this morning. He said you wouldn't mind if I crashed here for a bit seeing as you've got a spare room. Seems like a good bloke.'

Pip would have dropped her drink, if it hadn't been wine, which meant she instinctively held on. Clutching the stem in a death grip. 'Mick said?' So it hadn't been Lottie, it was worse. Mick had sent him here. She took a deep breathe. Mick, why would he do that?

And Mick had said there was a spare room? Was it worse than not loving her? Was he so bored he was thinking of a threesome? No, that was totally out of character, and anyhow men always went for the two-girl sandwich, didn't they?

Or maybe Lottie had asked Mick. Yeah, that would make more sense. Except she wouldn't do that, would she? That would be sneaky and not like Lottie at all, however desperate she was.

Letting Mick move in a while ago, so he didn't have to use the groom's flat at Rory's, had seemed like a good idea. Now, all of a sudden, it didn't. It was confusing. 'He what?' She needed this spelling out, just in case she'd misheard.

'Ahh, isn't that lovely?' Sam obviously liked the idea, even if she didn't. 'It means I can get to know you. I'm here all the time, aren't I, Pip?'

'Mick said what, exactly?'

'I could crash here. That's not a problem, is it?'

Inspiration struck. 'You can use the groom's flat, Mick's old place.' Making sure Todd didn't get under Lottie's feet was one thing, having him under her roof was altogether different. She'd act as childminder in the day, not the night.

'Afraid not.'

'What do you mean, afraid not?'

'Tab's moving in,' Todd grinned, 'after all she is the groom and she's getting fed up of being with her dad. She's ready to fly the nest. I mean, a girl that age doesn't want to live with her old man, does she? Watching her every move, if you know what I mean.' He winked at Sam, who giggled.

Pip glared and tried to think of something to say, but she'd been wrong-footed. In an hour or so on the yard he'd found out all kinds of things that even she didn't know.

'And all that horse stuff isn't really me, you know, more of a water type myself.'

'Are you a Pisces, babe? Two little fishies.' Sam snuggled in.

'More a Taurus, me.'

'Yeah full of bull, I'd say. Look, you can't get away from horses here, Todd. You'll hate it.' Pip sighed, at least if he hung around for a bit she'd have a kindred spirit in the house, and she had to admit he wasn't that bad. As daft and irresponsible as Lottie, maybe, and he probably hadn't given being arrested another thought. Couldn't comprehend the resulting meltdown for Lottie – which Pip suspected had come more from confusion than a real pain of losing Todd. Losing Todd had meant Lottie had just lost her alternative, had to face up to the truth of what she really wanted. Tippermere.

And she would be helping ease Lottie's burden. Lottie, who had found her a job when she'd moved here, introduced her to everybody, was as generous and undemanding as a friend could be. Payback time.

'Oh, you can escape the horses if you come over to our place at Kitterly Heath, Todd, we don't have any, just dogs.' Sam was practically clapping her hands with glee. 'Are you going to be around for a bit, then? I can plan stuff, introduce you to some people if you like. You'll love the girls.'

Todd grinned. 'Yeah, that would be ace. Might even see if I can find a job round here for a bit. Must be some apple-picking or something I can do, eh?'

'But why?' Okay she sounded pathetic. 'You'll be bored. I mean a week or two is more than enough for most people. And it's the wrong time of year for apples.'

He shrugged. 'Bartender? I'm sure I can find something to fill the time in. You did, didn't you?' His blue eyed widened and Pip knew she was being made fun of.

'That's different.'

'Hey, you never know, I might find some long-lost rellies in the UK.'

'Rellies?'

'Yeah, folk. Y'know, family. Aren't we all related to your royal family, or something? Six times removed?'

'Oh God, not another one.' Pip was on the verge of putting her head in her hands and wailing. 'I think you need to go over and see Tom and you can both dig up the past together. He's obsessed with long-lost relatives.' Which wasn't entirely true. When Tom Strachan had arrived in Tippermere he'd been drawn to Folly Lake Manor, unaware that it was his birth place. But his obsession with the place had nearly driven her nuts, and had caused more than one raised eyebrow in the village. For a long time rumours had been rife about him and the current owner of the place, newly widowed Amanda, until her relationship with Dom had come out into the open, and the wily Elizabeth had finally revealed the truth. 'You have met Tab's dad I take it? Tom?' She paused. 'And no, you can't be related to the Queen. No way.'

'Dad? Well we didn't exactly discuss him.'

'No, I bet you didn't.' Her tone was dry.

'You'll love it here, you won't want to leave, will he babe?' This time Sam did raise a toast, delighted at the prospect of parading her newfound buddy around the area.

Although, thinking about it, he'd probably be a hit in Kitterly Heath. Maybe she should actively encourage him in that direction.

'Never knew everybody would be so welcoming. Any chance of a drink, then, Pippa? Can't wait to get to know you all better.' Todd gave Sam the full-on beam, and Pip could have sworn she blushed. Oh God. It was getting worse by the hour. The man had barely introduced himself and he'd already done who knew what to Tab and now looked like he was setting his sights on Sam. The only advantage, she supposed, was that he genuinely didn't seem to be here to sweep Lottie off her feet, so why was he here?

'Mind you, I could do with a change of clobber – think this is a bit stinky.' Todd pulled the t-shirt, which he'd had on yesterday on his horse-riding challenge, away from his body and gave it a sniff. 'All that wrestling with the gee gees I guess. Can't imagine why you lot do it for fun.'

Sam giggled and Pip raised her eyebrows. 'Don't you dare strip

77

off here Crocodile Dundee, I'll show you the spare bedroom.' Which she supposed meant that she'd accepted he was staying. 'But if you as much as leer at Lottie I'll put you on a plane myself.'

***

Todd dropped his battered rucksack on the floor of the bedroom and stooped to peer out of the small sash window. To the immediate rear of the cottage was a small well-kept garden, overflowing with the type of colour only a British garden can boast, and beyond it the lush green of grass and trees.

He rested his knuckles on the sill and had a sudden longing for the wide-open spaces of his home town in Australia, and the sea. Homesickness was a new one for Todd, and he didn't acknowledge this feeling as that. He just put it down to claustrophobia.

The cottages might be quaint around here, but they were dark and crowded with heavy furniture, and an expanse of flat green pasture didn't compensate for the surf and blue-to-the-horizon life he was used to.

What was he doing here? Sure, he'd felt a heel over the whole splitting up with Lottie thing and he did owe her an explanation and an apology. Being a bit careless and forgetful was one thing, but the whole charge of bigamy had knocked him sideways. He might be irresponsible at times, but he'd never meant to hurt anybody. And he'd never really been one for breaking the law. And if his second rushed marriage had been carried out formally, he guessed the whole misunderstanding would never have happened. Not that his first wife called it a misunderstanding. He'd seen the look on her face when his lawyer had finally declared the divorce absolute.

He stared out over the fields, not really seeing them. He'd married the first time in a mad lustful rush of youthful impatience, but within days the cracks had appeared. Marrying his English wife in her home town had been part of the plan, as had a move back out to Australia. But, they'd both soon realised that the day-to-day reality of living the dream was a nightmare.

After a year of hell, she'd headed home to her family and filed for divorce. And then changed her mind on seeing the decree nisi and realising what she was losing. So she had never filed for the absolute.

Except Todd hadn't realised. As far as he was concerned it was done and dusted and he'd moved on. He'd been on a trail of proving his manhood and repairing his ego.

Coming back to the UK to tie up the loose ends had been one thing, but there was far more to it than that. He had to stay and fulfil the promise he'd made to his brother. His conscience wouldn't let him escape from that obligation. Having good intentions was part of his character; being responsible wasn't. And right now every bit of him was screaming out at him to leave this place and head back to the waves.

But he had made a promise, and it was one he didn't want to break. Sometimes in life you only had one key chance, an opportunity to do the right thing, and he was pretty sure this was his.

Todd suddenly remembered why thinking wasn't a good idea; it never made anything better. He turned back to the tiny room and, stripping his t-shirt over his head, realised that being six foot tall wasn't a good idea in a cottage either. 'Struth.'

'What are you up to? Oh!' He barely registered Pip's brief knock on the door as he'd whipped his top up and received an unexpected rap on the knuckles as they'd made contact with the very old and sturdy beam that straddled the bedroom ceiling. She was now grinning at him and staring at his exposed midriff. 'Just need a hook up there and I could hold you captive, at my mercy.'

'Any time, hun. You get on and have your wicked way.' He winked, then let his arms drop down to his sides, the t-shirt slithering to the floor. Both of them knowing it wasn't going to happen, but the blood had rushed straight down to his crotch anyway. All these girls in skin-tight jodhpurs and designer gear was playing havoc with his libido. Bikinis he could cope with, but hidden delights was a new one on him.

'I would, but,' her head dropped to one side, exposing her long, lightly tanned, neck, 'Sam is waiting. You did say you'd take us out for some grub.'

There was something about this English rose complexion and countryside thing that could make for an interesting summer, Todd decided. After he'd sorted what he came here for, although he could always run the two alongside. Why suffer more than he had to?

'And you do know that Sam is out of bounds, don't you? She's very happily married.' She stressed the 'very'. 'To a very rich and famous footballer.'

'So you said. Looks like pretty much every woman in the county is out of bounds, eh?'

'You got it.'

'No harm in a bit of fun though, doll.' He laughed at her annoyed expression, which he remembered well from Barcelona. How Pip and Lottie had ever met up he didn't know, and how they'd become such close friends was even more unfathomable. 'Ah come here for a hug, Pippy.' He held out his arms.

Pip froze, her eyes fixed firmly on his naked torso, and took a gulp, not quite sure where a hug against that might take her. 'I think you need to put some clothes on.' As she scarpered down the stairs casting a 'and don't call me Pippy' over her shoulder, he laughed to himself. He'd not expected that reaction. He genuinely adored the prickly Pip because he just knew that under that protective layer there had to be a warm heart. Or Lottie wouldn't love her. And she was funny, entertaining and witty. Which had to be a bonus.

He pulled a clean t-shirt from the rucksack and put it on, taking more care not to fling his arms about this time. That Mick she was shacked up with was an interesting character too. A good craic, as the Irish would say, but touchy. Very touchy. He'd had a 'don't you dare' look about him last night, then had been offering bed and board this morning. Which had been unexpected, but perfect. Well it looked like he might not have the surf to keep him occupied, but there were plenty of other distractions. But if he wasn't careful, the way this lot partied, he'd have trouble keeping his eye on the ball.

He had one more try at lifting the sash window and letting a bit more air in the place, then admitted defeat when he managed to lift it barely two inches. He guessed this place could be more of a challenge than it looked.

Chapter 7

Lottie sat on the bale of hay, her gaze following Mick's every move.

It wasn't just that he was supremely fit, stripped to the waist, his dark hair plastered to the back of his neck and a tantalising bead of sweat trickling between his shoulder blades. It was also soothing. The watching bit. Well, that was her story and she'd rather like to stick to it.

The muscles in his arm flexed as he eased the shoe away from the horse's foot, and then he straightened the kinks out of his spine in what could have been slow motion until he was upright. He winked and gave a half-smile.

'You're quiet, treas.' He leant one arm on the horse's broad, polished rump and studied the normally bouncy Lottie, who was wrapping strands of straw around her finger and twisting the ends until they tightened like a hangman's noose. 'Freud would have had something to say about that.'

She'd glanced down, embarrassed to be caught watching, but the deep chuckle made her look back up, straight into those deep eyes. There was something about Mick that had always frightened her, and something that was almost magnetic. She didn't exactly feel like a rabbit caught in the headlights. More like one of those swinging silver balls that kept clanking against the others until it was torn loose. Only to be dragged back, almost against its will.

'Freud what?' It was a good job Mick was Pip's man and not hers. Pip could handle him. Lottie always felt she'd drown in a man like that.

He grinned and nodded in the direction of her finger, the tip of which was rapidly losing colour as she cut the blood supply off. She let go abruptly.

'So you met this Todd in Barcelona, then?'

'Australia.' She sighed, and he wasn't quite sure if it was a dreamy look in her eye, or dust from the hay. 'And then we went to Barcelona together. He said he wanted a change of scene, but maybe he was hiding from his wife.'

'Which one?' Mick lifted an eyebrow, which made him look deliciously naughty, before tossing the horseshoe in a bucket and moving round to the other side of the horse. He clicked and it obligingly lifted its hoof as he bent down. 'But he didn't break your heart, did he, darling?'

'No.' Lottie stood up and leaned on the horse so she could study the top of his head. The horse turned and nipped her bum, which was so unfair when all she was doing was standing there. It obviously didn't appreciate anyone barging into its 'me' time with the farrier. 'No,' she grinned, 'but he did seriously piss me off.'

'You came back to Rory.'

'Well, yes.'

He tapped up and snipped off the clenches, then started to lever the second shoe away.

'So him arriving out of the blue isn't a problem?'

'Well, no.'

It wasn't exactly a problem, but she didn't get why Todd was here. Okay, maybe he did want to explain, although it was a bit late, like somebody delivering a Christmas present in August. When you know you should be grateful but the moment has gone, and it's just a present. For no reason. Which can be spooky. When it's an ex. And all of a sudden what was a nice private adventure had been announced to all your friends. And your boyfriend. She'd moved on from Christmas and into the realms of 'this could be so embarrassing'.

'But?'

'It's just a bit weird. And why is he here?'

'Boredom? Curiosity?'

'He's not the curious type.' Although she didn't really know that, did she? Just as he'd remarked that he didn't know her at all, she didn't know him. Their fling had involved first names, sexual kinks and that was about it. Not that she was kinky – maybe preferences was a better word, except she'd told him about the chocolate sauce. Oh God. What if he told everybody? You see, that was the problem. It was all well and good having a no-holds-barred fling with a stranger when you were in a foreign country, but it wasn't supposed to follow you home. There was a reason holiday flings were so much fun, and it had nothing to do with being held accountable.

'Maybe he's after your massive inheritance.'

'Well, he'll be bloody disappointed. I'm not inheriting a country pile, more like a pile of debt. Have you any idea how much it costs to repair a roof that size? I hadn't until the other day.' That had been a real shock to the system. You could buy more than one good horse with that type of dosh. 'And do you know how much it costs to keep even just the East Wing heated?' She hadn't known that herself either until Dom had very gently started to introduce her to the less glam side of being a Lady, and the spreadsheet. But Todd didn't strike her as a gold digger either (if you called men that, or were they prospectors?). But there again, he hadn't struck her as a bigamist, or even a husband (ex or otherwise) at all, which was a bit worrying.

'Not a clue. Did you know he's staying with me and Pip?'

'What do you mean? Why didn't you tell me?' She banged one palm down without thinking, the horse swung its rump around in retaliation and Lottie found her own bum in the bucket of cold water that Mick had set aside to cool the horse shoes down in.

'I am doing. You didn't know, then? Rory didn't mention it?'

Lottie grimaced and went to stand up, only to find the bucket went with her. Which was her own fault for having a big arse. Although if she took over her inheritance she wouldn't be able to afford chips and chocolate, so that would solve that problem. Maybe that was why a lot of rich people were thin, because they weren't actually rich.

'I'm stuck.' She giggled as the horse nudged the bucket with its nose and sent a new cascade of water into her boots. The seal broken, it fell off with a clatter, the horse faking alarm reversed onto Mick's foot and the terriers arrived at full belt, eager not to miss any of the fun.

Mick, armed with steel-toe-capped boots pushed the horse forward good naturedly and watched as the dogs circled them, barking with excitement.

What had ever brought him to this mad yard? Lottie was love-able but as scatty as they came, Rory was good natured but too easy-going and forgetful for anybody's good, and the dogs just about summed it up. Chaotic.

Home with Pip was different. Tidy, ordered, animal-free. But he had to admit, the last bit bothered him. He didn't have any particular need for a canine companion, but horses were his live-lihood. His life. In his blood. A day without a horse was a day wasted. And the fact that not only did she not want to share that affection, but she was obviously beginning to get irritated by it, loomed like a large black cloud on the horizon. Her bossy nature and challenging outlook on life, plus her immaculate turn-out, had been what had drawn him to her in the first place. The challenge more than anything, if he was honest. But an insurmountable challenge was an altogether different prospect. He went back to looking at Lottie, which was always a nice experience. Even if she did have a habit of wearing mismatched socks with her breeches, and polo shirts adorned with horse slobber and hay.

She stared back at him, looking hurt. 'Why's he staying with you?' Mick had an urge to cuddle her, make it better, so he shoved his hands in his pockets out of harm's way.

'Is it a problem?' He spoke softly, willing her not to care. Mercurial was the word for Lottie; wild and spirited one minute, lost and hurt the next. A girl who needed the space to run free, but a man who could nurture her, understand her.

'Well I'd kind of assumed he was making his way to the airport after he'd had his breakfast and a last fondle with Tab in the tack room.'

'Fondle?'

'Shag?'

'Now, why on this earth would he be shagging a kid like terrible Tab when he came over to see you, treasure?'

Lottie shrugged. And blushed. He had that effect on her, with his earnest gaze and Irish brogue. She'd once fallen asleep while he was talking to her, not because he was boring but because she was tired and she just loved the sound of his voice. Irrespective of the words.

He took his hands out of his pockets and went back to pulling horse shoes off. 'Rory asked if we'd put him up, so I said yes. Didn't think it would be an issue, but say the word...'

Lottie stooped down and gazed at him, under the horse's belly, aware of her cold, damp breeches clinging to her bum. 'You offered, you bugger.'

'You want me to un-offer?'

The horse was nibbling her hair, which was sending goose bumps down her neck and making it hard to think. Well it was that, or the way he was looking at her. 'You can't do that. It would be mean. Wouldn't it?' She added the last bit in a hopeful tone, hoping he'd say no. But he didn't.

'I doubt he'll stay long, darling. Pass me the file.' She passed the file, and didn't miss the slightly guilty look on his face.

When Todd had mentioned he needed a place to crash, Mick

hadn't been about to offer. But when Rory had put him on the spot, it had seemed like a good idea.

Todd sparked something off in Pip and Mick had sensed it right from the start, even if Pip hadn't. His fooling and antics punctured the air of impending gloom that hung around them these days, which meant if the Australian stuck around it would lift the pressure for a bit, give Pip somebody to talk about stuff other than horses with. And hopefully she'd lighten up and go back to the tenacious journalist that he'd fallen for in the first place. Instead of the frustrated and increasingly snappy city girl.

She'd chilled since moving out of London and settling in Tippermere. In those early weeks when he'd first met her and Lottie, she'd been edgy, but she'd got more laid back by the day – less twitchy and acerbic. But still funny and sharp. But that was then, and now he had a feeling they were heading for a car crash. Now she was looking for a fight. Unhappy. With him. Because she was nobody's fool.

Mick sighed inwardly, but it had been selfish to say yes to Todd. He should have asked Lottie first.

'Never mind.' She was scratching the horse's withers, in apology for the earlier outburst. 'You're right. I'm sure he'll soon get bored. No sea and surf here.' The grin was genuine Lottie, tinged with optimism. But he wasn't convinced himself. Mick had a horrible feeling that Todd wasn't just here to issue an apology for whatever happened last time he saw Lottie. Maybe he was after making up and rekindling the lust. And what if Rory, in his normal easy-going fashion, missed the signs?

Rory was blind as far as Lottie went. He could spot a problem with a horse at fifty paces, but with her he just expected things to be fine. The man honestly didn't deserve her. He'd told him before and probably would again. But would he do anything about it? Which reminded him, he'd still not discovered what went on at the wedding, and why Rory had gone from wanting to kill the man to offering him bed and board to hang around.

'You sure you want this mare barefoot?'

Lottie nodded, a worried frown creasing her brow, and chewed the edge of her thumb. 'Rory said it's the last resort.'

'Thanks for that vote of confidence in my abilities.'

'I didn't mean that.' She lightened up and grinned. 'He wants her sound because she's got this incredible jump in her, but nothing seems to work.'

'This might not either. It's not a miracle cure, you know,' he winked, 'even with my skill.'

'I know. Last resort. We're going to put her in foal if it doesn't work. But I'm sure it will because you're just so bloody clever.' And she reached up and kissed him, sending a waft of floral scent his way before waving and heading over to Rory, who'd just got back from a hack with Flash.

Mick wished he could switch off and not like her quite so much. Be ambivalent. But he couldn't. And even Pip wasn't distracting him as much as she used to. He really had to get them back on course. Talk to her. Before the relationship went the same way his previous one had with Niamh.

Niamh leaving him to bugger off to America had been a blow to his pride as well as his heart. And he'd sworn never to get that involved again. And he wasn't. But maybe that wasn't helping right now.

He watched Lottie, bouncing up and down in welcome like one of her dogs. Watched Rory lean down and kiss the tip of her nose. Then he turned his concentration back to what he did best. Trimming hooves and talking to horses.

***

'Why did you ask Todd to stay?'

88

'I didn't.' Rory swung out of the saddle, narrowly missing landing on one of the dogs, who yelped then jumped into his arms and proceeded to try and stick her tongue into his mouth when he opened it to speak. 'Stop it, Tilly, you're a tart.' She wriggled her little body enthusiastically, her tail whipping from side to side. He dropped the ecstatic bundle and grabbed the rein just as Flash made a bid for freedom. 'He asked.' He loosened the girth a hole. 'Said he wanted to hang about for a few days and wondered if I knew anywhere cheap.'

'But, don't you...' Lottie paused. 'Mind' might suggest there was still something going on.

'Mind?' Mick said it for her. She hadn't heard him come up behind her.

'Course not, I trust you, darling. Why would you be interested in him when you've got a hunk like me?' He winked. 'Run the stirrup up on the other side, love.'

Lottie pulled the stirrup up and pushed the leather through. Maybe it would have been easier if Rory had actually caught and killed Todd yesterday. Well not killed, because that would be murder, and she wasn't that keen on the idea of conjugal prison visits. And did you get them if you weren't married?

'You sorted that footie mare, Mick? She'd be a bloody good prospect if I could keep her sound for more than five minutes at a time. Like riding a ballerina. Suppose you're going to tell me to take it slowly.'

'Rory, what did he say to you?' It bothered Lottie that Rory seemed happy for Todd to hang around, and it bothered her that she hadn't been there when Rory had caught up with him. The jump-off at the wedding might have been fun, and a bit of alpha-male competition. But really? What were they playing at?

'Who?' Rory had already moved on.

'Todd.' Mick said it with her. 'You know, at the wedding, after you caught him.'

'Oh, not much. He's a nice guy, and I know nothing really went on between the pair of you. Right, come and help me with these jumps. We need to put Black Gold though her paces before we fill that entry form in.' He was already striding across the yard, Flash trailing behind him like a docile donkey.

Lottie sighed and admitted defeat. Was it good or bad when your man didn't have a jealous bone in his body? He trusted her. Great! But if one of his exes turned up asking for a bed for the night, she wouldn't have been quite so generous. Men were weird. The whole Mars-Venus thing was right. They were on a different planet.

'Are you sure it's a good idea? Entering Gold?' The horse had been a present from her father, who obviously either hated her or wanted to challenge her. When she'd got back from Barcelona, hoping for some TLC or at least a bit of sympathy, instead he'd told her to pull herself together and sort out the youngster, who wanted to kill her, or so it seemed.

Her first outing in public had been a draghunt, and Mick had babysat them on a big borrowed hunter, who knew the ropes and was as steady as they come. That was the horse, not Mick. In fact, if she hadn't had Mick at her side the St John's ambulance brigade might well have had their first customer of the season, seeing as Rory had buggered off at the front of the field with Flash. A year on, Gold had settled a bit, but still liked to surprise her. The novelty was starting to wear thin.

'She needs a challenge.' The soft voice made her jump. Lottie had almost forgotten Mick was actually there, not that it was possible to forget him altogether. 'Like you do.' The warmth of his hand seeped into her skin, then was off before she could really register it. Lottie felt a flutter deep inside her, then looked up and it was straight into the eyes of Rory, who was gazing at her from across the yard, wondering what the hold-up was. She loved him. She really did. He was there for her, he understood her. He was fun. So why did the prospect of Todd hanging around worry her more than it did him?

Half an hour later, all thoughts of Todd had been swiftly banished from Lottie's mind. After Rory had set the jumps up and Gold had deposited her in the middle of them.

In a way, she had to admire the black horse. She was fast, unpredictable and refused to be consistent. On a good day it was funny, on a bad day it hurt. Like now, when she was lying face-up in a tangle of poles, and the long black face, with its white stripe, was peering down at her in amazement as she blew gentle puffs of warm air through her large nostrils.

'Ouch! That hurt.' She pushed the soft nose away from her face and tried to work out a way to breathe without it hurting her ribs.

'Well, don't fall off.'

'Very funny. She swerved.' Rory raised an eyebrow. 'And bucked.'

'Maybe we should enter her in the next class up. Higher jumps; that could work.'

The words 'suicide mission' leapt unbidden into Lottie's mind as she struggled to her feet and gathered up the reins.

'She can clear much higher than that, might concentrate her mind. I could ride her for you?'

Yes, yes, say yes. 'No. I'm fine.'

'There's my girl.' He gave her a leg up into the saddle and eyed up the poles, before raising them to a height even she could belly dance under.

'Cool, this looks like fun.' Tab had appeared, and fun to Tab, who was known for her goth appearance and outlook – total black and doom-laden prophecies of the type only a teenager could make with a straight face – was not Lottie's type of fun. It was bad.

Lottie, against all her self-preservation instincts, wheeled the mare around to face the first jump. Black Gold pricked her ears forward and tossed her head, keen to get the bit between her teeth and out of her rider's clutch. For a second they fought a battle of control, before the mare charged, swishing her tail, then her head was down and her back arched as she threw a sly buck in one stride out from take-off.

Closing her eyes, Lottie hoped the horse didn't do the same. She felt the power ripple through the great body – felt the brief hesitation and kicked on. The horse soared, hit the ground and bucked again, then headed for the next jump of her own accord. Out of the corner of her eye she could see the unmistakable figure of Mick and the thrill of that first hunt came back in a rush. She pushed on into the next jump, keen to show him that she could manage without his hand-holding.

'Tilly, come here.' Rory's voice carried loud and clear, and the little dog, which had been darting from jump to jump, wheeled around obediently, shooting out from the base of the jump into Gold's field of vision.

The mare was gathering herself for take-off, her weight in her strong hind legs as the brown and white terrier flashed out from her blind spot and across her line of sight. For a moment it seemed to the onlookers that she hung suspended, then her head swung to one side as the flight instinct gripped her body. Dangling forelegs followed, her whole body twisting as the forward momentum was lost and she reared up.

Lottie, all her concentration on the poles ahead, barely registered Rory's shout, didn't notice the small dog. Already committed to going over the obstacle with the horse, she was caught unawares.

The strong neck came up, knocking her hard in the face as she leant forward, numbing her. Instinct kept her weight forward, but the horse kept rising, past the point of no return. For a moment, horse and rider teetered and then Gold lost the battle. Lost her precarious balance as her body weight, twisted to one side, took her down. All Lottie saw was the gleaming black of the horse above, then nothing as Gold hit the ground with a ground-shaking thud.

Chapter 8

The whole of her head throbbed and felt huge – at least twice its normal size. Which, Lottie gathered, must mean she was still alive. Although it did smell strangely of heaven. She gave an experimental swallow, which made her throat hurt.

'Hey, you're awake.'

'I'm not dead?' It came out as a bit of a raspy croak, so maybe she'd been reincarnated as Kermit. Although, given the way everything felt enormous and swollen, maybe not. She ran her tongue over dry lips.

'You're not dead, no.' The voice was familiar, but not normal. It had a tremble, which could be her hearing, or his voice. She gave in, stopped trying to talk or listen, let the great wave of tiredness engulf her.

It hurt more the next time she tried to open her eyes. It wasn't just her head that was vibrating like a train going through a tunnel, it was her whole body.

'Where am I?'

'Hospital.'

'What day is it?'

'It's still Tuesday.'

'I feel like Elephant Man.'

'No big ears or trunk, but you've got one hell of a shiner.'

Which explained why her eyes didn't want to open.

'But I still don't half fancy you.' She squinted and the dark splodge that was Rory wobbled its way in and out of focus.

'It's the hospital nightie isn't it?'

'Well, actually, you haven't got one on.' Rory chuckled.

'What?' It came out as a bit of a squawk, more parrot than Kermit.

'Kidding. You're right. It's that and the purple legs, very attractive combination.' He had a lopsided grin on his face when she managed to turn her head and look at him properly, and seemed almost relieved. It was the look he usually wore when he turned to look back at the jump poles and confirmed he'd got a clear round.

'Can we go home?'

'Tomorrow. You didn't break anything, just got a smack in the face and a slight squashing.'

'You smacked me?'

'Gold. You don't remember?' Now he sounded worried.

'Oh, Gold, yes. Jumping…'

'You were lucky.' He held her hand in his, stroked his thumb over the back, again and again, and for once, instead of giving her a fizz of excitement it was comforting. Rhythmic, warm. 'She was as quick getting back to her feet as she was falling, like a cat and careful. Never touched you.' Rory knew as well as Lottie did from experience that when a horse went down it was the rolling body and flailing hooves that could do the most damage.

'She's okay?'

'She's fine.' He turned her hand over, traced a finger down her lifeline. 'Came off better than you, she's just a little shook up.'

Lottie closed her eyes again and wallowed in his touch. 'How long have you been here?'

'I came with you.'

Which didn't answer the question, as she wasn't sure how long that had been.

'Don't you need to do the horses?'

'Mick and Tab are sorting them.' He stopped stroking and wrapped her hand in both his warm ones. Lottie let go of reality and slept again.

***

'I think you should do a big upstairs-downstairs thing, with a butler. You know, go the whole hog. People lap that kind of thing up. They'd pay a fortune.'

Lottie stared at Todd and wondered who was the most deranged. Her for letting him visit, then asking him what he thought. Or him for just being him. He was beginning to sound a bit like Sam. And she hadn't really expected him to suggest anything, there had just been an awkward gap in the conversation, which she'd tried to politely fill.

But as she was still aching all over, and had obviously been trampled by a herd of cows (Rory's version of events had to be wide of the mark), she was a captive audience. A very captive audience. She'd got up earlier to go to the bathroom and been shocked at just how wobbly her legs felt – not quite jelly, more like being on stilts in a high wind.

'Y'know, theme days, weekends.' He plonked his feet on the edge of the table and put his hands behind his head, warming to the subject. 'People pay and get the whole works. How about murder-mystery things? Mr Green in the library with the candlestick and all that. And your old Gran could turn up in her tiara and nightie, like a ghost.'

Maybe this was some weird kind of pre-death hallucination thing, where you're between death and life, and maybe she hadn't actually lived through the whole waking up and coming home.

It was a dream. Todd wasn't here. And he wasn't talking about butlers. But if he was, murder mystery was always an option. With him being the one mysteriously murdered.

'Gran doesn't want people in the house.' She'd go with it, assuming she was alive and not pre-death hallucinating. Just in case. 'And nor do I. You've been talking to Sam, haven't you?' Only Sam could come up with stuff like that. 'Or Pip?' He was living with Pip.

'Now, that would be telling.' He grinned.

'You like her, don't you?'

'She's a laugh, a smart cookie. I reckon she's warming to me.'

'Doesn't Mick mind you being there?'

He pulled a face. 'Hard to tell. It was him that invited me, but he's a bit of an uptight kind of guy, isn't he?'

Lottie, who would have said 'unsettling', or 'brooding', or 'dark and dangerous' rather than 'uptight', decided it was safest not to comment. Particularly as she was very confused when it came to Mick. He gave her confidence and made her feel strangely safe, but at the same time she felt as if she was running on quicksand when he gave her that look. She hoped that the little shudder that ran through her was just on the inside, and Todd hadn't spotted it.

'Anyhow,' it was Todd who changed the subject back onto safer ground, 'you could have some wild raves in that place of yours. The guys back home will never believe I shagged a real Lady.'

'Shush!' Lottie looked at him, horrified, and glanced around, even though she knew Rory was out at a show. Okay, he knew she'd been with Todd for a while, but... 'Anyway, what do you mean, a real lady?' Had he thought she'd had a sex change?

'A ladyship, the real deal. So does the Queen visit?'

'Only at Christmas.'

'Really, wow.' He narrowed his eyes. 'You're having me on, right?'

'You're as daft as Sam. Have you any idea just how many lords and ladies there are, Todd?' Not that she had a clue herself. And not that she actually was one herself yet.

'Guess you'll go weird and eccentric soon, like old Lizzie.' He chuckled, and she assumed he meant Gran, not the Queen, but either one would be appalled.

At least he wouldn't still be around to see her turn into her gran – not that she intended to, of course. Would he? 'So how long are you staying at Pip's place, then?'

'Aww don't worry about me, Lots. If it gets awkward, I'll soon find somewhere else.'

Which wasn't quite the answer she'd been looking for.

***

Amanda hadn't meant to get pregnant. In fact, she'd more or less forgotten that it was a possibility she ever would. And so far, it wasn't going well. Apart from Dominic's reaction. He'd gone from open-mouthed shock, straight through to delight in about five seconds flat. And then he'd been so incredibly sweet and attentive she'd felt a complete fraud for not being more enthusiastic herself.

Her late husband, Marcus, had said he'd treat her like a princess, and she'd thought he had, until now. Dom had shown her what it was to be truly adored, but his attention to detail and precision had meant that he was too preoccupied to notice just how wretched she looked, with the daily puking, until she really did look appalling. He was more bothered about her inner self than her outer self and, for once, she was thrilled.

'You're in good company, darling.' He kissed her forehead as she eyed up the toilet bowl and felt as if it had been her closest companion (Dom aside) for what seemed like a lifetime, though it was only for a few weeks.

Marcus might have put her on a pedestal, but he wouldn't have sat on the bathroom floor and brushed her hair back as she fought the urge to throw up. He would have gone off to play golf.

'I can't do it.'

'You can, Amanda. The day Kate Middleton came out the other side she looked much more her old self.'

Once the consultant had pompously informed them that she definitely did *not* have morning sickness, but the much more official-sounding *Hyperemesis gravidarum* (which actually sounded far more terrifying), Dominic had a label that he could research, which made him far happier. The fact that royalty had suffered from it as well was by the by as far as Amanda was concerned, but it somehow made her pathetic state more acceptable to the Stanthorpe's, who believed in a stiff upper lip and getting on with things. Even if you had a leg hanging off. Which she didn't; she just felt like the entire contents of her insides were about to tip out.

Her relief that the state she was in had a name, was soon scotched, though, when the sickness got worse, at which point she just wished it hadn't existed in the first place.

She summoned what she knew was a weak smile.

'When I said I can't do it, I didn't mean the puking-and-being-pregnant bit.' The way she felt, even knowing the Queen herself had felt like this wouldn't have helped. 'I'm perfectly capable of coping with that.' She stared at Dominic's drink and wondered if she'd ever enjoy an aperitif and stuffed olive again. 'I meant the cricket match.'

'They're not expecting you to lift a bat.' He stretched his legs out and pulled her onto his lap. 'Sorry, bad joke. Nobody will expect you to be there.'

'Well I am, darling. I've got to be, it's important.' Since falling in love with Dom, Amanda had taken her duties as wife of the caretaker Lord of the Manor very seriously. One of the traits she and Dominic shared was a sense of responsibility and a need to carry out all duties to the best of their capabilities.

Dom sighed. It was important, she was right. The annual celebrity cricket match was the one fundraiser that Tipping House

Estate had hosted for years – unfortunately, though, it raised funds for the church, not the Estate. But acting as magnanimous host was one of the Stanthorpe's duties. The Lord and Lady had a duty to look after the villagers, even if these days the roles had rather reversed. The ancient church would have its new modern stained- glass window (not that he altogether approved), and his mother would continue to suffer from a central-heating system that was all noise and no warmth.

Yes, the village would love Amanda to play the hostess, as she did it so brilliantly, but they would cope without both her and her Ladyship, Elizabeth, who played the role in her own inimitable fashion.

In fact, Dom reckoned as much money was raised on the bets that were placed in relation to her consumption of gin, and choice in hats, as was via the raffle. Without his mother and Amanda, somebody else would have to step in as mistress of the manor and give them the show they all loved. And it was time for Lottie, Lady-in-training, to perform her first official duty.

'It is important, darling, but so is your health.'

'But Elizabeth can't do it, you know what the doctor said.'

'No, but Charlotte can.'

Amanda sat up abruptly, then regretted it. 'Lottie? But she can't.'

'I know she hasn't got a brilliant track record,' he paused, Billy's wedding still fresh in his mind, 'but if you look at it logically, what could possibly go wrong? All she has to do is oversee and act like a Lady.' Dom looked at Amanda, just as she looked up at him, and they both burst out laughing. 'Oh dear Lord, what do I mean, all she has to do?'

'But it's not that – she's still in hospital, isn't she, darling? That's why I thought we really needed to—'

'No, she came out last night. She's tender but fine, nothing broken, which might be a good thing. It might restrict her potential to cause mayhem, and with any luck Rory will be looking after her instead of riding horses down the wicket.'

'Oh, Dominic.' Amanda laid her head back on Dom's chest and rested a hand on her stomach. Lottie wouldn't say no, she was quite keen on taking her duties seriously. But it didn't stop Amanda worrying. The thought of Lottie in mismatched socks and grass-stained breeches just somehow wouldn't translate into an image of ball gown and high heels. Although maybe it didn't have to. Maybe Lottie, like her gran before her, would just do things her own way.

Charlotte was nothing like Amanda or Dom, but that could be a good thing. Conventional thinking wasn't going to save Tipping House Manor, but maybe Lottie, who had everybody's love and support, could somehow pull it out of the bag. 'We probably underestimate what she can do.'

'I'm sure we do, and we overprotect her. Charlotte is tough and resourceful. She had to be when she was a child. No mother, and Billy as a father could have been a disaster, but she came out fine.' More than fine, thought Dom. 'I think it's time we all took a back seat, darling, and let her shine, don't you?'

'But we'll help.'

'We'll be there if she needs us, but I'm sure once she's cleared this first hurdle she'll be away, and it might help clarify some of her money-making ideas.'

'You're right, and I think I might be okay to move again now.' Amanda started to straighten out, and halfway up changed her mind. The doctors might have a fancy name for it, but the morning sickness from hell was something only the most avid dieter could welcome.

Chapter 9

She could get used to this Ladyship lark, thought Lottie, as she eyed up the massive jug of Pimms that was sitting in the middle of the table and watched her very favourite cricketer, Jimmy Sanderling, run up and launch a surprisingly fast ball at a local stand-up comedian.

The annual celebrity cricket match was one of the highlights of the Tippermere calendar (all horse events excepted), and the fact that she'd woken to find hardly a cloud in the sky had to be a good omen. Lottie had to admit she'd got what Tiggy referred to as the collywobbles when Dom had reminded her that her first duty as Lady of the Manor (or substitute in Elizabeth's absence) was to oversee the annual celebrity charity cricket match and auction. Not because she didn't want to do it, but because cricket was a mystery to her. And what if somebody put her in charge of the scoreboard? Until Rory pointed out that neither Elizabeth, nor half the players seemed to really understand what was going on. And Elizabeth had never, ever taken on the role of umpire or scorer.

Lottie did, in fact, attend the game most years (as everybody in Tippermere did), but she was still none the wiser about how the scoring worked, what a googly was, where you found your inside edge (which sounded like a documentary) and if square leg was a medical condition or something related to sharp work in the slips. But how hard could it be to oversee the game, applaud in the right places and serve a few nibbles?

Sam clapped enthusiastically at the dashingly tall bowler, who happened to be a neighbour of hers in Kitterly Heath, and there was a collective gasp as, by some chance in a million, the ball glanced off the comedian's bat, bounced off the captain's Bentley and landed at the vicar's feet. The vicar glanced heavenwards, as though it was a divine gift, and somebody yelled at the batsman to 'shift his arse and run like hell'.

The Very Reverend Waterson raised an eyebrow, the comedian ran, minus his bat, which had been all but knocked out of his hands, and Dominic ruined his pristine whites by diving at the stumps, ball in hand.

'There's something about a man in whites, isn't there?' Lottie gazed dreamily at the cricketer of her dreams and fished a piece of strawberry out of her drink, along with what looked suspiciously like grass.

'Definitely something about an Australian cricketer, whatever colour he's in,' remarked Pip.

'Isn't that racist, or country-ist or something?' She couldn't quite get to the bit of kiwi, which was ironically just out of reach.

'Sexist.' Pip topped up their drinks and pointed at the tall, blond figure, who was heading down the pavilion steps with a long, determined stride. 'You have to admit, it does suit him. Look at that bum!'

As far as Lottie could see, it was his box not his bum that was on show, although seconds later, as he strode on towards the wicket, the bum in question was on show, coated in surprisingly tight whites.

'Has he got knickers on?'

Unfortunately, although Todd did, in fact, look the part, he didn't play it. He swung wildly at the first ball, which had been bowled by a genuine cricketer, who knew exactly what he was doing. As Todd swung, the ball landed with a resounding smack right in the middle of what Sam politely referred to as his middle stump. Lottie flinched. Todd looked down, as though to check that everything was still intact, before falling in spectacular slow motion onto his wicket.

'Is that BBW? Balls before wicket as opposed to leg?' Lottie finally managed to capture the elusive strawberry, which had been stuck to the bottom of her glass.

Pip laughed. 'And there was I thinking Australians were born with a cricket bat in their hands.'

'Just like Englishmen are born with a silver spoon?' enquired Dom, who for some reason had retreated to the boundary and was listening in.

Lottie giggled and Pip shook her head. 'You thought he was going to whack it, or you wouldn't be over here.'

'He was born with a surf board under his arm. Do you think he's okay?' Lottie was the only one who looked concerned.

'Poor babe, he could have been debagged.'

'I think you mean castrated, Sam. Debagged means having your trousers pulled down.' Pip laughed.

At which point Dom shook his head in disbelief and headed off to check that no lasting damage had been done to the wicket, which he had been checking religiously for the last two days. It was one responsibility that he definitely hadn't been prepared to hand over to Lottie. Standards had to be maintained.

'Does it, babe?' Sam grinned. 'I think he's about to be debagged anyway. Looks like Tab is going to check out his tentacles.'

Pip nearly spluttered her mouthful of Pimms across the table, redirecting it at the last minute towards the grass, where she stayed for a few minutes, her back shaking with what Lottie knew was giggles and Sam assumed was choking. Pip resurfaced. 'She's the one with tentacles, he's got the testicles, or not. I think we might find out soon.'

'So what exactly is a sticky wicket?'

At this point, Lottie, who really hadn't got much clue about cricket, decided that Sam probably had. 'What Todd has been hoping for – probably.'

After Todd had been pulled to his feet and all his bits accounted for, Dom declared there would be one more over, then it was time for tea, which sent Lottie scurrying for the pavilion door, determined to demonstrate what an effective hostess she was.

'Oh, bugger.' She gazed at the table before reaching for the nearest Pimm's jug and pouring herself another large glassful.

'What's up?' Pip peered over her shoulder and then started to giggle.

The artistically arranged cucumber sandwiches were now parted like the Red Sea, except this was green, and through them could be seen Bertie's black nose and doleful eyes, a triangle of crust-free bread still protruding from his gentle mouth, a crumb bouncing on the end of one of his whiskers, as he raised and lowered his eyebrows in silent apology.

'Oh shit, what do I do now?'

Bertie, the larger of Elizabeth's Labradors, belched, and lifted his head from the table, backing off, his tail doing a slow, solemn wag.

Lottie pushed two mismatched triangles of bread together and poked a sliver of cucumber back inside. 'Do you think they'll notice?'

'You'll have to say they're the latest in deconstructed food. Nobody will dare question it in case they look silly. They'll think they missed a critical episode of *Bake Off*.'

'Really?'

'No, not really. A deconstructed sandwich is a loaf of bread and a cucumber, and it doesn't generally have teeth marks in it.'

'Told you that you should have had a barbie.' Todd appeared to have made a miraculous recovery and, despite the absence of runs, had built up an appetite.

'Bugger off, Todd, or there'll be chestnuts roasting on an open fire.' He laughed. 'Go and support your team and don't you dare tell anybody.'

'I'll go and distract them, shall I?' Pip, who wasn't into catering of any kind unless it only involved a packet, scissors and a bowl, headed out of the pavilion. 'Come on, Crocodile Dundee, come and help me.' She linked an arm through his and Todd obligingly went outside, cracking jokes about Englishmen and the Ashes whilst simultaneously attempting to flatter Sam by adding the odd comment about football, which clearly he knew nothing about.

'He's such a card, isn't he Pip? I hope all your bits are okay, babe?'

'Not so sure, always willing to let a lady check them out.'

Pip rolled her eyes as Sam giggled. 'His bits will be fine, but I'm not sure about Lottie's.'

Sam looked alarmed. 'She wasn't playing was she? Did I miss her?'

'This is more of a catering disaster. Will you go and help her out? I really don't do fancy food.'

Sam went and Todd sulked for a second or two before deciding that teasing Pip could be just as entertaining.

***

'Men don't like green stuff anyway, babe.' Sam had found a bin bag and was hastily shovelling the most deconstructed parts of 'tea' out of sight, before rearranging the remainder, which involved shoving vases of flowers into the middle of platters to make them look full.

Lottie was impressed. 'That's brilliant.'

Sam grinned, happy that she could be of use. 'Well, at all these posh things we go to they don't give you enough food to feed a mouse. It's all just in silly little bits on massive plates. And we're all having a big nosh-up later anyway, aren't we – at your auction thing?' She paused. 'Should he be doing that?'

Lottie turned around to find that Bertie, unobserved, had taken the opportunity to move on to the cakes and now had a rather large chocolate muffin, complete with wrapper held carefully between his jaws. He rocked back on his haunches, watching them watching him, then with careful deliberation he tried to swallow. Labradors could swallow most things, but this was a new experience. Brown crumbs shot out to both sides, as brown drool ran from his jaws and he valiantly tried not to choke on the paper.

'Bless.'

'What do you mean, bless?' Lottie decided it was time to step in, although she wasn't sure if it was to try and rescue the cake or the dog. Bertie clamped his mouth shut, determined not to give up any more of his prize. 'Help me get him out of the back. Quick before anybody sees him.' Smuggling a big black dog out of a cricket pavilion when half the village are on the front steps, and the other half milling around with drinks was, Lottie decided, not her brightest idea.

They had got to the doorway, Sam pushing him from behind and Lottie at his collar, when Bertie realised that he was soon to be banished from the remnants of his party. He dug his heels in, leaning his portly body back, so that he landed squarely on the toes of Sam's very high-heeled shoes. With a giggle she sat down abruptly. Lottie, taken unawares by the Labradors change of tactics, lost her grip on the dog's collar and found herself going in the opposite direction, landing outside on the grass at the feet of Mick.

'You could tempt him out with food, babe.' Bertie turned around and gave Sam's cleavage an appreciative snuffle, smothering it in chocolate dribble, his mouth still full of cake.

'I'm not sure that will work, I think he's totally stuffed.' And so was she, Lottie decided.

'I'll put him in the Landrover shall I, treasure?'

At the sound of his voice, Lottie glanced up, into those deep, dark eyes and had never been so pleased to see the farrier in her life. 'Oh, please.' What she really meant was please, please, please, but instead she struggled to her feet and wrapped her arms round

106

her saviour's neck, giving him the type of affectionate kiss that Bertie had just bestowed on Sam. 'You always rescue me, don't you?'

Mick shook his head slowly and grinned. He'd watched the sandwich fiasco from a safe distance, not sure he should interfere. He'd once told Lottie that her feet would lead her back to where her heart belonged, and unfortunately his own feet kept leading him to her. Which was something he really had to find a cure for. He should be at the front of the pavilion, sharing a joke with Pip, not at the back eyeing up the lovely Lottie and sexy Sam, who he'd say was a lot sharper than she let on.

But it had got too much when the two girls had started to slide the uncomplaining dog across the floor. Help was obviously needed. So he'd grabbed a rope from the Land Rover and arrived at the back of the pavilion just as Lottie had fallen out of it. Making his whites tighten uncomfortably, which was another reason he should have refused to play in the match. He should have stayed on the yard and trimmed horse's feet.

He regretfully disentangled himself from Lottie, who went bright pink. Then looked at the dog, who had dropped the remnants of the cake and was now licking his lips, and Sam's toes.

'So where's the grub, then?' Rory, who had decided he'd had enough of Pip and Todd, had managed to sneak past them and into the pavilion. When he was bored he got hungry. And as no horses, hair-raising or hell-raising was involved in cricket, he needed food. Although he did know from previous years that a 'cricket tea' wasn't quite the same as a burger van at a three-day event. 'And I'm not drinking tea.'

'Not so sure you'll be eating or drinking anything.' Mick winked at Lottie. 'Come on, Bertie.' The dog didn't need a rope attached, he ambled off after Mick as though he was going on an afternoon stroll and eating cake had been the furthest thing from his mind.

Rory went to grab a sandwich off the nearest plate and got his hand slapped by Sam. 'Stop spoiling the arrangement. It took ages for us to do that.'

'I thought the caterers from Kitterly did it?'

'We re-did it.' Lottie grinned and succumbed to a bear hug. 'I suppose,' she looked at the food doubtfully, 'I suppose everybody can come and get it, if you think it looks alright?'

'It looks good enough to eat, just like you do, gorgeous.'

Sam hastily shoved a sandwich that had been squashed by Bertie's ample rear under the table with her foot and grabbed the jug of Pimm's, which by now was half empty. 'You tuck in, Rory love, come on, Lottie, we've got more serious stuff to attend to.' And she grabbed Lottie, who she was sure was just about to tell Rory everything.

'Can you catch anything from dog slobber?' Lottie hissed in the general direction of Sam and Pip, as the three of them sat around a table as far away from the door as they could. Lottie was working on the principle that if they weren't near, then they couldn't be blamed.

'Shush.' Pip giggled. 'They've all got iron-clad innards. It'll be fine. Anyway, shouldn't you be up at the house checking everything has been done for tonight?'

'Shit.' Lottie, who'd been distracted by the disastrous tea, glanced at her watch and suddenly remembered that her duties had only just begun. The cricket match was the easy bit. The ball and auction were the main event, well they were as far as raising money went, and although Amanda had promised to check up on the caterers, it was only fair that she was there to help her.

***

Amanda may have been constantly on the verge of throwing up, but her mental faculties were still surprisingly intact and functioning.

And she had known that Lottie wouldn't cope on her own. So she'd tied her hair back, put on a summer dress and a good spritz of perfume, and headed over to Tipping House Estate with her tablet and back-up notepad. She'd been in Tippermere long enough to know that the Wi-Fi could be as reliable as the horses. Just when you thought you were in control, it ducked out for no fathomable reason.

The title Lady of the Manor was something Amanda had never coveted. She found draughty country houses played havoc with her complexion, couldn't understand for the life of her why anybody would want to stand in a river and call it sport, or shoot the wild-life, and was petrified at the idea that she would be expected to provide an heir and a spare. And as for leaky roofs and gurgling pipes, even the much more modern Folly Lake Manor would, she felt, benefit from an overhaul.

But organisation and precision, along with a need to have everything in its place, came to her naturally. As did looking perfect and having an instinct for social etiquette. Over the years she'd built up an encyclopaedic knowledge of what to do when, and to whom. In fact, she had been accused of swallowing Debrett's guide to etiquette and manners by one particularly bitchy gold-digger at her engagement party to Dominic. And years of looking after her by-now-deceased former billionaire husband, Marcus, and entertaining his often dodgy clients, had taught her how to deal with the most difficult company without getting flustered.

And although Amanda was as close to the perfect hostess as you could get, she was still so likeable that everybody who knew her got on with her. Even the difficult Elizabeth (who always called her by the correct name as a mark of respect that shouldn't be underestimated) and the scatty Lottie.

She'd already organised the caterers, checked the flowers and was busy co-ordinating sound checks when Lottie rushed in.

'Oh my God. I'm sorry I'm late. Gosh, should you be here? Do you feel alright? Oh I am so rubbish at things like this, and you will never believe what happened at the cricket match.' The rush of words came to an end and Lottie grinned and gave her friend a hug.

'You're not late, relax.' Amanda smiled back. 'I promised you I'd be here and I am. Everything is going exactly to plan, and I'm fine. Nobody is expecting you to do everything, Lottie. Elizabeth has always had lots of help. She just turns up and drinks gin. And as long as I've gone before any food appears I'll be okay. Luckily Dominic isn't that bothered about food.' If she'd have been ill like this when Marcus had been alive, he would have employed a chef and she would have been unsure if it had been out of concern for her, or for his own stomach. Life with Dominic was so different. He might not be flashy or demonstrative, but he cared. And he was a dab hand at omelettes and beans on toast. Although thinking about that was making her whole body stir with something very different to lust.

'You look a bit funny, are you sure you should be here?' Lottie was looking at her with concern and she made an effort to pull herself together.

'I'll go in a minute, if you're sure you'll cope?'

'Of course I will. I mean, what can possibly go wrong that hasn't already?'

What indeed?

'Here.' Amanda pressed a neatly written list into her hands. 'I think that covers absolutely everything. I hope you don't think I'm being bossy, but it's the list I made last year, and' she grinned apologetically, really not wanting to appear too forceful, 'I thought it might be useful. But you might have a list of your own…'

Lottie tried not to look horrified at the length of the list. She did have one of her own. It was much, much shorter. Would it be rude and ungrateful to throw it into the Aga – once Amanda had gone, of course?

'Oh, how lovely, you're so organised.'

'You're on point 15, here, look. Check the champagne has been put on ice.' Amanda identified the look on Lottie's face and laughed. 'You don't have to do everything – it's up to you. I only write every single thing down because I know if I don't I'll forget something.'

'Right, er, ok. I'll go now then, shall I? The kitchen?'

'Everything is in the main one.'

'The main one. Of course, the main one.'

Not sure if she was doing the right thing, Amanda picked up her handbag, gave Lottie a quick hug of encouragement and waved goodbye.

As Amanda left, Lottie heaved a sigh of relief. She loved Amanda, and she was so grateful for her help. But the level of efficiency was scary. And she really was not going to actually double-check everything everybody else had done, and she definitely wasn't going to go and check that the housekeeper had pleated the end of the toilet paper.

When the bell in the butler's pantry clanged for what had to be the sixth time, Lottie decided she really should go and see what was wrong with Elizabeth before she got changed for the fundraising dinner. She'd got to the kitchen and checked the champagne (which was important), then realised that she'd already lost Amanda's list. A quick look in the dog's basket (which was where most things ended up) didn't help, and she'd shifted all the canapé trays around and was just reaching out to try one of the mini toad in the holes (even if it was cold, it looked damned tempting) when she realised that as she was the only person in the kitchen, she really should check who it was. How on earth did cook put up with the racket?

It was her gran, of course. The bell that somebody had labelled very clearly with LADY E. even though nobody else lived here and it seemed a bit over the top.

But, there again, it was probably Uncle Dom who had labelled it. Lottie's hand hovered over the little Yorkshire pudding for a moment, until the bell clanged again, as though her gran knew, and she decided that cramming it into her mouth probably wasn't the done thing. She'd have enough trouble getting into her dress for tonight as it was. Stretchy jodhpurs were much more comfortable than 'gowns'. And why did people call them that anyway?

Both of her gran's dogs were staring at her, tails slowly wagging. Expectant.

'Doesn't she know I'm busy?' Bertie cocked his head to one side and lifted an eyebrow. Holmes did a very slow, funereal tail wag. 'Oh, hell, you don't think there's something wrong, do you? Gosh, what if she's feeling ill?' With one last regretful look at the food, and trying to ignore her rumbling stomach and the slightly light-headed feeling that the Pimm's had left behind, Lottie checked her watch, then set off in the direction of Elizabeth's room, which was up two flight of stairs and in the west wing of the house. She hadn't liked to scoff any of the cricket tea, as there wasn't that much left. And although Sam's flower arranging had helped disguise the fact, it would have soon become obvious once half the players had helped themselves. Maybe she should have eaten a few of the sandwiches that had been unrecoverable due to doggy teeth marks?

Hurtling up the wide staircase with the Labradors at her heels, Lottie wondered, not for the first time, why the place had to be quite so big. Although she would lose weight living here, just walking to bed and getting up for a midnight snack would work off the calories – a definite bonus.

She was out of breath by the time she got to Elizabeth's room, bursting through the door (by now quite worried – it was surprisingly what terrible thoughts could go through your head on the way up the imposing staircase) to find Elizabeth sitting by the large leaded window with Pip, who had a cup of tea in her hand.

Holmes, the slightly slimmer of the two Labradors, charged in, nearly knocking the tea tray flying in his rush to get to his mistress.

'Oh, you're okay.' Lottie sank down onto one of the wing-backed chairs, then glanced from her gran to Pip. 'I thought you were still at the cricket?'

'Mick was getting arsey and expecting me to wash up, so I came for a chat. I'm filling Elizabeth in on Australia's opening batsman, and I thought she might like a cup of tea.'

The pair of them looked too smug and happy for Lottie's liking, which made her suspicious. Pip and Gran together could be bad news. They just liked mischief-making and she had a horrible feeling that this time it could be at her expense.

'What are you up to?'

'Nothing.' Pip grinned, and made Lottie even more suspicious.

'So why did you keep ringing the bell?'

'I wanted to check that you were actually here, dear. And that you were on top of everything. Speaking of which, shouldn't you be thinking about getting ready?'

Lottie suddenly noticed that Pip had managed to get changed since she'd last seen her at the cricket, her immaculate bob of hair shining and her make-up perfect.

'Oh sugar. Is that really the time?'

'Everything will be fine, Charlotte.' Elizabeth patted her hand. 'You're doing a splendid job. I really think putting a comb through your hair wouldn't go amiss, though. I mean, what if *Cheshire Life* turn up? I do believe that slip of a girl who is in charge of editorial now said she'd sponsor us.'

Elizabeth watched as her only grandchild ran from the room and a wave of affection swept over her. The girl was so like her mother had been, the beautiful and wild Alexandra, scatty and loveable. Except Alexa had possessed a flintier edge that had no doubt been inherited from Elizabeth herself, and manners and grace came naturally to her, much as they did to Amanda, whereas Charlotte had a good dose of her father in her – not the gruff side, but definitely the disorganised and slightly uncultured edge.

She turned back to Philippa, who was a different kettle of fish altogether. She loved the journalist, with her enquiring and slightly devious mind, like a daughter. When Charlotte had come back from Barcelona and brought Pippa with her it had been a breath of fresh air for Elizabeth, who felt she was in danger of getting old and lonely. Not that she would have ever admitted such a weakness to herself or anybody else. But the girl was a kindred spirit, someone who thought on the same wavelength and could be relied on to stir things up when required. Except now she was troubled. Matters of the heart were an alien concept to Philippa and she was finding them hard to cope with. Emotions were such fickle and unmanageable things. Unlike headlines and people.

'So, Philippa, tell me about Michael's arse.' That was, she was sure, the real reason for the girl's visit. 'And what you intend to do about it.'

Pip stared into the tea leaves at the bottom of the cup and wondered where the hell to start. 'I think I love him, but he doesn't love me.' That seemed a good point.

'Do you love him, or the man you'd like him to be?' Elizabeth stared out at the expanse of once bright green lawn that was beginning to fade as the summer months took their toll. 'You can't pin a man like him down, you know. He needs his freedom, even if he doesn't know it.'

'I've never tried to pin anybody down.'

'Before. But you've never let anybody in before either, have you, Philippa?' Her tone was gentle, because she knew what it was like. The first time. However old you were. 'A man like Michael isn't easy to get the measure of, but he will beat himself to death like a bird if he's trapped in the wrong cage. He will do the right thing, he's an honourable man, but,' she put her liver-spotted hand over Pip's slim, young perfect one, 'ask yourself if this is the right thing. You already know the answer to that, my dear, and only you can decide to listen to it. If you can bear it, trust your heart and let him go. And if you can't, then as an old lady I'd advise you do it anyway. Everything happens for a reason, child, but unfortunately not always one that benefits us personally. As humans, our ego means we assume it will. Now,' she took the cup from Pip's hands, 'go and party – enjoy yourself.'

Pip gave a twisted grin. 'That hasn't made me feel any better.'

'Only you can do that, dear. That colour suits you.'

Which she took as it was meant from Elizabeth – a signal of approval, a compliment.

'You're sure you won't come for a bit?'

'Oh no, dear, tonight is Charlotte's, and if I'm honest, though, don't you dare tell another soul, it is quite a relief. I've wanted to let the Estate go for a while now, but I didn't want to burden poor Charlotte until she was ready.' She smiled, a small secret smile. 'I can't let Dominic think I want to hand over the reins, though, can I? He'll think I'm going soft. But, it's time I made the right decisions as well. Isn't it?'

All Pip could do was nod. The older woman had said what she knew she would, and in very few words. Maybe it would be a relief when she accepted the way things were and bowed out gracefully.

Elizabeth stroked Bertie's head as she watched Pip pull the door quietly shut. Yes, it was decision time. Time for Lottie to accept her inheritance and help Tipping House Estate move into the twenty-first century, but hopefully minus the wild ideas she was sure would be suggested. And it was decision time for young Philippa. The Irish man was passionate, deep, and the pair obviously challenged each other, which she was sure was what had held them together until now. But until death us do part? Death from misery and a broken heart was not what either deserved. Although death from boredom was worse.

And poor Philippa did obviously care for him. He was the first man she had let into her heart, the first man who had shown her a glimpse of what life could be. She was agitated, sad, even though she was trying her best to hide her feelings with her normal front. But he'd given his heart to somebody else. And that was a problem. A problem that had to be used, not ignored.

115

Chapter 10

Lottie stood in the cavernous entrance hall and stared at the showered and brushed-up Rory. Her stomach did that shivery thing that it had done the first time he'd kissed her. She hadn't actually had time to stop and just look for ages and now she fell for him all over again. Not that she'd ever stopped being bowled over by his looks – not for a second of her life since she'd found out what hormones were about.

Falling in love with Rory had happened when she was about fourteen years old, and being in love with him was why she'd left Tippermere to go on her travels. Because she'd always felt she was just another of his adoring groupies, as besotted as one of his terriers. So she had decided the best thing to do was go and do just exactly what she wanted rather than what Rory, her father and everybody else expected. It wasn't that life had been boring – Rory could never be called predictable – she had just felt everybody took her for granted.

Todd hadn't had any expectations, he'd accepted her as she was, which was a new kind of liberation. Until the whole beach incident had sent her scurrying back to Cheshire and into the arms of a Rory who'd convinced her he cared.

His dark curls were damp from his shower, the pristine white shirt hugging his toned torso was just begging to be stripped off and he smelled gorgeous. Gorgeous enough to unwrap like a forbidden bar of chocolate, although thinking about chocolate made her stomach rumble. It had been a long day with only a makeshift fruit salad, extracted from the jug of Pimm's, for sustenance. She straightened his bowtie and hung on a bit longer than necessary, wondering if a good shag would distract her from the hunger pangs.

'You're looking sexy.' He twirled one of her ringlets around his finger (she'd not really had time for the perfect hair-do, so she'd decided that the curly out-of-the-shower look had to be worked *with* rather than *against*), then his finger slipped lower down towards her cleavage. 'Very wanton.' The dress hadn't been her idea, it had been Sam's. She was a bit worried that the combination of a few extra pounds, wearing a new, rather forceful, bra and a plunging neckline could lead to dangerous spillage. Her nipple, which was responding to Rory's attentions, seemed to be in a dangerously high position.

'Oh God. I don't do I?' 'Wanton' didn't sound right. 'I'm supposed to look like a Lady.'

'Stop worrying, you're taking this Lady stuff far too seriously. You look gorgeous.'

'So do you.' She tried to wriggle away and her boobs wobbled alarmingly, like two puppies making a bid for freedom.

Rory put one warm, steadying hand on her buttock and pulled her closer. 'Can we just go off and be naughty somewhere?' He grinned, his dark eyes shining with wickedness. 'Those heavy curtains look ideal for shagging behind, Your Ladyship.'

Lottie giggled and was glad she wasn't just like Amanda, who would never find herself in this position. 'What have you got in your trouser pocket, Rory Strachan?' She wriggled her hips experimentally and he groaned.

'Something I've been keeping just for you, Charlotte Brinkley.'

'It might have to keep a bit longer.' Lottie put a hand on his chest, knowing that if he carried on she really would be tempted by the heavy curtains. Sadly she had to try her hardest to be sensible now that she had responsibilities. 'Did you win the game?'

'The cricket? No, although your Todd did redeem himself a bit as a fielder.'

'He's not "my" Todd.' She toyed with his shirt button and glanced up. He didn't look as if he was bothered about Todd, but it was better to make it clear.

'He was crap with a bat, but great on the boundary, and bowled a googly that even caught one of the pros out.'

Lottie hadn't got the foggiest what he was on about, and suspected he didn't either. 'Do you even know what a googly is? You're making it up, aren't you?'

'I know all about bowling maidens over.' Rory nuzzled her neck and a shock of goose bumps ran down her arms and chest. She grabbed the top of her dress, although 'top' wasn't an accurate description, with one hand, suddenly sure that her bright-pink bra was going to pop out and it really wasn't for public consumption, just for Rory's.

'I bet you do.' She giggled.

'Spoil sport.' He put one hand over hers and traced a finger over the swell of her breast.

'Stop it.'

'It'll only take a minute.'

'No, I mean it.'

'It only takes a minute, babe.'

As he crooned the lyrics of the song in her ear, he slipped one finger down her cleavage and Lottie, knowing that if he went one inch further she'd be lost, clamped her hand around his.

'No.' Oh bugger. That came out wrong, she sounded as if she was telling one of the dogs off. 'I do want to, but we've got to be here to greet all the guests. They'll be here any second.'

'I dare you. A quickie.'

'We can't.'

'I hope you aren't going to turn all stuffy like Dom.' His tawny eyes were inches from hers, still glinting mischief. A challenge.

'We really can't.'

Rory raised an eyebrow, then let his hands drop down by his sides with a sigh. Which made her feel rotten. He looked like a rejected puppy.

'It's not that I don't want to, you know that, it's just—'

'Put her down, you don't know where she's been.' Pip, chirpier than she'd been for quite some time, had a very sexy but much more manageable dress on, and Lottie looked at her well-contained chest enviously. Then shot a sidelong look at Mick, who looked as dangerously dark and handsome as he always did. Then dared to look at Rory, who winked, which meant she'd been forgiven.

'I've got a good idea where she should be going.' He squeezed her bum and Lottie thought it was a good job that they'd all arrived when they had, or she really might have forgotten all about her duties.

'Oh you are a naughty boy.' Sam giggled. 'Wow, that dress looks amazing on you, babe. Doesn't it, Davey?' She tugged David closer so that he nearly fell into Lottie's bosom, and the assorted crowd observed her chest, which was going blotchier by the second. 'I wish I had your pins – they go on for ever.' Sam, as generous as ever, air-kissed Lottie, being careful to keep her lipstick to herself and displaying her own perfect breasts, which she'd very proudly told Lottie she'd picked out last summer after seeing one of the other footballer's wives with the perfect pair. 'When you see them you've got to grab them, haven't you?' Lottie wasn't sure that was the best way of putting it and studiously avoided Rory's eye. 'I mean it's like when you see a perfect dress, isn't it?' Had been her parting comment.

Sam, Lottie had decided, went out to select breasts and noses in the same way she went out to buy horses. Minus the auctions, of course. It really wouldn't do to be buying breast implants and plastic surgery under the hammer.

'What do you think of the nails? Amazing aren't they?' Samantha's smile was broad, and her blue eyes bright as she waved a set of perfect nails in front of Pip and Lottie. They were in David's team colours, sparkling with diamantes in a way his shirts would never do. 'David's just signed a new mega contract, haven't you, Davey? He's my hero.' She was up on tip toes and kissing him, one arm linked through his. 'We're celebrating, I've even bought Scruffy a new blingy collar – all sparkly and everything – although they're not real diamonds, of course.'

'Of course.'

'Cos he's a boy. Aww I wish I could have brought him to show you. Bless him. He looks so sweet in it. But I was worried her Ladyship's dogs might not like him. I mean,' she leant forward to whisper conspiratorially, 'I wouldn't say it in front of him, but he's not got their class has he? He's just a mongrel.'

Lottie did appreciate that Scruffy the dog was like a baby to Sam. She loved him, and the term 'pampered pooch' had been taken to a whole new level. But the thought of him in costume jewellery was a picture that was too weird even for her head. He was scruffy and it suited him.

After a glass or three of champagne Lottie forgot all about the threat of her boobs making a break for freedom, although several mini toad-in-the-hole canapés and burgers made it more than likely. The cricket players, who had noticed a shortage of food at tea time had tucked into the snacks on offer with enthusiasm, and washed them down with vintage bubbly and more than a few bottles of beer. What she lacked in restrained elegance, Lottie made up for in her generosity with refreshments. As the evening wore on she was having so much fun with her well-oiled guests that she'd completely forgotten about the main event, the auction.

'Aren't you supposed to be the compere?'

'What?' Lottie looked blankly at Pip. How could she have missed something like that? Ever since Dom had told her she was in charge, she'd worked her butt off, determined to make this the most successful auction they'd ever had. In fact, she'd been very quietly pleased with herself when she'd looked through the impressive list of items that had been donated. Even she was shocked by what she'd achieved. But she'd just assumed someone else would run the actual auction. She was sure she'd never seen Elizabeth or Dom with a gavel in their hands.

'Who's running the auction?'

'Oh shit. Really? Am I supposed to do that as well? I wish Amanda was about, she's brilliant at all this, but she's gone from perfectly poised to perfectly pukey. She gave me a list, but I lost it.' She grinned apologetically.

Rory hugged Lottie into his side and lowered his mouth to her ear. 'She's teasing. Somebody has been paid to do it. Dom told me at the match that he always gets a professional in and he knew you'd forget. He got Amanda to book the same chap we had last year. All you have to do is stand next to him and smile.'

Lottie groaned and put her head on her hands. 'Why didn't I remember that?'

'Because you're remembering lots of other things.'

'Oh, Rory.' She kissed him full on the mouth, drinking in his unique taste and for a moment wishing they could just run down to the stables and be naughty. 'I do love you.'

'I know.' He grinned.

'Next time is going to be so much better.'

'It's all good now. And you are totally gorgeous from where I'm sitting.'

'That's because you're looking at my boobs, Rory.'

'Well lift that skirt a bit and I will eye up your legs as well.'

'I can't.'

'Aww, come on.'

Rory had got fed up with canapés and drink and was fidgeting, waiting for the action to warm up. He knew from previous experience that the auction could turn into a competitive and rowdy affair (even more competitive than the cricket match) and he

121

was champing at the bit. If it wasn't about to happen he needed a distraction. He put one hand on Charlotte's knee. She giggled.

'No, I really can't.' She glanced up and her eyes locked onto those dark dancing Irish ones of Mick's. He'd noticed her problem the second he'd walked through the door, even though she thought she'd got away with it. And his whispered, 'Loving the footwear, treasure,' had said it all.

'Do you think anybody will notice?'

'Only if they ask for a dance.' And he'd grinned as they'd shared one of those illicit moments that had left her feeling confused. He'd asked for a dance once, long ago. In fact it seemed another lifetime ago now. Before she'd known she was to be Lady of the Manor, before she'd moved in with Rory. They'd danced and he'd done his best not to complain about squashed toes, apart from saying he wished he'd known steel-toe-capped boots were obligatory at hunt balls.

It wasn't that Lottie had actually forgotten to put her high heels on, she wasn't that daft. But she'd been in such a hurry to get ready and she'd been trying so hard to look the part, which was pretty difficult given the time scales. In fact she'd ended up feeling exhausted and wishing she could go to bed.

It hadn't gone well from the start, when she'd attempted to straighten her hair, which had taken so long she'd been forced to give up and go for ringlets. Then the distinct smell of burning, which she couldn't quite locate, sent her into a tizzy. After five minutes of wandering round sniffing the air she realised that she'd nearly burned the room down (what was an odd singed chair between friends?) after forgetting to turn off her curling tongs (which she was using to straighten rather than curl her hair).

It was only after unplugging the hair accessories and doing her best to hide the damage that it dawned on her that she'd put her dress on before her knickers. Which was something of a problem, as although she'd tried she couldn't roll it up high enough because her hips seemed to have spread. Then she wasn't sure she'd put deodorant on so she'd had to peel the dress off again just in case. And then there was her make-up – and the new liquid eyeliner that Sam had lent her. This was 'the thing' and guaranteed to give you the perfect cats' eyes, but had actually made her look more like a weird oriental panda – and it wouldn't come off. And the un-smudge-able smudged.

With only minutes to spare before the guests arrived, she had promised herself she'd be in the entrance hall all poised and perfect (like Amanda would be) at least ten minutes early. All she had to do was put her shoes on.

Slipping her foot into the first one hadn't been a challenge, but then she'd hit the problem. She'd been wobbling on one foot because she couldn't work out how to do it in the sheath dress without bursting the seams, and she'd just been so close, so incredibly close, to being ready when she'd wobbled a bit too far and as she'd fallen back onto the bed the heel on her shoe had gone.

Snap.

Completely – as in snapped right off.

Lottie stared at it. And briefly considered trying to find some sticky tape or string, or super glue (but her last experience with super glue had been bad, luckily they didn't make it as super any more), but she couldn't go out with just one high heel could she? So, she'd done the only thing she could. She put her boots back on.

Obviously it had been a mistake arriving at Tipping House with an overnight bag containing make-up, one toothbrush, one posh frock, two pairs of knickers (pink), one bra (matching pink), toiletries, contact-lens solution and one pair of shoes (posh with high heels). Amanda would have had a spare of everything or Dominic would have driven home.

Whereas Rory was playing cricket and had lost his mobile phone again, along with everybody else in Tippermere it seemed. Still it could have been worse, she might have arrived in her Converses or wellies – at least her favourite boots would be comfortable. And everybody said sensible shoes were important, didn't they? And they were clean – she'd stuck them in the bath and given them a quick rub over with the nailbrush to be sure. Now, though, they might be a problem.

Rory, who loved Lottie's legs nearly as much as he loved her hips and boobs finally managed to tug her dress up so that he could ogle her ankles. 'You are kidding me?' He gave a loud guffaw, then stuck his head down again to take a closer peek. 'God, you are brilliant. Only you could do that.' And gave her a smacker of a kiss.

Everybody else made a dive to look under the table.

'I did have proper shoes, but my heel broke off.'

'Don't panic, babe. I've sorted it for you.'

Lottie looked at Sam and wondered if she'd turned into some kind of fairy godmother and was about to wave her wand. 'Davey has gone to tell Gerald.'

'Gerald?'

'He's driving us tonight and I bet he's bored – he won't mind at all.'

'But he doesn't know where I live, and he won't be able to get in.' Lottie had a sudden image of Sam's chauffeur bursting into their cottage bedroom and finding the normal mess of clothes, knickers and shoes on the floor, and thinking they'd been burgled. 'And it's, er, not very tidy.'

'Oh no, he's gone to get some of my shoes for you. You will love them, hun. They'll look amazing on you, and they've got heels like this.' She held her thumb and finger apart to demonstrate.

Lottie gulped and hoped Sam was prone to exaggeration or she'd be suffering from vertigo. Or more likely fall off them at a critical moment.

'Louboutin's – they are so gorge. Bright pink and glittery, with this music thing on the front instead of a strap.'

'Piano?' What had she let herself in for?

'No, silly. You know, er, a triple cliff.'

'Treble clef?'

'That's the one, Pip.'

Lottie was none the wiser.

'They'll match your knickers.' Sam grinned.

'How do you know?' Lottie tried to peer down the front of her dress in a bid to work out how anyone could see her undies.

'Saw them hanging out of your bag at the cricket, hun.'

Oh Christ. That's why she'd had a string of comments when she'd arrived at the cricket trailing dogs, and it seemed knickers, behind her. And she just thought they'd all been excited about the cricket match.

'I asked Gerald to bring Scruffy too so you can see his bling. In fact his collar matches the shoes. How's that for co-ordination?'

By the time the shoes arrived there was barely time to strap Lottie into them (that's what it felt like to her as Sam took one foot and Pip the other) and hoist her to her feet before she had to go and introduce the auctioneer. Once he was standing next to her, the safest option seemed to be to lean slightly against him in a bid to stay upright. Unfortunately the five-inch heels meant Lottie towered over the poor man, so for the sake of his dignity he kept trying to put a gap between them. She felt like the leaning tower of Pisa as she went with him. Sam gave her a thumbs-up of encouragement, around the hairy mass of Scruffy, who had now joined the party and was doing his best to sit on his mistress's knee and scratch behind his ear at the same time.

Lottie tried to smile and not look worried, while the auctioneer, still sidling away, announced lot one: the opportunity to be owner for a day at the races of a particularly striking racehorse, who belonged to an ex-premiership footballer who was a friend of David Simcock. Bidding started low, until Sam shouted out that it included lunch in the owner's tent with her and David, at which point half the horsemen of Tippermere decided they were game for a day at the races, and the aged rock star from Kitterly Heath (who'd put in the first low bid) upped his bid as she winked his way.

His very young current wife (who Lottie was sure was younger than his granddaughter) was not amused – until she realised who David was. And after doing a quick mental calculation on the goal keeper's life expectancy and earning potential, judged both to be far greater than her husbands, so she started to egg the Keith Moon look-alike on, accusing him of watching his wallet when he lost enthusiasm.

Pip nudged the photographer from *Cheshire Life* with her elbow. She'd already done a deal. He could keep the society photos; she wanted to buy the more opportune ones off him.

The fact that the photo of the racehorse was two years out of date and the poor animal, who had never yet seen a winners' enclosure, was looking forward to a life out at grass at the end of the season, was irrelevant.

The rock star won. The Tippermere lot, who knew a losing horse when they saw it, and also knew that Sam could quite easily be caught lunching in their local pub, kept their wallets firmly shut.

There was a brief lull while the rock star took a bow and then ordered himself a double brandy, before the next lot was announced. A private cruise over to Cannes for the film festival, with entry to a private party in celebration of the actor who had donated the lot.

'But how does he know he'll get nominated?' Pip, never one to be in awe of another's fame and credentials, was sceptical. There was a murmur around the tent as a first bid was requested. This was slow in coming, mainly because nobody was quite sure who the guy was, until one of the footballer's wives triumphantly waved her mobile phone in the air.

'I've found him, I've found him! He was a hobbit.' There was a louder muttering. 'A stand-in hobbit, I mean, but they didn't need him in the end.'

'I didn't know hobbits had stunt doubles, did you Davey?' Sam looked confused.

'And he was in a James Bond movie.' There was an expectant intake of breath.

'Don't tell us, he was the cat that sat on the bald geezer's lap?'

The auctioneer frowned at the hilarity and pushed for an opening bid, reminding everybody that this was for charity and the church.

'Oh 'ang on, I don't think this wiki page is right. Here, here, he was in this movie trailer. Wow, look at the abs on that!' The abs settled it, even if the hobbit talk hadn't.

'So where did he get a yacht from, if he's a hobbit stand-in?'

'His wife – she's a princess or something. Cor, would you look at this house?' The link to the wiki page spread from phone to phone, some people eyeing up the actor's abs, some his wife and others the Hollywood-style mansion. 'That's not in Kitterly is it?'

The auctioneer banged his gavel down and looked at Lottie for inspiration. Lottie tried a cough that didn't get anybody's attention, then went for a full wolf whistle straight into the microphone, which gave a kick of resounding feedback, effectively silencing the crowd.

'He can't be here because it's his mum who donated the prize, but he's agreed to do it, apparently. She said so.' Lottie cleared her throat and looked sheepishly at the auctioneer, who had decided to let her lean on him. They had to be in this together.

'Who will start us at £5,000?'

'Me.' A hand shot up behind Sam, and the lady in question glared when her escort shot her a look of disbelief. 'I need to be on that yacht.'

'But—'

'I have to be. For my portfolio.'

'Well, I need my hand on those abs.' A recently widowed, and very, rich lady, known for her fearlessness on the hunting field, and sexless quality everywhere else shocked everybody into silence. 'Ten thousand.'

'Do something.' The starlet-in-the-making, who had been

responsible for the opening bid, glared at her much older companion, who hadn't realised just how deep he was expected to dig into his pocket.

'Is the wife part of the deal?' bellowed Billy from the back and Tiggy giggled.

Lottie blushed and looked at the man beside her, who checked his notes and shrugged.

One of the footballer's wives waved her mobile in the air. 'I've never been to Cannes and you promised after the World Cup that we'd have a trip. Fifteen thousand.'

'No way.' The starlet saw her chance of a portfolio slipping away. 'Do something, or I'll, I'll, I'll leave you.'

'But I don't like French food! All those bloody frogs' legs.'

'You don't have to come. Do it. If you loved me you'd do it. Do it!' She had nearly reached screaming pitch.

He eyed her up and down. 'I must be fucking stupid. Twenty grand, but it better be going to a good bloody cause. I could buy the frigging yacht for that much.' He glanced around the assorted crowd. 'Anybody want to go with her?'

By the time they got to the last lot, Lottie was swaying on her feet and seriously concerned that she would never make it back to the table. Scruffy had abandoned his bling and gone on a food-scavenging trip around the tables. The rock star had gone for a lie down.

Billy had bid on a makeover for Tiggy, Rory was miffed he'd missed out on a case of cigars and malt whiskey, and Mick had unwisely helped Pip bid on a helicopter trip to attend next season's catwalk show in Milan and interview a particularly reclusive designer, who had agreed to come out of hiding for Tabatha's ex-model father, Tom, provided Tom agreed to come out of hiding himself and model the 'older man's' range. Tom wasn't sure whether he was most bothered that he'd been categorised as old, or that catwalk 'old' was more likely to involve leather collars and ripped jeans than comfy corduroys and cardis.

Getting her feet out of the shoes without Sam noticing involved Lottie having to prop her chin on the table, trying not to look as though she was completely drunk (even though she was decidedly merry), and carrying out minor contortions whilst pretending she was just trying to find a dropped earring.

'Are you sure you don't need a hand, babe?'

'No, no, it's just here. No prob, honest.' She wrestled with the buckle, trying not to grit her teeth and nearly fell under the table as it was finally loosened. 'Yes.' She couldn't stop the triumph escaping, and was very afraid that it sounded like sexual release rather than just a gasp of pleasure as her feet were allowed to straighten out back into their normal shape. She stayed under the table for a moment and eyed up the shoes. Gorgeous as they undoubtedly were, she had never really mastered high heels. And as she was actually quite tall, she felt less of an ungainly giant if she stuck with just an inch or two.

Shoes like this were for special occasions, short ones, preferably, which involved a lot of sitting down, not standing up in front of an audience, who could observe every wobble. She sensed from the wriggle of thighs opposite that Sam was just about to join her under the table, so she straightened up abruptly, catching her head on the table on the way up. 'Ouch! Sorry. What were we talking about?'

'How ace tonight has been. I never knew cricket could be this good. Isn't Lottie amazing?'

Lottie looked at Pip, who was doing her best to keep a straight face, then looked back at the dreamy-eyed Sam.

'It's not always like this, you know. I mean the bit with the bats and everything is, but not the auction. And normally the village cricket team just has old fogeys on it.'

'But, I agree, Lottie is amazing. This just has to be the best auction night ever.' Pip gave Lottie an uncharacteristic hug. 'It's been a huge success.'

'Don't Rory, Tom and Mick normally play then?' Sam looked slightly shocked.

'Rory and Mick don't. I think Tom does, though, doesn't he?'

Pip nodded. 'Yeah, he's aspiring to be an old fogey.'

Sam giggled. 'Ah, bless. He's so sweet.'

'He'll be wearing jumpers with elbow patches next.' Pip, who'd had high hopes for Tom when he'd first moved into Tippermere, was obviously disappointed with how he'd turned out.

'He's a real gent. Don't you love him? It's hard to imagine him modelling knickers now, though, isn't it?'

Lottie decided she was probably right. When the ex-underwear model had moved into the village he'd been Armani-suited and had (from what Pip had told her) a very respectable six-pack. But his intention had been to blend into country living and he'd done it admirably well. His daughter, Tab, brought up on London life, had not been impressed.

'You have to admit it's been a success, though, Lottie. You must have made a record amount tonight.' Pip looked impressed as she raised a glass to toast her friend. 'Shame it's all for charity.'

Lottie, who had actually started to enjoy her role as Lady of the Manor, suddenly felt glum when she remembered that this was only a practice run. She was supposed to be saving her inheritance, raising thousands of pounds, when the most money she'd had to raise in the past was a few thousand for a horse she'd seen for sale that she just had to have.

Killer high heels and events like this weren't going to be just a once-a-year thing any more. 'Bugger. I forgot about that. Do you think they'll let me keep some of the dosh?'

'I know what the answer is.' Sam looked at Pip and Lottie triumphantly. They both looked back blankly. 'You know, to raise money? It's simple.'

'It is?'

'We'll have a big auction, a proper one.'

'But this is a proper one.'

'No, I mean get some big names in, real money. Even more than this. We can put you on the map and raise money for the mansion as well. It'll be the start of something massive. We can have a summer ball to remember.'

Lottie, who was quite sure she'd remember this one for quite a while looked up at the crumbling ceiling, then back down at the designer-clad Sam, who had a bottle of champagne in one hand and a glittering dog's collar in the other. She didn't like the sound of the word 'massive'. She bit the inside of her cheek and tried to work out if it was possible to say anything and not sound ungrateful.

'Can we help you do it, Lottie? It would be so fab. Please?'

Lottie looked at the smiling face, big blue eyes that were gazing back expectantly. Well, if things were as bad as Uncle Dom said, then she was going to need all the help she could get. She took a deep breath, which unfortunately made her cough. When the fit subsided and she'd blinked back the tears that were threatening to fall, Sam was still waiting.

Well, why the hell not? There was no way she could do this on her own, and she didn't really have to, did she? 'Yes. I mean, well, I'd love you to help. We can have some kind of committee? And maybe have some kind of ball, though maybe not a massive one. Thank you. It will be, er, fabulous.' She paused – they were obviously waiting for more. 'First meeting tomorrow, for ideas?'

'Woohoo!' Sam tossed the collar into the air. 'We are going to bring glamour back to the manor, babe.'

Which wasn't quite what she'd meant, but it would do for now. And it would be tasteful, appropriate, fitting for the grandeur that surrounded them. And not massive. Or glam.

Chapter 11

'We're going to have a baby.'

Lottie burst into the tack room with a squeal, nearly running headlong into a startled Mick, who had been searching for a rasp that somebody (probably Rory) had walked off with. He caught her with a grin, then dropped her just as quickly as the words sunk in.

Moving to Rory's small eventing yard, Mere Lodge, had been more by accident than design, but when the eventer's sometime-girlfriend Lottie had returned from her travels she'd brought a ray of sunshine into his slightly cloudy life. There was something about Charlotte, with her love of life and scatty nature, that reminded him of his home back in Ireland, and something about her that he had to admit wasn't good for him.

'Oops sorry. I thought you were Pip.' A blush of pink spread over her cheeks as she gave a little giggle, totally oblivious to the fact that his brain was having a major problem with taking her words in. 'What are you doing here?'

He held up the rasp, which had come to hand seconds before she had and took a step back. Having Lottie pressed against him wasn't doing him any favours at all.

A sudden vision of a mini version of Rory trailing behind Lottie filled his head and left his heart feeling surprisingly empty. Maybe all those months ago he shouldn't have told Rory to get his act together and show Lottie how much she meant to him. And Lottie would have moved on. But she wouldn't have been happy. She loved Rory. It was totally wrong to think that way. The man was going to be a father. They, the two of them, were about to become parents. And after all this time, he should feel differently. After all, he'd never thought there should ever be anything more than friendship between him and Lottie, had he?

'Really?' He looked at her, not quite sure what he should be feeling, but pretty damned certain that it shouldn't be what he was, which was a mixture of shock and disappointment.

'Really, definitely.' Lottie squeaked like an affectionate puppy and flung her arms around him, then as he stiffened, backed off sheepishly. 'Isn't it wonderful? I'm so glad you're one of the first people to know. Where's Pip? I've got to tell her – and Rory.'

'Rory doesn't know?' He knew their relationship was pretty casual and unconventional, but it was like sending out wedding invites before you'd been proposed to. Although, knowing Lottie, she'd be perfectly capable of doing that. Her life consisted of lost lists and forgotten messages. How she and Rory ever managed to run a successful eventing yard beat him. 'Shouldn't he be the first to know?'

'Well, probably. But he was pretty sure anyway. He said you can always tell. Could you tell? Did you know before I told you?'

Mick fought the urge to look at her gently rounded stomach, which to him looked like it always had, and wondered if the infamous Irish tendency to have large families had anything to do with her assumption that he'd know. Something deep in his gut tightened as he acknowledged the look of undisguised pleasure on Lottie's face. He wouldn't exactly say she was blooming, but she was brimming over with something. 'It never occurred to me to be honest.'

'Really?'

'Truly. I suppose I should say congratulations.' It was the shock – once he got used to the idea it would be fine. Lottie dragging her tousle-haired toddler behind her as she inspected a cross-country course flitted through his head before he shut the door firmly on it. 'You're pleased, then – and he will be?'

'Rory? Well it was his idea.'

So the man was already intent on filling Tipping House with his offspring before they'd even moved in – something that Mick had never imagined had been on the agenda.

Lottie bit on the inside of her cheek and stared at him through those lovely wide eyes of hers. 'You think it's a mistake, don't you?' She looked worried, the elation of seconds ago dimming in the face of his lack of enthusiasm, which made him feel guilty.

'Nothing to do with me.' He shrugged. 'I'm sure it'll be wonderful for you, treas., if it's what you want?'

'We just thought it might, you know, have a settling effect.'

'A settling effect.' He echoed her words and was just about to say that he wanted her to stay just the way she was, when it dawned on him that something was off-kilter. 'Why?'

'Well after I had that accident he said he couldn't see me getting Gold round a cross-country course in one piece.'

So the man was putting his girlfriend out to grass rather than risk her neck on a horse that was as impetuous as she was? 'Wouldn't it be easier to get another horse?' were the words on the tip of his tongue.

'Don't you think it will work, then? Dom thought it might. And maybe if it doesn't, then her foal will have the same jump in it, I mean that stallion is gorgeous, but much more solid and sensible than she is. I saw him jump at Hickstead and he was awesome before the accident. Coming down the bank he was just so steady. Do you remember? Did you see him?'

As she spoke, Mick could feel his heart return to its normal rhythm and the pain that had settled over his sternum like bad indigestion dispersed. 'Gold.' The tension slid from his body. 'You've put Black Gold in foal.'

'Yeah, Gold. Why? Who else would it be?' Lottie gave him a

funny look. 'We haven't got any other mares, silly.'

'Haven't got any other mares for what?' Pip stomped into the tack room, a saddle in her hands and a bridle over her shoulder. 'Here, take this will you, Mick, and put it up there. Why the hell Tab can't put saddles away is beyond me.'

She watched critically as Mick took the saddle and effortlessly slung it up on one of the racks, and wondered if it was too early to go to the pub.

'She had to go straight out on the next horse or she wouldn't be finished before Rory got back.' Lottie said reasonably. 'Hey, guess what, we're having a baby.' Pip, who had by now been partly smothered by a hugging Lottie, who was also somehow jumping on the spot, raised a questioning eyebrow at Mick, then caught on – quicker than he had.

'A baby. As in baby what?'

'A foal, of course, Gold is in foal. Isn't that fabulous? The vet just confirmed.' She grinned, good humour restored.

'Fabulous.' Pip dipped the bit from the bridle in a bucket of water and hoped whatever had hit Tippermere wasn't catching. 'What is it about you lot in the countryside and breeding? I get the fornication part, but…. what with Amanda puking up every-where, Sam going all broody and bloody Tiggy filling the country with mad spaniels. Is everybody around here set on increasing the population? I think Tippermere needs a controlled breeding programme – a limit on the number of permissible births per year.'

'Tiggy?' Lottie stopped mid-hop, then realised and put her foot down.

'The spaniel. Is it something in the water?'

'She's not had her puppies, has she? Why didn't you say? Oh God, they'll be so cute, I've got to go and see. Come on, come on. Have you seen them already? Where's my phone? I need to text her.'

'I did say. Apparently they just popped out like little corks.' Pip shuddered. 'Later. Come on, Sam's waiting in the kitchen.'

'Sam?'

Lottie looked at her blankly, which was how Mick felt.

'You're hopeless. She's come over so we can put together your plan of action. You know, the one we discussed after the cricket auction?'

'Oh hell.' Lottie glanced at her wrist, then realised that, yet again, she'd mislaid her watch, she grabbed Pip's wrist. 'How can it be that time already?' In her head she'd been busy trying to put together her own plan most of the day, in between all the other things she'd been doing. And she'd been rehearsing her 'this is what we're doing' speech, except she hadn't yet hit on the perfect solution. But she'd then been so preoccupied with the vet's visit and side-tracked by the thought of puppies and how she could persuade Rory that a spaniel would make a lovely addition to the terrier trio, that she had completely lost track of time.

'I'll leave you to it, then.'

'No you won't.' Pip grabbed hold of Mick's arm as he made a bid for freedom. 'Stay. We need all the help we can get.' She hung on, hoping that they could, just for once, do something together that didn't involve horses. 'Don't we, Lottie?'

'Why on earth would you need me?' The shock of a pregnant Lottie had shaken him more than he liked, and now the idea of contributing to an action plan designed to set Lottie and Rory up in Tipping House, with or without a brood of children, was a step too far. He needed some distance. He needed to persuade Pip to go back to Ireland with him, where they might stand a chance of rescuing what was left of their relationship. And he could tell from the look on her face that his prickly attitude was showing. 'Isn't it Rory who should be there helping, not me?'

'I'd like you to be here. And Rory will be when he gets back from the gallops.' Pip wasn't going to give him a let-out. 'We're a committee and you are on it.'

'Says who?' Lottie and Mick spoke in nearly perfect unison. Both alarmed for different reasons.

'You honestly don't have to be there,' Lottie said, seeing her

136

committee of four ballooning in size like badly behaved dough – if she wasn't careful. Then she saw the frown on Pip's face and dithered, 'Unless you really want to, of course.'

Mick shook his head. Long ago he thought he'd accepted that Lottie would never be anything more than a friend. He'd moved on, and the relationship he'd had with Pip had been good. But lately the sparks between them had turned to shrapnel, and the lack of common interests, which had given them independence at the start, was now a chasm that became harder to cross each day.

It was easier to be apart than together and he hated it. Pip was bossy, and that had worked at first, but they'd started to act like an old married couple, nagging and niggling as they fought to share the same path. It wasn't fun now, it was getting too serious. And as each day passed he became more certain that she wanted more from him, wanted something he couldn't give. And he couldn't pretend, didn't want to live a lie. The harder she tried to pull them together, the more he became sure they were better apart.

'Says Her Ladyship,' Pip threw Lottie a semi-apologetic look, 'Elizabeth.'

'I thought I was supposed to be in charge?' Lottie, who was in the habit of trying to avoid being in charge, suddenly realised that she was in danger of being an onlooker in her gran's and Pip's master plan. Which Mick thought was probably Elizabeth's idea, to put her in a position where she actually wanted to take control.

Pip dug in her pocket and found a scrap of paper. 'She gave me this and said she's not lost her marbles so she wants a weekly update.'

Lottie shook her head. 'Weekly update?' This wasn't how she wanted it at all. Take charge, her uncle had said. Take the reins. She wanted to, she needed to, and Gran was starting to behave like a youngster fighting the bit. She swallowed hard, then raced in. 'I'm not having a committee, and I'll tell her things as I decide them.' Pip raised an eyebrow. 'I'm really grateful everybody wants to help, but I know what I don't want to do, and I've got a few ideas for what I do.' She drew breath and Pip's eyebrow went higher. 'I do want to know what everybody thinks, of course.'

'Well, she's made a note of what you can't do as well. I think "let bloody people stomp through the house" was top of the list. Now can we stop faffing about and get on with it?'

Lottie tried to walk, talk and read the list, which, given the spidery writing and uneven yard, made it a pretty near impossible task.

Sam was already in the kitchen waiting when they got there, with Scruffy at her feet and the terrier that Rory had left at home circling them with suspicion. Amanda was sitting opposite and was obviously being interrogated about pregnancy disorders, and Dom was standing by the Aga looking uncomfortable. Mick and Pip squeezed in, moving entry forms off chairs and Lottie realised that a tidy-up was probably long overdue.

She glanced around, and apart from the obvious solution of chucking everything in the other room, she couldn't see any way of making the place look remotely presentable. The terrier started scratching at an old horse rug, which Lottie had brought in from the tack room, meaning to mend a tear, and Amanda sneezed as hairs were sent in all directions.

'We'll sit outside.' A decision that wasn't one of Lottie's best. True it meant there was more room and less chance of a dogfight, but it also meant there were flies and country smells wafting their way from the muck heap, which had been due to be emptied that week, except the tractor had broken down. 'We'll light the chiminea.' That would get rid of the flies, smoke always worked.

'Charlotte, sit down. Some of us have got work to do.' Dom looked pointedly at his watch.

Well do it, was on the tip of her tongue. She imagined he'd driven Amanda (who really wasn't comfortable behind the wheel these days) over. 'You really don't have to stay Uncle Dominic, unless,' she gnawed at her bottom lip, 'unless Gran told you to?'

'And some of us have pints to drink.' Mick put a match to the contents of the chiminea, which unfortunately had been there some time, and the black smoke that billowed out threatened to get rid of Amanda as well as the flies.

Lottie tried to ignore it and spread the note that Pip had given her, now more than a little bit crumpled, on the table.

'Did somebody mention a pint?' Rory had arrived back at the yard unnoticed and Lottie, with a squeal, forgot all about the task in hand. She scrambled over to meet him, the precious list drifting off the table and into the dog's water bowl.

Dom sighed and sat down next to Amanda.

'Guess what, we're pregnant.' Mick cringed as Lottie jumped on Rory with glee and shared her news.

Sam looked on worriedly as all three terriers, the pack reunited, regarded her dog with interest. He, however, was unperturbed, and with a loud woof tore himself free of her hold and launched himself over the garden wall, with Tilly in close pursuit.

Disentangling himself from Lottie, Rory deftly caught one of the little dogs that was scrambling for attention and doing his best to avoid the dog's tongue, he spoke around the bundle of fur. 'So, why's everybody here? Are we having a party?' He frowned. 'Actually, I thought you were going to come for a pipe-opener on the gallops, then we were off to the pub.'

'Oh hell, I forgot that. But I told you I had to do this.' The frown deepened. A short sharp gallop would have cleared her head as well as the horse's lungs. But she couldn't. She just couldn't. Not right now. 'Rory, I did tell you. We've got to put together a plan.'

'Mother felt that Charlotte might need some,' Dom paused, 'pointers. So she sent a list, which appears to have got,' he stared at the list as the ink slowly blurred into one, 'wet.'

'Oh my God.' Lottie fished it out and held it over the chiminea in a bid to dry it, which just made it sooty and even harder to read. 'But I don't need a list, I know what she hates and I wouldn't do that anyway.'

'Right, if you're too busy with your lists to ride, I'm off to the pub.' Rory stood up, Tilly the terrier, suspecting he was on the move, forgot all about her new canine friend and came hurtling back. 'How about it?' He made a move to grab the sheet of paper and Lottie clutched it to her chest protectively. Rory leaned in closer, his tawny eyes dark. 'Let's have some fun and forget the boring stuff, gorgeous. It's quiz night and we've got to stuff Tom and his London pals.' He winked. 'You can do your lists tomorrow.'

Lottie sighed 'I'm sorry.' And she was. Fun with Rory was tempting. 'But I do need to get this sorted. Stay and help? Then we can go for a drink. Please?'

'You don't need me.' Rory shook his head ruefully and backed off. 'You know I'm allergic to paperwork, darling. Come on, you're much better at the music questions than me and Mick.'

'But you promised to help.' Lottie wailed. Out of all the people surrounding them, it was Rory she wanted to support her in the task and help her hold off the batty ideas. And she couldn't do this on her own, without him. She didn't want to.

He planted a kiss on the top of her head and ruffled her hair. 'And you promised to come for a ride. Anyway, too many cooks and all that. Looks like girl stuff to me. You get your plan together, darling, and then I'll look at it with you, okay? Promise. Coming Mick? Dom? Let's show the townies what we're made of. I'll text you if we're stuck.'

'Rory.' But he wasn't listening, he'd blown her a kiss and was already heading for the gate. Lottie sighed and resisted the urge to run after him. Why couldn't he see how important this was to her? 'And texting is cheating.'

Dom hesitated, torn between his sense of duty, his wife and the knowledge that staying might frustrate the hell out of him. He was used to being in total control, taking charge. If he was honest, he would probably find it more difficult to hand over the reins to Charlotte than his mother would. At least she was taking the sensible route and keeping her distance. He unfortunately felt obliged to oversee his niece's journey from spurs to stilettoes.

'You go, darling.' Amanda smiled up at him, serene and composed, understanding his predicament as she always did. 'We'll sort out some ideas for the event and then we can always discuss them later. And I'm sure Pip or Lottie will drop me off home.'

'Definitely. And now can we please go back into the kitchen, Lottie? I reckon it's still a smoke-free zone.'

At the cricket auction, after several bottles of wine and relieved that she'd survived the day, Lottie had thought Sam's idea for a huge summer ball and auction was feasible, with a few modifications. But in the cool, and sober, light of day she'd had doubts. It wasn't just the fact that she hadn't even been able to keep cucumber sandwiches safe – a full-scale dinner and enough celebrities to stage a film festival would be a major challenge. Her instincts, which she always relied on when it came to horses, were telling her it wasn't right. The trouble was, knowing what *wasn't* suitable was the easy part. But hitting on what was suitable had escaped her until now. But getting a diplomatic word in to divert Sam towards something more apt was never going to be easy.

'It will be fab, babe. A man auction.'

'Sorry?' How did the word man and auction go together? Lottie had been thinking yachts and tickets to the golf.

'We can auction off the hottest men in town. I mean we've got Davey and the boys, and Tom must have some modelling friends who are young and hot. We can have them stripped and oiled and…'

'No.' It had come out rather more forcefully than she'd intended. Sam's mouth dropped open, a very small smile tugged at the corners of Amanda's mouth, and Pip rather uncharacteristically failed to throw in a smart comment. She was too busy pondering about Mick and his earlier uptight behaviour. It was one thing to not want to stay with her, but he'd been rather more forceful than was necessary. In fact he'd been almost as grumpy as he had been the night of Billy's wedding.

Lottie tried a softer approach. 'No stripping and oiling. We can't have naked men, *Cheshire Life* would never set foot in the house again. Would they, Pip?'

Pip dragged herself out of her musings. 'A lot of other people would, though.' Lottie frowned. 'No, sorry, you're right. And you do need their kind of coverage.'

Sam shut her mouth, then opened it again unperturbed. 'Well that rock-star chap that was at the auction promised me he could get the Rolling Stones.'

'Are they still alive?' Pip was bemused, but listening again now. As self-appointed head of PR she wanted to know just how hot the material could get.

'I don't think they all are,' Lottie looked doubtful, 'and I'm not sure they're the hottest men in town still, are they?'

'I was thinking more of them doing the music, babe, not being auctioned, although that song's about not getting satisfaction isn't it – we don't want people thinking that, do we?'

'We don't, no.' Lottie was glad there was an easy way out of that one. 'We'll cross them off.'

'How about a bit of "Sex on Fire"? You like those Kings of Leon don't you, Lottie?' Sam giggled. 'Sizzling steamy bits – you'd need a fireman. Oh I do love a fireman!'

'And his slippery pole, of course,' added Pip, sensing that Lottie needed help in steering Sam back on course. 'Very funny. But you do realise that we need to get this together quickly, before the summer is out?'

'I know.' Lottie had already studied the calendar, desperately looking for a suitable date, which mainly involved working out which three-day events she and Rory were supposed to be attending, and what she had to do with the horses to prepare. 'But we're not having poles or any sex either.'

'September's a lovely month, when everybody is back from their hols.' Sam, with a wink in Lottie's direction, went back to thoughts of 'the event'. 'But Kings of Leon are good, and they're much younger, too, aren't they than Mick Jagger? I wonder if any of the girls know them?'

Lottie still had her mind fixed firmly on dates. 'But that only gives us eight weeks.'

'No probs, babe, I know lots of people and so does Davey. All the girls will help, especially when they know it's for a real Lady, in a *real* mansion. I mean, it's just like being invited to Buckingham Palace, isn't it? It's so posh, and money talks, isn't that what they say?'

'But I haven't got any. That's the point.'

Sam was undeterred. 'Have you got a tiara? You know, family jewels and stuff, like Princess Di wore.'

'I don't know, should I have?' This was getting worse by the minute. Lottie couldn't remember any mention of family jewels, apart from the sapphire and diamond ring she'd been given when she was eighteen.

'Don't worry, babe.' Sam patted her hand. 'They'll adore the idea of you being poor and them being able to help. I mean it's perfect, isn't it? You can say you had to pawn the family jewels and want to get them back.'

Lottie wasn't so sure. 'I don't want to look desperate, do I? And it's a new roof we need really, not diamonds.'

'Have you got a pen, love, to write a list with? It is just so hard to put things on my tablet since I got these nails done. I mean they are lovely, but look.' She tapped ineffectually.

'So what did you mean, a man auction?' In amongst thoughts of fireman and family jewels, Lottie was trying to get her head around the idea of buying an actual man. Despite firmly dismissing the idea as far as Tipping House went, she was intrigued. Where would one keep him? And wouldn't Rory mind? Was it like a timeshare?

'You know, babe, you bid on a hot man. I went to this charity thing once and they had all these men stripped and oiled up and the girls loved them. And your men are better, real, like famous – not just models and stuff.'

'Apart from Tom.'

'Well he's a posh model, isn't he? And we could get them glam mags here, couldn't we, Pip? And the *Sun*. Do you think we can get in *Hello* or something? The girls would love that.'

Sam was on a roll and there seemed to be no stopping her. Lottie knew from experience that the best thing to do was wait until she'd run out of steam, before even attempting to add an opinion of her own. Samantha had a heart of gold, and was generous to a fault, but sometimes, Lottie knew, her ideas were a step too far for tranquil Tippermere.

'Sam we need *Tatler*, *The Lady* and *Cheshire Life*, not,' not what? 'not the others.' Which seemed the safest way to put it. 'And no nakedness.'

'Do we? Well we can do the place up, real glam with proper butlers and stuff. Hey, how about getting those caterers in that have topless waiters?'

Lottie felt her mouth open in horror, then realised Sam had said waiters not waitresses.

'They are gorg, all fit and just in, like, dickie bows.'

'Just dickie bows?' Pip raised an eyebrow and Sam giggled.

'On the top half, silly, they have trousers on.'

'Shame.'

'So, this bidding on a man…' Lottie had barely registered the conversation about topless men and dickie bows. She was still trying to work out A) What the auction involved, and B) Whether it was an idea she could salvage anything from – though obviously without the oil.

'You bid to go out with them, you know, for a meal, or a day or,' Sam grinned and winked, 'whatever they're up for.'

'I think Rory might mind, wouldn't David?'

'Course not, babe, he trusts me and it's for a good cause, isn't it?'

'I was just wondering, I mean it sounds wonderful, but,' they all turned to look at Amanda, who'd been listening quietly, 'maybe we need some kind of highlight? A main prize. I was just thinking that this is all for the women, and maybe we need to get the men involved as well? There are some very rich men in Cheshire, who I'm sure would donate generously.'

They all looked at her and she coloured slightly.

'Go on.'

'It's only a thought,' she glanced at Lottie, who wasn't really concentrating, 'about offering lunch with the Lady of the Manor. Just lunch, of course.' She added hastily.

'You know what, that's a brilliant idea. Lottie as the main prize.'

'Sorry?' Lottie, whose mind was still wrestling with the idea of what to do with any man she bid on, caught the end of the sentence with horror. 'I'm the prize for what?'

'All the men bid on you.' Sam laughed, pleased to see that everybody was joining in now.

'What?' The horrified gasp was ignored. 'I don't want anybody bidding on me.'

'The Lottie Lottery.' Sam clapped her hands. 'And Magnificent Man auction.'

That did it. 'No way. I'd be the most unladylike lady in Cheshire.'

Pip grinned. 'The Lady Lottie Lottery.'

Lottie glared at Pip. 'I thought you were my friend?'

She laughed. 'I am.'

'So, can we do it?' Sam hugged herself with enthusiasm.

Lottie shook her head and wished she could say yes, but she couldn't. She just couldn't. Tipping House was old and grand, a majestic lady who had stood guard over Tippermere for many years. Being inventive was one thing, but it had to be, well, dignified. Elegant.

'I kind of like some bits of the auction idea,' she said tentatively, 'but then what?' They all looked at her. 'Well, I mean, what happens the rest of the year? How does the auction make everybody come back?' That was the part that was really worrying her.

'I see what you mean, babe.'

'We need to use something that only Tipping House can offer.'

Which was about as far as she'd managed to get, despite thinking of very little else.

'The whole posh country-mansion thing.'

'Exactly.' Relieved that they were now on her wavelength, Lottie relaxed slightly.

'So we need to be thinking about country weekends, or fishing, or clay shooting or something like that?' Amanda tapped on her tablet. 'And maybe have an auction or summer ball to launch it?'

'Yes, but it's got to be something with wow factor, so people who come will spread the word and we'll get in the press.'

'I like wow factor.' Sam grinned, not at all put out by the fact that her other ideas hadn't been welcomed with open arms.

'Shall we all go away and try and think of "wow", then?' Amanda grinned and switched her tablet off.

'Perfect.' Lottie, who hadn't realised she was holding her breath, started to breathe again.

'Want a lift, babe? Hang on a sec while I find Scruffy, then we'll be off.'

It was only once Pip had headed off to the pub in search of Mick, and Sam had found her dog and headed off with Amanda, that Lottie decided they hadn't really made any progress at all. Mulling over what to do with any man she won, and worrying about whether anybody would even want to bid on her, was spectacularly unproductive. She really needed to get a grip on the situation and do the one thing that Gran and Dom had been unable to – find a way of easing Tipping House into the twenty-first century without spoiling it in the process.

She spread out Elizabeth's list, which had dried out, but was speckled with soot and was an inky smudge in places. Squinting at it helped with some of the words, but her gran's neat but old-fashioned writing had been transformed into a bad example of modern art in places. She really must remember to destroy it in case Elizabeth saw what she'd done.

And then she glanced at Sam's, which was scarily legible in its modern rounded lettering (minus any water damage) and knew that this really wasn't the type of glamour that the manor needed.

The thing was, Lottie did love Tipping House, and she happened to like it just the way it was, in all its slightly shabby splendour. The ancient scratched oak floorboards told tales of a hundred Labradors wagging their tales after a good day out, and of scores of ladies in high heels calling in for sherry or afternoon tea. Hair-covered chair covers that had a musty smell and slightly singed rugs in the snug told of winter days when cold children would rush in from the grounds, discard their wellingtons and curl up with the dogs, roasting chestnuts and heating sticky marshmallows in the large open fireplace until they oozed sugary sweetness tinged with smoke.

The fact that the wobbly Chippendale writing desk, which showed signs of teething puppies on its legs, a chip in the corner and a scratched top, but was the real deal, and that the Chesterfield oxblood sofa was 'distressed' through years of wear and not some artificial manufacturing process made it home. It felt like home, smelled like home, wrapped itself around you, even though the central-heating pipes gargled alarmingly and the cold permeated the thick walls all year round. In fact, Lottie was convinced the house was often colder in than out.

When Samantha, in her well-meaning way, talked about bringing some glamour in, Lottie was very afraid that it would mean transforming the ballroom into something that resembled one of the chic wine bars of Kitterly Heath. Or worse. She could just imagine her ancestors, who adorned the walls larger than life, looking down their aristocratic noses at the revelry and wondering what it had come to.

She knew full well that she had to raise some money before the rising damp rose high enough to meet the seepage of rain coming in through the roof, but she wasn't entirely convinced that her gran meant she should sell her body to the highest bidder and fill the place with film stars, rock stars and footballers' wives. But would she let everybody down if she didn't?

Chapter 12

Lottie poured a coffee and decided that Pip was right. Mick was being weird. He hadn't been himself in the tack room, and he'd been totally grumpy when Pip had tried to get him to help with 'the plan'. She's caught him more than once glaring at her as though she'd done something seriously wrong. He must think she was a complete idiot, like everybody else did. Oh Christ. She'd just put salt in her cup instead of sugar.

Maybe he had the male equivalent of the menopause. She had read in *Cosmo* or somewhere that it actually existed and wasn't just an excuse for running off buying Porsches and shagging teenagers. Except he was a bit young – he was more or less her age. It could be that he was worried about Pip, and Pip had said she thought he didn't love her anymore, and maybe he thought she'd gone off him. God, she was a crap friend, she'd forgotten all about that until now and just worried about her own silly problems – like working out how to become Lady of the Manor and raise the same amount of money as the entire population of Tippermere and Kitterly Heath together spent in five years. But she would. She had to, it was her problem and with the help of her friends (and maybe her boyfriend) she was convinced they'd sort that.

But, what about her friends? Maybe she should try and get Mick to confide in her – she could be his shoulder to cry on.

In between the fundraising events. Not that he seemed to want any shoulders to cry on – he was more the type of man that you unburdened problems on, not took off. He was just so good at solving her problems. He had this way of looking at things that made them seem so much simpler.

Lottie absentmindedly took a bite of toast, just as one of the dogs, which thought she wasn't concentrating, made a grab for it. They met nose to nose and Lottie giggled and grabbed the little animal. 'Guess what, Tilly, we're going to have a foal.' Nobody else seemed that bothered to share the news. 'Shall we go and tell Tigs – and we can see her puppies?' And maybe ask her what she thought about Pip and Mick.

Lottie loved her father's new wife – she'd always been a bit like a mother to her. In a very abstract way. To find out there was something going on between Tiggy and Billy had been a bit of a shock, but once she'd got used to it, she could see the bonuses. Tiggy had always mothered Billy anyway, running around after him and doing everything he wanted from levelling the arena (which she was crap at because she was too easily distracted – it was always more uneven at the end than it had been at the start), to putting horses out (except she was always so vague they ended up in the wrong fields). But he seemed happy and willing to forgive her, which he didn't do with anybody else. And she just ignored him when he was gruff and grumpy, or told him to cheer up. They were in fact, Lottie decided, a very good match.

Which was more than it seemed could be said for Mick and Pip. Lottie didn't like arguments – she was all for an easy life and the niggles between her two friends put her on edge. She loved both of them to bits, and even though Pip and she were so very different, they just got on. Pip made her laugh, and in her logical way made everything seem straightforward. And Mick was even-tempered and calm enough to make even the biggest jump or most difficult horse seem within her capabilities. He grounded her, and yet never criticised or made her feel silly. But together what had seemed like banter at the start, all those little differences that made them better together, now seemed to make things worse.

She sighed. Pip had wanted to talk to her about Mick, she was sure, and then Rory had arrived and it had all been forgotten. She was a crap friend. Pip had always been there for her, and although she might not be very good at advice, she could at least listen and try to help. She could have sworn that Pip said she didn't think Mick loved her, and she couldn't have made that up, Pip must have said it. And Pip never talked about love, she steered well clear of that particular four-letter word, which meant... Lottie paused mid-bite and stared at the dog. 'It means she loves him, doesn't it?' The dog wagged its tail and eyed up the last bit of toast. 'She wouldn't have said that unless she really cared. Oh, God. What are we going to do, Tilly?' For Pip there could only be one worse thing than actually being in love, and that was not being loved back.

Lottie fed the last bit of toast to the dog and glanced up at the kitchen clock. Seven o'clock, which meant she had time to go and see her dad and Tiggy before Rory got back from the pub. And she had to go out to collect some chips anyway, as the fridge seemed to be bare. Again. So she could combine the trip: see the pups, ask Tiggy what she should do about Pip (because Tiggy was good at stuff like that, even if she was a bit batty) and get the dinner. Perfect. Provided Rory did just stay for a couple of pints, and if he didn't, she'd eat the chips herself.

Billy Brinkley stretched out his legs and, nursing a large glass of whiskey, watched his daughter as she picked up one puppy after another, her eyes shining and a wide grin on her face. She picked the plumpest one up, giggling as it wriggled and tried to push its wet nose against hers.

The unexpected lump in his throat made him feel old and sentimental, and he didn't like to think he was either. But she was the spitting image of her mother, curled up happy on the floor surrounded by animals. A lady by birth, but more like a

151

gypsy by nature.

Billy had always feared for the future his daughter would grow into. When her mother, Alexa, had died, it had released her from a future of onerous duty. But Lottie was to have no such escape. And yet Elizabeth had found a way to cope with it, her own individual eccentric way, and Lottie took after her grandmother in more ways than were immediately obvious.

Watching Lottie now though was like seeing a young Alexa, the one he'd always loved and hoped he'd grow old with – except he'd never had the chance. The old familiar pain bit into his chest and Tiggy squeezed his hand, understanding that even though he was happier than he'd ever been in his life, the past could never be erased. Forgotten. And although he never wanted to forget his darling Alexandra, and never would, as she'd left a legacy in the shape of her daughter, he wished the pain that came when he least expected it would mellow.

These days the nightmare sharp sound of a hoof slipping on uneven cobbles, the sound of happiness changing to a cry of pain, didn't wake him from his sleep quite so often, but he still sometimes could swear he heard sweet laughter on the wind when he was out on the horses, smell her heady scent as he galloped over the fields early in the morning, see her dark eyes staring out at him in the darkness, sense her soft words telling him he could do anything, be anyone….

'This one looks like you, Dad.' Lottie held up the fattest and most squirming brown- and-white puppy of the litter and laughed as it did its best to bark. 'And it sounds just as grumpy, too.'

'Less of the grumpy from you, missy.'

'We could call it Sweet William?' Tiggy was grinning, too, as she took the complaining pup from her step-daughter.

'And less of the sweet. You're not giving them names because we're not keeping them.'

'Ahh this one is tiny – we could call it Horatio.' Lottie picked up the runt of the litter. 'Get it? Seeing as the dad's called Nelson.

Half Nelson?'

'Very witty. Haven't you got more than enough dogs to fill that cottage of Rory's?'

'Well,' Lottie sighed, 'if we move to Gran's, we're going to have lots of space.'

'Ah. So you are moving soon, then?'

'Gran said,' she tugged gently at a loose thread on the rug, 'she wants to move into one of the wings, and she said she thought it would be an idea for me to be there. But Rory's got so many competitions, and we don't want to upset the horses, and Tab can't manage on her own on the yard, and Pip is so well, preoccupied.'

'You do know you need to get on with it, don't you? It's not fair on your gran to leave things too long, Lottie. The horses will cope, Rory will cope.' Billy didn't want to push his daughter into anything, but the fact that she was here meant she wanted to talk. Wanted somebody to make the decision for her. She was honest, hard-working and, despite the outwardly chaotic appearance, Billy was proud of her. He knew she could make it work, knew that she had enough of her mother in her to take on the challenge in her own sweet way and make things happen. The wild streak that had led Alexa astray wasn't as deep in Lottie. She liked to have fun, but Billy could see in his daughter that same sense of duty that shone from Dominic. Her uncle.

Lottie stroked the puppy, which was trying to scramble up onto her knee.

'It's your inheritance.' His voice was soft. 'And you do love the estate, don't you?'

'I do.' Her voice was soft as she stroked the pup's soft curls, but the worry lines furrowed her brow. 'But you weren't happy there, were you, Dad?'

'That was different. Your gran wasn't ready to let the place go, and we were just lodgers. If things had worked out differently,' he paused and fought the lump in his throat. Oh, yes, if things had worked out differently, if she hadn't ridden that horse, hadn't fallen, hadn't died. He looked over the top of his whiskey glass and Tiggy was watching him, smiling encouragingly, as she always did. 'We would have all gone back there one day, Charlotte. Your mother loved that old place, it was her home. I always remember the time she rode one of the ponies down the long hallway, all your gran did was to tell her to take its shoes off the next time so that she didn't leave marks on the oak floorboards.' He chuckled. Elizabeth could be stern and forbidding at times, but she'd had the measure of her children. 'Your gran gave us the space to enjoy ourselves, to enjoy you.' But that was then, many years ago. And now things were different. Elizabeth, and the Estate, were getting older. Time attacking each in different ways. 'And you love Tipping House, don't you?'

'I do, I really do, but what if I can't do it, Dad? I'm hopeless at organising stuff.'

Tiggy smiled. 'You organised our wedding.'

'And that wasn't exactly a huge success was it?' She kissed the pup and wished her life just consisted of playing, eating, sleeping and making funny noises. Well, maybe not the noises bit.

'It was the best wedding ever, wasn't it, Tiggy my love? And the horses were a stroke of genius.'

Lottie, who always tried to be honest, sighed. 'But they weren't actually in the plan at all.'

'Sod the plan, love, the whole day was one to remember. You can plan your own next.'

'I think Rory has to ask me first.' She avoided his gaze.

'Better tell him to get a move on before somebody else jumps in.'

'Dad!'

'Like that Aussie fella.'

'He was just a friend.'

Billy shook his head. 'What's the problem, love? You know you can manage the place, we all know you can.'

'It's just…'

'Rory? Is that what bothers you? I'm not expecting you to get married, love. I'm joking.' His voice was soft, he was worried. Lottie deserved to have fun, even if she wasn't exactly going to have freedom. 'Show the lad the place properly, darling, he's only really seen the stable yard.' He raised an eyebrow as she blushed. Oh, yes, that stable yard had seen a fair bit of action, it had been his and Alexa's favourite place, and now it seemed it was Rory and Lottie's. He'd seen them head over there more than once, seen them on the night Elizabeth had explained to Lottie about her inheritance. The same night that he'd realised he didn't want to lose Tiggy. The night Dom had told them he was marrying Amanda. Three events that looked set to shape their futures.

'I just sometimes wish he took it a bit more seriously, like Mick does.' Mick who was always there to help out, who was happy to stand still and listen. Who took her seriously too.

'Ay, well Mick's a different kettle of fish altogether. Look, love, you can show young Rory why you love that place just like your mum showed me, and if he's not won over then,' he put the empty glass down, stood up and kissed her lightly on the tip of her upturned nose, 'you've got some decisions to make, haven't you?'

'But I love Rory.'

'And you love Tipping House, too. Right, I'm off to check the horses.' He shook his head in mock dismay. 'Horatio, my arse. Funny bloody name for a dog.'

'Funny name for a posterior, too.' Tiggy raised an eyebrow and Lottie giggled.

'Oh shit, is that the time?' Lottie glanced up at the clock on the mantelpiece in dismay. 'Rory will either be pissed in the pub by now, or home and wondering where I've got to.'

'Won't he ring if he's worried?' Tiggy couldn't imagine Billy without a mobile attached to his person. He was constantly on the phone if she as much as disappeared from sight and he needed something doing. Some people might have hated it. Tiggy loved it.

'He's lost his mobile again.' Lottie grinned. 'I've got a horrible feeling Tilly put it on the muck heap.' She looked at the pup who had fallen asleep on her foot. 'Can I have him?'

Tiggy grinned. 'Course you can, love. If Rory won't mind?'

Rory wouldn't mind. He never minded about much at all. She chewed at the inside of her cheek as she gently moved her foot from beneath the sleepy animal.

'Do you think it's normal in a relationship for one person to love more than the other?'

'I think it's how a lot of us feel. It might be that it just seems that way, though, but it actually isn't really? I thought my first husband loved me to bits, until he ran off with somebody else. In fact, I thought he loved me more than I loved him. But maybe he did and got fed up of trying.'

'He was an arty type, wasn't he?' Lottie wracked her brain trying to remember what she'd been told about Tiggy's first husband.

'An author, dear – ran off with his agent. Agents are usually very smart and assertive, not at all like me. They'd remember to iron his shirts and stock the wine rack.'

Tiggy was definitely more the starving artist, if you went by appearances. Forgetful, with a wardrobe of favourite pieces, which unfortunately didn't go together and a mass of hair that she pinned up or tied back in the most abstract way possible. She was totally scatty, but very well meaning. No doubt, Lottie thought, when she'd met her first husband they had shared ideals, until he'd started to make money and moved on.

'Although that wasn't his first dalliance. Don't you love the word dalliance? Almost poetic – much nicer than affair or fling. We had a bit of an open marriage, very bohemian.' She grinned. 'We were very trendy.' Then giggled in true Tiggy style. 'Oh well, dear, I suppose I'd better go and warm the bed for your father.'

Lottie looked up startled. The image of Tiggy spread out naked on the bed for when Billy got back from evening stables was not one she wanted occupying her bed space – head space – she hastily corrected herself.

'He does love his electric blanket.'

'Oh.' That was a relief. 'Pip doesn't think Mick loves her, well not as much as she loves him.'

'Ahh, we're talking about your friends are we? Now there's mess in the making, like a cock and a bull facing up to each other, aren't they?'

'Cock and bull?'

'Well maybe that's not my best metaphor, but they're totally different, aren't they? And they both like a challenge. Not a match made in heaven is it? More a potential bloodbath.'

'Tiggy!'

'Sorry, dear, just thinking out loud. I'm sure they'll be fine. Now do you want to take that podgy thing with you now? And are you coming back to see the new puppies tomorrow? I am sorry Beth wouldn't let you see them, she's been a bit insecure about them and they are so young.'

'What are you going to do with them all, Tiggy?' Lottie had been quite surprised when the first of Tiggy's dogs had delivered a litter of healthy puppies, and shocked when Tiggy had told her that the second dog was due seven weeks later.

'Oh, they'll find homes. It just seemed mean to let Blossom have puppies and not let Beth. I do try and treat them both the same. Maybe Beth is frightened that Blossom will steal them, and that's why she hid them under the dresser?'

Lottie didn't know, but she was more than a bit worried that if the pups grew at the same rate as the first litter, then they'd be stuck like corks in a bottle and the only way out would be to lift the dresser off their little fat tummies.

Chapter 13

Lottie steered the horsebox along the narrow country lane that trickled its way through Tippermere and tried to ignore the warmth on her knee that could have been more than just cuddly puppy heat. More like leaky puppy over-excitement.

It was all she needed, the day really hadn't gone awfully well at all so far. She'd not actually spelled it out to Rory, to be fair, but she had expected him to be excited about the move and there to help her. And instead he'd been cross that she wouldn't cancel everything and go and look at a horse with him. The fact that he absolutely refused to understand that she'd promised Dom and her gran that they'd move today, and couldn't change the arrangements, had led to an impasse, and them staring at each other. Until he'd snapped and strode off, with a muttered comment about her not being much fun at all these days.

She sighed, they had kissed and made up, but she would have felt much happier if he'd been sitting beside her.

'You've not had a wee on me, have you?' The puppy squirmed in excitement and nearly slipped into the foot well. Which could have spelled disaster. Lottie made a grab for him, the horsebox lurching dangerously close to the ditch amid whinnies and stamps of indignation from the horses in the back.

But even that couldn't dampen her excitement, even if it had dampened her legs. Although when she lifted the fat brown-and-white puppy with one hand there didn't appear to be signs of leakage. Which was a relief. Turning up at Tipping House after being peed on by a dog was so not the image of Lady of the Manor.

'We're really doing it, aren't we?' The puppy squirmed and tried to lick her chin, toppling over backwards and nearly falling onto the floor again. Lottie grabbed him just in time and put him next to her on the seat, where he rolled over to show his fat pink, mottled puppy belly before sliding inelegantly off the leather seat head first. Lottie laughed as he struggled to his feet and started to hop up and down in an attempt to get back up. 'You're hopeless.' She pulled him back up and then turned her concentration back to the road.

Lottie loved this time of the year, when the hedges were looking overgrown and slightly wild, just before they were cut, when the trees were covered in leaves and the wild flowers littered the side of the roads with untidy splashes of yellow, white, pink and blue. The puppy clambered back across her knee and tried to look out of the cab window, before losing its footing and nearly slipping between the seat and door. Common sense should have told her that taking in a puppy the day before she moved into Tipping House was probably a silly idea, but surely the mistress of the estate needed a dog? And the terriers were really Rory's. And Tiggy had said they could call him a moving-in present, which kind of validated it.

Lottie rarely thought things through that thoroughly before jumping in – it was one of the things that made her so adorable. And something that made her life a tad tricky at times. Like saying 'yes, of course I'll train your horse' when it was known by everyone in Cheshire to be a confirmed bolter with a love of bottom-biting, or 'yes, come to dinner, we can always squeeze another one in', when the chicken dinner for two was already at a stretch seeing as Rory could, pardon the expression, eat a horse and more often than not Tab would steal a chicken leg and Mick would have his hands on a Yorkshire pudding before she had a chance to stop him. And then there was the 'Yes, I'll move into the Manor and raise enough money to keep it going for the next five hundred years.' Well, she hadn't exactly said that, but she might as well have done. She sighed and the puppy leaned against her in sympathy, or maybe it was because its stout little legs weren't up to the horsebox suspension.

Turning in between the large gate posts Lottie eased her foot of the accelerator and let the reality sink in. One day this would all be hers. For now she was caretaker, taking the first proper step into a future that was as scary as it felt it was meant to be.

It had been a game up until now. The dog sat still, sensing something different, softly rounded fluffy ears pricked forward as they edged their way up the long driveway, finally turning the corner so that the Manor sprung into view. They rolled to a halt just before it, by the large archway that led into the stable yard.

Of all the parts of Tipping House Estate, this was where Lottie felt most at home. Stepping through that archway had always felt like moving from reality into the perfect dream, her own Narnia.

On one side of the archway were the immaculate lawns and the sprawling rhododendrons, the rolling acres an emerald green carpet that spread down to the river, past the small copses of trees that formed dark green splodges on the tapestry of the landscape. And one step away on the other side was the quiet perfection of a time gone by.

She fished the puppy off the seat and climbed down from the cab of the horse lorry, walking until she was standing under the brick archway, poised between the present and the past, between her own present and a future that had felt unreal until now.

As she walked through into the cobbled yard the only sound was the reassuring chomp of horses chewing hay and the tinkling water of the fountain that stood in the middle of the circular cobbled yard. All around were the stable doors, over some the elegant noses of Dom's horses, over others the familiar faces of the ones that belonged to her and Rory, and at the far side lay the entrance to the small indoor school that had seen the horse masters of the past work their magic.

As she hovered, on the brink of the future, the tall familiar figure of her Uncle Dominic stepped from the school. Dom, elegant and poised, looking so much more a part of the place than she felt she was. In fact, he looked like a page out of *Tatler*. She might love it here, but sometimes she felt not quite good enough, not quite the lady she should be. Her Uncle Dominic, just like his mother, Elizabeth, oozed good breeding and aristocracy, whereas Lottie felt more like the puppy that was struggling in her arms, its whole body wriggling ecstatically at the sight of another person.

'Don't worry, I won't be going anywhere for a long time, Charlotte. As long as you need me, I'll be here.' He looked at the pup wriggling about in her arms. 'Another delinquent addition to the family?' The pup immediately stopped its fighting the second he took it. 'He can go in the tack room for now and I'll help you unload the horses, shall I?'

Taking charge came naturally to Dom, and Lottie instantly felt some of the pressure ease.

The first horse out of the box was Black Gold, who she had loaded last as the mare had flatly refused to go anywhere near the horsebox ramp until she was convinced that all her mates were going too. Even then, the horse had gone into reverse at the sight of the ramp, nearly ending up in the water trough, followed by a quick surge forward that had taken Lottie perilously close to a gatepost.

Now she flatly refused to unload, digging her heels in and looking at Dom like he was the devil and Tipping House was her idea of hell. Which posed a bit of a problem as until she was out none of the others were going anywhere.

'Come on Gold. She's having a baby you know.' She yattered to Dom as a way of passing the time and trying to hide the fact that she couldn't budge the horse. Dom was unimpressed.

'I heard she was in foal. Let us hope that it's a bit more obliging than she is.'

Black Gold took exception to his comment and decided to make a plunge towards freedom, reaching the end of her lead rope before Lottie realised that the plan had changed. By a skip and jump she managed to keep her footing, just missing falling off the edge of the ramp, but by the look on Dom's face he was under no illusions that she was in any kind of control at all. Especially when Gold kept going instead of turning under the archway. Lottie dug her heels in, taking a firmer grip of the rope and the mare spun round coming to a stop nose to nose with her. 'Please don't show me up.' The horse rolled her eyes, ducked her head, nearly yanking Lottie down with her and took a mouthful of the lush grass that was part of the manicured lawn before taking a step back, leaving a far from dainty footprint in the grass. Lottie was just wondering how much damage a horse skittering backwards would do to the lawn when the mare suddenly had a change of mind.

Lottie hadn't noticed that Dom had started to unload the next of her horses, but Gold had, and seeing the rump of her stable mate disappearing under the archway she set off in pursuit, nearly trampling Lottie under foot.

Half an hour later the four horses were safely installed in neighbouring stables and were alternating between grabbing mouthfuls of hay and hanging over their stable doors, eyeing up the other horses, ears pricked and nostrils flared as they took in the new sights and smells. Lottie rubbed her toes and wondered if they were all intact; one or two definitely felt squashed and she was pretty sure she had a big bruise on her arm, where Gold had squashed her against the stable door on the way in.

Dom, who liked his horses to have impeccable manners and steady natures, didn't comment as Gold bellowed across the yard, her red-lined nostrils flared and her ears flat to her head.

'She's highly strung.' He nodded. 'But she has a massive jump in her.'

Unlike most of the horsemen in Tippermere, Dominic wasn't particularly impressed by the size of obstacle a horse could clear. Dressage was his sport, which was all about beautiful paces, controlled power and biddable nature. His horses were often far from easy, but his calm approach and understanding made it look effortless. In his hands a horse directed its strength and speed into impulsion and a performance that could be magical. If all four feet left the floor at the same time, it was for a reason. But he respected Lottie as a rider and though she was far from conventional and far from the type of rider he was, he knew she had to do things her way.

'I'm sure she has.' He turned his attention away from the mare. 'I meant it about not going anywhere, Charlotte. I know what it's like, this place, and it's not meant to be a burden.'

'It's not. Well, I mean it is, but I don't mind. It's just,' the cat, which had been alternately stalking the puppy and looking at it in mock horror with arched back, jumped up onto the rim of the water fountain and the pup tried to follow suit. It bounced on little fat paws while the cat watched, only inches away, with disdain.

'Just?'

'I don't want it to change. I love it the way it is, all—' She waved a hand, encompassing the old stables, the cobbled yard, the horses.

'Old and worn at the edges?' He smiled, waited.

'Peaceful, warm – it's kind of like an old blanket. Do you know what I mean?'

'Familiar.'

'I'm scared that if we do what Sam and Pip were suggesting, we'll spoil it.'

'The yard doesn't have to change, you won't lose the magic here.'

'But I don't want any of it to change. Well, I know the roof needs to change and maybe the water pipes.' She looked at him. 'But I like it tatty, I like the flaky paint.'

'Really?' He raised an aristocratic eyebrow, but she knew he understood.

'Well maybe not the bits where it falls on your head if you as much as sneeze. But, I don't want it, well, glamorous.'

'It can be old-glamorous, not Kitterly Heath type glamorous. Faded glory, don't they call it?' His tone was dry. 'You don't have to transform the place, Charlotte. But it's not enough to have a hunt ball once a year.'

'We have the celebrity cricket match.'

'That's for charity.'

'Oh yes. See, I'm rubbish at this. And the whole thing that Sam has in mind is just so over the top.' She put her head in her hands and tried to remember the vivid description that had overflowed from the lovely and generous, but very over-the-top, Samantha. More *Footballers' Wives* than a *Move to the Country*. 'I prefer being in my boots to being all dressed up.'

'So we noticed.' Oh, so he had, too. Everybody, it seemed, had noticed her foot attire at the cricket auction, before Sam had supplied an alternative. 'You're more satin and spurs.'

'That's clever. I like that, actually. Apart from the satin bit, unless it's a cravat. Oh God! What am I going to do? She's unstoppable. I think she's been lying awake at night planning the big event, with me as main prize. And,' she paused, 'stilettoes will ruin the floor in the Great Hall.'

'True. But you can't have them all coming in Hunters and Barbours, darling.' At that moment the podgy puppy, after scooting around the end of the fountain, barking his little squeaky bark and jumping up and down, managed to clamber over the rim of the fountain and was now suspended, rocking. Two front feet in the water and his wriggly-tail-wagging back end hanging on the other side. After an alarmed spit from the cat, he tumbled backwards and landed back where he'd started.

Lottie giggled. 'Come here, Harry, come on.'

'Harry? As in Prince—'

'No, silly.' She gathered up the pup. 'I was going to call him Horatio, because his dad was Nelson.'

'As in half Nelson?'

One thing she did like about her Uncle Dominic was the way he was in tune with her weird sense of humour. Nobody else had got it, and she had thought it was quite clever. 'Although, now you mention it, there are certain similarities with the other Harry.'

'I do hope he doesn't cause as much trouble.' Dom stroked the curly head. 'So what do you really want for this place, Charlotte? Get to the root of that and you might know what to do next.'

'I don't want it glammed up – I want people to love it as it is. So how can the ideas we've got possibly work?'

'I know, but I think you do need something a tiny bit radical, which is why Elizabeth thought you'd be much better at this than me and Amanda.'

'Did she?' Lottie brightened up at that the thought that her gran actually believed she could do this.

'She did. I'm far too straight-laced and old-fashioned, aren't I?' He smiled.

'But isn't this a bit, well, drastic?'

'Well tone it down. Samantha is correct about one thing – people want a slice of our life. Well, the life they think we lead.'

'She thinks I might invite the Royal Family.' Lottie looked glum and Dom laughed. 'And she thinks we've got family jewels.'

'Well we have, and we can dig out some Lords and Ladies. Give them your idea of a celebrity bash, not hers, Charlotte. She'll love it. Amanda is keen to help and she has incredible taste.' The pride echoed in Dom's voice, and Lottie was pleased for him. She'd never actually been able to imagine him happily settled, and although most of the event-riders had speculated on a regular basis about his sexual leanings she'd never thought he was homosexual either. Even if his mother, her gran, had remarked that she had wondered. But although she'd now got used to him being married, she really couldn't imagine him changing nappies.

'Is Amanda well enough?'

'She's not being quite as sick these days, we're hoping it's coming to an end. And you need to think more long-term. This event has to be the launch, not the finale.'

'I know.' She went back to feeling glum.

'Won't Gran mind? You know, the noise and people.'

'Mother trusts you to do the best. Although, mind you, she does hope that you will eventually get married. Rory has got to help you with this, you need to work together, Charlotte. That is, if he wants to?'

'I'm not sure he wants to get married. Why does everybody keep going on about that? I mean, I'm not actually bothered, but everybody keeps…'

'Everybody loves a wedding, Charlotte. Even your gran.'

'I suppose they do. But we can't just…'

'You don't have to be married, but it would help you enormously if he wanted to support you with this. Will he be there by your side?'

'Well,' Lottie gnawed at the inside of her cheek, 'he's a bit cross with me at the moment. I think,' she paused, trying to be fair, 'he just wants things to stay the same. And today he wanted me to go and look at a horse with him, which is far more exciting than moving, isn't it? He said it was a bargain, slightly tricky, but a star in the making.' He'd left before she had, not even helping her load the horses onto the lorry, so it had been a relief when Mick had stepped in and helped persuade the reluctant Black Gold up the ramp.

'All tricky horses are stars in the making.'

Dominic had a feeling that his mother's agreement to let Charlotte take over the reins was down to more than just her failing health. It had been too easy to persuade her, which meant she was up to something. Maybe, in her own way, she was forcing the issue. Trying to get Lottie to make her mind up and see if Rory really was the man for her, or not. And Elizabeth knew all too well that Tipping House Estate was a responsibility that had to be shared.

They'd all thought that Lottie had returned to Tippermere to settle down, but Dominic wasn't so sure. Her relationship with Rory was easy-going and familiar, but his niece was so like her mother had been, what would happen when the fun had to take a back seat and she had to commit and act responsibly? He knew she wasn't like him, that she would never take life as seriously, but he feared that Rory wasn't the stabilising influence she needed.

Although his mother had always outwardly appeared to only grudgingly accept Billy Brinkley into the family when he married Alexa, Dominic knew that she had been happy with her daughter's choice. She'd married for love, and the often-gruff Billy knew how to party as well as he knew how to work.

'I'm sure he'll be fine once he gets used to the idea.' Lottie gnawed the edge of her thumb and looked far from sure, then looked up abruptly at her uncle. 'I don't want Gran to die. She isn't going to, is she? She wouldn't have asked me to do this if she was well, would she?'

Dom put his arm around her shoulders and stared at the fountain, the splash ruffling the water's surface. He couldn't answer because he didn't know.

'She won't live forever, Lottie.'

***

Lottie stood in her socks in the grand hall and felt about as sophisticated and glam as a bag lady: green spotted socks, cream breeches that had been darned and a polo shirt. She rubbed absentmindedly at the stain that seemed to highlight her stomach and wondered if it was jam from this morning's toast or ligament ointment. Sniffing it didn't help. It didn't smell of either.

Moving some of the horses in had been part one of the exercise, partly because where his horses went Rory followed. Not that all of his horses had been moved. He'd insisted that until they'd sorted out some gallops he was better off leaving his two star eventers where they were. Part two was trickier – moving the pair of them. It was bloody draughty in Tipping House. Outside it was a lovely summer's day, inside it felt more like February. The terriers, though, were acting like all their Christmases had come at once (although, thinking about it, it was nearly as cold as December inside), running up and down the grand staircase and along the myriad hallways with their noses to the ground. No doubt, Lottie thought, on the scent of a rat or two in addition to the smells of her grandmother's Labradors.

She hoped when she shook their bowls they would hear and come running for food or they might be lost for ever, especially if they managed to dig any holes between the rotting floorboards. Which reminded her, she needed to move the rugs around to try and hide the moth-eaten bits, and cover the worst bits of the floorboards. Who'd have thought that becoming a Lady (well, taking one step nearer to it) would lead to a life worrying about woodworm and mothballs?

Lottie's own puppy, Harry, was altogether different from the terrier trio, and was practically glued to her calf, which was a bit hazardous on the stairs, particularly as he hadn't really got the hang of them and tended to slip halfway down, ending up on his back with his paws in the air. She's nearly put her foot on his tummy more than once.

'Any idea what I did with my best jacket?' Rory arrived, the terriers at his heels (which solved the lost-dog problem) and the large cat, which was far too lazy and smug to demean itself by chasing rats and mice, shot out of the front door followed by the pack of dogs.

It had been hard enough keeping track of his stuff in the small cottage – it was going to be a nightmare here, Lottie decided, as he had a habit of wandering around the place and dropping stuff wherever he happened to be. But surely a jacket was too big to just lose?

'Do you think I need to smarten up, in case anybody arrives? They might think I'm the cleaner.'

'No, everybody loves you just as you are.' He wrapped an arm around her waist and pulled her closer so he could nibble, then lick, her ear.

'Stop it, that's disgusting.' Lottie giggled.

'You let that puppy do it. Anyhow, who could possibly come round that doesn't already know you?'

'True, I hadn't thought of that.'

'And they all know you can't afford a cleaner.' Rory moved on to nuzzling her neck, which sent a rush of goose bumps down her chest and arms. 'You're gorgeous just the way you are. You don't need to change one bit.'

'Even in this polo shirt?'

'Even in that, so easy to rip off when I shag you.'

'Even in my socks?'

'Especially in your gorgeous green socks – green for the luck of the Irish. Talking of which, where the hell has that moody sod got to?'

'Mick isn't moody.' Lottie shivered as Rory's hands found her boobs. 'More moody and magnificent. Oo, stop it.' His thumbs had found their way to her nipples and she was finding it very hard to concentrate on anything.

Rory raised an eyebrow. 'I'm the magnificent one, darling, don't you forget it.'

'Oo you are,' Lottie decided giving in to temptation might not be such a bad idea after all, 'Take your shirt off and show me your muscles, Mr Magnificent.'

'Oh you're such a trollop, come here then and left me ravish you.' The words were muffled as he was stripping his shirt off over his head, but Lottie got the general gist.

'You'll have to catch me.' She took a step back as he rolled his shirt into a bundle and flung it in her general direction. Lottie ducked.

'Shit. The priceless Ming vase.'

'But we haven't got a... Have we?' She spun around to see exactly what he had hit, to see the shirt on the floor.

'Gotcha.' And he had, so no chasing involved then. 'Catch you, my arse.' He'd got his fingers hooked in her waistband and Lottie started to giggle. 'You deserve a good spanking, m'lady.'

'Shhh, Gran will hear.'

'Old Lizzie is ensconced miles away, in the other wing.'

'It isn't miles, and you know you can't call her Lizzie.' She giggled.

'And she's deaf.'

'Only when she want to be.'

'Well she won't want to hear this. Come on, let the dog see the rabbit.' Which sent Lottie into a new fit of giggles as he swept her off her feet and did his best to throw her over his shoulder. The dogs, who had miraculously reappeared at the sound of Rory's voice, started racing around in excitement as he smacked her bum and headed towards the grand staircase. He made it up about three steps before losing his balance and crashing to the floor, which luckily was carpeted.

'Bloody hell, have you been at the pies again?' It wasn't that Lottie was fat – more statuesque and strong. Throwing her over his shoulder on the flat was one thing, tackling stairs quite another.

'Cheeky bugger, you're just a wimp. And you told me you were magnificent.' The dogs, by now thoroughly overexcited, jumped on top of Lottie and knocked the remaining air out of her, and even Harry, sensing that everybody was happy, decided to get over his reticence and scrambled onto her neck so that he could lick her face. So Rory decided to join in, which was about as undignified, unladylike and unromantic a situation as Lottie could imagine.

'Eurghh stop it.'

'I could drag you up, I suppose. Or sort you out here?'

Lottie tried to prop herself up on her elbows, then gave up when Rory lay beside her on the stairs.

'Rory?'

'Hmm.'

'Everybody keeps going on about getting married. Do you think we should?'

'Do you want to?'

'Well, I'm not really bothered at the moment, are you? And there's so much to do here, and I want to do it properly when we do, not just because everybody else says we should.'

'Then we shouldn't.'

'But you don't mind if we do?'

Rory shrugged. 'Doesn't bother me either way, darling. Whatever you want.'

'Oh, I don't know. Why does everybody make such a big thing of it?'

'People like weddings.' He put a warm hand on her thigh. 'Well, girls do. And boys, if they're going out with some sweet virgin, who's waiting for the Big Day. They're desperate.' His fingers edged higher up her thigh. 'I mean, I'm a bit desperate at the moment, but not because you're a virgin, or sweet. More the sexy wanton hussy.' The fingers tightened. 'But if it's wedding they want, then give them a wedding.'

'You're right, that's what they want.' Lottie suddenly struggled upright. 'You know, you are right.' It was, Lottie remembered, just what Dom had said.

'Aren't I always?'

'No. But you are this time, why didn't I think of that before? They all want a wedding. Everybody does. You're brilliant. That's it. You're bloody brilliant.' And kissing the astonished Rory she jumped up and danced down the few steps before doing a twirl with the dogs running with her. 'Genius.'

'Don't I get a shag for that, then?' Rory had propped himself up and was watching her with a smile on his face. Their lives had always been busy, but lately he seemed to be seeing less and less of Lottie. And when he did see her she had a list in her hands and a frown on her face, even in bed. He'd had a feeling that ever since Billy's wedding the girl he loved had been trickling away from him. And it wasn't another man vying for her affections, it was Tipping House. And it had been driving him nuts. Except right now he could see the old Lottie that he loved. Spontaneous, carefree, fun.

'Later.' She picked up the bemused Harry, who couldn't keep up with the terrier antics and clutched him to her. 'I need to talk to Uncle Dom. I've got to tell him it's going to be okay. And I need to tell Sam quick before she makes up an even more way-out plan.' She gave a skip then giggled. 'Promise, later. God, I do love you Rory Strachan.' The kiss she blew in his direction as she reached the doorway wasn't exactly consolation, but Rory was relieved that the uptight girl had gone and the fun loving one was back.

Maybe everything was going to work out after all. Now all he had to do was kick Mick out of the grumps, which he might as well get on with, seeing as a fumble had been struck off Lottie's agenda. The only thing that worried him was he wasn't sure if he'd actually proposed without really knowing it, and been accepted, or not. Although that should cheer Mick up. The miserable git was always saying that he didn't show Lottie he cared. Well, if he had actually asked her to marry him, what more could a man do?

Chapter 14

'You don't get anything like this back home.' Todd stretched his long legs out in front of him and took a swig of his lager. 'Bloody entertaining, isn't it?' He winked at Pip, who was partaking of one of her favourite activities: people-watching.

She grinned back. It was nice to have somebody who genuinely got it, which was a bit unexpected with Todd, who she'd initially, rather grudgingly, accepted into her home. Mick had said he thought it would do her good, and it looked like he was right. As usual.

The trouble with most people in Tippermere was that they wouldn't sit still long enough to do a proper job, and they were usually far too engrossed in talking about horses, or planning their next escapade, to actually watch.

'Bet you a beer she's got six-inch heels on.' Todd inclined his head towards a silver Mercedes, which had stopped a few yards away as the driver worked out whether she could actually park it in the available space.

'Too easy.' Pip shook her head. Todd was quite happy sitting, and he actually seemed to see the entertainment value. Sitting with Sam wasn't quite the same, either, she was too busy waving at people. It astounded Pip just how many friends Sam had made in the short time she'd lived in upmarket Kitterly Heath,

173

Tippermere's neighbouring and much classier village. Tippermere was old money, land, horses and hunt balls. Kitterly Heath was just money. Lots of cash and everything it could buy. Glamour was obligatory, but unlike with the wellington and riding-boot inhabitants of Tippermere, taste could be dubious.

If Pip made a comment, Sam tended to take it literally, not realising how much the skill of people-watching involved a vivid imagination.

'What made you come here then, Todd? You've never really said.'

'Well I did owe Lots an apology, I reckoned.'

'Never heard of phones? Aren't they that advanced Down-Under?'

'Watch it, cheeky.'

'Nobody comes all this way just to say sorry, do they?' She raised one eyebrow and watched closely as a frown flickered across his features and disappeared.

'It's complicated.'

'So am I.'

He laughed then – his easy, full laugh. 'You're bloody nosey. Well, first off I had to come over to sort out the divorce.'

'She was British?'

'Yup, my wife was a Brit. Lives down Oxford way.'

'A posh Brit.' Pip settled into her seat, anticipating something better than she'd originally expected.

'Tall, blond, finishing school, expert surfer. I met her at a competition back home. Haven't got a clue what I saw in her.'

He smiled, but this time there was tension, and Pip, who had been relaxing in the sun sat up a bit straighter. 'No, can't see the appeal at all, a fit, posh, good-looking girl.'

'She thought she fancied a life Down-Under, competing, living it up, working on her tan. But,' he shrugged, 'the reality doesn't always match the dream, does it? And I guess I didn't live up to her expectations. She threw my cheap wedding ring in my face and came back to daddy.'

'And?'

'And filed for divorce, then changed her mind. I couldn't believe it when the police turned up in Barcelona.' He ran a finger around the rim of his glass. 'I was livid, in fact. I'd been such an idiot, that's why I told Lottie to go. It was easier to be nasty to her, seeing as I couldn't be nasty to my ex. And I was worried I was really going to lose it if she started asking questions, like you girls have a habit of doing.'

'You weren't really that nasty to Lottie, though, were you?'

'Well, I acted a tosser, pretended it was a joke even though I could see she was cut up. I never tried to explain. I had to come back here to finalise stuff with the divorce, so thought I'd see if I could find her.'

'You could have texted and asked for her address.'

'Deleted her number when I was raging. Stupid twat, aren't I?'

'A bit daft, maybe.'

'Have you any idea how many Charlottes there are in Cheshire?'

'Probably not as many as in Oxfordshire,' Pip paused, 'or Berkshire, or—'

'Okay, smart arse. It got easier once I remembered about her dad. I didn't realise she had a pile in the country, though.' He gave a low whistle.

'Would it have made any difference?' Pip looked at him shrewdly, already knowing the answer, but asking anyway.

'No, she's still Lottie, isn't she?'

'Missed your chance, didn't you?'

'Guess I did.' He grinned, this time the genuine article. 'Not that we ever really had one, did we?' He didn't wait for an answer. 'We were both out for a good time, a few laughs and a beer on the beach. We would have driven each other mad in the end. She wasn't really upset, was she?' The earnest look on his face took Pip by surprise. Okay, he'd said sorry but he was happy-go-lucky, out for a laugh most of the time. Now he looked like he genuinely cared. Which she supposed maybe he did if he'd spent time trying to track Lottie down.

'She was gutted, well pretty hysterical at the time. But, to be honest, I think that was a mix of shock, and having to face up to what she really wanted before she was ready. With you gone, her natural reaction was to flee back here, to this place, and I guess she hadn't wanted to admit, even to herself, that she desperately wanted to come back.' Pip shrugged. 'Maybe she felt a bit of a failure running back after only a few months.'

'I'm glad she's happy, though. She is, isn't she?'

'I think so.' Pip drained her glass of wine and waved for another one. 'So, what's next, and why's it complicated? Tippermere isn't exactly your scene, is it?'

'Miss Merc has given up,' his attention was back on the car, 'we'll never know about the heels.'

'Stop changing the subject. Anyway she won't give up, women like her don't. Look.' Pip nodded as the woman abandoned the car at an angle, its rear end jutting into the narrow road. Completely ignoring the flurry of car horns, she flung the door open and got slowly out, waving imperiously at one of the waiters, who had obviously carried out car parking duties before. A small, fluffy white dog in one hand and a large handbag in the other, she stalked past Pip and Todd, stopping at the prime table on the terrace, where two immaculately made-up, and to Pip's experienced eye, recently Botoxed ladies greeted her with copious air-kissing. The dog was placed on a chair and presented with olives, whilst champagne was poured.

'Six-inch heels, told you.'

'Bet she walks all over her rich banker husband in them while he's handcuffed to the bed, and the dog will be running round licking everything.'

'Treat 'em mean.' Todd raised his glass and looked far too interested in the idea of being walked over.

'Into the kinky stuff are we?'

'Not sure about the dog bit.'

'You are into it, aren't you?' Pip was really intrigued now, and more than a bit turned- on. She was seeing a whole different side to her beach bum today. Caring but daring, which could be a killer combination in bed.

'No pain, no gain – isn't that what they say?' He was still flashing her his grin, but looked strangely serious.

'I don't think that's what they mean, though.'

'Come on, you're not telling me you've never stepped off the vanilla trail.' He was looking at her speculatively and Pip felt herself colour up.

She liked sex, lots of sex, and for its own sake. Not just as part of a deep and meaningful relationship. But her experiences had been surprisingly straight-laced. In fact it was probably down to the fact that she scared most of the men she'd slept with. They'd enjoyed the experience, but wouldn't have dared risk her wrath by suggesting anything as untoward as bondage or spanking.

'You're kidding me.' His eyebrows were raised and he was close to laughter. But he stopped short, another low whistle escaping. 'Thought you were the work-hard-play-hard type, like me.'

'You've never worked hard in your life.' She grasped the chance to get back on an even keel.

'Don't kid yourself.'

'What do you do, then? When you're not running around apologising to people or surfboarding.'

'I work at a university, lecturing.'

'You're kidding.'

'If you say so.'

'You're not, though, are you? So you're not just a pretty face.'

Todd was starting to enjoy himself. When he'd met Pip in Barcelona she was obviously a workaholic desperately trying to chill, and she had managed to unwind a bit, but he still felt he hardly knew her at all. You only saw what she wanted you to. But since he'd moved into the cottage she'd been surprisingly amenable, although he put that down more to her relationship with Mick than anything to do with him. They didn't argue, they obviously had a lively, and satisfying (from the noise levels) sex life – which was probably why it was on his mind now. But there was a friction – as though the pressure was building up inside a volcano. He guessed he was a pressure valve.

She was entertaining, though – clever, sharp and he didn't mind the abrasive edge, or what could be taken as a judgemental tone at times. Pip was cocooned in a layer of something approaching armour, protecting her feelings at all costs. By keeping them to herself.

'So what was up with the man this morning?' Todd guessed that Mick was probably fairly easy-going, but he was a deep one too. The combination of the pair of them, both with their barriers up, was a weird one. But the Irishman had been positively monosyllabic, even by his standards, this morning.

Pip shrugged.

'Nothing to do with me being there?'

'No, it's not you. It's us.'

'I don't really do deep relationship stuff, not in touch with my inner female side.' He downed the rest of his drink in one. 'But you can always let off steam at me if you want.'

'Thanks, not sure it'll help, though.'

'You're good?'

'I thought we were, but,' she paused, 'I'm not sure he is. He just won't admit it to himself. Wants me to go to Ireland with him.'

'Run away?'

'Something like that. But it's not my style. My experience is that your problems catch up with you sooner or later.'

'Tell me about it.'

'Ahh, yes. I'm talking to an expert. So,' he saw the change in direction before she spoke, deflecting attention away from herself, 'what do you lecture in?'

'Astrophysics.'

'I'm impressed.'

'Don't be, it's my ideal job, plenty of time off in the summer.'

'To be a beach bum.'

'Yup, and—'

'Plenty of attractive students to chase.'

'I think you've got the wrong impression of me, Philippa.'

'I saw you ogling Sam, and Tab.'

'All these tight jodhpurs are sending me nuts. There's bits of me that don't know whether they're coming or going.'

'Tab's only a kid.'

'So people keep telling me. She's a big kid though.'

'And Sam is married.'

'Gorgeous, isn't she? I would have thought my ex would have put me off polished blonds, but she's—'

'Nice?'

'Very nice. Polished but not too posh.'

'I'm not sure she'd be into walking over you in high heels – she'd be scared of hurting you.' Pip grinned.

'You wouldn't mind, though, would you? Hurting?'

'Giving or receiving?'

'With pain and pleasure, it doesn't always matter.' Todd watched as the grin slipped from Pip's face and her eyes darkened.

'You two looks cosy.' The fact that they were staring at each other probably wasn't good, Todd decided, as Mick dropped his car keys down onto the table between them. Pip jumped with a guilty start, knocking the table and nearly losing her glass of wine, which made the Maltese terrier choke on its olive. Having the ladies at lunch stare across at them wasn't good, although Mick seemed fairly oblivious.

'We were just chatting.'

'Oh, I heard.'

'Here, have my seat, mate. I'll leave you two to it.'

'Don't let me break things up.'

'You're not breaking anything up, don't be stupid.'

At the 'stupid', Mick raised an eyebrow, and Todd was pretty sure it was a bad choice of word.

'There's nothing to break up.' Pip was on her feet. 'You know that, not that you care anyway.'

'Says who?'

Todd shot an apologetic grin in the direction of the ladies: one was busy consoling her spitting dog, the others were transfixed, their analysis of cosmetic surgery temporarily suspended.

Mick had shoved his hands in his pockets, his face dark as he looked at the flustered Pip. 'It's not me who's talking about pain and pleasure, is it? From where I'm standing it's you who doesn't care.'

'It's you who invited him to stay.'

'I was just offering him a bed.' He paused. 'An empty one.'

'You bastard, that's totally unfair. Why are you doing this?'

Todd watched and suddenly got a hint of why Pip had got together with Mick in the first place. She was always in control, always a step ahead, but Mick had taken that away. He figured that Mick was different to the other men she'd met, all those 'yes' men willing to do things her way, this times the rules had been his and she'd liked it. The sex was probably good, but that two-way connection wasn't quite there. It was more the ongoing challenge that kept them together. Pip had met her match, a guy who met her head-on. And she'd fallen in love. And it hurt. Todd knew what that felt like when you dropped your defences and wham, somebody jumped underneath them and destroyed you from the inside out.

Mick shook his head. 'Forget it.' He picked up his keys, took a step back.

'You don't care at all?'

'I said forget it.' He was heading away, but Pip was after him, not wanting to let go.

'You spend more time with Lottie than you do with me, you care more about her, don't you?' Then she stopped dead, and Todd could see that the meaning of the words she'd thrown were sinking in, making sense. 'You do.' Her voice had dropped. 'Christ, you're still infatuated with my best bloody friend, aren't you?'

'Bollocks.' And he was off, then, striding out of the place and heading up the road towards his Land Rover.

Mick got back in the Land Rover and banged the steering wheel with the palm of his hand, as a twinge of guilt twisted in his stomach. He was a bastard. She was right. He didn't know what had got into him lately. But, whatever it was, it wasn't Pip's fault. He looked back up the road towards the bar, and she was there, staring at him. Even at this distance he could see she was on the verge of tears.

'Shit.' He was out of the car and striding back before he had time to stop and think, and the second he wrapped his arms around her slim body he saw the single tear find its way down her cheek.

'I'm sorry.' He rested his chin on her head and wished he had the gift of the gab like he was supposed to have. The sharp tang of shampoo did nothing to take the bitter taste from his mouth. 'I stopped by to tell you I'd be late and something snapped when I heard you flirting like that.'

'I wasn't—'

He held her tighter. 'Shh. You used to flirt like that with me.'

'But—'

'Then it got too serious.' Her body tightened defensively beneath his touch. 'It's my fault, Pip, I'm not ready to get involved. Not right here, not now. Come to Ireland with me, I need to get away from this place.'

'No, Mick.'

'Please. This is the closest I get to begging, Pip. I'm not sure how many more weddings I can stand.'

'I can't go with you. I love you, you great Irish eejit. But you don't love me. And I'm not ready to be second-best.'

The dampness that could only be tears was warm against his chest and he held her tighter and wished he had something clever to say. 'You mean a lot to me.'

She took a deep, heaving breath, her voice soft when she spoke

181

again. 'I know. But you mean everything to me and it's not the same.' Pulling herself away from his body, she let the cold air come between them. 'And Lottie means more. Running away won't change anything, Mick, you know that as well as I do.'

'It might not change things, but it might be the right thing to do, treas.' He paused. 'I'm not ready to be second-best either.'

'Oh, Christ. What am I going to do with you?' She gave a shaky laugh.

'Go and talk to your Aussie. He's waiting.' He put his hand over her slim, perfectly manicured ones and just felt too big, too rough. 'I won't go anywhere, promise. Not without telling you. Honest, go on, we'll talk later. When you get back.' She let him go, watched as he got back in the vehicle and slammed the door behind him. Then she gave him that little half-smile, which was usually accompanied by a grin, but this time there was just sadness.

What was she going to do with him? Mick grimaced. More like, what was he going to do? Because if he stayed here he was afraid he'd do something very stupid indeed.

'I settled the bill,' Todd gave a small smile, 'reckoned a walk was a good bet.'

'Then we don't scare the posh locals?'

'Something like that.' He winked at Pip. 'Little woofer was choking on its olives.'

'Can't have that can we?' She sniffed and concentrated on the path ahead, trying not to think about Mick driving away.

'Is it better if I move out?'

Pip sighed and wished it was that simple. 'It really won't make any difference at all. I think that's why he offered you the room. It's called avoidance tactics. Deflect attention from the real problem. I'm guilty of it too.' And she was, she knew that. Todd had been the diversion they'd both welcomed in. 'How about you tell me about your complications?'

'I reckon you and him are both pretty good at avoiding stuff.'

'Not so bad at it yourself, and you don't want to move on from here, yet, do you? Spill the beans, cheer me up.' Having her mind on somebody else's business would do wonders for her mood. 'No, not that way.'

Todd had automatically followed the road to the left, the road that led up to The Edge – home of witches and ghostly tales. The place Mick had taken her that very first day. Gulping down the tears and shoving her hands deep into her pockets she nodded and hoped she didn't sound like a strangled kitten. 'Straight on.' What had happened to her? She never used to be one for tears and right now she felt like curling up and wailing, which wasn't good at all, especially when she'd known that this day would come, and she'd been doing her best to dodge it.

Todd put one large warm hand on her shoulder and leaned in until he could talk into her ear. 'I don't want to move on, but if I tell you why then you have to keep it to yourself. Or I'll have to kill you.'

'A bigamist and a murderer, eh?' She looped a hand through his arm. 'I'll risk it. Tell me.'

'I'm looking for my brother's dad.'

Which wasn't what she expected him to say. 'Your brother's?'

'Yup.'

'So why hasn't he come himself?'

'He can't, so I said I would. I promised him I'd find out what I could.'

'And your mum?'

'Died a couple of years ago.' They were striding up the road now, and as he spoke Todd seemed to quicken his pace, his long stride eating up the ground, which left Pip close to jogging alongside. Pip slowed, but the pull on his arm didn't seem to register.

'She died? I'm so sorry.'

He shrugged and finally slowed down. 'An accident. It took a long time to sort through all her papers, but we found these letters. Love letters.'

'From somebody who lives around here?'

'They were postmarked Cheshire. And,' Todd stopped abruptly, and had to catch Pip as she cannoned into him, 'they talked about witches, ghosts and classy wine bars.'

'Oh shit. You're kidding.'

She never found out if he was kidding, because at that moment there was a yell and they spun around to see a herd of heifers heading their way at a trot. 'Oy, you two, head 'em off.'

Pip looked at them in horror. Cattle-herding was not something she had on her CV, or had the faintest intention of adding. Todd, though, was far more game, jumping out in front of the cattle. The leader of the herd, now only feet away, made a move to dodge around him, and Todd made a lunge after it. The animal sped up, doing what cows do best and shooting a trail of green slime out behind it. Pip couldn't help it, she giggled as he jumped back, desperately trying to stay out of firing range.

'Wave your arms at them, you gormless bugger.'

Too late, Todd, in his haste to avoid a smelly shower, caught his heel in something another cow had left behind and fell, as if in slow motion, onto his bum in the middle of the road.

Pip forgot she was scared of cows and felt herself going weak at the knees as hysteria hit her. It had to be the wine, or the scare, or the emotional turmoil. The cows fanned out either side of Todd, and all she could see was his waving arms.

'Bloody townies.' The farmer shook his head in despair as the heifers galloped on up the road, heading for the M6 motorway and trouble. 'I'd have a bath if I was you, daft sod.'

Pip could have sworn that a smile was threatening to split open the weather-beaten face.

'Away with you.' For a moment she thought he was shouting at Todd, then as the black and white collie streaked past she realised he had a dog, which meant that carnage on the northbound carriageway might not happen after all.

She wiped the tears from her eyes. At least they were from

laughter this time. Straightening up, she caught her breath, then walked over to where Todd was still sitting stunned in the road. 'I'll give you a hand to find him – your brother's dad. I'm good at things like that.'

'I know you are. I was hoping you'd say that. Give us a hand to get up as well, will you? I'm sure one of those cows thought it was a performance of the *Nutcracker*. Bloody feels like it anyway.'

'You smell a bit.' Pip wrinkled her nose, looked at the muck-spattered Todd and tried not to laugh.

'Cheeky minx.' He took the proffered hand, but before she knew it she was on his knee.

'Oh God. You really do stink.'

'He was okay, wasn't he? Mick?'

She looked into the deep-blue eyes, let herself place a hand on the smeared cheek and took a sobering breath. 'I don't know. Why does everything have to get fucked up?' She slipped off the muscled thighs and onto the road beside him. 'It's not just me. What about Lottie? Oh shit.'

'I'm not here to mess things up for Lottie. I just needed to see her again.'

'So why,' Pip looked straight into those clear-blue eyes, 'did you stampede into that wedding like some medieval knight?' It had actually been quite impressive, but she wasn't going to admit that right now.

'Ah well,' Todd grinned, in what looked like embarrassment, 'that was a bit of a cock-up. I asked little Tab if she knew Lots and when she said she was at her wedding and started going on about why did ancient people have to embarrass themselves like that? Well, I guess I jumped to the wrong conclusion.' He shrugged. 'Tab said the guy was old enough to be her granddad and it was all too creepy, and the thought of sex was like, so sick.' He rolled his eyes in a fair imitation of Tabatha, and Pip tried to keep a straight face.

'Sick can mean "good" these days, you know. Don't you talk teenage-speak?'

'No way did she mean "good". Finger down the throat is not "good" in any language, kiddo, and "gross" was one of the words too. And anyhow, how was I to know she was talking about Lottie's dad? I only came here to bloody explain things. Honest, not to mess things up.'

'Nobody wants to mess things up for Lottie.' Pip forced her face into what she hoped resembled a smile.

'And from what your man said, Lottie's going to do it anyway, isn't she? And good on them. Cool. It was only the thought of some rich old letch getting his hands on her that wound me up, not her actually being with somebody else.'

Pip stared. Mick had just said something about not being able to stand any more weddings, but, she'd know. Wouldn't she? She'd be the first to know, well, the second, after the groom. If Lottie was… 'What are you talking about, Todd?'

'Well I assumed he was a dirty old man, you know one of your lord types that are always in the papers. All posh accents and doing what they want.'

'No, not that bit. The bit about them doing it anyway.'

'Lots? Well her and that Rory of hers. They're getting married.' He looked at her, slightly confused. 'Aren't they? He seems like an okay guy to me.'

'Are they? Who said?'

'Rory, and he'd know, wouldn't he? Your man said he'd bought a round of drinks at the pub to celebrate.'

'Mick said that? And this was when, exactly?'

'Last night, I reckon.'

'Come on, I need to get to the bottom of this. Let's go and get a shower.'

Todd raised an eyebrow.

'Not together.' Pip scrambled to her feet. 'But I will help you find your brother's dad.'

'You're a star. I'll show you the letter when we get back, see if you know the guy.'

'Unlikely, but I know somebody who will.' Pip grinned. 'Elizabeth knows everything and everybody.' She stopped dead and frowned. 'You don't think Rory's proposal has got anything to do with her, do you? She is just so damned sneaky and determined to get her own way.'

Todd grinned back. Frankly he couldn't give a monkeys. Right now his body and mind were more interested in just how helpful Pip might be now that Mick had thrown his cards on the table, hopefully closely followed by his front door key.

Chapter 15

'You're leaving aren't you?' Pip had never been one to avoid the truth, even though she had to admit she'd given it a damned good try lately. But enough was enough. After insisting Todd had a shower alone, despite the fact that right now a no-strings-attached shag and shared cigarette had a certain appeal, she'd given him instructions to go for a long walk, preferably via a few pints in the pub.

Letting Mick discover another man boosting more than just her ego wasn't the way she wanted things to end. Not this time. So she'd sat, facing the door, and waited. Like a convict awaiting sentence.

Mick had spent way longer than he should have done tidying his tools, while he tried to work out exactly what he was going to do about the whole mess. But he should have known she'd be in there first.

'I do love you, Philippa. You're an amazing woman.'

'That sounds like a tribute, not a declaration of affection. You could put that on my gravestone.'

'You know—'

'I'm kidding. I know what you mean.' Being serious hurt. It would be easier to make light of this, or just be logical. But he was saying the wrong things to make her want to be logical.

'I wanted this to work, treas.' Mick sat down heavily. And when he stared at her, there was as much confusion and hurt in those dark eyes as she felt in her own heart.

'But it's not done, has it? How can it, when you're in love with somebody else?'

'I'm not—'

'You hurt when you look at her. Well, I bloody hurt when I look at you.' So much for logic and distance. 'It's not fucking fair. I don't want to like you this much.'

'Come here.' He dragged her closer, held her, unresisting, on his knee.

'I don't want to get upset.'

'I know. You don't do tears, do you, pet?'

'Or make a scene – it's not me.'

'I know.'

'Stop smiling.'

'I'm not.'

She glanced up. She wasn't going to crumble into a pathetic emotional heap. She wasn't. And he was smiling, she knew he was. Even if it was a sad smile.

'It's okay to make a scene now and then, darling.'

It would be okay to reach up and stroke that strong face, kiss those firm lips, too. But she couldn't, wouldn't. 'What are you going to do, Mick?'

'Nothing.' He shrugged, gazed past her at something she could only guess at. 'Or go back to Ireland.'

'That's running away. That's what other people do – not you.'

'Turn to the bottle?' He gave a short laugh.

'Love sucks, doesn't it?'

'All the tough things in life do, treasure, or they wouldn't be worth going after.'

'Then, go after her.'

'No. The tough bit is "not doing".'

'It won't make you a better man, you know, resisting temptation.'

189

He laughed properly then. 'It might make him one, though.'

'Do you think Rory loves her, you know, properly? Enough to get married?'

'It's not for anybody else to say what "properly" means, is it?'

'I should be mad at you.'

'You should. Feel free to rant and rave.'

'I thought I'd want to, but I guess it's not my style.'

'One of the things I love about you.'

'I should be mad at her too.' She sighed.

'She doesn't know a thing about this, Pip. She's only ever had eyes for one man. Whatever you do, don't be mad at her.'

'I used to watch you watching her, and I used to wonder what was going on in your head.'

'I've never touched her.'

'I know.'

He paused. 'Is it easier if I just pack and go now?'

'It's easier if you stay, but,' Pip got up reluctantly. One step at a time. 'Better if you go.' Freedom and space had always been her thing, she'd thought. But now she wanted to grab, hang on and beg him not to leave. So much for independence. 'I guess I like you too much. Never a good thing.'

'When you get to too much it's not good, darling.'

'"Can we still be friends?" sounds lame.'

'"Can we still be friends?" sounds nice.' He raised an eyebrow, the corner of his mouth quirked in that sexy way he had. 'I'll put my stuff in a bag.'

'I'll go and see Sam, I'm not very good at this kind of stuff.'

***

'So, we're not going to auction some sexy men off?' Sam looked concerned.

'And we're not going to auction you off?' Pip, her chin, balanced on her hand, was giving Lottie the type of penetrating stare that normally only came from her grandmother.

'No, you're bloody not. I told you that wouldn't work. Anyway I've got a new idea. Well it was kind of Rory's idea.'

Lottie, who had only slowed down long enough to pull her boots on over the spotty green socks, had dashed straight over to Sam's house and been pleased to find that Pip was already there.

At least this way she only had to explain her idea once, and if they both thought it was daft she'd have to go back to the drawing board – even though she happened to think it was brilliant. Well, she had done when it had been buzzing about in her head on the way over. Now that she was trying to put it into words she was beginning to think she might just sound deranged. 'It's not that I didn't like your ideas, Sam, it's just,' she had been thinking a lot about just how unsuitable she thought the auction idea was, and hadn't been thinking at all about how to explain it diplomatically to Sam. 'It's just I'm not sure what Gran would think. And Uncle Dom says it has to be a long-term plan, and we can't just keeping finding men to auction off, can we?'

'Can't we?' Sam looked confused.

'There aren't enough around here.' Pip's tone was dry. 'Believe me, nobody would want to bid on some of the farmers and poachers you find around here, even if they do think they're God's gift. Smelly gumboots and a twelve bore aren't everybody's idea of a good night out, and let's not even talk about what they keep in their pockets.'

'But there's the football team, all of Dave's mates.'

'True, and I for one would bid on all of them.'

Lottie fought to get the attention back on her before she completely lost control and ended up accidentally agreeing that the only way forward was to pimp out England's finest footballers. 'Look, listen.' She tried not to jiggle up and down on the spot like a child trying to attract attention. 'What's been the best day of your life, Sam?'

'Best day? Now you're asking. Well, when me and Davey went to the World Cup and I met David Beckham, that was pretty good.' Sam looked dreamy. 'He's so sweet you wouldn't believe, and his voice is quite deep, now, you know, not like when he first went on the TV. He was a bit squeaky then, wasn't he? Not that I didn't love him to bits, but I think somebody should tell you stuff like that, don't you?' Lottie gave a weak grin and forced herself to stay still and not fidget. 'And we went to that film premier for that Vinny. I mean, he's not sweet in the films, is he? But when you meet him for real he's a right softy, and a right gent. He likes doing the country lord stuff, too, you know. And then when—'

'One day, if you had to pick one special day?' Lottie had expected an instant correct answer, and was beginning to get worried that she'd got over-excited about her idea for nothing. Maybe it was just her who was interested in weddings – some Freudian thing that she hadn't caught on to.

'One day? Like a whole-day thing? Well your cricket auction thing was lovely, babe,' she glanced at Lottie to see if she was on the right track. Lottie had buried her head in her hands. 'But when we got married that was spesh. I mean the wedding thing we had here at her Ladyship's, not when we were already actually married, although that was lovely too. But all of my friends were here the second time, and even Scruffy. Ah bless, he's such a poppet.'

'Your wedding day?'

'Yes, hun. Is that the right answer?'

'Thank God for that.' Lottie grinned triumphantly. 'Everybody loves a wedding, don't they? I mean everybody has been going on at me and Rory to get married.'

Pip crossed her arms, raised a questioning eyebrow, and glared. Which was a bit disconcerting.

'You're getting married?' Sam jumped on Lottie with unbridled delight and wrapped her in the type of hug that wasn't often seen in the Brinkley household. When Lottie finally managed to get free and breathe again she felt guilty saying that, no, actually she wasn't. But she had to say it anyway.

'Well, no. Sorry.'

'No?' Pip really was behaving strangely. It almost sounded like an accusation. Lottie decided it was probably best to ignore it and crash on regardless with her explanation.

'But people love weddings, and lots of people have them, don't they?'

'But you don't?'

'Well, no,' Lottie stared at Pip and wondered if the heat was getting to her, or maybe the whole relationship crisis with Mick was worse than she realised. She really must make sure she talked to Pip about it soon. Like today. After she'd managed to explain her idea, if she ever did. 'Not me, but other people.'

'Okay.' It was drawn out, and sceptical. 'Assuming it isn't you, but somebody else. You can't make people pay to come to weddings, Lottie. Not exactly an earner is it? Unless you've got some celebrities under the bed who have granted you exclusive coverage.'

'You haven't, have you? Who, hun? Or is it a secret?' Sam's eyes were gleaming. 'Is it George, tell me it's George Clooney.' She paused. 'Oh no, he's got married, hasn't he? Is it somebody Royal? Prince Harry? Wow, I would so love to meet him. He's so cheeky. I bet he's a right laugh, isn't he?'

'No, er, no it's not Harry, and I don't know if he's a right laugh or not, to be honest.' Lottie still hadn't got used to the idea that Sam assumed she personally knew every member of the Royal Family. 'It's not anybody. And not me.' Lottie, who suspected Pip was winding Sam up on purpose, decided she needed to get to the point quicker than she was. 'A wedding venue. I'm talking about using it as a place to get married for other people, not me, or George Clooney specifically.' She looked from Sam, who looked blank, to Pip, and back again, then decided to bash on. 'I want to make Tipping House Estate the best wedding venue in, well in, anywhere. What do you think? You know, get people to have their weddings here. They'd pay for that, wouldn't they? It would be different? Good?'

'So if Prince Harry did want to, you'd let him babe?'

'Well, er, yes, if he wanted to, but I think his gran has a bigger place than mine, actually.'

'Are you sure, hun?'

'Probably better if you have got some surprise celebrities under the bed as well.' Pip swirled what was left of her coffee around in the bottom of the mug thoughtfully. 'Actually, I think that could be the best idea you've had so far.'

Lottie suddenly realised that the tips of her fingers were throbbing because she'd been gripping the edge of the breakfast bar. She let go with relief. 'And I thought maybe we could kick off by having, like, a big summer party, an exclusive launch event to show people what it could be like. A bit like the auction,' she saw Sam's eyes light up, 'but without the auction, or the men.' The look turned to mild confusion.

'I could get some good coverage in the glossies, I reckon. You are right, people do love a good wedding.' Pip stared. 'So we'd have a big event like a staged wedding, to showcase everything, well, like a wedding fayre.' She paused. 'And you're not getting married?'

Sam, who had been sitting looking between Pip and Lottie silently, trying to make sense of the auction that wasn't actually an auction, suddenly smiled. 'I get it, babe, we're going to have, like, a fake wedding, the full works at the party, make it really posh. Although,' she paused and looked at Lottie, 'if you did actually get married it would be better.'

'No.' Lottie, who had no particular urge to say her vows quite yet, and who really didn't want an over-the-top, specifically-for-an-audience, type of wedding, shook her head as decisively as she could.

'No?' Pip, Lottie decided, was beginning to sound like a stuck record, which wasn't like her at all.

'Okay, babe. No probs. But you could be the bride,' she saw the look on Lottie's face, 'as in the fake bride. We've got to have a fake bride and groom, haven't we? And you'd look gorg in a big white dress. You could have, like, a big tiara and a train like Princess Di had, or was it Kate had a train?'

'It would grab more headlines.' Pip nodded, still giving Lottie 'the stare'. 'You being the bride.'

'No.'

'Only fake. We'd make it quite clear. And you could pick the groom. It doesn't even have to be Rory. We could find you somebody really buff.' Pip who seemed to have perked up a bit, grinned wickedly. 'Elizabeth will love this idea.'

Lottie, who wasn't sure whether she meant Gran would love the whole idea, or just the 'not Rory' bit was beginning to wonder if she should just let them auction her off after all, along with a group of fit and no-doubt topless men.

'I love it, I love it.' Sam clapped her hands. 'I can't wait. Are you going to have a horse-drawn carriage? Oh, let's open some bubbly and celebrate, girls. Oh no, I know, we'll have Pimm's on the terrace. I'll get Alice to make us a jug.'

'Alice?'

'Davey reckoned I needed somebody to help hoover all Scruffy's hair up.' Sam smiled. 'And he said it's helping with employment in the area, it's our duty. And she wants to learn English, it's like having an au pair really, and,' she lowered her voice, 'he thinks maybe I can't get pregnant because I'm too stressed with all the stuff I do. Isn't he a darling?'

'You're serious about a baby?' Pip sounded shocked, which Lottie reckoned was a good thing – it distracted her from obsessing about a wedding. 'Even now you've seen the state poor Amanda's in?'

'Not everybody is like that, are they Lottie? I bet you'd like a baby, wouldn't you? You could have a real cute one, all curly-haired like Rory.'

'Well I'd rather have a foal, if I'm honest.'

Sam giggled. 'You're funny.' Lottie, who wasn't trying to be funny, but was deadly serious, let it pass. 'And Amanda is much better now. Alice could be my au-pair for real, too, couldn't she?'

Sam led the way through the patio door onto the terrace and minutes later, Alice, who wasn't actually called Alice but had a foreign name that she knew Sam wouldn't get to grips with, came out with Pimm's and glasses. From the speed they arrived, it looked like she'd had plenty of practice. 'Pimm.'

'Pimm's.' Sam corrected her automatically.

'It is one jug of, it is one Pimm.'

'But there are lots of glasses in it.'

'Ah. So I pour you one glass of Pimm? Like beers, you have one beer, yes?'

'Well yes, but no.'

'Like wine, you have one wine, yes?'

This obviously flummoxed Sam, who turned to Pip for support. 'It's called Pimm's, on the label, look on the bottle.'

Alice didn't look convinced, and Lottie wasn't entirely sure that coming to learn English at Sam's was going to give her the education she expected.

Alice was the least of her worries, though. By the time the second jug of Pimms had been plonked on the table she'd actually started to think that being the fake bride was a good idea, which was all very disturbing. And drawing up a list of possible grooms was even more of a worry, especially when her mind kept going back to just how sexy Rory would look in top hat and tails. Which probably meant she'd diverted to a Fred Astaire-type fantasy, not a wedding.

'Here's to lots of big weddings, then. Oh, I do love a wedding. I can't wait to pick the dress.'

Lottie groaned inwardly, and made a mental note to ensure that Sam didn't choose any of the clothes. But when she glanced in Pip's direction she didn't get the expected grin. And Pip didn't raise her glass. She had, Lottie realised, gone uncharacteristically quiet.

'Sorry, Lots, it's a brill idea, really, but right now I'm not really in the wedding mood.' She put her glass down. 'I probably should go home.'

'Pip? What's happened?' She reached out, but Pip flinched away. 'I'm sorry, I'm just not in the mood.'

'It's Mick, isn't it? Oh Pip, you've not had a row have you? I know you said—'

'He's gone. Over.' She held up a hand. 'And right now I don't want to talk about it.'

***

She was drowning. The whole country was baking in a heatwave and she was surrounded by water. In her ears, her eyes, cold all around her. Her hair was wet against her neck, clinging, strangling her.

Lottie woke up from her dream with a start and realised it wasn't actually a dream. Her ears really did have water in them and when she moved her head on the pillow there was a definite squelching sound. As a large drop of water landed on her nose she shot upright. Fully awake and freezing. Even though it was the middle of summer.

A second drop of water sploshed on her head and Lottie glanced upwards towards the high ceiling that had a dark patch directly above her.

'Bugger.'

'Oh you're awake, are you?' Rory wandered into the bedroom, naked apart from some tight breeches. His hair damp against his skull, which she was sure was a result of a shower and not a soaking from the bed.

'It's raining. In the bed.' Lottie rolled out and shook her wet hair.

'Not raining outside, darling. Are you coming out for a hack with me, it's a gorgeous morning, look.' He threw the large heavy curtains back, and the dust scattered on beams of sunlight.

Which could have been quite pretty and romantic, Lottie thought, if it didn't make her nose itch. She sneezed and Harry fell off the bottom of the bed.

'Where's all the water come from? Don't you think I should sort that before we go riding?'

Rory shrugged.

'Or the bed will still be wet tonight.'

'True. Have you seen my polo shirt, Lots?'

'In the drawer. Aren't you cold?'

'Hot shower. Come on, get your act together. It'll be a burst pipe, the way they gurgle it sounds like there's something in there trying to force its way out. Looks like it has now.'

'I'm bloody freezing, and soaked.' Lottie was starting to realise now why her gran had always let the dogs sleep in the bedroom. In case emergency measures were needed to keep you warm.

'It was your idea to move in here. We could always go back to the cottage.'

Rory hadn't exactly complained about moving into Tipping House, he rarely complained about anything unless horses were involved. But, Lottie had the distinct feeling that he would have been happier to stay where they had been. In the cottage. Cosy, comfortable in their own self-inflicted state of mess and chaos. True, at times it could be a bit cramped, just because they had so much stuff, but it was comfortable, and it was theirs. Well his. And Tipping House wasn't. It was enormous, cold and draughty and belonged to somebody else. And now it was damp as well. She sighed and pulled a sweatshirt over her head.

'I do need to be here.'

'I know.' Rory hugged her to him. 'Hurry up, I've spotted a great place where we can make some gallops.'

'Not in the middle of a lawn?' She looked at dubiously.

'Nope, although I'm not quite sure anyone needs that much grass just for looking at.'

'We could have garden parties?'

Rory was grinning at her with a look of mock horror, his little finger cocked in the air as he held an imaginary tea cup up, so Lottie did the only sensible thing she could think of, and threw her shoe at him, which unfortunately hit a painting of a severe-looking aristocrat and knocked him to a much more attractive angle. He rocked slowly from side to side before coming to rest, and Lottie giggled.

'Come on, lazy arse, I want to show you. Race you to the stables.'

'But I've got to—'

'No you haven't, you've got to meet me at the stables. Ten minutes.'

Rory stared in horror at the room that Dominic had assigned to him as a temporary tack room. He could see the floor. Actually see it. Somebody had tidied it. Every bridle was on a hook, all the saddles were neatly placed on the racks, and the floor was completely clear of the rubbish he'd left strewn everywhere yesterday.

Which left him in a bit of a quandary. He knew he'd left his favourite whip right there in the middle of the floor, and now it wasn't. And he could have sworn he'd left one of the horse's passports on the upturned bucket in the corner, and he needed it. He was in the midst of chucking the contents out of the tubs and drawers as he searched, when Dom walked in.

'Making yourself at home?' His tone was dry.

'I'm not convinced this is going to work. No offence, Dom, but...'

'Amanda thought it would help, tidying up for you. She presumed you hadn't had time yesterday.'

'Ah.' Rory suddenly spotted the small vase of flowers on the table in the corner. It was Amanda's doing. Effeminate as Dom sometimes appeared, it didn't extend to picking flowers.

'She didn't realise it was how you always had things.'

'I can find stuff if it stays where I leave it.' Normally. Rory had to admit that he did quite often misplace things, but having somebody tidy up after him had to make it worse. 'Any idea where she'd have stashed the horse passports?'

'Desk drawer?'

'Desk?' Rory looked round in desperation. He wasn't used to a tack room with a desk, even if it was old cast-off from the house (which was probably a priceless antique). His tack room at the cottage was just big enough to store his riding gear and tack, with some plastic trays that were overflowing with plaiting bands and competition entry forms. He tried the drawer, and, sure enough, his paperwork was neatly stacked. 'Maybe we should just call in one of those antique programmes. You could mend the roof with the proceeds.'

'*You* could do the roof.' Dom said a little pointedly. 'It's more Charlotte's than mine. I'll leave you to it, then, shall I?' He backed away from the door, and Rory suddenly felt a bit guilty. He hadn't exactly done a great deal to help yet, but in a way he'd felt he wasn't part of the big plan any more. It was Lottie's inheritance, she who was trying to work out how to save it, and her family who were there at every corner. 'She needs your support, Rory.'

'I know.' He dropped the horse papers back on the desk. 'I know.' And held his hands up. 'But, to be honest, I'm not really sure where to start.'

'Just be there for her. Or somebody else might be.' And with that cryptic comment Dom wheeled away and headed over to the other side of the yard with his large stride.

'Did I just see Uncle Dom?'

'You did. Here, hold this.' Rory dropped a saddle onto Lottie's open arms, and hooked a bridle over the top. 'Tack Flash up for me, we're going out.'

Rory hadn't needed Dom to prod him into action, he'd been concerned about the move even before it happened. They had never been very good at finding time for each other, for their relation-ship. Life was too busy. A whirlwind of schooling horses, feeding horses, grooming horses, mucking out and going to competitions, and it wasn't until Lottie had left him to go on her travels that he'd realised how much he relied on her, needed her beside him. Loved her. And when she'd come back to Tippermere, and him, he'd done his best to do what Mick had told him he needed to do – show her he cared.

And they'd been doing fine, until now. When he'd stopped to think about it, he'd realised that the empty feeling inside was because he could feel her slipping away, out of his grasp, like sand trickling between his fingers.

Todd arriving in Tippermere had unsettled him, the easy-going Aussie had seemed up-front enough, but the Lottie he'd described hadn't been the one Rory thought he knew. And now it seemed there was another Lottie, too. The one with responsibilities. He'd seen the look on her face when Todd had landed in their midst, and he'd seen the blush on her cheeks. And he'd been trying to forget it and keep busy.

He threw a saddle onto the back of one of the horses and tightened the girth. Not so long ago Mick and Pip had been telling him to whisk Lottie away, but she hadn't really wanted that. Or at least he hadn't thought so. He thought they'd been happy as they were. And now that he had accidentally proposed, she did seem to be. They did seem to be back to normal. Which is just how he liked things.

The clatter of hooves on the cobbles outside broke into his thoughts and he slipped the bridle over the horse's head and grabbed his hat from where he'd propped it in the feed bucket.

'Where are we going?'

'Surprise.' He picked up the rucksack from where he'd dumped it outside the stable and swung onto the saddle.

Five minutes later they were cantering across an open field and Rory had to admit that this was much better than boxing up to go the gallops, or hacking out on the roads. Lottie grinned at him, then eased forward out of the saddle, urging her horse into a gallop. How could he not love a woman like her? With a holler he pushed his horse on faster, matching her pace.

Turning off the path, the horses picked their way down the slope, between the trees, weaving their way down, the smell of flowers and leaves crushed beneath their hooves floating up into Rory's nostrils. The faint sound of running water reached their ears, a gentle shimmer of noise that broke the quiet air up into a million tiny pieces. And then the ground levelled out and they reached the clearing that Rory had found the day before.

'Oh, I love it here.' The wide smile and shining eyes told him everything. 'I used to come down here when I was little to hide.'

And that was the problem, the one he was trying to ignore. It was her place. Every little secret spot that he discovered, she had probably been there before. With somebody else. It shouldn't bother him. He wasn't possessive, and she'd been happy to move into the lodge with him. But somehow this seemed different. He shook the thought from his head and pulled the bottle of champagne from the rucksack.

'I thought we deserved some time to ourselves.'

'That is so romantic.' Lottie wrapped her arms around his neck, bouncing up and down as she did so, which wasn't quite so romantic. 'Oh, I do love you.'

'Bloody good job! I love you too.' He popped the champagne cork, one arm still around her waist. His fingers crossed behind her back. 'And I am going to buckle down and help you, Lottie.'

'I know.' She rolled on to her stomach and propped herself above him, eyes shining. 'It's going to be perfect, isn't it?'

Chapter 16

Lottie cocked her head on one side as she tried to work out exactly what the large, red-headed reptile was and why it appeared to have a green Mohican. It didn't help that she could only see half of it properly, the other half having disappeared down the low-slung, faded, denim jeans, ending up God knows where. At least she could see what the head end was up to.

'Admiring the scenery, love?'

She glanced up, no doubt looking as guilty as a Labrador that had been caught with half a chicken in its jaws, straight into the bright-blue eyes set into a chiselled face, topped with an alarming shortage of hair. The muscled-up and shaven look had always slightly scared Lottie, who was more accustomed to the tightly toned lean physique of the men who spent their lives on horseback, and usually had something to run her fingers through under their riding hats.

She sneaked one more look at the creature that had been tattooed over most of his torso and wondered if it would sound prudish to suggest he put his t-shirt back on.

'Where am I supposed to be putting this, then, love?'

Up until that moment, the mini scaffold tower that he had his hands on had completely escaped her notice (which had been firmly fixed on his body art), and now she looked at it in horror, wondering what on earth it was doing in Tipping House. Surely scaffolding went outside? Not that this would be much help in even reaching the windows, let alone mending the roof. She was still trying to work out exactly what it was for, and why she'd know where he should put it, when she realised that Reptile Man's attention had been diverted.

'Hey, babe, isn't it brill?' Sam grinned. 'I can't believe we're actually doing this.'

Nor can I, thought Lottie, then glanced over at Mr Muscle Man, who was staring slack-jawed at Sam, obviously under the impression that he was the 'babe' in question. He'd be asking her to oil him up any minute now, and then what would happen to the reptile? Maybe it would curl up and disappear beneath his belt.

'Be a doll and put it in that corner, will you?'

'Happy to put it wherever you'd like it, darling.' The 'doll' winked and pushed off with his metalwork.

'It's to put the speakers up.' Sam offered an explanation to a confused Lottie.

'I'm so sorry, Sam, but we can't mount speakers, they'll damage the wood panelling and it's been there for years.' Lottie looked worriedly at the walls of the Grand Hall and bit the inside of her cheek, just as a large man with a tape measure pushed past her. 'What on earth is—'

'Don't worry about him, babe. He's just measuring up for the stage.'

'Stage?'

Lottie would have felt much better if Amanda, arbiter of good taste, had been the only one there with her. Instead, Sam (who, to be fair, had been allotted responsibility for organising the workmen, as she had a natural aptitude for it) seemed to be taking charge and modifying things as she saw fit. She was fairly sure that if she didn't keep an eye on her a disco ball, or worse, would materialise. 'Don't worry, hun, it's more of a catwalk.' She giggled. 'And we're not sticking any speakers on the walls, or lights, they're going on the tower things – that's what they're for. See? Amanda thought of it, isn't she clever? She thinks of everything. I'd have just thought we had to nail them up.'

'Catwalk?' Lottie looked blankly at Sam as the barrage of unwelcome words bounced around inside her brain. Catwalk, lights, speakers? Had she actually imagined being at Sam's and discussing the new plan, the wedding plan? This sounded more midnight rave than bridal fayre. Tipping House was about to be transformed into a strobing, pulsating, head-banging rock venue. With a catwalk. 'You do know? We're not doing the auction, Sam? It's more of a pretend wedding.'

'Of course it is, babe, but everybody will want to see the dress, so this is my little surprise. I mean, that's the best bit, isn't it? I can't wait to see you walk down there all glam. I know somebody who does brilliant makeup. You won't recognise yourself.' Sam gave Lottie an impromptu hug and looked as excited as she had on her own wedding day. Lottie, who didn't think weddings normally involved speakers or catwalks, or not recognising oneself, wished she'd never thought of the idea. She looked at Amanda, who nodded encouragingly.

'No.'

'Sorry?' Sam's smile slipped the tiniest bit.

'We're not having a catwalk or a stage.'

'Not even a little one?'

And now she felt rotten. But she had to do what she knew was right. And if it didn't work, then at least she'd know she had given it her absolutely best shot. 'I'm so, so sorry Samantha. I do appreciate everything you're doing, you know I do, but we do need to stick to the plan.' Her plan. 'It's got to be like a real wedding, so everybody feels like guests.' As time went by Lottie had got more and more attached to 'the plan', adding tweaks here and there until she just knew it would be a success. It had to be. 'I don't want them to feel like customers, I want, well,' she fished around for the right word. 'I want it to be magical, a fairy tale.' Which was what

Tipping House had always been to her as she was growing up. A place of mystery, where anything could happen. Her home was the key to the whole thing. She was selling the type of wedding that normally money couldn't buy.

And after many hours of mulling things over as she'd been exercising the horses, she'd realised that Pip had been right. If she, the next Lady Stanthorpe, was the bride, it would catch the headlines far more effectively than anybody else would. She was selling a dream – of being a Lady.

'A fairy tale.' Sam sighed. 'It is going to be magic, babe, I just know it. So, who's the lucky man going to be? Oh, I can't wait! I just love weddings.'

Amanda smiled and gave Lottie a gentle squeeze. 'They'll be queuing up, but, to be honest, you don't have to pick one if you don't want. Although it might be nice to have somebody to hang on to when you walk in? Unless you'd like to walk in with some other brides and we can showcase a few dresses that way?'

Amanda had secretly been delighted when Lottie had come up with her wedding idea. As a young girl she'd spent hours looking through bridal magazines, picking out the perfect dress, the perfect cake and the perfect honeymoon. Her own first wedding had made her fairy tale come true (even if the groom turned out to be lacking in some areas), no expense spared and planned down to the finest detail with military precision. Her second, to Dominic, had been a quiet and dignified affair that was as beautiful as it was perfect. To be cast in the role of wedding planner had been handing her the perfect profession on a plate. And working with somebody like Lottie was wonderful – it was just curbing Sam's extravagant tendencies and Pip's mischief-making that was the problem.

'It really has to be like a proper wedding, not a kind of fashion show for bridal wear.' Lottie glanced over at Reptile Man, who had now risen to the top of his scaffold and was stretching up, displaying an alarming amount of extra creature that had been hidden earlier.

'Okay, that's good, one bride and one groom.' She made a note. 'We're only here to give you more ideas, but we do want it to be just how you dreamed it up, Lottie.'

'The trouble is, my dream wasn't very, er, thought-through at the start. I'd kind of stopped just after the 'let's host weddings' bit.' Lottie admitted. 'But I have got a better idea now. I'm just missing a final bit.'

'And a groom.' Sam added.

'I think Rory will do it.'

Sam squealed.

Lottie frowned at her. 'Pretend of course.' And she had kind of assumed he would, even though she hadn't actually asked him outright. In fact, he'd been pretty positive every time she mentioned the wedding, and had even asked once or twice if he needed to do anything. 'I've never actually thought about weddings that much before. I mean, you don't if you haven't had one, do you?' She looked at Amanda with a worried frown. 'Or do you?'

Amanda laughed. 'Well I had, but I'm a bit strange. I'd been dreaming about weddings since I was about twelve.'

'I'd been dreaming about jumping at Hickstead.' Lottie felt slightly glum, she was completely out of her depth. Did she really know what she was doing or was she seriously deluded?

'How about horses? Are they the missing link?' Amanda smiled encouragingly.

'Horses?'

'Yes, Lottie, horses. You wouldn't be you without a horse. And you've said yourself that you're offering the type of dream wedding that nobody else can offer, the type you don't see in normal bridal magazines. That's your USP.'

'Is it?' Lottie, who hadn't got a clue what Amanda was talking about, nodded. 'USP, that's something to do with computers?' Rory was always losing his, but what it had to do with weddings she wasn't quite sure.

'Unique Selling Point, you noddle. It's what makes you different.'

Amanda took Lottie's hand in her own and tugged her gently over towards the table, then pushed her into a chair. 'Right,' she knew Lottie was onto a good thing, but had sensed that she was already feeling out of her depth. 'This is all sounding brilliant, but let's work out the final bit. What is the best thing about Tipping House?'

'The courtyard.' Lottie answered, without thinking. 'Why?'

'The courtyard – is that the bit where the stables are?'

'Well yes, but—'

'Why? Tell me why that's the best thing.'

Lottie looked around. This really wasn't the best time to have a chat about things, when they had so much to do. Maybe it was hormones. People blamed most things on hormones. And Amanda's pregnancy had been so horrendous, she'd been so sick, maybe it had affected her brain temporarily. She probably should humour her, or it could affect the baby. Stress affected babies – she did remember reading that somewhere, even if she knew very little else about being pregnant. Apart from the fat bit, and the debate about sex (having it, as opposed to the sex of the baby), and the fact that pregnant ladies had weird food fads and burst into tears. In fact, now she thought about it, she did know quite a lot about pregnancy, just not birth.

If Amanda flipped right now it would be a disaster on the wedding-planning front. Sam would be in charge and turn the Great Hall into Disneyland, or maybe an adult version of Hogwarts, or more like a completely over-the-top version of how people thought Downton Abbey should look. Apart from that, she really did love Amanda and wanted her to be happy and not at all unhinged.

'Well?' Amanda was tapping her pen on the clipboard, just as a nudge, not violently, like impatient Pip would have been doing by now.

'It's magic. I've always loved the courtyard. You go in and it's like stepping into the past. I used to go and hide in there when I was little, and I think Mum and Dad did too. It smells of horse,'

Amanda wrinkled her nose slightly, she couldn't help it. Lottie noticed and smiled, 'nice horse, and fresh hay. And water.'

'Smells of water?'

'I know it sounds weird, but it does, when the fountain is going. And I just feel free when I'm there, like a kid again.' She glanced over to where Sam was in deep discussion with the tape-measure man. He was looking disgruntled as he put the measure in his pocket. 'Shouldn't we be helping?'

Amanda ignored her. 'It sounds like the perfect place to get married.'

Lottie thought back to the times when she'd run around the fountain with Rory in pursuit, the times he'd made love to her with only the moon and stars as company (apart from a few dozing horses), the days she'd led a horse under the archway and felt like she was stepping into another, more perfect, part of herself. The lump in her throat meant she could only nod and forget Sam, and reptiles and catwalks.

'Then,' Amanda's voice was soft, 'that's where we'll do it. We'll film your dream wedding in there, show it on a screen here and then have the perfect reception.'

'And there isn't going to be a catwalk.'

'Nope. Although,' she grinned, a twinkle lighting her steady eyes, 'we will need a grand entrance to appease Sam. Maybe a red carpet?'

'What's that about a red carpet?' Rory had entered unnoticed amongst all the toing and froing and strange men, and dropped a kiss on her neck. 'Making a right bloody mess in here, aren't you? Don't let Lizzie catch you – she'll kill you.'

Lottie took a swipe at him and missed. 'Rotter, you know she doesn't like you calling her that.'

'Have you seen my new white dressage pad? Brought it in to wash and can't remember where the hell I put it.'

'Boot room?'

'Doubt it, I didn't want the dogs to chew it. Bugger. Oh well, you don't fancy coming for a bit of target practice to cheer me up?'

'Target?' Amanda looked concerned, her mind flitting over the prospect of Rory taking pot shots at her contractors, or standing out on the front lawn with a rifle and scaring the magazine editors away.

'He's being rude, ignore him.'

Rory blew her a kiss, then spotted the photographs of the wedding gowns, which Lottie had somehow completely missed, spread out on the table. 'Good tunnelling practice finding your way under one of those – would have to send a terrier in first.'

'Rory!'

He laughed. 'So you're not up for a quick game of hide and seek under your skirts?'

'Go away.' Lottie gave him a shove with her foot and he pulled a sad face. 'And I've not got any skirts.'

'Right, then, I will play alone, while you girls play weddings – any garters going spare?'

'Go.' Lottie, who'd been feeling a bit overwhelmed, was so pleased to see Rory and be the butt of his jokes she was tempted to beg him to stay, but she knew it would end in disaster, and possibly Amanda and Sam accidentally agreeing to a jousting event in the library – or worse. 'Go, go, go, now! Unless you are going to help?'

'Are you sure you can't come and find my dressage pad?'

'No, Rory, I've got to do this.'

'Please? I do really need to find the damned thing, I'm sure they can manage without you for a bit.'

'I can't, Rory, I really can't. I'll look later. I need to be here.'

'And I need you to be with me for once.'

'Rory.' Lottie glanced up to see his normally happy face filled with frustration.

Loving Rory was easy when they had no distractions, only each other to worry about. But lately being happy had been harder. She knew he hated it when she was too busy to play, but surely he should understand that things weren't so simple these days. That her gran and Dom were relying on her, that this had to be the most important thing in her life right now. She had to save her home, had to do the very best she could. The empty feeling in the pit of her stomach spread as she fought to find the words to explain, to beg him to understand.

'Aww can't he stay?' Sam, who had got over the initial disappointment of the 'no catwalk' decision, and had been busy discussing with the florist a rose-scattered red carpet that would make Chelsea Flower Show look like it had skimped on colour, spotted Rory and rushed over to give him a kiss. 'You will make such a gorgeous groom, darling, won't he, girls? Look at those muscles,' she ran a loving finger over his bicep, 'and a grin to die for – you are so lucky, Lots.' She giggled. 'If I didn't already have my Davey I'd be tempted myself.'

Rory, who'd been staring at Lottie with a sadness that had brought a lump to her throat, suddenly took on the look of a startled racehorse and took a nervous step back.

'And you're such a tease. I love a man who can make me laugh. I nearly wet myself the other night when Davey was winding me up. It's what it's all about, isn't it?'

'Incontinence?' Amanda, who'd been watching with quiet amusement, couldn't resist.

'No, silly. Having a laugh. He doesn't even take shagging that seriously, my Davey, he put a red ribbon on it for Christmas.' She giggled again.

Lottie put her hands over her ears. 'Nooo. Too much information, Sam.'

'Bloody hell, they do that at studs so you know you might get a kick in the balls.'

'Oh, I don't kick, I mean that would be dangerous in these heels, wouldn't it, babe?' Sam balanced precariously on one foot, so that she could show them a six-inch heel.

'Castration.' Rory, a protective hand over his own privates, gave a shudder and shot out at a gallop, back to the safety of bucking horses and lost saddlery.

'I'm glad he's gone.' Amanda linked an arm through Lottie's. 'I've been dying to show you something.' Sourcing flowers, food and tableware had been one thing, but looking for the perfect wedding dress to showcase Lottie's wonderful figure, big green eyes and cascade of thick, dark hair was at the heart of her creation.

She loved Lottie and wanted to give her the ultimate reality of the dream that had been in her head, and she also recognised that Lottie *was* the key to everything. She was the selling point; she was what would make this a success. Without Lottie – her breeding, her looks, her lifestyle, her spirit, her passion – this was just another event. Another wedding location. Lottie was the dream that others aspired to.

So Amanda had sourced the best independent wedding-gown designers in the country (thanking God that Baby Stanthorpe had now settled now and was no longer playing havoc with her innards) and offered them something they couldn't refuse, the opportunity to have their dresses showcased in a country house, modelled by the next Lady of Tipping House herself, at an event that would be covered in glossy magazines with the type of circulation that would reach the richest.

With Pip's help she'd shamelessly dropped names like *Tatler* and *Vogue* with careless abandon, stressing that she could make no promises, but expected much. And then she'd moved on to the luxury car market, the champagne suppliers and purveyors of good food. Offers of everything you could desire at the dream wedding had poured in, and the ornate tickets (supplied, of course, for free) in the style of wedding invitations, had been snapped up despite the heavy price tag.

With the last of the contractors gone, including the very distracting reptile, Amanda could finally share what she saw as the highlight of all her hard work so far.

'Come on, follow me.'

When Amanda flung open the door at the far end of the large hallway, Lottie was seriously concerned that baby brain had struck. Okay, the bathroom facilities in Tipping House were fairly grand, and this one was large enough to host a party in, with ornate and heavy fittings that dated back to God knows when. But chilly and ancient fittings did come with their own special sound effects, which echoed alarmingly in such a large space.

But they weren't there to look at lavatories.

Just inside the door was a life-sized mannequin (well, actually, a Lottie-sized one), which was wearing the most amazing dress she had ever seen.

'Elizabeth said it would be safe in here.' Amanda paused, trying to work out if the look on Lottie's face was surprised awe or horrified shock. 'What do you think? I mean, I know it's not everybody's taste, but I think you'd look wonderful in it. It was one of the ones you said you liked in that magazine?'

'It's…' Lottie tried to find a word.

'That's gorg, babe, and you can always put some nice jewellery on – and your tiara to glitz it up a bit. I've got this diamond choker you can borrow – it's a real dazzler.'

'Beautiful.'

'It's your size if you want to try it.'

'Are you sure?' Lottie glanced down worriedly. 'I'm not sure I'm quite that shape, I've got a tummy, although I'm sure I can diet a bit to fit it.' She added guiltily.

'I'm sure it will be a perfect fit.' Amanda patted her own stomach. 'It's me that's bulging, not you.'

Lottie sighed and reached out tentatively to touch the soft fabric. 'I wish Pip was here to see it.' Pip would tell her if she'd look overdressed, or a dork, or as if she was about to split the seams.

'Yes, where is she? I thought she'd be here today.' Amanda, glanced at her watch. Pip was one of the more reliable people in Tippermere. For one, she actually wore a watch, and secondly, she ran her life along the same efficient lines that Amanda did.

'I don't think she's coming.' Lottie let the heavy satin fall between her fingers, then traced the scalloped edge with the tip of her finger. 'Actually, I don't think she's really in the mood for weddings, even pretend ones.'

'Really?' Amanda who'd been watching Lottie and hoping her hands were clean (how did one explain stains on satin if one had to return the dress?), tried not to worry about it. 'But I thought she loved the idea?' They'd worked as a team: Lottie, her, Pip, Elizabeth and Sam. All equally enthusiastic, even if they all had slightly different ideas and motivations.

Lottie shrugged. 'Oh, I think she's happy with the idea, but, well,' she was feeling so guilty that she'd never realised what was going on, how serious it was, hadn't found the time to talk to the girl who was her best friend. Even though Pip had made a point of trying to discuss it, which would have taken a lot of effort, considering Pip just wasn't the type to discuss her personal problems – ever. 'I think she's split up with Mick, you know, for good. She told me and Sam that he'd gone, moved out. I mean, that's serious, isn't it?'

'After you left,' for once Sam wasn't smiling, 'she rang me and said she was going to end it all.'

'What?' Amanda and Lottie spoke in shocked unison.

'She said he didn't love her, and she knew it, poor babe.'

'Oh crumbs, I better…' Lottie looked around in alarm, trying to spot her phone and keys, which she was pretty sure she'd had with her and put down for safekeeping somewhere, 'I've got to stop her before she does anything stupid.'

'Stop her?' Sam looked shock. 'Well, it's too late, that's why she's sad, she brought it up with him and I think he just agreed. She said she'd always known he was infatuated with somebody else, but just hoped he'd get over her. Must be that Nev he used to go on about. '

'Ah.' Amanda put a steadying hand on Lottie's arm. 'End it all,

214

as in the relationship?'

'Of course, babe. What did you think I meant?'

Lottie, who'd been having visions of her normally logical and sane friend standing dramatically on the edge of a cliff (not that there were many in Cheshire), preparing to throw herself off in the name of love, blinked at Sam. 'Nev? Who is Nev?' She could never remember Mick mentioning a Nev – and a Nev meant he was gay. No wonder Pip was distraught. She'd heard of situations like that before. I mean, it was bad enough being mad about someone only to find out they didn't feel the same way, but then to find out they fancied another bloke. 'Oh God, poor Pip, I never realised. Does she know Nev?'

'I don't think so. You know it's that girl that he went out with when he was back home in Ireland, before Rory persuaded him to come here? She got fed up with him messing with horses and said he had to go with her to the States, or something. I thought it was you that told me.' She leaned forward conspiratorially. 'He is very sexy, but I think Pip was a bit fed up of him spending all his time with the horses too. Very dark and mysterious, isn't he, like Darth Vader.'

'He's nothing like Darth Vader.' Lottie stared at Sam. 'You mean Niamh?'

'Probably, yeah, that could be her name. Oh, that dress is absolutely gorgeous, you have just got to try it on, Lots.'

Lottie let go of the fabric, which she'd had a death grip on, and hoped it didn't crease too easily. She didn't want Mick to still be in love with Nev, or Niamh even. She wanted him to love Pip. She wanted them to be happy, to set up home in the little cottage and be surrounded by small, dark-haired brooding boys and perfectly poised petite madams. She wanted them both to stay in Tippermere forever. Even if that seemed a bit bloody selfish.

'Pip will be fine.' Amanda gave her a quick hug. 'She told me the other day that he'd been the sticking plaster she'd used over a great big hole of insecurity, and he wasn't big enough or sticky enough.'

'Pip said that?'

'Well, it's not the type of thing I'd normally say, is it?'

Which was true. 'I do hope she's okay.'

'And she said, if she was honest with herself she'd been getting bored at trying to be the perfect partner. She isn't ready for domestic bliss.'

The toddlers that Lottie had been wishing on Pip and Mick disappeared off the scene with a plop.

'She was trying too hard because she really thought it was time she had a proper relationship. And Mick had been the closest she'd ever got to a man she could imagine having more than three shags with.' Amanda flinched slightly as she said 'shags'. 'And maybe she was more in love with the idea of love, than the actual doing of it. I suppose it must still be dreadfully difficult to talk about weddings, though.'

'I told her to cheer herself up with Todd.' Sam gave a naughty little shrug of her shoulders accompanied by a wide smile. 'Can't get bored with him, can she? Now, please try the dress on and find Rory so we can see what a gorgeous couple you make.' She clapped her hands. 'Shall I go and find him? This is SO exciting.'

'Oh flip,' Amanda, tuned in to the polite buzz of her mobile, picked it up before the screen had even lit and stared at the reminder that flashed up, 'We've got a meeting at my house with *Glam* magazine. Must dash. Do you mind if we leave you with the dress, Lottie? We can sort it tomorrow. Oh, sugar, do you want to come, Sam?'

Sam, who had been desperate to see the lucky couple in wedding togs, hesitated. But the word '*Glam*' was too tempting to miss. 'Can I bring Scruffy as well, babe? I left him in the car. I hope he hasn't chewed the seats again. Davey gets so mad, but he gets bored, bless him.'

Amanda paled, images of the energetic mongrel weaving in and out of her priceless ornaments, rolling on the immaculate rugs and launching himself onto the chaise longue filled her head.

'I'll put his new collar on. They will love that, they might even take his photo.'

'We'll see.' Amanda had a quick look around to check she had everything, then gave Lottie a quick kiss on the cheek. 'Pip will be fine, I'll ring her later. You go and see what Rory wants.'

'I know exactly what Rory wants.'

Lottie waved them off and closed the front door with a sigh of relief, then her gaze was drawn back to the dress. It really was gorgeous. Stunning. And it looked as if it might even fit. It really wouldn't harm to just slip it on before she went down to the stables, would it?

Chapter 17

'You've got to tell me what to do.'

'Tell you?' Mick, who had been stuffing hay nets as though his life depended on it, stopped and sat down on the nearest bale, intrigued by the note of panic in Rory's tone, which echoed clearly from his mobile phone.

Yesterday he'd felt much the same way. Today, with the air cleared between him and Pip, he felt a massive sense of relief. And a sense of, he reluctantly admitted, freedom. He'd been brought up to believe that honesty was a virtue, but he'd felt he'd been living a lie, which wasn't fair on anybody. 'What am I, your father now?'

'She came in wearing a bloody dress and saying on the phone I had to help her choose.'

'Choose what?'

'The dress, the right wedding dress.'

'Isn't that a girl's job? I thought you weren't supposed to see it before the day.'

'I don't bloody know, but I don't think I can do this.'

'Do what? Are you drunk?'

'I need bloody rescuing. It's all too quick.'

'Man up, you idiot, you sound like a girl. What the hell are you on?'

'I don't know.'

'Speak up, mate, I can hardly hear you. Where are you, in one of the cellars?'

'In the walk-in wardrobe.'

Mick, who had been expecting a more general location, waited for inspiration and none came. 'A wardrobe?'

'I'm in Lottie's, our, bedroom, but I need to get out.'

'She's shut you in?'

'Keep your voice down, she'll hear. And stop asking frigging questions. Haven't you heard a word? Of course she's not bloody shut me in. Oh, Christ. When I said I'd marry her I never thought it would be like this,' there was a long pause, 'I can't do it, Mick. I fucking love her, but I can't cope with all these bloody meetings and lists, and I can't live in this bloody decrepit house. How the hell do I tell her to stop?'

'Well, for a start you need to get out of the wardrobe, I'd say. Why are you in there?'

Losing things was a daily occurrence for Rory, but when he'd been living in his small cottage, there had been a fair chance that things would turn up, eventually. Living in Tipping House was existing on a whole different scale. He wasn't even sure that he'd lost his stock at the house. It could well be in the horsebox, tack room or, frankly, anywhere that he'd visited in Tippermere in the last twenty-four hours. Which was why he'd been in the closet, chucking things out of drawers, when Lottie had entered the bedroom.

Proposing had been half-hearted, but her excitement, plus a return of the old carefree Lottie he loved, had made it worthwhile. Until he'd realised just how seriously she'd taken him. He'd imagined a wedding sometime in the distant future. But being accosted by Sam, who was ready to shoehorn him into a suit and shoo him up the aisle as quickly as possible, and then hearing Lottie on the phone saying she'd already got a wedding dress, had brought home the enormity of the situation and sent him into a panic.

He hadn't dared come out of the closet in case she'd grabbed him and whisked him off to the altar right there and then – with Sam and her beloved Davey as escorts.

Just peeking out of the door and seeing her adjusting the flouncy white skirt of what had to be the most over-the-top dress he had ever seen in his life had been enough to give him palpitations. He'd come out in a sweat, despite the fact he was only partially clothed. He couldn't do it. He'd rung Mick, expecting camaraderie, which wasn't what he'd got. As the phone went dead in his hand he stared out of the open window. There was only one thing for it. He had to make a run for it now and explain later. Once she'd ditched the dress.

Lottie, flying down the imposing staircase, a veil billowing behind her, was not what Mick had expected to see. Deciding that Rory needed a talking-to he'd dumped the haynets and set off for Tipping House. Arriving to see Lottie in all her bridal splendour left him open- mouthed. She was a vision – a perfect vision of tanned skin and virginal white.

Her focus was on the stairs so Lottie didn't see him until it was almost too late to stop. She slid to a halt just inches from him and then gazed up, eyes wide with surprise. Mick did the only thing that he could.

Kissed her.

It was like coming home for Mick. As her soft, full lips opened slightly, her warm breasts pressed against his chest and a sweet smell filled his senses. He would have swooned, except he had other, more pressing, needs – like wrapping his arms around her body and pulling her tighter against him, like tangling his fingers through that glorious mop of curls, like tasting her, his tongue exploring her mouth…

'Shit.' He was horrified and elated. Fighting a hard-on that had shot up the second he touched her, like he was some love-lorn teenager having a first grope. 'Christ, I'm sorry.' He shut his eyes and ran a hand through his hair, desperate to get his act together, willing it to not have happened. He opened his eyes. She was still there. Inches away. Looking slightly shocked. 'Don't marry him, treas. Think about it, take your time. You don't need to rush into it.' He shouldn't have said that, he really shouldn't. That was definitely his dick talking and not his brain.

'Oh.' The way she ran her tongue over her lips was just so unfair.

He took a step back. 'Christ, what am I saying? What the fuck do I know about being in love? Marry him, do what you want, it's your business.'

'I can't.' She teased her bottom lip between white teeth. 'Even if I did want to, and I don't really know…' Her big green eyes were fixed straight on him for a second, then her gaze wavered and flickered over towards the open doorway behind him. 'The bugger just jumped out of the bedroom window.'

'I only wanted to ask him if he liked the dress.' Once Lottie had worked out how to get her feet working again she headed for the front door, out of which Rory could be spotted, halfway across the lawn. Striding along, Tilly at his heels. It was pretty hard to look dignified when your shirt only just covered your boxers, and you had one sock up and one down. But Rory was doing his best and looked oblivious to the state of his attire.

'Stupid twat. Where's he headed?'

She looked out of the corner of her eye at Mick, who had returned to his normal non-smouldering state. She must have imagined it. He hadn't kissed her. None of that had just happened. Had it?

'He just climbed out of the window. I think he's going to the stables.'

'In his socks, boxers and shirt?'

'I think he was about to have a shower. Can I ask you a question?' She glanced down at her dress and, not waiting for an answer, asked anyway. 'Seeing as Rory has gone. What do you think?' She did a twirl. 'Sam reckons I should go for full impact, over-the-top.'

'Figures.'

'Amanda says sophisticated is best, very Lady of the Manor, and I daren't ask Pip.' She paused and gave him a meaningful look. 'It wouldn't be fair.'

She swished her hips from side to side and he tried not to look at the way her bosom threatened to pop out, and tried to forget how nice it had been having his hands on her waist.

'And Rory says?'

'He didn't, he just climbed out of—'

'The window. You don't think you're rushing this a bit, treas?'

'We've only got until September. Honestly, you should see the bank statement. And summer weddings really are best.' Lottie frowned. When Dom had shown her the latest letter from the bank, the sheer length of the numbers had been astounding. She'd never seen so many digits after a pound sign, and she'd said so. 'That's what we owe, Charlotte, not what we've got,' had been Uncle Dom's comment as she'd stared open-mouthed, one finger trailing along the line as she tried to work out the true size of the figure. She couldn't begin to imagine what that much money looked like, let alone what the negative amount signified. It was an awful lot of money not to have.

'Getting married won't solve it, though, will it?' Mick's voice was soft, as though he was talking to an idiot or a skittish horse.

'But I'm not. Why does everybody think I should get married?' She tried not to stamp her foot. 'You're all obsessed.'

'We're not obsessed. Rory told me you were, treas.'

'Sorry?' She frowned. 'Rory told you I'm getting married to who?'

'Him, of course. He did propose.' The frown had deepened. 'Didn't he?'

'Did he?'

'Well he told everybody at the Bull's Head that he had – he even bought a round.'

'You're kidding?' Lottie suddenly grinned, then started to giggle.

'Rory bought a round?' Mick's eyes narrowed, which made her laugh even more, until she had to hold on to his arm or fall over. 'He thought? The idiot! I'm not picking a dress for me. Well, I am, but it's not for our wedding, it's for the Wedding Fayre. You know, to raise money. You do know, don't you?' Mick was just staring at her as though she'd finally lost her marbles. 'Well, that just proves Rory never listens to a word I say. Doesn't it?' She shook her head and picked up her skirts, giving Mick a flash of tanned and toned leg. 'I suppose I better get changed and go and talk to him.'

'I'd let him stew.' He dropped a kiss on her head and squeezed her arm. 'The great eejit. He really doesn't have a clue what he's losing, does he?'

And on that confusing note, Mick marched out and headed down to the yard to give Rory a piece of his mind.

***

Rory, however, wasn't down at the stables, and nor was his car. He'd picked up a few belongings and headed home, back to his small eventing yard and cottage, where Mick eventually tracked him down. 'I can't do it.'

'The dress wasn't for your wedding, you silly twat. She doesn't think you're getting married.'

The still trouser-less Rory had his feet up on the Aga and a dog on his knee. 'The idea of walking down the aisle scares me shitless.'

'Listen to me, man. You're not going to.'

'I don't think I'm the marrying type.'

As Rory obviously wasn't in the listening mood, Mick changed tack. 'So you're running away?'

'I don't run away from anything. I don't belong in that old heap, but I'm really afraid that she does.' For the first time Rory looked

Mick full in the eye. 'It's her home and it's bloody Bleak House. It's old, big, empty and serious. So fucking serious.' He took a deep breath. 'I've lost my loveable Lottie, Mick. And if you're going to say that's part of growing up, then I'm not ready.'

Mick looked down at Rory's hairy legs and shook his head in disbelief. 'You can say that again, mate.'

'I'm moving back here.'

'You never moved out, did you?'

Chapter 18

Pip had not slept well.

The first Pimm's-assisted night on her own hadn't been too bad. She'd been too unhappy and too bothered about the gap in her heart and her life to notice the gap in the bed. The second, despite avoiding an afternoon of wedding planning with Sam, Amanda and Lottie, had been hell. There had been a vast emptiness in the bed next to her and thoughts of Mick and Lottie together running through her mind on an X-rated loop.

Not that Mick and Lottie were together, or that she was ever that dirty and smoochy in real life. But one particularly heartfelt groan had woken her fully from the half-dream state, until she'd realised it was Todd banging his head on the beam at the bottom of the stairs, en-route to the fridge. She'd been sorely tempted to go down and find him, then follow him back to his bed, just for a cuddle and human contact. But she had resisted.

When she'd told Amanda and Sam that she'd always known that her relationship with Mick had been on the skids, she'd not been kidding. It had been a diversion, for both of them. And if she'd applied an ounce of common sense she would have never got so involved. But knowing it, saying it didn't help – she still felt wounded. Rejected.

Todd, oblivious to his missed opportunity, was busy sloshing tea into mugs and egg onto plates by the time she'd been under the shower for long enough to make herself feel vaguely human again.

'You're a messy bugger.'

'And you're a grumpy cow. Here you go.' He served up breakfast with a flourish. 'And don't forget to go and see Lottie.'

'Sorry?'

He dropped her mobile phone on the table. 'She called, needs you to pick up a bridle or something for Rory on your way over there. Then Rory called asking the same thing.'

'You answered my phone?'

'Well, you were in the shower so bloody long, it was either that or drop it in the sink to shut the bloody thing up. Do you not get water shortages in this country?'

'Water shortage? Are you bloody kidding? Anyway, why didn't he take the stuff himself?'

'Well, Mick told me Rory's moved back to the cottage.' He sat down opposite her and took a mouthful of his breakfast.

'To the cottage?' Pip stared. 'To his cottage. The yard?'

The answering mumble through a mouthful of scrambled egg didn't enlighten her.

'Stop eating for a minute. And how do you know? You've been talking to Mick as well? You've spoken to all of bloody Tippermere before I'm even up. Christ, you're worse than Elizabeth.'

Todd laughed and carried on eating. 'Spoke to Mick at the yard when I left Tab this morning.'

'You're a tart.'

He shrugged good-naturedly and winked. 'She's a sweet, generous girl.'

'Innocent.'

'I wouldn't bet on that. Daddy apparently went ballistic when he saw her latest t-shirt.'

'I thought they were always black with some heavy metal additions.'

'This one had *Sticks and stones will break my bones, but whips and spurs excite me.*'

'Mm, I bet they do.'

'Hard for a man to resist.'

'Impossible.'

'Apparently her old man's decided he actually misses the goth look.'

'I bet he does, poor Tom.'

'Oh, and your man Mick said to let you know he was trimming at Rory's first thing, then heading over to Lottie's after that if you needed him.'

'Huh.' Pip took a mouthful of too-hot tea and tried to ignore her smarting eyes. 'He's not my man. Anyway, what's Rory doing back at his yard? Has he really moved? What about Lottie?'

'Dunno. Just him, I think. You'll have to ask yourself, Miss Nosey. I can't keep up with you lot.'

Pip grimaced.

Lottie and Rory had always been unconventional, but a wedding proposal followed by moving to different addresses, all in one week? 'They're my friends. I'm not being nosey I'm being caring. Oh, and be here at three o'clock. I'm taking you over to Elizabeth's for afternoon tea.'

'Tea?'

'As in G&T.'

***

'Are you going to move back to the yard with him?'

Lottie looked at Pip and was relieved that her blue eyes were as clear as ever, and she didn't look as if she'd had sleepless nights over her break-up with Mick. 'Back? Well, er, no, I can't—'

'You've not split up, then?'

'God no. Well, at least, I don't think we have. Have we?' Pip shrugged and Lottie frowned. 'He's just relocated for now. I think.'

'Relocated?'

'Well lots of people in relationships live in separate houses these days, don't they? Like, like…' She gave up when she couldn't immediately think of anybody.

'Not when they've inherited a country pile and are trying to keep it afloat.'

'Well, I haven't actually inherited it yet, have I?'

'You could have separate wings if he wants his space.'

'I don't think he wants any more space – that's half the problem. Too much. He can't find anything now. Do you know how much time he spent the other day looking for his jacket? And that's something big. And I think he'd quite like a dry bed and hot water, which, to be honest, so would I. Anyhow, I can't move now, can I?' Lottie, who had been cutting carrots into ever-decreasing-sized chunks, pointed at the piece of paper she'd just pinned up in the tack room. 'That's mine.'

Pip stared, screwed her eyes up a bit, tried squinting and then finally admitted defeat. 'What is it? Your latest dressage score?'

'My debt.'

'Your…?' Pip looked at it again. 'All of it? It isn't just two numbers stuck together?' Although even split into two it looked alarming. 'Bloody hell, Lottie! Ever thought of an insurance job? You know, quick splash of something highly inflammable around and a well-placed match?'

'I can't afford that much petrol.'

'True. It's a lot to burn down. Oh, Lots, I'm not being mean, but I'm not surprised Rory got cold feet and ran away.'

'He hasn't even seen that, although he has got cold feet. It's actually colder in the house than it is outside. He actually ran away when he saw the wedding dress.'

'Wedding dress?'

228

'You know, I was trying it on, the one Amanda had got hold of for me. It is gorgeous, all sleek, but I would need to lose my tummy, I suppose, or I'd look like I was pregnant, which I'm not. And I did want to see what Rory thought, then next thing he was out of the window. It's quite high, you know. I don't think he real-ised I'd seen him. He kind of balanced on the balcony bit, then—'

'Lottie, stop.' Lottie stopped. 'Climbed out of the window?'

'Yes, didn't I say that? In his socks and boxers.'

'Why?' This was getting more ludicrous by the second. 'Just because you live here doesn't mean you have to turn eccentric, you know.'

'Mick said—'

'Mick was here too?'

'Well he arrived because Rory had rung him. He said Rory had got cold feet cos he thought it was *the* wedding dress – as in mine, for real.'

'Oh yeah, Mick told me and Todd that Rory had proposed to you.'

'He told you too? But he didn't. I mean propose. Ahh,' the penny dropped, 'that's why you kept asking if we were getting married. You thought?'

'That's what everybody thinks.'

'You mean, I'm the last person to even know about my own wedding?'

Pip laughed. 'Looks like it.'

'I thought maybe Mick had got it wrong when he told me. And Rory didn't actually say that when I spoke to him last night, although,' she paused, 'he was going on about it being too rushed. I thought he meant all the plans, everything, moving in, you know.' She waved a hand around to encompass 'everything'. 'Well I missed it if he did actually propose. But I'd definitely remember if he went down on one knee.'

Pip was still grinning. 'Only you could miss a proposal.'

'I suppose he was the one that suggested the wedding thing.

229

Do you think when he said it he was kind of talking about us in a roundabout way?'

'Well, if people talk about weddings…'

'But I thought he was talking about letting other people get married here. I told him he was a genius for suggesting it.'

'Oh, God you are funny. I bet nobody has ever been called a genius before for proposing. Not exactly the response you expect, is it?'

Lottie stopped frowning and shrugged shamefacedly. 'Oops.'

'Oops, my arse. Oh, Lottie.' She shook her head. 'What are you like? So you're not bothered he's got cold feet? Have you told him it was all a misunderstanding and it's not your actual wedding dress and you didn't actually think he'd proposed?'

'Well, no, not yet. I never realised what he thought. And I never thought I was getting married, so I don't suppose I can be bothered if I'm not now, can I?' Lottie absentmindedly threw a few more bits of carrot into the feed buckets, then stopped when she realised there was more veg than horse nuts. 'I don't know.' She stared across the yard. 'But we'll manage, he'll help me, he said he would. I don't know when he's coming back, though.'

'I don't think Mick is coming back at all.'

'Really, are you sure?' Lottie started chopping again. She was a crap friend. All she'd done was think about herself, Rory and Tipping House. She'd thought Pip and Mick were fine, even though Pip had tried to talk to her about it, and now it was too late. And she was sure that the little that Pip had told her and Sam the other night was only a part of the story. 'It is completely, definitely over?'

'He never actually was mine, we were kidding ourselves. I was. I actually thought I was in love. Me, can you believe that? Even when I told you he wasn't, there was still a tiny bit of me hoping.'

'Oh, Pip, I'm so sorry. Are you sure you're okay?'

'Elizabeth tried to tell me, but I didn't want to hear it.'

'Gran?'

'Yeah, I think she's been reading *Wuthering Heights* again.'

Lottie giggled, despite herself. Then blushed and her fingers went up to touch her lips. He'd kissed her. Or hadn't he? Crumbs, he'd split with Pip and then snogged her, and according to Sam he was still in love with Niamh.

'Anyhow, how can I not be okay when I've got Todd to entertain me? It was time to finish it, so I did.'

'You finished it?' That must make it better – the him-kissing-her bit. Maybe he was feeling hurt about Pip and just wanted, well, needed a kiss.

'Yup, I finished it. I haven't completely lost my marbles, Lottie, unlike you. Why are you cutting even more carrots up?'

'Oops, sorry.'

'It was over, like those veg.' She grinned, but Lottie was still worried.

'But.'

'No buts, unless they belong to sexy men. I'll survive, honest.' She took the knife out of Lottie's hand. 'I did really fancy him, more than anybody I can remember, but he really fancies somebody else. So I guess I need to pull my big-girls' pants on and get on with life. Let's face it, it never was the love affair of the century. More Wallace and Gromit than Wallis and Edward.'

'That's so not true, Pip. He loves you, I know he does.'

'Ah, but he isn't in love with me.'

Lottie pouted and wasn't quite sure what to say next. 'Who does he fancy?' Sam had said he was still mad about Niamh, his ex. But he'd told her ages ago that was all over and that they'd been wrong for each other.

'Later.' Pip stabbed the knife into a carrot with rather more force than she'd intended. She'd done a lot of thinking about Lottie and Mick, but knew he was right. It was all in his head. Nothing to do with Lottie. So she'd forced herself to come here, pretend everything was normal, before a chasm of distrust opened up between them and she ended up losing her best friend as well as her lover. But she had to do it in small doses. Time was up. 'Come on, get

231

feeding those horses. I've got to get over to Rory's and help Tab muck out. You know how hopeless both of them are.'

'Oh, Pip.' Lottie hugged her. 'It'll be okay.'

'It will. Now, where's that bridle – or whatever I'm taking?'

'Oh, that. Well, I think he's actually already got it. It was in the horsebox all the time – which is at his place.'

'Oh, Lottie,' she shook her head, 'God, you two are incredible.'

'I know.' Lottie giggled. 'Good, isn't it? I told Rory I'd ride over later, so I'll see you there, shall I? Oh cripes. Is that the time? Elizabeth usually comes out with the dogs, so I need to sweep up. She hates the yard looking a mess. Dom had it looking like something out of *Country Living*. Oh, shit, I'd better hide my debt in the drawer, too.'

'It's her debt, Lottie, not yours, and I'm pretty sure she knows it down to a penny. If you see her, remind her I'll be over later, will you? I'm taking Todd to entertain her.'

Lottie wasn't entirely sure why her grandmother would find Todd entertaining, but she didn't have time to think about it. Within minutes of Pip leaving the yard, there was a throaty diesel rumble, announcing Mick's arrival.

'I'd forgotten you were coming.'

He raised an eyebrow and turned to open the back of the Land Rover so she could admire his broad back. 'Nice to feel wanted, treas.'

'Pip said you don't love her – you fancy somebody else.' She probably shouldn't have said that.

'Is that a fact?'

'It isn't any of my business, is it?'

'Some things are probably best left.'

'But most things are better sorted out there and then, Charlotte.'

Lottie had been staring so intently at the muscles rippling under Mick's t-shirt as he took his tools out that she hadn't heard Elizabeth arrive. Not that she often did, her grandmother was an expert at arriving unannounced, which meant that she gathered all kinds of information she would have otherwise missed.

Harry whimpered at the sight of the two Labradors and was instantly on his back showing a pink tummy. He was already missing Rory's terriers, and the sight of other canines made him squirm with delight. Holmes gave the pup a shove with his wet nose, which was met with a happy yelp.

'Sort out your problems as you go along, dear, that's what I always say and then you're not leaving a mess in your wake for other people to deal with.'

'Sorry, I was going to sweep up when I'd finished feeding, and then Pip came, and she'd only just gone when—'

'You're right, the yard does need a sweep as well.' Elizabeth switched her gaze from the courtyard to Mick. 'I'm glad you're here. Perfect timing, young man.' Lottie suspected that the perfect timing had been due to her gran, not Mick. 'I understand from young Philippa that you're looking for somewhere to stay.'

'No, I'm no—'

Elizabeth ignored the interruption. 'Now, obviously Charlotte needs a man around here and so at least until Richard comes to his senses I suggest you move above the stables, young man. There's a nice room up there, though it might have the odd cobweb.'

'Gran, what—'

'Well he does need somewhere to sleep, don't you? And he can't sleep in the house. That would be most unacceptable.'

'Well, I…'

'Good, that's settled. Why you youngsters have to make things so complicated these days I don't know – a song and dance about nothing.'

'I can't stay here.' Mick shook his head, face resolute. 'Thank you for the kind offer, though.'

'It's not a kind offer. It just makes sense. You can't sleep on Rory's sofa, you're far too tall. Heaven knows why he's run back there, though, silly man. What did you say to him, Charlotte?'

She tapped her stick on the ground and looked him in the eye. 'Give me one good reason why you can't stay here, Michael? It's the perfect solution.'

Mick opened his mouth, thought better of what he was about to say, which was along the lines of *because I've got a desperate urge to jump your granddaughter*, and shut it again. Elizabeth smiled with satisfaction. 'Exactly. Right that's settled.'

Which didn't reassure him, as now he wasn't sure if she'd mind-read or he'd said something he shouldn't out loud. 'And I do need one of the old metal gates welding, so you can do that when you've finished these horses. Charlotte will pay you, of course.'

'Will I? I mean, I will.'

'And, Charlotte, I really do agree with Amanda that you need to arrive on a horse for your wedding, and that dress does hitch up nicely.' She gave Mick a sly wink. 'Doesn't it?'

'Very nicely.' What else could he do but agree?

'You're doing very well, darling. I'm so proud of you. I can't wait to see you walk down the aisle.'

'But Gran, it's pretend, I'm not actually…'

'Right, I'll be off. Philippa is coming to see me later with that young man of hers – Tom, Rod – whatever his name is.'

'Todd.'

'Ah yes, Todd. What's that short for? Nice young man, he looks like fun. She needs a bit of fun, that girl. Far too serious.' She frowned in Mick's direction. 'Come on, boys.'

Lottie watched open-mouthed as Elizabeth set off back towards the house, the dogs at her heels, and when she glanced at Mick he had his arms folded and a grin on his face.

'Long live the Queen, eh?' He went back to sorting through his tools, found what he was after and straightened up to find Lottie still looking at him.

'She's terrible, isn't she?'

'Terrible.'

'She didn't mean that *you* weren't fun, you know when she said that about Pip, she just says—'

'The first thing that comes into her head?' He smiled. 'That lady says exactly what she means to say, and she isn't wrong.'

'You don't have to do what she says and move in, you know.'

'Would you mind if I did? I quite like it here. Nice scenery.'

'Well, er, no. But when she said cobwebs...'

'A few cobwebs never killed a man. Shall we have a look when we've done the horses?'

Chapter 19

'I can see why your feet brought you back here, treas.' Mick sat on the edge of the fountain in the middle of the courtyard and ruffled the curls on the top of Harry's head.

Lottie squirmed and hoped she didn't look as shameless as the dog. It seemed a long time ago when Mick had told her that she'd been right to come back to Tippermere; that her feet would always take her back to where her heart belonged. Except she'd thought he was talking about Rory, not this place. Or had that just been her – hoping that all along she and Rory would work out, that it wasn't just her infatuation?

She glanced up and the dark gaze was fixed on her, one eyebrow slightly lifted, as though waiting for a comment.

'I do love it.' She looked down at her feet. 'But I never understood why until I came back and Gran explained about Mum and the inheritance and everything. This has always been my favourite place in the whole world, though, right here, in this yard. Even though Mum died here. Is that weird?'

'No, it's not weird. Maybe it was her favourite place too.'

'Would you think I was mad if I married Rory?'

'Not if you love him. Love is a special form of madness that's completely acceptable.'

'Did you ever love Pip?'

'I like Pip a lot. She's very special. And I really do wish I'd fallen in love with her, but, like she said, it's not supposed to be hard work. The falling bit, that is, not the staying bit. Now, are you going to show me the cobwebs? That's if you're sure you don't mind having me as a lodger?'

'I don't mind. As long as you don't mind mending gates for Gran.'

'I'd stay with Rory, but he's got Tab in the groom's flat now.'

'I know.'

'And Pip needs her space.'

'And Gran already seems to have labelled the space here with your name. If she remembers it, that is – your name.' She smiled. 'She'll probably come up with some alternative for you.'

He smiled, the grin lighting his features and sending a look of mischief to his eyes. Pure naughtiness. 'Nick or Dick?'

Lottie led the way across to the tack room, which Amanda had so lovingly tidied, and Rory had already trashed again, and was pleasantly surprised to find that the key hanging above the desk opened the door that led to the groom's flat. She'd never actually been up there. In the old days, when she'd been a child, it had always been kept locked, and it wasn't until many years later that she found out it had been her parents' hideaway.

When they'd had enough of life with Elizabeth they'd spend the afternoon above the stables. Or so Uncle Dom had told her. Her dad, Billy, never mentioned it, and as far as she knew after Alexa, her mother, died, the room had stayed out of bounds to everybody.

She opened the door to find a proper staircase when she'd half expected a ladder or at least open treads, and although there was no carpet, the old oak steps were dust-free, as if they'd been swept only yesterday.

'Do you want me to go up first?'

Mick had noticed her hesitation, but she wasn't worried, just surprised. 'No.' The soft word echoed in the small space, bouncing gently against the old worn wood, the bannister smooth against the palm of her hand felt almost warm, as though a hundred hands had touched and left a trace behind. As she unlocked the door she'd almost felt she was intruding on a past that should have stayed hidden, but with each step her heartbeat slowed and the magic of the stable yard wrapped itself around her.

'Oh.' She stopped abruptly on the last step, Mick's body bumping gently against her in surprise. But she hardly noticed. The room spread out in front of her was small, but flooded with sunlight from the window set into the roof.

'No cobwebs, then?'

'Oh My God, it's beautiful. I think I want to live here.'

She could sense Mick smiling, his breath against her neck sending a rush of goose bumps down her body. 'I'll give you visiting rights.'

'Oh God, look.' On a small table, lit by the beam of sunlight, was a single picture. Her parents. Billy much younger than she'd ever seen him, his grin broad but his stomach flat, his arms wrapped around Alexa. Lottie fought the sudden rush of emotion that sent tears to her eyes, fought the lump that threatened to take her breath away. Her mother was laughing, her head back, a cascade of dark curls over her shoulders, her laughing eyes looking up at Billy. 'She's gorgeous.' It came out as a whisper, and she sensed rather than felt the warm hand that came down on her shoulder.

'She is indeed. Like mother like daughter.'

'I could never be like that.' Alexa looked full of mischief, but something more shone through. A poise that Lottie never felt. Alexa would have made the perfect Lady of the Manor – Lottie didn't come close. And as she studied the picture, the way their bodies matched perfectly, the way their eyes met, Lottie felt a sudden pang, an ache in her chest, so deep that it hurt.

Nobody would ever love her like that. Billy had built this love nest for Alexa, Billy had hung around in the big dusty house, Billy had promised to love her till death had parted them. 'Sorry.' She spun around to find Mick blocking the way. In a panic she dodged around him, blocking the hand he held out. 'Sorry, I've got to go.' And she went, as fast as she could, down the stairs, slipping on the cobbles, finally stopping at the fountain and taking deep steadying breaths, willing herself not to cry.

How could she do this? How could she take on this wonderful place and solve all its problems? She wasn't Alexa. She'd never be perfect. And she'd never have a Billy of her own to make it all worthwhile.

She glanced down to find Harry staring up at her with big, brown doleful eyes, scooped him up and held him close. She needed to walk. A long walk. A walk that was far enough and fast enough to clear her head and take her to a better place.

***

'Todd has got a problem.'

'And so have I, dear, not enough gin. Dominic is such a fusspot, watches my every move. When he's got time to, that is.' Elizabeth sniffed dismissively. 'Pour us all a drink, Philippa, and then we can think straight. He's hidden a bottle in that cupboard. And sit down, Rod, you look uncomfortable towering over me. Here.' She patted the seat next to her. 'You can tell me all about little Tabatha and the bad influence she's been on you.'

Todd chuckled and did as he was told. 'Well, I'd like to say she's a bit of a goer, Liz.'

Pip cringed and waited for a response, which didn't come.

'But I reckon she's never had a proper boyfriend, she's a real softy underneath all that spit and snarl. A real cute kitten, that one.'

'Cute?' Pip raised an eyebrow and didn't miss the little smile from Elizabeth.

'Aw, come on, give the kid a break, Pips, you know she's a good one. Come on, admit it, you like her.'

'I do.' Pip poured gin, wondering how little she could get away with.

'If you can't pour a proper measure I'll get a man to do it, Philippa.'

She poured a bit more. 'I get on with her fine. It's not a secret. But she's growing up, and we've all noticed the way she follows Rory around, and how, er, impressed she was with your riding.'

Todd laughed, loudly.

'Her dad's going to have a heart attack soon.'

'Only because she's like her mother and he know *exactly* what Tamara was like at that age.' Elizabeth's tone was dry. 'He was on the receiving end.'

Todd, who had been slightly overawed when they'd been shown into the large drawing room, felt his spine relax another notch. And a swig of one of Pip's G&T's, once he'd got over the initial splutter, made him feel as if he could do this any day of the week.

'Christ, that's got a kick.'

'No good if you can't taste the gin, young man.'

'Drowns the taste of the tonic.' Pip kept her voice low, but it carried clearly to Elizabeth.

'Tonic is fine in small doses, but it kills the flavour of everything. So, what have you come to chat about?'

Clearly the pleasantries were over. But Pip was used to Elizabeth and her imperious tone. She knew full well that they weren't a bother. In fact, they probably wouldn't be allowed to leave until Elizabeth's curiosity had been satisfied.

'Todd is looking for his brother's father. He's got a love letter.' She nodded at Todd, who grinned. He could see why this pair got on, they were two of a kind.

'We found a pile of these after Mum died and I promised Greg I'd try and find this guy.'

'And your brother couldn't come over himself?'

'Well, I was here anyway to sort out the divorce, and see Lottie,

240

of course.' Todd paused. 'And Greg's not up to it.' He took another swig of the drink. 'He's ill. If I don't get him an answer soon it could be too late.'

Pip opened her mouth, then closed it, and stared at Todd in astonishment. It had all been delivered in such a matter-of-fact tone that she could have got it wrong. Misunderstood. But one look at the hand holding the letter told her she hadn't. The tremor was only slight, but Todd normally had a steady hand. A very steady hand.

'Your mother was English?' Elizabeth took the mention of death in her stride.

'No, I think she worked over here for a while. She was an artist – liked to travel for inspiration.'

'And it looks like she got it.'

'Got more than she reckoned on, from the sound of these letters.' He nodded at the one that Elizabeth had taken from him. 'Signed himself Will, as far as I can tell – the handwriting's terrible.'

'Will?' Pip, who had recovered her power of speech shot upright. 'Will? Why didn't you say? Oh God, it can't be Billy? Lottie will die, but he was terrible, he—'

'Philippa.' Elizabeth's voice, firm and authoritative despite her age, rang out and stopped Pip dead. 'William liked to have fun, as so many young people do.' She looked pointedly at Todd and then Pip. 'But he was not terrible. There isn't a single shred of evidence that he was ever less than one hundred per cent faithful when he was married to Alexandra.'

For the second time in a few minutes Pip found herself speechless.

'Just because a man is photographed with his clothes off does not mean he's been fathering illegitimate children.'

'Well somebody has.' Pip said reasonably.

'Indeed. You need,' Elizabeth slowly and carefully refolded the letter and handed it back to Todd, 'to talk to Victoria.'

'Victoria?' Pip was confused.

'Tiggy, dear.'

'What's this got to do with Tiggy? I thought you just said that Billy didn't go…'

'This is a different William, this is Will. Totally different, a womaniser if ever there was one. I was glad when he left the village. The man never did fit in here.'

'Who? Who was he?'

'Ask Tiggy. So are you planning on leaving once you've spoken to her, then, young man?'

'Well, I hadn't got any firm plans.'

'You should take Philippa with you, she's getting stifled here, aren't you? Tippermere isn't the place for you if you're frightened of horses.'

'I'm not—'

'All people talk about, apart from shooting and bridge, of course.'

'Sam doesn't talk about horses.'

'That's different. One more drink, I think, then I really must get on. Lottie is having supper with me so that we can have a little chat about how things are going.'

'Does she know she's having supper with you yet?' Pip tried to ignore Todd's grin.

'I doubt it, dear, but she's not doing anything else now that Robert has run back home.'

'Rory.'

'He's such a nice man, but so disorganised. I can see the attraction, I suppose, and he does have rather fine legs – like a lot of horsemen.'

'Elizabeth.' Pip laughed, despite herself. 'And when have you seen his legs?'

'When he was climbing down the drainpipe, dear. Very nearly lost his pants, snagged on the downpipe. Now that would have been entertaining. I doubt he has the staying power, though. Men like him are so easily distracted. Such a waste.'

Todd spluttered into his gin and Pip sighed. 'You're being

naughty now.'

'Well, why do you think gardeners have always been popular? Staying power, that's what. Lady Chatterley's lover wasn't the figment of somebody's imagination.'

'Yes, he was.'

'The inspiration had to come from somewhere. I think with Ronald, though, it's probably just a case of zero powers of concentration.'

'Rory. You know he's called Rory. You made them move in here on purpose, didn't you? You knew he'd crack.'

'I don't know what you're talking about. It was Dominic's suggestion, if you remember, and I went along with it.'

'You never go along with anything that isn't your idea in the first place.' Pip grinned. 'You are so bad.'

'And you, my dear, should take a trip to Australia with somebody reckless and fit.' She looked at Todd. 'I'm sure you can, what do they say? Ride the waves?'

'Whatever you say.'

'A change of scenery will do you good, and then you can come back and tell me all about it. You can let yourselves out, can't you? I need to rest my eyes before supper.' She shut her eyes, as though to demonstrate the point and Pip, with a shake of her head, stood up. 'And let me know what Victoria has to say, won't you? And,' Pip paused at the door, 'don't upset her. She's a nice girl and William seems very content. We don't want any unpleasantness, do we? Not on top of all this other business.'

'Right, we won't.' Pip, who hadn't got a clue what she was talking about, pulled Todd from the room and shut the door quietly behind them.

'So, do you fancy coming with me when I go home?'

'For a holiday?'

'Whatever. Could be a laugh.'

'I've got to help Lottie sort her Wedding Fayre out first.'

'Sure you want to stay and watch her get married?'

'It's only a fake wedding.'

'Sure. We'll go straight after, then. So, where do we find this Vicky, then?'

'Tiggy. God, you're as bad as Elizabeth.' She rolled her eyes and tried to ignore the fluttering of unease in the pit of her stomach. 'Nobody calls her Victoria. We'll go tomorrow morning when Billy's exercising the horses.'

'Fancy going out and getting slaughtered?'

'You and me?'

'Yeah, no strings, no sex, just enough drinks to put the world to rights.'

'And fish and chips.'

'You've got some weird ideas.'

'Steak pudding and chips?'

'You do know the way to this man's heart is definitely not through his stomach? You have to shoot a bit lower.'

'I do, so it's perfect, seeing as I don't want to find the way to your heart.'

'What about any other bits?'

'Dream on, Todd.'

'I know you're tempted.'

'What have you been doing with Tab, if she's such an innocent?'

'Educating her.' He grinned.

'I was afraid you'd say that.'

'She's a blank canvas, an empty vessel, virgin territory.'

'Stop it.'

'Uncharted waters, an enquiring mind, thirsty for knowledge.'

'If you don't shut up I'm going to push you in the lake.' Pip glanced over towards the stable block and wondered if Lottie was still with the horses. Wondered if Rory had left a gap, in the same way that Mick had left a hole in her life.

'Don't.' Todd took her hand, gave a gentle tug. 'Stop over-thinking it.'

'She can't marry Rory, can she?'

244

'I don't think she ever meant to, darling. It was just everybody else that assumed she would.' He shrugged. 'Maybe she's not ready.'

'I thought we were all getting our lives sorted, all moving on, but nothing's changed.'

'Lots has changed, I reckon, from what you guys have told me, but not in the way you thought it would. Life's like that.' He shrugged. 'Who'd have thought we'd be standing here now? Things just happen and you either go with it or stress yourself out.'

'Who'd have thought, indeed? So what are we doing standing here now? What the hell are you doing in Tippermere, Todd? You and Lottie didn't just happen. A bloody coincidence that you meet her, and then end up coming to the very same tiny village she lives in to look for your brother's dad.'

Todd let go of her hand and stared across at the lake, putting his hands in his pockets. 'Okay.' He seemed to have come to a decision. 'Up front. My brother spotted Lottie's name in a local paper. He'd been researching on the internet about this place, trying to track down his pa, and if you put the name Will into Google with Cheshire, then out pops Brinkley, doesn't it? Old Billy is one of the most famous names in the county, isn't he? Greg was so flaming excited, it was the first lead he'd had and he was too ill to come traipsing over here, so he couldn't believe his luck. This report said she was visiting Australia, so he rang up every hotel, every surf school, every bar until he tracked her name down at the surf school, which I tell you was bloody miles away. A right trip-and-a-half in my vacation.'

'So you targeted her?'

'I'm not a bloody private eye. We jumped to the same conclusion you just did, had this mad idea that the Will in the letter could be Billy, but I wasn't going to just barge in and say come and meet your step-brother was I?'

'Considerate.'

'I didn't go in with the intention of chatting her up, I thought she'd be some long- nosed, posh horsey type, so I drove over with the crazy idea of introducing myself, having a bit of a dig to sort some facts and then explain. I promised him I would. Not much to do for your brother is it? But I knew the moment I talked to her that her dad couldn't be the right guy. Real bummer.' His voice had dropped, lost its normal buzz. 'None of the dates worked, nothing. There was just no way Mum could have met him. So I kind of forgot about it, but I didn't want to forget her. She was cool. We just clicked straight away. We got on. She's fun.'

'So that was supposed to be that?'

'The girl needed a break, she was seriously wound up about life and her guy Rory. Thought nobody really loved her or wanted her, and she didn't know what to do in life. I thought we could have a good time for a couple of months, chill, and I'd half got it in mind to come back here with her after Spain and ask if she'd help me. But then, as you know, things got a bit out of control.' He turned back to face Pip. 'But I promised Greg I'd try and find something out, so once I'd got the divorce sorted I thought I'd risk Lottie kicking me from here to kingdom come and stop off.'

'Lottie isn't the kicking type. So why didn't you ask her?'

'Well, this might sound stupid, but I thought there was still that tiny outside chance that it was her Dad. How could I do that to her? So I reckoned I'd ask you.'

'So that's everything this time?'

'Unless you want my dental records.'

'I'll only need those if your body needs identifying. Right, let's go and get slaughtered, then.'

'I did like Lottie, you know, that's the only reason I chatted her up, no ulterior motive. She's sweet. Honest.'

'Everybody likes Lottie, including Mick. And right now, that's not helping me. Is that mean?'

He draped an arm around her shoulder. 'Come back to Oz with me. I'll show you "mean". As in mean surf, a mean steak...' He grinned. 'The world is your mean oyster.'

Chapter 20

'Christ, sorry.' Pip, who had wandered into the tack room to find a pitchfork, shut the door hastily at the sight of the couple in a clinch. Then opened it again just as quick as she realised who they were.

'What the fuck are you two doing?'

Todd grinned. 'Didn't think I'd need to explain that to you, of all people, Pippy.'

'Don't call me Pippy and put her down. You can't do that with her, she's, she's...'

'All grown up from where I'm standing.' He had let go, though, which was a minor point in his favour, she reckoned. 'Stop being a bloody spoil sport, she's over the age of consent.' He frowned. 'Aren't you?'

Tab scowled, and aimed her best glare in Pip's direction. 'I thought you were my friend, not my mother. What is it with you lot? Aren't I allowed to have any fun?' The arms were folded. 'Actually my Mum wouldn't be so stuffy. I'm not a kid, you know.'

'Your dad still thinks you are.'

'Oh stuff Tom. He's only grumpy cos he isn't getting any at the moment. Even you ditched him because he's so fucking boring.'

'He isn't boring, and don't swear, and I didn't ditch him, we weren't...' Pip shot a glance at Todd, who looked as though he was enjoying himself immensely.

'Fucking? You were, I heard you.' Tab did a good imitation of the type of noises Pip had been known to make just before she came.

Todd laughed.

'And you can shut up.' Tab rolled her eyes, gave Todd a prod in the chest and then straightening her t-shirt as she went and pushed her way past Pip, who had been effectively blocking the exit.

Todd held his hands up in mock surrender. 'She jumped me, honest. What can a man do? It would have been rude to push her away. I reckon she's frustrated and horny cos she can't get—' He never got to say what Tabatha couldn't get, because there was a shriek of dismay from the yard.

'Oh sheet! Nooooo! Come here,' they both rushed to the door, colliding against the door frame, 'they're my best ones, you little sod.'

Tilly the terrier was standing yards away, her head high and something pink dangling from her mouth, her small body coiled and ready to take off the moment Tab made a move. Tab jumped forward, Tilly dashed off, muffled yaps coming through the scrap of material.

'Her best?'

'Knickers, I'd say.'

'And I bet you're an expert.' Pip tried to look stern. 'Did you take those off?'

'No way, I never unwrapped. I think she left them dangling somewhere for Rory to find. She's seriously got the hots for that man.'

'Come here, you little shit.'

'Language, Tabatha!' Todd's voice rang out clearly across the yard, but Tab didn't care, she was scrambling over the fence into the paddock as Tilly shot under it. A horse, which has been watching the proceedings quietly, took alarm at the invasion into its field and spun around, kicked its heels into the air, then shot off across the grass, his tail high. Tilly, by now in the middle of the field, lay down, dropping her prey, her tongue lolling from her mouth.

Tab started to stalk, her voice soft, wheedling as she edged closer. Tilly pawed.

'It's never going to work.' Pip shook her head.

One step closer – another – Tab could almost sense victory. 'Nice dog, good Tilly.' Tilly slowly shifted position, wriggling forward, her back end going up, her tail a slow pendulum of a wag and her mouth edging closer to the knickers as the anticipation of a chase rippled through her muscled-up body. Tab took a step, Tilly leaned in, her dark gaze never leaving the girl as her white teeth snatched at the lacy edging. The final leap was the mistake. Tab never got close as Tilly, grabbing her prize, took off back towards the fence, shaking the knickers in delight as she jumped onto the edge of the water trough, her cat-like paws curling as she balanced.

'Knickers like that deserve to see some action.' Pip giggled.

Tilly shook them like she'd shake a rat.

'Well, they're seeing some now, though probably not what Tab had in mind.'

'This is so unfair. Come back you bugger.' Tab, forgetting her previous strategy, hurtled across the field towards the dog, who dipped her head into the trough.

'She's drowning them.' Pip laughed as the knickers resurfaced and were plunged back into the water, the little dog growling as she did it.

'Stop laughing, you sods.'

'Did I miss something?' The sound of Rory's voice sent Tab the same colour as her poor distressed undergarments and sent Pip slithering to the floor, clutching her stomach, which was just when Tab, sensing that Tilly had been distracted by her master's voice, made a final lunge and managed to grab one end of her by now sopping knickers.

Tilly hung on.

Tab pulled.

Pip cringed, waiting for the inevitable sound of tearing.

The little dog, now on the floor, one eye fixed on Rory, kept her jaws firmly locked.

'She'll fight to the death, you know, never lets go.' Rory was grinning. 'I've lifted her clean off the floor before now when she's had one of my boots.'

'I think they're already dead.' Pip keeled over completely.

'Sopping for the wrong reasons, mate.' And Todd's contribution didn't help at all.

'Do something.' The wail was so far from Tab's normal fighting talk that it stopped them all dead, the last of the giggles dying away into nothing, the only sound that broke the silence being Tilly's snuffles and growls as she fought to get her trophy back, digging her back feet in and leaning back as far as she could go.

Rory clicked his fingers and the dog, with a yelp, did the very opposite of what Tab expected. She stepped forward, twisted her little body, taking off in a new direction and snatching the satin from the tips of Tabatha's fingers, set off at a proud trot towards Rory, head held high for all to see.

'Oh, shit.' Tab, who had been kneeling on the ground, sank down face first and kicked her feet with embarrassment.

'Who's a clever little girl, then?' Tilly, squirming with pleasure at Rory's feet, finally loosened her grip on her prey, licking her lips as she glanced adoringly up. There was nothing that Tilly liked more than her master's approval, and she could tell he was pleased. Rory grinned as he dangled the soggy scrap from one finger.

'I think Tab wanted to give them to you herself, actually, mate.'

Tab, who had recovered and moved with remarkable speed across to where they stood in the yard, scowled. 'Give them back.'

'Please?' He laughed.

'Rory.' She made to grab them, but Rory was too quick, shoving them deep into his pocket as Tilly jumped up and down barking, then leapt into his arms and smothered him with doggy kisses.

'I think she wanted to do that as well.'

'Todd stop being mean.' Pip punched him, suddenly feeling a twinge of guilt.

'You lot are so immature.' And with that parting comment Tabatha stalked off towards the tack room.

'Poor Tab, she's infatuated with you, Rory, and you're just so mean.' Pip didn't know whether to laugh or scold.

'I thought she was in love with Todd. He's the hero on horseback isn't he, rescuing the damsel in distress?' Rory had a look on his face that said he still hadn't quite forgiven Todd.

'But you're the real thing.' Pip shook her head. 'Well, in her eyes anyway, personally speaking I happen to think you're a bit of an idiot.'

'Seems to be a common feeling between you and your boyfriend.'

'Mick is not my boyfriend.'

'Really? That probably explains why he's even more grumpy than normal, then, not getting enough.' Rory grinned, unperturbed and fished Tab's underwear from his pocket. 'I suppose I better give these back or I'll be in trouble with Lottie as well.' And whistling the dogs up, he set off after Tab.

Todd watched thoughtfully. 'She jumped me in the tack room to make him jealous.'

'How do you know?' Pip, who knew that it was highly likely, as Tab had been after Rory since the day she'd set foot in Tippermere, watched as Rory disappeared from view. 'She was giving you the eye the day you arrived.'

He grinned, unconcerned. 'I was just a passing fancy.'

'I know that feeling.' Pip sighed and shook her head as the giggles started in the tack room.

'Doesn't Lottie mind?'

'He's always been like that, flirting.' Pip shrugged. 'Women are always throwing themselves at him, his groupies. That's why Lottie left this place, then she came back and he declared his…'

'Undying love?'

'Well, I'm not sure about that – undying lust, more like.'

'But he proposed, didn't he?'

'I'm not sure he meant to. I reckon that when she got so excited about him mentioning weddings, he thought that Lottie thought he'd proposed, if you see what I mean. So he just went along with it. Anything for an easy life.'

Todd gave a low whistle. 'Even getting married? The guy's mental. Reckon she actually loves him?'

'Lottie adores him, she has done since she was a teenager, she's nearly as bad as Tilly. As long as she gets a pat on the head she's happy, or she was. I'm not sure now.' Pip withdrew her gaze from the tack-room door and looked at Todd. 'I think taking on her inheritance might actually be the making of her, you know. There's finally something more important in her life than horses and Rory.'

'A girl with a mission.'

'Yeah. And he doesn't like it, which is why he's back here. Rory likes to be the centre of attention.'

'And what's your mission, Pip?'

'Sorting out your life. Come on, let's go and see what Tiggy has to say about your letter.'

***

'Of course I'll help you, ask away.' Tiggy, resplendent in the type of flowery cotton smock that Pip thought had gone out of fashion in the late sixties, stuck her bunch of flowers in an old jug and tucked her hair behind her ear. 'Come in, come in, do you want a cup of tea? Oh, I do love a mystery.' She beamed at Todd, who thought any second now he was going to get a hug. 'Oh dear, hang on a sec, I think that's the phone.' She looked around the kitchen for inspiration. 'Wherever did I put it? Oh, here it is, hang on, no not you, dear, I was talking to Pip, and,' she looked at Todd.

'Todd.'

'Todd. Was I?' She rearranged the flowers, Billy's voice carrying

252

loud and clear as he shouted over the phone, obviously annoyed and trying not to show it too much. 'Oh dear, oh never mind I'm sure he'll come later, he's so good. Don't worry, love, I'll sort it. You do the horses. What? Of course I know you need the feed. But you can make do just for now, can't you? Share it out?' There was another outburst at the other end. 'More hay and carrots?' She said it hopefully and then blowing a kiss rang off before he could say anything else. 'I'm sure it's not good for his blood pressure – all this shouting. I forgot I was supposed to order some horse food for today.' Tiggy forgot all kinds of things and lists were a waste of time. She forgot she'd written them. The fact that Billy, who ran his yard with military precision, put up with it was a constant surprise to his daughter, Lottie, and indeed everybody who knew him. But Tiggy adored him with such openness and forgave his grumpiness with such good humour that he found it hard to stay angry for long. She just wanted to look after him, and had done it in her dogged fashion from the day he'd returned to competition after his wife, Alexa, had so tragically died.

Everybody else had been wary of the volatile Billy that had emerged from grief, but Tiggy had known that the old Billy would return, the Billy whose bark was far worse than his bite. She loved his gruff nature and his stout body with all her heart and when he'd asked her to marry him her life had been completed. Looking after Billy was why she was there, and she had no qualms about helping out with the horses (even though she often forgot which stables to put them in), and she understood that the grand passion he'd had for Alexa would never fade. She accepted that she just wanted him to be happy. And he was, with her, even if at times she frustrated the hell out of him.

'Do you want to order the horse feed now, before you forget?'

'Oh no, Pip dear, it'll wait. I'm sure he's exaggerating, men do that, you know.' She winked at Todd. 'Right, where were we?'

'Elizabeth thought you might know who wrote this.' Pip took the letter from Todd and laid it flat on the table, smoothing it out. She'd never really appreciated the phrase 'hear a pin drop' until then. The whole room seemed to quieten and an unsettling stillness came over Tiggy. She didn't move a muscle.

'Where did you get this?' The happy edge that always rang out in Tiggy's voice had gone, and Pip felt guiltier than she could ever remember. She went to refold the paper, but Tiggy's hand came over hers, stopping her.

'I'm sorry, we...'

'It was my mother's.' Todd looked from Tiggy to Pip and back again. So Elizabeth had known, this hadn't just been a random guess. Pip was right, the old woman knew everything.

'Your mother's.' It was a statement, not a question, and Tiggy looked up, her gaze searching as she studied Todd properly, as if seeing him for the first time. 'I bet she's pretty isn't she?'

'She was. She died.'

'I'm sorry.' The brief flicker that was the closest Tiggy got to anger dissipated and was replaced with what had to be disappointment. 'Pretty and blond, like you?' She didn't wait for an answer. 'He did like delicate blonds. Slim and pretty, nicely made up, not at all like me.'

'Who did, Tiggy?'

'Oh sorry, didn't I say?' Tiggy turned to look at Pip.

'It's from Billy?' Pip hadn't want to say it, but the look on Tiggy's face, there was only one person Tiggy loved, who could do this to her... Elizabeth must have been wrong, it had to be Billy Brinkley.

'Oh gracious no.' She gave a short, fond laugh. 'Don't be silly, this isn't from my Billy. I'm sure Elizabeth told you that.' Pip breathed again. 'This letter is from Will.'

'Will?'

'Will is my ex-husband.'

Pip didn't need to ask if she was sure.

'I'd recognise that writing anywhere, and the poetic turn of phrase. He did love his words, did Will. In fact I think most of the fun for him was the chase, the wooing, not the bedding. He was terrible in bed. At first I thought it was because I was young, then I thought it was all my fault and I wasn't attractive enough.' She gave a sad smile. 'I mean I *wasn't* attractive enough, I do know that, but it just wasn't his forte – the whole touching thing.' She folded the letter up, with a slightly shaking hand, and passed it back to Todd. 'I don't know where he is these days, dear. We lost touch. In fact, we never real were in touch, he really was on a different planet. He ran off with his editor, you know, a very attractive young man, which made it easier in a way.'

'A man?' Pip, who was not often surprised, was shocked. She'd heard tales of Tiggy's author husband leaving her to run off with his editor, but had assumed that it was a woman.

'Oh yes. I don't think he particularly liked women. I mean, he had so many affairs I lost count, but he did like to impress, prove he could have whatever he wanted. And it was so unfashionable to be gay when we were young, it wasn't the done thing at all, not like it is now.' Tiggy's voice had strengthened with every word, and Pip was relieved that she'd recovered. Although it was obvious that the hurt had run deep, however lightly she spoke.

Love was like that, easy to dismiss on the surface, but impossible to remove the mark it had left deep down. Words just covered the wounds, like sticking plasters, until somebody came along and ripped them off.

'You're telling me that I've been running around like a blue-arsed fly to find the man, and all along Greg's dad is gay?'

'You've not been running like a blue-arsed fly,' said Pip reasonably, 'for one they don't run, and for another you've not exactly been scouring the country have you? Not even the county.'

'He's gay, you want me to go home and tell my brother on his death bed that all these words were just flannel and Mum was unfaithful with some bloke who just liked writing poncy letters and shagging blondes?' He suddenly saw the look on Pip's face. 'Sorry, Vic, er Tiggy. No offence meant, it's just a bit of a shock and all.'

'Your brother?' Tiggy frowned. 'Oh no, dear. Will can't be his father, he's infertile. He couldn't leave a child behind so he was determined to leave a legacy in his words, that's what drove him on with his writing I think. What on earth made you think he was your brother's father?'

'But the letters. There's a whole bloody pile of letters.'

'Oh I'm sure they had an affair, I could paper the house with love letters he sent to other women when we were together, so much purple prose and to think that's why I fell for him. Girls can be so silly can't they?' She looked at Pip who wasn't quite sure if the remark was aimed at her, or a general statement. 'I do love a nice romance though, makes you all warm inside doesn't it? And a knight on a charger to rescue the damsel.' She giggled at Todd.

'Sorry about that.' He didn't look sorry. 'Looks like I got that one wrong too.'

'You did look rather dashing. No wonder Rory and Mick got in a tizzy.'

'Mick?' Pip looked at Tiggy.

'Well all the men did, dear. I mean, it was just like in the films, wasn't it?'

'Bad rom-coms.' Pip's tone had an edge. The remark about Mick brushed her up the wrong way. She would have given anything for him not to have been bothered about Todd riding in to rescue Lottie, but he had been. And it explained why he'd been so out of sorts at the wedding. But that was all old news – and she hated old, tired news.

'Sorry about all this, Tiggy. I didn't mean to bring back bad memories.'

'It's okay. It was just a bit of a shock seeing one of his letters again. And I am sorry to disappoint you, dear,' she patted Todd's hand, 'you came all this way for nothing.'

'So who is his dad? Mine buggered off well before Greg was born.'

'I can't help you with that. Are you sure you wouldn't like a cup of tea, love?'

Todd closed his eyes and very gently lay his forehead down on the table.

'Will did like Australia. He used to go off on his little book tours and they all thought he was a famous author. Well, he did tell them that, and how were they to know any different? He didn't like it here – all damp and cold and no adoration. I really try not to think about him, though, not a nice man. Here, I'll write his name down for you and you can get in touch if you want and see if he knows anything. Although he'll probably just send you his autograph. He thinks everybody is a fan.' Tiggy scribbled on a scrap of paper and handed it to Todd. 'Now, was I supposed to be doing something?'

'Horse feed?'

'Ah, yes, and I did promise Billy I'd put the washing on.' She grinned. 'He had to go commando this morning, his knicker drawer was empty.'

Chapter 21

'Sorry about the mess.'

'I'm sorry, I should have texted and let you know I was coming.' Lottie looked around but couldn't see anything that remotely resembled mess. 'I just called in to drop off some horse nuts for Dad and thought I'd come and say hi on the way.'

'Oh, don't be silly, I'm so pleased you're here.' Amanda had never felt so pleased to see anybody in her life. Living in the gorgeous Folly Lake Manor had been a dream come true, but since her enforced rest she'd felt isolated. And now she was feeling better, and not rushing to the bathroom every five minutes to be sick, she'd started to feel trapped. True, she had now been able to start to turn the Wedding Fayre plans into reality, but her life hadn't really got back to normal yet.

She'd watched the dust cloud that announced a visitor moving closer to the house and was pretty sure that even if it had been a double-glazing salesmen (not that she had anything against them per se, but one had to be very careful with how one maintained a place like Folly Lake Manor), she would have grabbed him and made him stay for a cup of tea. 'To be honest,' she lowered her voice conspiratorially, 'I'm a bit bored.' She straightened a cushion (did a cushion at the wrong angle count as a mess, wondered Lottie?) and smiled. 'Dominic is being a bit over-protective. He wants me to take things easy and frowns at me if he catches me with so much as a duster in my hand. You know what he's like.' Lottie didn't. She'd never known her Uncle Dom to be protective of anything, apart from his horses, until he'd met and married Amanda.

'You're feeling okay now?' Lottie didn't mind the dogs puking on the carpet, or blood pouring out of a horse's knee, but people being ill made her feel queasy.

'I'm fine now.' Amanda beamed and patted her stomach. Even after a few horrendous months of sickness, she looked the picture of serenity and control.

'You should be looking after Tipping House, not me. You'd make a perfect Ladyship. I'm crap at it.' Lottie slumped onto the sofa, then remembered the cushions and sat up again. 'All the stuff you've done for the Wedding Fayre is brilliant. I wouldn't have known where to start.'

'Don't be silly, you've done everything – and come up with that fabulous idea. All I've done is ring a few people, like you asked. That's your home, Lottie, and you love it, don't you? I know you do, and you'll make a wonderful job of looking after it. I'd never know what to do, apart from fill in spreadsheets.'

'But you're so calm and organised.'

'And you're so brilliant and passionate.'

'And even Rory's left and gone back to his yard.'

'I heard.'

'Does everybody know?' Lottie chewed the inside of her cheek and looked at Amanda, who nodded. 'He just needed a break. He said I needed to lighten up and all I ever talked about was what we had to do. He said I don't even help him with the horses as much now and he missed me. And he didn't think he wanted to get married any more, and I'd been rushing into it just to please Gran.' She drew a breath. 'But I didn't even know he thought we were getting married. I was just rushing into doing the pretend wedding.'

'You don't need to get married, though, do you? Did you really want to?' Amanda sounded worried.

'I don't need to, no. I don't know why he said that.' Lottie gave up on trying to keep the cushions tidy and sank back. 'And I never said I wanted to, did I?'

'Not to me, you didn't. Poor Rory, he does get himself in a mess, doesn't he? Come on, I want to show you something upstairs.' Amanda, Lottie decided, was somebody she'd normally be jealous of. She was so together, so – perfect. She sat with her knees together (like a lady should), walked properly, didn't squash cushions, only said polite swear words (if there was such a thing) and was perfectly made-up even though she hadn't been expecting anybody to call round. But she was also very nice, and kind. Like a tidier and more organised version of Tiggy.

'Ta da.'

'Wow.' Lottie followed through the open doorway and it hit her. Amanda was going to have a baby. Okay, she'd known she was pregnant, but the reality of it hadn't hit her until now. When she saw the nursery laid out with everything a new-born might need. 'It's gorgeous.' And it was. Although everything Amanda did was – she had the type of taste that people paid vast amounts of money for. 'Oh my God, I had one like that.' Lottie smiled as she spotted the little rocking horse in the corner of the room.

'You do like it? Really?'

'Really.' Lottie hugged her friend. 'I've not seen enough of you lately, but I am so pleased, you know. I am sorry, Rory's right, I haven't had time for anybody and all I talk about is the house.'

'You've been busy, and I've been puking.' Amanda pulled a face. 'But now I'm better we can party. Well not exactly party, but you know. And Rory isn't right, although you do need to make sure you find time to get away and ride the horses. I mean, you know they're not my thing,' she grinned. Lottie knew. Amanda had come to her for riding lessons so that she could share Dom's interest. But she was terrified of horses and gave up the moment he told her he didn't care if she ever sat on a horse again or not. 'But they are your thing, you've got to do something just for yourself. And by that I don't mean for Rory.'

'Oh.'

'Lottie, he's big enough to look after himself, in fact he's big enough to be looking after a baby and you as well, but can you imagine?'

Lottie couldn't. She giggled. 'He's good at looking after Tilly. Oh, this is wonderful Amanda, but I still can't believe you're having a baby.'

'Nor can I. And it's going to be your cousin, isn't that weird?'

'Very. Amanda,' she played with the edge of the blanket that was draped over the crib, 'does Uncle Dom mind about Tipping House? You know, that I'm inheriting it, not him?'

'No.' The reply was soft but definite. 'Dominic never expected to inherit. He just wanted to help Elizabeth out until you were ready. It never was his and, to be honest, I think the thought of having to run it petrified him.'

'Uncle Dom isn't petrified of anything.'

'He is of failing. He likes to be in control, to know he can succeed and Tipping House isn't like that. It needs somebody like you, somebody who can let it be what it is, can accept it will never be perfect. If things don't go quite right you'll forgive them, Lottie, Dominic would find that very hard.' She smiled fondly. 'He'd kill himself worrying about every little detail, and there are far too many little details in that place.'

'I like it how it is. I like the shabby bits.'

'I know, and so does Dominic. We all know you can do it, Lottie. You and Tipping House Estate will be perfect together, just as Elizabeth was perfect, and so was your mother.'

'Dad wasn't too keen.'

'But he was willing to support her.'

'What if my idea doesn't work? What if nobody wants to get married here?'

'Then you'll think of something else. Won't you? Let's go down, I want to show you what me and Sam have done, the details we put together after we met up the other day.' She smiled. 'Reptile Man is actually very good at his job, he sorted out all the speakers and lights.'

'Sam hasn't gone mad, has she?' Lottie bit the inside of her lip slightly too hard with worry and winced. 'She's not made any little additions of her own, has she? No topless waiters or chocolate fountains. I have nightmares about a strobe-lit red carpet with a karaoke stage and Scruffy being guest of honour in his diamante collar.'

'Diamond.' Amanda giggled. 'It's tasteful. Honest.'

'Gran says I should arrive on a horse.'

'We've added that in too, Lady Godiva.'

'I'm not doing it naked.' She stopped dead in her tracks and Amanda cannoned into her. 'No, no way.'

'Joke, Lottie, it was a joke. Did you like the dress I found? You never said.'

Oh yes, the last time she'd chatted to Sam and Amanda she'd taken the wedding gown that Amanda had found for her, taken it up to try on. Shocked Rory to the extent that he'd jumped out of the window, and…. She'd kissed Mick. Her whole body heated up.

'Are you sure I want to do this?'

'Yes, you definitely want to do this.' Amanda gave her a friendly shove. 'Downstairs, let me show you what we've done. Sam is seriously good at this, you know, once you bring her down to earth. She is so driven, and she knows so many people. What Samantha wants, Samantha gets.'

Much as Lottie trusted Amanda and her impeccable taste, the thought of Sam wanting and getting scared her to death.

'And I'm not arriving by parachute.'

'Impossible in a wedding dress. I promise we haven't changed your plan at all. All we've done is finalise a few bookings, like you asked us to. And put it all in a nice, simple spreadsheet so you can see where we're up to.'

'And I am not pretending to marry a footballer.'

'No, we're leaving the choice of groom entirely up to you, Lottie.'

'Or wearing those six-inch heels again.'

'Okay.'

'Or letting her dog be my bridesmaid.'

'Lottie trust me. Okay?'

***

Lottie took one look at the sheet of paper and burst into tears.

'Oh no, you hate it.'

'I,' she picked the sheet up, crumpling it to her, 'I think, oh God, now I've made a mess of it,' she put it back down quickly and ran a shaky hand over it, which added new wrinkles, 'sorry.'

'Forget the paper, it's me that should be sorry. Don't cry, please don't cry, we'll sort it. I thought that was what you wanted us to do, but—'

'Oh Amanda, you're incredible.' Which was all she managed to say through her tears and splutters.

'Oh, Lottie, are you okay? Here, have a tissue.'

'Great,' sniffle. 'I'm so happy.' Sob. 'I really am.' She snuffled into Amanda's arms. 'Don't do it again.'

'No, we will.'

'No, I mean don't. I don't want you to. I love it, it's brilliant.' She looked up and took a deep steadying breath and said it again in case the first time hadn't come out properly. 'I love it. They're happy tears.' But they weren't exactly happy tears – it was more pure relief.

She'd laughed off the fact that Rory had gone (mainly because the way he'd done it had been funny) and not thought for one moment they wouldn't work it out somehow between them. Until Gran had told her she needed a man about the place and nominated Mick. Which kind of meant Gran didn't expect Rory back any day soon. But she'd managed to stick her head in the sand and ignore that.

She'd stuck her debt up in the tack room because it was amazing, not sobering, and she wanted a goal. Then Pip had been speechless, which was quite an achievement and meant it really was as scary as she'd known deep down.

And she'd thrown herself into the 'save the mansion' project because, well, she had to, and it would be fun. But as she'd looked at Amanda's spreadsheet, all meticulous and neat, it hit her. It was real. It was her task, her inheritance. It was more than one sheet – it was pages. It was mammoth, unimaginable and impossible. All too much.

And yet, maybe it wasn't. Rory had run because he could, and he'd made her feel selfish and obsessed, and alone.

But she wasn't. Amanda and Sam had already done all this, itemised everything that they'd discussed, pulled together all the scraps of paper she'd given them. Ticked everything off, so they knew what had been done, and priced every last item. For her. Just for her. The tears welled up again and her nose started to run. Which was so unladylike.

'You think it will work?' She wiped the tears away with the back of her hand.

'I know it will work. Sam thinks it will work, Pip does, Dom, Elizabeth.' She waved an all-encompassing hand. 'It's a brilliant idea, Lottie, and like I said, if it doesn't work, then I just know you'll come up with something else.'

'It was Rory's idea.'

'It was Rory who gave you the idea, but it's yours, and we all know you can do it. Although I'm not sure you'd get on a horse in any of the dresses I've been loaned.'

'Oh shit, the horse feed.' She glanced at the clock on the

mantelpiece, 'Is it really that time? Dad will go ape. I promised him I'd be there an hour ago. Sorry, sorry.' She headed for the door, then swung back to give Amanda another hug. 'Thank you, really.'

Amanda smiled and wondered if Lottie needed a lecture along the lines of the hare and the tortoise. And then decided that nothing really would change the way she was, which was why they all loved her and wanted to help her so much. She was strangely strong, but vulnerable. You wanted to help her when she struggled, and yet just knew she'd work it out on her own if she had to. 'You're welcome. Er, I think you're ringing.'

Lottie was, or rather her mobile phone, which was shoved deep into the pocket off her cut-off denim shorts, was. The muffled but distinctive ring tone that announced her affection for Kings of Leon also announced more trouble. 'Christ, I really am in trouble if that's Dad.'

She fought to pull the phone out, dragging the pocket lining with it, jumping on the spot as though it might help and making Amanda feel curiously maternal. Which considering there wasn't much of an age gap between them was a bit worrying. It must, Amanda decided, be her hormones.

'Oh, it's Mick. What does he want?' The phone stopped ringing, then started again.

'Well, there is one way to find out, Lottie. Don't you think you should answer it?'

Mick's warm tone carried clearly across the room, and even though his voice was as steady as it always was, even Amanda could sense the urgency. 'Lottie, you need to come home. Rory's lost the plot, he's taking all the horses – everything.'

Chapter 22

'Rory?'

'Oh good, you're back, darling.' Rory, who had two bridles over his shoulder and a saddle in his hands, kissed Lottie on the cheek and carried on walking, towards the horsebox. Her horsebox. 'Be a darling, grab that box of bandages.'

Lottie picked up the box, which was at the side of the fountain, without thinking, and hurried after him. 'Where are you going, did I forget an event?' Which wouldn't have been unusual. More than once they'd been up late into the night getting horses ready for an event the next day, which meant an early start. It wasn't that she was completely disorganised – there was just so much going on and paperwork had a habit of going astray.

'Nope.' He went to take the box from her, but she hung on. Suddenly reluctant to let go, but not sure why. 'I'm taking you home.' He pulled at the box and she hung on tighter, until it became a weird push-and-pull game. 'This is stupid, we can't live like this.' Rory gritted his teeth and dug his heels in, which reminded her weirdly of Tilly, his terrier. Which made her giggle and let go.

Rory landed with a thump on his backside, the contents of the box spilling around him, which made it even funnier – in a hysterical kind of way. 'God, you are so sexy standing there.' His fingers closed around her ankle and before she had time to react

266

he'd pulled her down beside him onto the gravel driveway. 'I need you at home with me. Christ, Lottie, I've missed you.' His fingers were tangled in her hair and he rested his forehead against hers, which sobered Lottie up. She stopped smiling, reached out to touch his face.

'I've missed you too.' I wish you'd stay here, she should say it, she knew she had to say it. But she didn't.

'Tabby is driving me nuts. I keep expecting to find her in my bed when I come out of the shower. You do need to come back and protect me.'

'I thought you were supposed to protect me?'

'And I can't find anything.'

'Well I'm crap at finding things too.' She said reasonably.

'It's no wonder that Aussie twat couldn't resist you.' He traced a path down her arm with one finger, stopping at the crook of her elbow. His gaze travelled over the long, tanned legs, sun-bleached curls and sexy hair for a moment, then he hooked one finger into the waistband of her denim shorts. 'He's still hot for you now.' Rory pulled her closer, his hand slipping down between her thighs.

Lottie wriggled and tried to keep her mind on what she knew she had to say. 'I thought he was hot for Tabby? Or was it Sam? No, it was Sam, I'm sure it was—'

'Shush.' He put a finger on her lips. 'Let's go home and I'll show you just how much I've missed you.'

'But,' Lottie paused, took a deep breath and hoped she didn't regret what she was about to say. The trouble was, she might. But she'd regret it even more if she didn't. 'I am home, Rory. This is my home, our home, and I want you here, with me.'

'Don't be daft. It's just a dream this place: a game. Can't you see that? No way in hell can you raise enough money to pay the bills. We couldn't even afford to have any heating on.'

'We can wear extra jumpers.'

'And there's the horses to feed, entries to pay.'

'I can take on more clients for riding lessons, and so can you.'

267

'The roof leaks.'

'That's why we're doing the Wedding Fayre – to pay for the roof.'

'And what about eating, drinking? Lottie it's imposs—'

'Noooo.' Lottie wailed to drown him out and put her hands over her ears, refusing to hear the word she knew he was about to utter.

'I've packed all your stuff, and now I'm going to load the horses up and we can go. Back to normal, back to you and me having fun.'

'Life isn't just about fun, Rory.'

'Please, Lottie. I can't function without you, I can't find anything, the fridge is empty.' He paused. 'The dogs miss you.'

It was the clincher. A blow that made something inside Lottie suddenly harden. Maybe it was resolve. She'd heard the expression 'harden your resolve' before and not really known what it meant.

'I can't, Rory. I haven't got a choice. You have.' This house needed her more than the bloody dogs, and since when had an empty fridge mattered? She shrugged and watched as he got up, staying where she was on the gravel as he brushed himself down.

'I can't believe you're staying here, in this dump, when you could have us.'

Then she watched as he backed off, turned on his heel and set off down the driveway on foot.

'And I can't believe you're going.' She knew he wouldn't hear her, but she had to say it anyway.

Lottie watched Rory until he was so far away he was just a dark, indeterminate figure against the blue of the sky. And she was still watching when two paws planted themselves firmly on her chest and a wet nose pushed against her face. 'Oh, Harry, where did you come from?' The dog wriggled in ecstasy at the sound of her voice, and when she glanced over his woolly head it was to see Mick, framed by the archway that led into the courtyard. One brief nod, then he disappeared from sight.

'What am I going to do, Harry?' Lottie let herself sink onto her back on the gravel and look up at the cloudless sky, and the puppy settled himself on her stomach, his paws balanced on her boobs as he tried to lick her face. 'I can't give up, can I?' The licking spread to her neck. 'Gran needs me, and she's done everything for me, looked after me when Mum died, kept this place going.' She put her hands around the fat body, trying to stop him from sticking his tongue into her mouth every time she opened it to speak. 'And I do love it here.' She sighed. 'It's not a dump, is it? You like it here, don't you?' Harry wriggled, trying to get free. 'But I do love Rory too, and I thought we wanted the same things. We always did before, you know.' The pup, who had found that struggling didn't work, tried to bark. Which he hadn't quite mastered yet.

There was a crunching on the gravel and Lottie shut her eyes and made a wish. He'd come back, he'd realised.

'Why are you lying there?' He hadn't. It was Pip. 'Why were you loading up the horsebox?'

'You've been spying on us. You're as bad as Gran.'

'No I haven't. I came to see Elizabeth and I couldn't miss seeing what was going on when I came out.'

'He wanted me to go back with him.'

'Ahh.' Pip sat down next to her.

'To protect him from Tab, and to find stuff.'

'Oh.'

'And to fill the fridge and because the dogs miss me.'

'Mm. So he didn't build a very good case?'

'I can't go, whatever he says. Can I?' Lottie turned her head slightly so she could see Pip, then looked back at the blue sky.

'Do you want to go back?'

'Oh God, I love him so much, Pip, but I can't, I belong here. Dad said to me a while ago that if I loved this place I had to show Rory why and,' she screwed up her nose, trying to remember exactly what he'd said, 'that if this place didn't win him over I'd got some decisions to make.' She ran her hands over the dog's body, slowly, trying to build her confidence up. Then she looked straight at Pip. 'I can do this, can't I?'

'Of course you can. Elizabeth said that Tipping House was the making of her and it would be of you. I think I know what she means now. Come on lazy bones,' she struggled to her feet and held a hand out to Lottie, 'let's get that horsebox unpacked.'

'Elizabeth said you were here.' Pip cast the type of assessing gaze over Mick that had scared off a good few men in the past, but he stood his ground. He liked a challenge, and he liked Pip, which was why it had been so difficult to admit that as a couple they'd been going nowhere. As friends it could be good. He hoped.

'She suggested it.' Mick dropped the hot shoe into a bucket of water, then hooked it carefully over the rim. 'Do you need a hand unpacking the stuff?'

'We're fine.'

They were like chalk and cheese, Mick thought, as he glanced past Pip to Lottie, who was fanning the bottom of her t-shirt.

Working in the heat had made her hair curl even more wildly than normal and he'd thought more than once that it had probably looked like that when she'd been on that Barcelona beach with Todd. The twist in his gut brought a scowl to his face, which he instantly regretted. This wasn't about him and his irrational lust – it was about Lottie. And it was about Pip, who was watching him closely. 'You're okay?'

'I'm fine.' Her gaze flickered over to Lottie and back again. 'Don't hurt her, she's my friend.'

'I'm not going to do anything.'

'Help her.'

'I'll try.' He picked up the horseshoe, which was now cool and checked it against the horse's hoof.

'You've got to do better than try, Mick, and Elizabeth must think you will or she wouldn't have offered you lodgings.' She paused, waited for him to look up. 'After the Wedding Fayre I'm going to Australia.'

'With Todd? Popular man.'

'With Todd. He's a very popular man, because he's not complicated like you. Elizabeth said she thought it was a good idea.'

'Then no doubt it's a good idea. She seems to be having a lot of them.'

'What's a good idea?' Lottie, who had been keeping her distance, not wanting to interfere if Pip and Mick were making up, finally gave in to her natural nosiness.

'Oh, just one of Elizabeth's madcap suggestions. I'm going to go and get a shower if we've finished unloading your stuff.' Pip lifted her top up and took a sniff. 'I stink of bloody horses, yuk.'

Lottie grinned. 'You muck out for Rory, you always stink of horses.'

'I always shower the minute I've finished. And you better get one too, Your Ladyship, because you're coming for a drink. We've not had a girly night out for ages and now Amanda has stopped puking, and Sam has been abandoned while David does his summer training, I've decided we need to let our hair down.'

Lottie groaned. She'd been quite keen on letting her hair down, in the comfort of her own home. With pyjamas on, the dog on her knee, a weepy film on the TV and a big box of tissues. And probably a pizza.

'And I know you're dreaming about pizza, so you can wipe that look off your face. You've got to get fit for your wedding, Charlotte.'

Lottie frowned, 'It's not my…'

'Even at a pretend wedding the bride has to look her best. I'll see you at Sam's at eight o'clock, okay?'

Mick, who thought Lottie looked as good as it got, decided to keep his mouth shut, in the interests of his own safety. Hammering the final nail into the shoe, he let the horse's foot go and straightened up.

'She's right.'

'About the pizza?'

'No.' He chuckled. 'About you needing to let your hair down.'

'Thanks for ringing me earlier.'

'You're welcome.' He started to pack his tools away.

'And, er,' she picked Harry up, 'thanks for being here. And, er, you know the other day, when…'

'It won't happen again. Do you want me to look after him for you – the dog? While you go out.'

'Mick, can I ask you something?'

'If you have to.' He took the dog from her, running firm fingers over its podgy body until it was looking up at him with the type of total adoration that all animals seemed to send his way at some point. He was steeling himself for the question that would require him to reply that Rory was a good guy, that, yeah it would work out, that the moon was made of cheese and that pigs flew around it every night.

'Is it just me that likes this yard, or do you think it's okay?'

'It's more than okay, Lottie.' He smiled, partly from relief that the question had been that straightforward, partly at the earnest look on her face. Which made him want to kiss her. 'I can see why your parents spent so much time down here, and I can see why Elizabeth wants you to look after it. It's a special place.' For a special person, he wanted to add, but that was fanciful.

'Thank you.' She grinned and leant forward to kiss Harry on the head. Great. Now he was jealous of a bloody dog, of all things.

Chapter 23

Lottie let Black Gold have a long rein and relaxed slightly more in the saddle than was probably wise. Except since being put into foal, the mare did seem to have mellowed, or that could be due in part to being at Tipping House.

It was different on the yard here, calmer and quieter, and all the horses seemed to respond to it. And she had to admit, even she did. Apart from when Mick was there, looking at her with that slightly too intense gaze. Nobody else had ever looked at her like that and made her so conscious of who she was and what she looked like – which was pretty rough at the moment.

Sam had been attempting to educate her, in quite a discreet way, all about under-eye concealer (after she'd stated that people like her didn't have facelifts). At first she'd been sure she'd said congealer, and couldn't for the life of her understand how that would help. Not that concealer would either right now. She didn't have bags, she had suitcases under her eyes after a late night out and a six-in-the-morning alarm call, which she'd been very tempted to ignore, until she'd remembered that she had to feed, muck out and exercise the horses, and be back in time to welcome Amanda and her interior design posse mid-morning.

And then there'd been the hair conversation. How on earth was she supposed to find time to end up with the effortless 'sleek' look? Surely 'effortless' involved not putting effort in? Which more or less summed up what had happened this morning. She'd even been known, in the past, to go out with a round brush stuck in her hair, because she'd been in a hurry and the damned thing had got stuck so high up that if she'd done her normal trick and hacked at it with scissors she'd have looked like a mangy dog, or had a reverse Mohican. Either way it wouldn't have been a good look. Although having a hair brush sticking out from your head probably wasn't normal behaviour, it was a good colour match.

But Sam's definition of the effortless look involved several bottles of shampoo, conditioner, anti-frizz, mousse, protector and two different brushes (not to mention the curling tongs, which would somehow give her far superior curls), which made it a complete no-go. No way would she keep track of all that lot. She had enough trouble finding the stuff to plait the horses' manes. Apparently, though, even bed-head hair these days was carefully crafted.

She nudged Gold off the main track and on to the grass. She did love Sam, but she could actually get three horses ready for a show in the time it took Samantha to get ready to face the world. And that included plaiting. And although she might not be good at doing her own hair, Lottie knew that making a horse look its best was something she was pretty damned good at.

It had been a good night, though, and Pip had seemed quite cheerful and back to her old bossy and funny self. She'd been right, she'd needed a break and a good girlie night. And even if Sam's mind had been firmly on her to-do list for the Wedding Fayre (it amazed Lottie how like one of the terriers Sam was, give her a challenge to get her perfectly enamelled white teeth into and she didn't let go) it had been a chat, not a chore.

'You need a hot man.' Had been Sam's opening comment as she smothered her in a hug and a good dose of perfume. Lottie came up for air trying not to splutter, which would have been rude.

274

'I'm the one that needs a hot man.' Pip was sat in the middle of Sam's large shag-pile rug with a glass of wine in one hand and a slice of pizza in the other, with Scruffy at her feet, his hairy head cocked to one side as he salivated and gazed adoringly at the food. He gave a gulp, then edged closer.

'Don't you feed this mutt, Sam?'

'Course I do, babe, but he never stops eating. Davey says he's on the C-plan diet – everything he sees he eats.' She giggled. 'Bless him.'

Lottie, who wasn't sure if the 'bless him' at been aimed at the dog or the husband took the glass of wine that Sam was holding out and sat down next to Amanda, who was on the mineral water. That, she decided, just had to be one of the worst things about being pregnant. How on earth did you manage without a drink for nine months? It would be hell when you were in a bad mood, or just knackered, or wanted to celebrate. Or maybe all those weird hormones whizzing around your body made you too deliriously happy to care – when you weren't being sick. She made a mental note to ask Amanda later. 'What do you mean, I need a hot man?'

Pip rolled her eyes. 'Well, I know what I mean. Do you know how hard it is to get a shag around here?'

'I bet Tom would be willing to help you out.' Lottie grinned and grabbed the last slice of pizza from the open box, beating Scruffy to it by a whisker, literally. 'Or Todd.'

'I meant, we need to ask some men, you know, to be ushers and stuff. And you need a groom.' Sam flashed her wide smile. She was busy pouring drinks in her normal hospitable way, but her mind was obviously on her list of essentials for the big night. Her dog's mind was obviously on pizza. 'And then it's more or less sorted. Should we get professionals? You know, models, do you think?'

'Tom's a model.'

'Impossible to get him out of his pullovers these days.' Pip's tone was dry. When he'd first arrived in Tippermere he still possessed his designer suits and matching stubble, but his intention had been to blend in with the locals. And he'd surpassed his aims.

He had, Pip decided glumly, become Mr Grey Man rather too successfully. 'Give him another six months and it will be pipe and slippers all the way.'

'Ahh, that's a bit mean. He's not that bad.' Lottie was trying to be fair. She'd never really looked on Tom as a sex symbol. He'd always been more Tab's dad, seeing as his daughter was all he ever wanted to talk about to her. He never failed to tell her that she had saved his life by finding Tab a job with Billy (he hadn't been half as keen on the plan for her to work for Rory, but had eventually accepted it).

Lottie had been completely oblivious to the fact that Tom actually lusted after her and Tab was his smokescreen. He was used to his fame and fortune as a top model giving him instant access into whoever's knickers he chose (male or female), and when Lottie was singularly unimpressed it had initially pleased him, then floored him. All his attempts to woo had fallen on deaf ears. Lottie, used to the very up-front approach of the highly sexed horsemen she'd been brought up with, had missed his subtle signals and thought he was just a very nice man.

'Maybe you should send him to the gym, then he'd be okay?'

'It's not his body that's the problem, it's his brain.' Pip downed her drink and held the empty glass out for a refill. Tom had been a surprising lover, with stamina that had topped most of the men she'd bedded and one or two tricks she'd never seen before. And he'd been surprisingly firm. It was just a shame that these qualities deserted him the second he put his trousers back on. Maybe, she thought, it was some kind of model complex, that when he was stripped down to his knickers (which he'd been famous for wearing) he was in show-off work mode. 'But people aren't paying to see just models – they want celebrities.'

Sam nodded. 'You're right, babe. Like a night with the stars, except in the day.'

'They are not getting celebrities or models.' Lottie, once she'd emptied her mouth of pizza, spoke surprisingly firmly, which brought a smile to Amanda's face. Lottie was changing. She was still as loveable as ever, but she was blossoming into the role she'd always been destined for. 'It's a wedding, not a film premier, and I want all the ushers to be from Tippermere or Kitterly Heath.' Which actually meant that quite a few probably would be celebrities, but ones she knew.

'It's going to be an amazing wedding – the best.' Sam expertly opened another bottle of champagne. 'With tiaras and white horses and your best family silver. Have you got family silver, Lots?'

Lottie, taken unawares, frowned. 'Well, I don't know. Well, I suppose there probably is some, if Gran hasn't sold it. But we've hired stuff. It would take far too long to get it all polished.'

'Oh right, babe, I forgot that. Aww, it's all so romantic.'

Lottie wasn't so sure. Her bedroom, with its leaky pipes, wouldn't be on her list of romantic destinations, and nor would the Great Hall or the grand entrance, with their dusty and moth-eaten curtains. Amanda patted her hand reassuringly. 'Don't worry, you've got an army of professionals coming in to make sure it runs like clockwork.'

It had amazed Lottie just how brilliant Amanda was at finding people to do everything. It would have taken her weeks. But Amanda, with her book of contacts and natural efficiency, had made it look easy.

'And the best bit is, none of them want paying. Once Pip told them the level of coverage we were getting from the glossy magazines they were falling over themselves to help. We've got enough flowers to start up a florists, top caterers, invites, everything. It can't fail, Lottie, and the interior designers are in tomorrow for a chat so that you can have those bedrooms spruced up.'

Lottie groaned, and suddenly remembered that she'd had good intentions to tidy a couple of the rooms in advance – or the interior designers would think they'd been burgled. The trouble was, Rory's arrival, followed by his rather abrupt departure, had completely wrecked her plan. She'd forgotten.

'What bedrooms?' Pip had missed out on more than she'd realised in the last few days. In fact, she was rather surprised at just how much Lottie had achieved.

'For the wedding party. You can make an absolute fortune if you book out rooms like these.'

'People adore four posters and old oak floorboards.' Added Amanda.

'And, apparently, noisy cisterns and woodworm.' It was the last bit that worried Lottie. She'd been desperately hoping that the water pipes would behave for the duration of the Wedding Fayre or it would be disastrous.

Amanda smiled. 'Even noisy cisterns and woodworm are popular if you've never had them.'

Lottie was nearly unseated and brought sharply back to the present as Black Gold ground to a halt and snorted.

'Oh gawd, I didn't realise we'd come this far. If we don't get back, Amanda is going to be showing Mr Fancy Pants around on his own.' She'd watched too many episodes of *Changing Rooms* not to worry that if she wasn't there her idea of olde worlde might be lost in purple paint and swathes of gold chiffon and satin. Although if she thought about it, she knew Amanda wouldn't allow that.

Lottie gave the horse a pat. 'Come on Gold, let's get back.' But Gold was staring, eyes on stalks, at the hedge. She took a step backwards, lowered her head and blew out of her nostrils. 'We really do need to get back. There's nothing there, you silly thing.' She gave the mare a nudge with her heels and the horse took another step back, her head shooting up into the air and her front feet leaving the ground. Lottie kicked harder. This really wasn't the time for horse hysterics, and the mare crabbed sideways, nearly taking them into the electric fence on the other side of the track, which really wasn't a good idea at all.

Having a hot seat wasn't something Lottie normally had a problem with, but an electric buzz up the rump was to be avoided at all costs. Two-thirds of the way round the route she was on, and already late for a meeting, meant that turning around really wasn't what she wanted to do. 'Please Gold.' She turned the horse's head away from the evil thing that lurked in hedges and tried to leg-yield past, but Gold had other ideas. The self-protective instinct was strong. Not only did she have to look after her own skin, she was responsible for her rider and her unborn foal. Taking advantage of the fact that Lottie had bent her neck, she let the rest of her body follow and with a stubbornness that Lottie had come to know well, completed a U-turn and set off determinedly towards home – back the way they'd come.

Lottie knew that it was a mistake to give in, but they were going at such a pace, and she was already so late, that to battle it out and turn around would take up far more time than she had spare. 'You're naughty.' The horse's ears flickered back in her direction. 'You know full well there was no monster, don't you? It'll serve you right when your baby is the biggest swine on earth and doesn't do a thing you tell it.' Gold snorted and kept up her pace.

By the time Lottie had untacked the horse, given her a quick brush-down and refilled her haynet and water bucket, it was already five minutes past the time she'd arranged to meet Amanda. She grabbed the hose and washed down her boots, hoping that would get rid of most of the smell, then peeled her chaps off, revealing bright-pink socks, which filled a gap between the top of her short boots and her green breeches, which they clashed horribly with.

'Bugger.' She stared at them, wasting more valuable seconds as she dithered about whether it was worse to be even later but with the socks changed, or to be just a little bit late but looking as if she was colour blind or already totally eccentric. 'Why don't I have short legs?' Harry, who'd been watching with interest, put his head on one side and wagged his tail, not helping at all.

The second alarm on her phone, which she'd set as an emergency measure in case she didn't hear the first one, which she hadn't, went off. So she was already ten minutes late. Lottie brushed the bits of hay off her chest, hoped there wasn't too much horse slobber on her shoulder and kissed Harry on his head before locking him in an empty stable. 'Be good, I won't be long, promise.'

Lottie sprinted the short distance from the stables to the house, skidding around the immaculate and highly polished soft-top car, which was parked very neatly at the bottom of the steps, announcing that, true to form, Amanda had arrived on time. In fact, it looked like it had been there a while. Taking the steps two at a time she ran through the already-open door into an empty hallway, the sound of Elizabeth's cut-glass tones echoing across from her normal reception room.

'Double bugger.' Being late was bad enough, but having Elizabeth in attendance was even worse. She took a sniff of her t-shirt to check she wasn't too sweaty and smelly, then slipped her boots off and pushed them under a chair, hoping that the dogs didn't find them. Her socks looked even worse now, with their purple toes and heels, and she was weighing up whether to strip them off and hide them in her boots when the click clack of nails on the oak floorboards announced that it was too late. If one of the Labradors knew she was there, then so did her gran.

'Don't you dare touch my boots.' Holmes wagged his tail and gave a doggy grin.

'About time, Charlotte, where have you been, girl?'

She sighed and headed towards the open door. Maybe if she smiled a lot and kept on the move, nobody would notice the way she was dressed.

'Good heavens.'

No chance of that, then.

Elizabeth tutted, then nodded towards an empty chair. 'We've been having a nice chat about your plans. And I've been telling this young lady that it's nonsense to use one of the rooms in here.' Lottie looked nervously past Amanda to a woman who didn't look at all like Lawrence Llewelyn Bowen, which was a huge relief. She looked completely normal, if slightly bemused.

'Sorry?' She seemed to be saying 'sorry' a lot lately. She really had to stop. 'But Amanda and I agreed we really needed to have at least one room, didn't we?' Lottie looked to Amanda for backup, who smiled reassuringly.

'I've told her we will utilise the room above the stables.'

'Mick's room?'

'The room Michael is staying in at present, yes. We'll move him.'

'Gran, you can't just move people like you do horses.' She'd got used to him being there, and it was nice, reassuring, especially now he didn't seem to be as moody and intense.

'Nonsense. The man can't stay there permanently.'

'And Dad might not like it, I mean it was his and Mum's...' What came next? Love nest?

'I'm sure William won't mind, but you may ask him first. In the meantime you need to show Amanda and this young lady around.'

'But people want four-poster beds and oak floorboards, and...'

'Indeed they do, which they can have. And there will be no damp or woodworm. It will cost a fortune to do a bedroom in here, Charlotte, and people will be traipsing,' how did anybody make traipsing sound like trespassing, wondered Lottie, 'through the house. Totally unnecessary. Right, now I have things to do. And you, young lady, need to hide those socks in some boots.'

Being late was definitely a mistake, Lottie decided. It gave Elizabeth far too many opportunities to run the show the way she wanted. 'And what about Mick?'

'Michael will be very welcome over at William's, I'm sure. Your father really needs somebody reliable over there. Victoria must be driving him to distraction. She completely forgot about the electric fence again the other day. That stallion of his was out again and very nearly mounted that flighty mare of your Richard's. Only thing that stopped it was the rider in the way.'

'Richard? You mean Rory?'

'Never seen him dismount so quickly.' Elizabeth wasn't smiling, but there was a definite gleam in her eye. 'That boy has quite a vocabulary when he's stirred, hasn't he?'

Lottie, who was still trying to get past the image of Rory nearly getting squashed between a squealing Flash and Billy's favourite stallion, found it impossible to comment.

'Anyway the man looks like he has gypsy blood in him, he'll be ready for a change.'

'You can't say that, Gran.'

'Well, he can move out for the day and then move back. Right, that's settled, then. Off you all trot before Bertie gets hold of your other boot as well.'

With a shriek of dismay, Lottie spotted Holmes, who was sitting quietly in the doorway, one of her boots between his front paws. His brown eyes were unutterably sad as his new find was taken from him, but in true Labrador fashion his soft mouth hadn't left a mark. Lottie patted him on the head and went in search of the other boot, which was still safely stowed in the hallway.

'This is Anna.' Amanda watched as Lottie pulled her boots back on with relief. 'Nice socks.'

'They're my best ones, no expensive spared. I'm so sorry I was late.'

'No probs, I think Elizabeth was pleased.' She smiled at the look on Lottie's face. 'And it is a good idea, isn't it? Or is it really bad? We don't have to, you know.'

'I know.' Lottie sighed. 'It is a good idea, but I don't want to upset Dad.'

'He didn't mind Mick moving in, though, did he?'

'Mick's different, he's not a stranger,' she glanced at Anna apologetically, 'and he's not giving the place a makeover. Dad might not want it changing.'

'Let's have a look, shall we, then decide?'

Anna, Lottie decided, was very nice. Nearly as nice as Amanda. She declared herself in love with the room, in love with the courtyard and declared that a coat of paint and a few finishing touches were all that they'd need to make the place perfect. 'Who designed this room? It's beautiful.'

'Mum and Dad, I think.'

'She must have loved the place.'

'I think she did.' Lottie looked out of the window and wished she'd been old enough to remember.

'You can always tell when a place has been renovated out of love.'

'And you can always tell when you're about to be evicted, can't you treas?'

Lottie bit the inside of her cheek and met the dark stare head on.

'Gran suggested it. But only for a day, that's all. You're not being evicted. And I'm not sure Dad will like it anyway, and if he doesn't actually mind, then we're only painting and doing a few—'

'Shh.' His soft voice, as steadying as ever, dried up the words. 'It's not a problem, treas. Don't you worry about me.'

'But I like having you here.' She blurted it out without thinking, then was pretty sure she'd turned pinker than her favourite knickers.

'And I like being here.' He nodded, the slightest quirk lifting the corner of his mouth. She liked that quirk – it made everything okay.

Amanda coughed, effectively stopping a hundred dangerous thoughts about his mouth. 'Shall we nip over to your Dad's, then, and see what he thinks? And I can give you a call and let you know, Anna, so we can make a start as soon as possible.'

'Sure, I'll pencil it in, then look at the colour charts and some bed linen.'

***

Lottie had turned down the offer of a lift in Amanda's car, saying

283

she'd have to get back and it wasn't fair to expect Amanda to ferry her around, seeing as Billy's yard at Folly Foot Equestrian Centre was actually part of Amanda and Dom's estate. And one glance at the pristine interior of the other girl's car had filled Lottie with horror. She was covered in hairs, which apparently were a sod to get out of car upholstery (not that she knew, as she never tried to remove them, which meant her own car seats resembled hairy rugs), and although her boots had seemed fairly dung-free she was pretty sure they'd leave the type of horse odour that would linger for months.

So they'd arrived at the equestrian centre in convoy and found Billy Brinkley in the school, astride one of his horses.

'Watch out, here comes trouble.' Billy was busy cantering one of his lazier horses around in the indoor school for a potential buyer, and Lottie knew better than to expect him to stop. 'What are you two plotting?'

Leaving Lottie little option but to tell him. 'You can say no, I mean if you mind. It was just an idea.' She glanced at Amanda for reassurance. 'But we can leave it, there are lots of rooms and…'

'Mind, why should I mind? Pop that pole back up will you?' He circled in front of the first jump, letting the horse have a good look then gave it a discreet smack with his whip whilst the buyer was distracted by Amanda, and as the animal shot forward he gave it its head and cleared the pole by a considerably larger margin than it had ever done before.

'Keen as mustard, but quiet enough for a girl to ride.' Before she had time to object he was out of the saddle and legging Lottie up, whispering a gruff aside. 'Keep him on the left rein or he'll duck out.' She took the advice and sent the horse back into a steady canter, wondering if he did mind or not, but then as the horse tried to grab the reins from her hands decided she better concentrate or she'd be in trouble.

What her dad considered too quiet, many riders would consider dynamite, and Lottie had a fair idea that he was actually trying to take some of the fizz out of the horse before the decidedly more novice potential purchaser got into the saddle. It was a fine line between showing a horse at its sparkling best and heating it up so much that it scared a jockey to death, but Billy knew his horses. This one could take an amateur rider as far as he wanted, but it wasn't up to competing at the level Billy did. Its concentration wandered far too often, which made for careless mistakes, and it hadn't got the sparkle and showmanship that a top show-jumper needed. But it was an honest horse and would do its best, when it could be bothered. And it liked Lottie's quiet style, which suited its nature far better than Billy's demands and bossiness. Billy liked to place a horse, tell it exactly what to do – Lottie was softer and happy to accept a compromise.

The horse cleared the jumps economically, and the buyer declared he'd seen enough and mistaking Lottie's quiet riding for that of a novice declared he didn't need to ride, he'd sign a cheque and be back the next day with a horsebox.

She sat on the horse, gnawing the inside of her cheek as Billy made the deal on a handshake.

'You really don't mind, Dad?' She swung out of the saddle and landed in front of him.

'That place deserves to be loved, darling.' He squeezed her arm. 'No point leaving it to rot now, is there?'

'But I thought...'

'Whatever you and your gran do to that place, I'll never forget what it was like. I'll take the horse, love.' He took the reins from her unresisting fingers. 'I think you're wanted.' And nodded over towards Amanda, who was waving her phone in the air distractedly.

'It's Dominic, he said,' her normal furrow-free brow had frown lines, 'tell Charlotte she needs to get back and bring all the horses in before the helicopter lands.'

Chapter 24

'Helicopter?' Lottie stared at Amanda and wondered if there was something she'd missed. Like an event she'd planned without realising it, just as she's apparently missed Rory's marriage proposal.

'The air-ambulance. He said not to panic, but he had to call it for Elizabeth. She's had a fall.'

'Oh God, I've got to get back.'

'He sounded more worried about the horses being frightened,' said Amanda reasonably, hoping that this didn't mean Lottie was going to try and drive her little car even faster down the narrow lanes than she had on the way to the Equestrian Centre. 'I'm sure it's nothing serious. You know what Dominic's like; he always errs on the side of caution. Look what he's been like over my pregnancy.'

Lottie, who still couldn't quite get used to Uncle Dom in the role of caring father-to-be tried not to be rude and shove Amanda out of the way so that she could get in her car. Flattening a mother-to-be was not how a Lady, or friend, for that matter, was supposed to behave.

But he'd called an air-ambulance. Why would even Uncle Dom call an air-ambulance if there wasn't blood pouring out of some gaping wound? He said 'fall' – maybe she'd fractured a leg and there was a splinter of bone that had pierced an artery, or a rib that had punctured a lung, or worse.

'He's just texted again. He knows you'll be thinking the gory worst, look, he says '*no blood, no heart attack, she's demanding medicinal G&T. Ambulance due in 15 min*', so you don't need to worry.'

Lottie stared at the text blindly and decided it must be true. She couldn't imagine any circumstance under which Uncle Dom would lie, unlike herself, who thought the odd tiny white lie to make things sound slightly better than they were was perfectly acceptable in certain circumstances. Like when Rory demolished three-quarters of a show-jumping course with Flash and she'd said it absolutely wasn't the worse round of the day, or when Tilly had buried the show entries in the paddock and she'd insisted they must have got lost in the post.

'She hasn't knocked her head and gone delirious?'

'She's asking for a drink, Lottie.' Amanda, judging that Lottie had now calmed down to the extent that it was safe to let her get into the car, moved out of the way. 'Which sounds like she's completely compos mentis, doesn't it?' She paused, knowing she couldn't not ask. 'Do you want me to come and give you a hand?'

'No, it's fine. Mick might be there anyway.' Lottie, well aware that Amanda had only made the offer out of good manners and her caring nature, saw the sigh of relief. 'And you're pregnant. I thought you were supposed to be taking it easy.'

Amanda rolled her eyes. 'If I take things much easier I'll forget how to walk. Now go, get your horses in and don't worry.'

It was only a few minutes' drive from Billy's yard at the equestrian centre, over to the Tipping House Estate, but as she pulled into the driveway it hit Lottie.

Elizabeth was going into hospital.

Which meant she wasn't going to be there. Which meant somebody else was in charge. Her.

'Cripes.' The up-until-now scary visions of Elizabeth lying injured were replaced by one of herself in the grand hallway,

Bertie and Holmes either side of her, and one of Gran's feathered hats on her head.

There were the dogs to feed, the bank manager to fend off, and who knows what other daily tasks that she hadn't yet encountered. Like instructing the game-keeper. All she'd done so far was buy him a pint in the Bull's Head, and she was probably supposed to do more than that, wasn't she? Gawd, was she supposed to wander around and check all the fences every day, or did somebody else do that? And there was the Wedding Fayre.

'Shit.' The car lurched and jolted her out of the nightmare as she strayed off the driveway and onto the grass, and as she wrestled with the wheel to get back on track the unmistakeable sound of a helicopter filled the car. 'Bugger.' She would have heard it earlier, she realised, if she hadn't pumped up the volume on her CD player as far as it would go. Clutching the steering wheel, she put her foot down, the little car bouncing painfully over the dips and bumps in the uneven road, knowing full well that if the horses weren't already in, it was now too late. They'd be galloping the length of the paddock, pounding the sun-baked earth and no doubt damaging tendons as they went.

Lottie and her car ground to a halt outside the archway that led to the stable yard. She winced at the plume of dust she'd thrown up and throwing the door open she was out and running before the engine had fully cut out. She careered in though the archway, suddenly realising that if Black Gold wasn't safely tucked away, a helicopter landing in the grounds would send the mare into orbit. Well, she careered as far as she was able before cannoning straight into a tall and solid figure.

Mick. She really must stop doing that, she thought, as she ground to an enforced halt and found herself gazing into the dark, smiling Irish eyes. At least he was smiling this time, unlike last time when he looked like he wanted… well it was better not to think about that.

'The horses—'

'Are all in, treas. Elizabeth apparently told Dom to stop being an old fussing woman, leave her alone and come down and help me. Well, that was my interpretation of what he actually said. That woman is a force to be reckoned with, worse than my ma, I'd say. You go up to the house, if you like, and see if you can catch her before they whisk her off.'

'Oh, Mick, thank you. What would I do without you? You're always here when I need you.' Lottie gave him a quick, impulsive hug then sped out of the yard as fast as she'd entered, leaving a bemused Mick in her wake. He sat down on the edge of the fountain and looked down at Lottie's spaniel, Harry, who had started to follow him like a shadow if his mistress wasn't about.

'What am I going to do with her, Harry?' He stroked the dog's curly head and was rewarded with a lick. 'I guess you don't know the answer to that one, do you, little fella? Well, I'll tell you something, neither do I. Neither do I.'

By the time Lottie had run in the imposing front door of Tipping House, Elizabeth had already been stretchered out of the back and into the waiting ambulance.

'Time is money. These chaps don't hang around.' Said Dom, rounding Lottie up and escorting her firmly back into the house. 'Get changed and we'll drive over to the hospital. Broken hip, they think.' He smiled. 'It's hard to tell with your grandmother. She was busy barking out orders to the poor men and telling them she'd suffered far worse out hunting, and carried on riding.'

'Oh.'

'She asked if you'd sorted out that Irish chap and booked the decorator in?'

'She's so bossy.'

'She is, indeed.'

'Oh, Uncle Dom, what am I going to do without her?'

'Well, for starters you can feed the dogs and check they're not raiding the kitchen. Maybe it's best if I go over to the hospital on my own and find out what is happening, although I'm sure by the time I get there she'll have them all organised. And then you can arrange with Philippa to visit tomorrow,' he winked. 'She said on no account should you turn up without her because hospitals are such boring places. Any messages?'

'You can tell her Dad doesn't mind if we use Mick's room, and nor does Mick.'

'But?'

'I think I might mind.'

'Oh, Charlotte,' he ruffled her hair affectionately and kissed the top of her head, 'you are so like Alexandra, you know.'

***

'Are you sure she's breathing? Should we call somebody?' Lottie moved closer, studying her grandmother's face for signs of life.

'Of course she is, although this place looks a bit like a morgue. I just never did understand why people have to send flowers when somebody's ill.' Pip picked up the vase of roses. 'Do you think she'd miss these? I really could do with some for Tiggy, to thank her for helping Todd.'

'Yes,' the tone was dry and surprisingly strong and Lottie jumped back from her position two inches away from Elizabeth's chest, which she'd been studying for movement and detected none. 'She would miss them, and she's not dead.' Elizabeth opened her eyes. 'I've broken my hip, not lost my sense of hearing or my wits. Although the way they talk to you in here anybody would think they all went together. Some silly slip of a girl,' which Lottie took to mean a nurse, 'suggested that from now on I use a stick all the time. What does she think I am, old?'

'She was probably trying to help. They'll tell everybody that.'

Elizabeth made a harrumph noise. 'Nobody is going to catch

290

me hobbling around the hall like some geriatric old dear. They'll be giving me a hearing aid next. Where are the dogs?'

'At home. Mick's taken them down to the yard to play with Harry. I didn't think they'd let them in at visiting time.'

'Nonsense. Last time I was in this place I insisted they came to visit. A bit of dog hair and a few germs never did anybody any harm.'

'Well they have been known to kill the odd person.' Pip put the vase of flowers back down where she'd found it. 'The germs that is, not the dog hair.'

'Only if they're ill in the first place.'

'That's normally why they're here, Elizabeth. I'm surprised they haven't sent you home already.'

'Dominic tells me that you think using the room above the stables for conjugal liaisons is a splendid idea.'

'Well, I didn't exactly say—'

Pip laughed out loud. 'Conjugal liaisons? I've never heard it called that before.'

Elizabeth frowned at her and turned her attention back to Lottie. 'Jolly good, I'm glad that's settled. And tell Michael he's welcome to stay until the first booking.'

'No conjugal liaisons for him, then.'

'Philippa.' Elizabeth shook her head. 'You can be crude. He is welcome to have them, which I'm sure he will, but not in that room. And how is Rod?'

'Todd you mean? Todd is fine. Tiggy has given him the last-known address of her ex-husband and told us that the man swings both ways and is shooting blanks.'

'Really, do you have to talk in terms like that? The one doesn't necessarily follow the other, you know. We had many fine friends that dallied with the boys as well as the girls and fathered strapping fellows. In fact, the hunt master was known for his dalliances, went after anything pretty, and he's a fine figure of a man if you ever saw one.'

291

'I know that.' Pip sat on the edge of the bed. 'But he is infertile according to Tiggy, but she said he might have some suggestions if, and I quote, you can get him to talk about anything but himself.'

'And then you will be going to Australia?'

'Are you?' Lottie, who'd been thinking about Mick's conjugal liaisons, looked up in surprise. 'You aren't really going, are you? Have you told Mick?'

'He's fine with it, but it isn't definite, I haven't booked a ticket yet or anything.'

'But what about,' *me*, had been on the tip of Lottie's tongue. But that was incredibly selfish.

'I won't go until after the Wedding Fayre, I promise.'

'Oh.'

'Philippa needs a change of scenery, she's getting bored.'

'Are you?' Lottie looked at her, suddenly worried that it was all her fault for not being attentive.

'She's done enough messing about here. She's the type of girl that needs a purpose in life.'

'Elizabeth, stop talking about me as though I'm not here.'

'A change from just mooching about bedding men and messing with horses will do you the world of good, girl. A change, that's what you need.'

'Can't you just take up sewing or something?' Asked Lottie.

Elizabeth laughed. 'Skydiving would be more like it, and I'm sure that Tim will join you. He looks the adventurous type. Did you bring me that flask I asked for?'

Pip grinned. 'No I didn't. Dominic frisked us before we got in the car. And you know it's Todd, not Tim. Tim? Where did Tim come from?'

'That boy never did appreciate its medicinal qualities, stops the nausea. Oh well, I suppose I better take some of those silly tablets. Now tell me about the plans for the room, while I just close my eyes for a moment.'

'You will be there, on the night, won't you, Gran?'

'I hope so dear. I do so want to see you in a wedding dress. It would make me very happy.'

Pip raised an eyebrow. 'That sounds like blackmail.'

Elizabeth opened one eye, just a tiny bit. 'Old ladies are allowed to say what they want – it's one of the few advantages that age brings. And it isn't blackmail, emotional or otherwise, it's a request. Alexandra looked so beautiful on her wedding day, everybody said so. She was so happy too.' She closed her eye and sighed, and Lottie looked worriedly over to Pip as they watched her chest rise and fall.

'Do you think she's okay?' The whisper stuck in Lottie's throat, and Pip nodded towards the door. And there was no summons as they crept towards it. No clearing of the throat, which told them that Elizabeth was actually conscious.

Lottie glanced back and her throat tightened. Her gran looked so vulnerable lying on the white sheets, and without the armour of her tweed skirts and thick jumpers and boots. For the first time Lottie could remember, she looked old.

Chapter 25

'I'm Stephen. That's with a PH.' His handshake was limp with a small L, thought Lottie, sitting down and trying not to be judgemental. But how could you feel positive about somebody when they kept sending you thinly veiled threats? 'With Lady Elizabeth in hospital, I do feel it's a good time for you to, er, take over the reins, so to speak.' He gave a small, embarrassed cough – and so he should, thought Lottie. As funnies went, it wasn't.

She decided she liked the old bank manager better, the one that called her 'little Charlotte', ruffled her hair up and asked if she'd fallen off any ponies today. This new one looked around her age, with a shirt collar that was fitted to the point of uncomfortable, and shoes that looked far too shiny and new. She glanced over at Dom's shoes, which looked as if they were old and quality, which they were. And, according to the business card he gave her, he was a customer advisor, not a manager. And he was staring at her bare midriff in the way an adder did before it struck.

Lottie had actually thought the combination of fitted dress with cut-out sections and pumps had looked smart and suitable for the weather – until Dom had ushered her into the bank, at which point naughty-child syndrome took over.

'So, have we made any, er, progress Miss Brinkley?' The brown-eyed gaze flickered up to her face and then back down to her abs, which she tightened to see what happened. He swallowed, hard, his Adam's apple jumping convulsively.

'I have a plan.'

His grip tightened on his tablet and she decided he was more nervous rabbit than adder. Or maybe ferret. 'We certainly can't lend you any more money, I'm afraid.'

'I'm not asking you for any money. We've got a plan, with,' she proudly put down the spreadsheet that Amanda had given her, 'projections.' As far as she could see they were a bit like predictions, the type you read in your horoscope. If the sun is shining and there's no trees to the west, or clouds in the sky, and an 'E' in the month, and Mick is happy, and the stallion hasn't escaped, then the good-luck fairy will blow kisses down on you.

But 'Stephen' with a PH, not a V, looked impressed. 'Very, er, good.' Maybe he believed in horoscopes too. In his line of work you had to believe in something, didn't you? Or all that money talk and big debts would drive you crazy, or to drink. Or maybe he was just shocked that she was able to produce a spreadsheet.

'And this does, er, include provisions to repay the existing accrued…'

'I think you'll find it all there.' She hadn't got a clue – she glanced over at Dom, who gave an uncharacteristic wink.

'I'll need to, er, check over your, er, figures.'

'Right, well, you do that. Now, if that's all.' Lottie stood up and hoped that neither her voice nor her knees were wobbling. 'Must dash! I've got an estate to manage in Grandmother's absence. Any questions, give my PA a ring.' And she bolted for the door, hoping she wasn't actually going at the speed she suspected she was.

'Your gran would be impressed.' Dom gave her a hug and opened the car door, watching with a smile the way she collapsed in.

'Really?' The hammering that was her pulse slowed a shade and she stopped feeling quite so worried that she was going to have a heart attack.

He grinned as he started the engine. 'She hates these sales people, wants her old- fashioned bank manager back, with manners and the power to make their own decisions. For that you can read 'let her have her own way'. But you certainly caught him on the back foot. I was certain the bugger was going to make demands we couldn't meet.'

'Oh.' Lottie bit her lip.

'Saving historic homes isn't on the agenda these days.' Dom pulled into the slow stream of traffic and headed back towards Tippermere.

'I think I owe Amanda a drink, and Sam, and Pip.'

'You're lucky to have such good friends, Charlotte. They count for a lot.'

'I know.' She leant her head back on the headrest and closed her eyes with relief.

'And now you just need to decide which man you're going to have by your side on the opening night.'

'Well, it won't be Rory.' She glanced out of the window, not seeing the houses as they gave way to lanes. Not seeing the familiar landscape. 'I think he's allergic to wedding dresses, and,' the worst bit of all, 'to Tipping House. Dad says I need somebody who loves the place like I do, and otherwise I've got decisions to make.'

'Billy's right.' Dom patted her knee then rested his hand back on the steering wheel. 'You will work it out. Come on, I'm taking you out for lunch. You deserve it, and after you've taken all that time to get ready and look decent.' He flashed her a warm smile. 'Even if you forgot to cover up all the right bits, as your gran would say.'

Lottie wiped her eyes with the back of her hand and tried to smile back. 'She is going to be okay, isn't she? She is coming home soon?'

'Of course she is.'

***

296

By the time they'd finished lunch, Lottie was feeling much more optimistic – although the glass of wine might have had something to do with that. In fact, she was feeling so relaxed and chilled that when she spotted Mick, who was putting the finishing touches to Elizabeth's gate, she just stood and stared. Unwilling to interrupt his concentration, but very willing to make the most of the sight.

He was stripped to the waist, his torso a dark, dusky brown from the hours he'd spent in the sun (and it had actually being a surprisingly good summer, for the UK).

A thin white scar, which she hadn't noticed before, snaked its way over his rib cage and she had a sudden urge to trace a finger over it. Instead she held her breath and hoped he didn't notice her. Well, at least not until she'd stopped gawping.

Worn jeans hung low on his lips, the denim bleached almost white where it was frayed along the waistband. Lottie took a step or two closer and admired the way his arm muscles moved as he worked. There was something about big, strong arms that suggested a very hot, capable man. She swallowed and blamed the lethal combination of alcohol and warm sun on the way the only thing she could think was 'what does he look like without the jeans?' She could ask Pip, but that would be terribly tactless right now – maybe in a few years' time.

'Everything okay, treas?'

Lottie all but leapt in the air as his voice interrupted her dirty thoughts. Then he looked up from his work, gave a lopsided grin and winked. Oh God, she wanted to jump on him. No she didn't. That was so immature. He was just a nice man and she was tipsy, and she still kind of had a boyfriend, and he'd been sleeping with her best friend, who was now off to Australia, probably. So, maybe she could… NO. Even if Rory didn't want to marry her, he still loved her, he just didn't want to marry her, or live with her, or help her….

Mick was studying her, waiting for an answer.

'Great. Everything is going to be great, I've decided.'

'What do you think, will her Ladyship be satisfied?' He nodded at the gate.

'Oh yes.' She'd be satisfied, even if her other ladyship wasn't. With him, well with the gate. 'Don't you have any horses to shoe?'

'Nope, I'm all yours.'

Lottie was pretty sure her eyes had opened a bit wider.

'How about I help you exercise the horses? We can take a couple out for a pipe opener down by the river, where the ground isn't like concrete.'

'I better get changed.' His dark gaze rested on her bare stomach, which was doing weird clenching things of its own accord. 'I've, er, got a skirt on. It's too tight to ride in.'

'You could take it off.' He hadn't moved. Was just watching her. 'While I tack the horses up.'

Lottie's gaze drifted down, over the ripple of abs, to what she had to admit was his crotch. And the leather working chaps just seemed to accentuate the area in question. Frame the bulge, was the only description she could think of.

'Sure.' She fled to the safety of the tack room, slammed the door behind her and leant against it. 'You're drunk, that's all. You do not fancy him and he doesn't fancy you.' She stripped the dress over her head and stood there in bra and knickers. There was a tap on the door.

'I need to get the saddles.'

'Hang on.' Shit, where were her spare riding clothes? She grabbed the pile of clothes, crashing into buckets as she tried to pull tight jodhpurs on. 'Hang on, won't be a sec.' Pulled the 'Born to Ride' top over her head, hopped about trying to pull socks on, and then finally opened the door, still breathless.

He squeezed past, raised his eyebrows as he studied the t-shirt and grabbed a saddle.

Okay, she did fancy him.

'Let's ride then, treasure.'

Then he went out again – which meant he didn't fancy her.

Bugger. Lottie trailed after him, a saddle over her arm.

Twenty minutes later, feeling slightly more sober, but no less randy, they rode out, knees bumping as they went through the archway.

'He's got a thing about her.' Lottie explained, as Mick's gelding edged closer to her mare.

'Nothing wrong with that.'

'Mick, will you marry me?' This was probably a bad idea. 'I mean not for real, Sam said I need a man.'

'Oh, Lottie.' Their thighs brushed together as he leaned in closer, put his large, capable hand under her chin, let the touch of his rough fingertips trace a path along her cheekbone. He hesitated. Then his hand was deep in her hair, cradling her head. He leant in closer, the dark, dark eyes, staring into hers. He was so close, he was about to…

'I can't treas.' His voice had a harsh edge she'd not heard for a long time, and he suddenly pulled back, took the reins in both hands and faced forward. 'I don't do pretend. I like my love to be real.' And with a nudge of his heels, the horse was away. Lottie's mare whinnied in dismay, then plunged after the gelding, desperate not to be left behind.

So, what had happened there? He'd nearly kissed her, hadn't he? Or had he just been having a good look to see if he fancied her enough or not? How could a man be so sexy and so bloody confusing?

Lottie tightened her grip on the reins as they caught up with Mick – not that she had any choice in the matter. Sulking and turning back wasn't an option when you were on a horse that was this determined.

'Who do you think I should ask?'

He gave her a funny look, then sighed and sat deep in the saddle so that his horse slowed to a trot, then into walk.

'Have you asked Rory?'

'He's so off the whole wedding idea, and Tipping House.' She sighed. 'I think he'd rather I didn't save the place and I went home to him. But it's not for me. Gran wants to see me in a wedding dress, she said so, and she's ill and I don't want to upset her. And Sam said I need a hot man,' he gave her another look, 'well, a man. Not that I'm saying you're not hot, you are hot, but it wouldn't matter if you weren't...'

The horses went back to bumping shoulders and flanks, which meant she went back to rubbing herself against Mick. Which he was polite enough to ignore. Good and bad.

'I'll do it if you can't persuade Rory, or find anybody else. For Elizabeth.'

'Thank you.' She would have kissed him, but it didn't seem that good an idea right now. His horse gave a little skip, frustrated that Mick was pushing it away from its girlfriend, which she could sympathise with. Her mare tossed her head, and Lottie copied and giggled.

Mick shook his head, and raised an eyebrow. 'You're a card. Race you back to the yard, my beautiful bride.'

They took off together, their horses in stride and she couldn't help but grin when he glanced her way. There was something about being with Mick, even when he was in a dark mood, which made her feel safe. Reassured. And she'd almost forgotten how good it was to be on horseback, speeding across open countryside with the warm smell of horse in her nostrils.

Lottie was still laughing when they slowed down as they hit the harder ground. She was incredibly lucky, she'd decided. She had it all. She glanced up at Tipping House as they drew closer.

'Happy to be home?' Mick had reined in his horse, and they both sat in front of the grand old property. The two horses, their coats gleaming in the sun, touching noses, their nostril flaring.

Lottie nodded, sobered a bit. Yes, it was home. And she'd make her gran proud of her. She'd look after the place, patch it up and make it better. It was a shame Rory couldn't call it home, but the realisation had slowly crept up on her the last few weeks. It was hers. It always had been.

'Like the salmon, you can't fight it.'

'Sorry?' She frowned, where did fish figure in this?

'They always go back to where they belong.'

'I'm not sure I like being compared to a salmon.'

He laughed, a short, full sound that made her smile. 'It's a favourable comparison, treas. And they're fighters too.'

'Hm.' She'd returned to Tippermere and her inheritance not because she had no choice, but because she wanted to be there. Once she'd realised that, of course. And it had taken a while to sink in.

'Come on then, fishy, let's turn these horses out before they decide to roll in the dust. Lottie?'

That one word held an uncertainty, a question that stopped her dead. He was staring at the house, not her. 'I don't know that I should be saying how I—'

'There you are. I thought I'd never find you.'

Lottie swung around in her saddle. A woman she'd never in her life seen before was standing a few yards away and the comment wasn't directed at her, it was aimed straight at Mick, who swore softly under his breath, then uttered a single word that sounded, to Lottie's ears, like so much more. 'Niamh.'

Niamh wasn't how Lottie had expected her, not that she'd consciously conjured up a picture. But whatever her imagination had come up with, it wasn't this.

The first thing Lottie noticed were the auburn waves that cascaded over her pale shoulders in a silky, soft, ordered way that her own curls never did. Her eyes were wide and green in the delicate, fine-boned face, her mouth wide. She was wearing the type of dress that made Lottie feel all wrong: neat, clean, tidy and simple but stunning. It showed off a slim figure to perfection.

Lottie resisted the urge to put a hand over the slogan on her own very old, but very loved, t-shirt.

'And why would you want to find me?'

Chapter 26

Niamh didn't seem at all put out by Mick's tone, she just smiled warmly. 'To give me a drink? I'm parched. And don't you look all Lord of the Manor?' It was said with a complete lack of edge that left Lottie glancing back and forth between the pair.

Mick, still astride his horse, was looking as if he had no intention of being sociable, though, which left Lottie feeling like a helpless dog in the middle of an argument that would quite like a cuddle for itself, but also wants everybody to love each other. At least now all traces of alcohol induced light-headedness, and knicker-twisting lust had been knocked out of her. She slid out of the saddle and put a hand on the reins of Mick's horse. 'Shall I sort the horses?' God, it was so lucky she hadn't got carried away and kissed him.

He still just sat. And Niamh just stood motionless (and very pretty with it), a half- smile on her lips. 'Your mam told me where you were.'

'Oh, she did, did she?' He finally spoke again and got off his horse, snatching the reins away from Lottie, then looked guiltily at her. 'Sorry, it's not your problem. I didn't mean that.'

Lottie shrugged.

'Don't go.' He put his hand over hers and Lottie froze. 'She shouldn't have told you, Niamh. Some things are best left.'

'And I thought you were the man who said they were best

discussed.'

'At the time, not when they're stale.' He folded his arms and Lottie felt like a little girl about to beg to be allowed to go to the toilet, just to get away.

'We need to talk.'

'You were the one who set the ultimatums, darling. You gave me a choice: my horses or you. You waved your airline ticket in my face,' Lottie had only heard a part of this before, and even though she felt a bit like an eavesdropper, she was transfixed, 'and told me the time for "fecking about" was over, I could walk you up the aisle and take the plane with you, or rot in Ireland on my own. I picked Ireland, darling, and you knew that. And now I've picked Cheshire. I thought I loved you, you know.' He grimaced. 'I'd have done anything if you'd asked, but ultimatums don't do it for me.' Lottie was suddenly reminded of the old saying that you could tell a gelding, ask a mare, but discuss it with a stallion. And Mick definitely didn't strike her as a gelding or a mare. 'I didn't need to run away to some strange country, I can get my thrills here.'

Niamh glanced at Lottie, then back to Mick and then seemed to take a deep breath before speaking so quietly that her words barely carried. 'My mistake.'

But did she mean her mistake in going, coming back or just trying to push him in the first place, thought Lottie?

She smiled at Lottie. 'It's wonderful to meet you, I've heard so much about this lovely place. You are so lucky.'

***

It wasn't until a good half hour after she'd gone and they'd untacked the horses and turned them out that Lottie got more than a nod and a grunt out of Mick. And it wasn't what she expected.

'Amanda and her designer friend have been to give the love-nest a makeover. I can move out if you want.'

'No.' Oops, she'd shouted that out slightly more forcibly than she'd intended. Seeing Niamh with her lovely hair and smile had made had made her feel a bit of a useless lump. 'I mean, you don't need to. It's fine. Gran said so too. Stay.' He gave her that probing look. 'Please.'

He didn't say yes, but he didn't say no either – which was something. 'Come and see what you think.'

The last time she'd followed Mick up those steps she'd been oblivious to the heat he was giving off, expecting cobwebs and finding something so beautiful she'd rushed off before she made a complete and utter fool of herself.

This time she was wondering just how firm his buttocks were (they were only inches from her face and well within squeezing range), and whether they still belonged to Niamh, and was expecting an immaculate makeover that had removed every bit of her parents and their love, and instead found...

'Oh my God, wow.'

From somewhere Amanda had found a photograph of Billy and Alexa that Lottie had never seen before, and now it had pride of place in the small room. Her father was sitting astride a horse that Lottie remembered from her childhood, an old stallion that had since died and he'd buried near the lake. The horse was a grey, one of the few Billy had owned, his Andalusian heritage obvious in the proud carriage and flowing mane. And in front of Billy was his bride, Alexa, in her wedding dress, the veil hanging down over the horse's shoulder, her gaze fixed on Billy, laughter playing on her lips.

'She looks amazing.'

'I think she was.'

'Like mother like daughter.'

He'd said something like that before, but this time a shiver went down her spine and she didn't dare look at him. Not when there was a large bed in the room.

There was a new chair at the side of the bed, fresh cushions and bedding and flowers on the chest of drawers that stood in front of the window. And there was a gorgeous view of the courtyard below, which she was trying desperately to concentrate on, but all she could think about was the fact that he was behind her.

'I didn't expect to ever see her again. Niamh.'

'I didn't expect to see Todd again.' Lottie gave a nervous laugh.

'How long has Rory been a part of your life?'

'Forever.' She dared to glance at him, watched as he ran his fingers through his dark hair. 'That's how it feels.'

'I'll be your best man, but I'm not sure I can be your groom.' He kissed her then, on the neck. 'Not yet.' Then quietly backed off. She counted the steps he took down the stairs, listened for the door to open and clunk shut. Watched as he walked across the cobbles without looking back.

**

'So you do like it?'

'I love it.'

'You don't sound sure.' Pip frowned at Lottie over the stable door, pushing Flash out of the way as the chestnut mare, fed up with her haynet, barged over to see if Lottie had anything more interesting.

Lottie fished into her pockets to find the packet of mints that usually lived in there and found only a soggy white-and-green mass. 'Bugger, they've been through the washing machine again.' The mare, smelling success, made a lunge and narrowly missing the tips of Lottie's fingers, managed to snatch what was left of the packet.

'You shouldn't feed her mints, it makes her nip.' Pip frowned disapprovingly.

'Oh, she always nips. Especially Rory's bum when he's putting her boots on.' Lottie giggled.

'Well, you'll make her worse.' Pip pushed the horse back, then opened the door. 'So?'

'So what?'

'I can tell there's more. You've got that worried look on your face.'

Lottie, who had no idea that her expressions were quite that open to interpretation, hesitated. 'I met Niamh.' She peered at Pip, who seemed slightly surprised, but not particularly upset, which was good. It meant she was getting back to her normal, pre-Mick, self. A good dose of Todd seemed to have done wonders. 'She came looking for Mick.'

'And?' She fastened the door and double-checked it as Flash was building a reputation as an escape artist.

'Mick had said he'd be my groom, then he changed his mind.'

'Ah.'

'What does "ah" mean?'

'Poor Mick.'

Lottie frowned, thinking about her lustful thoughts that had gone to waste. Although that could have been a lucky escape, she was on the verge of throwing herself at him, which was probably partly down to wine and relief that the meeting with the bank had been a success. And all he'd done at the end of the day was talk about Rory. Maybe he thought she was a complete tart. Maybe he was right and she was just getting so bloody frustrated with Rory because he was avoiding her and making her feel like she used to: unloved and not needed.

'He's not here.'

'Who?'

Innocence didn't cut it with Pip, who raised an eyebrow. 'He's gone to look at a horse.'

'He never told me.' Lottie was miffed. Not only did he not want to live with her, he now didn't want to share anything. Did that mean it was over? That finally, after all these years of her chasing him, he was trying to tell her (well, avoiding telling her) that he'd had enough?

'He got a phone call and sped off straight away. One of his buddies was there when this horse threw a complete wobbler and tried to mash the rider against the wall. Told Rory if he got there quick he'd get a bargain.'

'I don't want Rory mashed against a wall.' Even if he doesn't love me.

Pip shrugged. 'Rory said it wasn't a bad horse, just a crap rider who thought kicking the shit out of horses was the way to get them to listen. Look, it'll be fine.'

'Not if it kills him.'

'I'm not talking about the horse. He loves you, Lottie, but he needs to grow up a bit.'

'What if he can't?' She chewed on her bottom lip and stroked Flash's soft nose.

'I don't know.' Pip sighed. 'Right now he's pretending nothing's changed, but he's missing you. He keeps going on about when you went to Barcelona, and muttering about losing stuff. He just wants you to come back here.'

'But I can't. And, he hasn't actually asked.'

'He isn't the type to ask, is he?'

Lottie thought for a moment. That hadn't occurred to her before. But he wasn't. Rory just grinned his schoolboy grin and people did what he wanted, without his actually asking. Until now. And she missed that grin. She'd rushed here to break the news of Niamh's arrival to Pip, before the village rumour mill kicked in, but she'd wanted to see Rory. To be reassured that he was still there, that everything was going to be okay (even if she'd been having totally uncalled for X-rated thoughts about Mick). In fact, it was probably because of that, she thought guiltily. She really shouldn't be apologising for something she hadn't actually done, and it was his fault. He knew she got randy when she was drunk, excited or triumphant (Rory loved nothing more than her winning any kind of horse-riding event because she was on such a high after. All he had to do was add wine.).

So he should have been there. And he should be her groom at the Wedding Fayre.

'Maybe I should just come back. I don't need to be up at Tipping House.'

'Yes you do, Lottie, and you know it. It's your home.'

'But he hates it.'

'I don't think he actually hates it.' Pip was sweeping the yard methodically, which helped her think. 'You know what? I reckon he's scared of it. He's scared of growing up and taking something like that on, and he needs to man up. Lottie I know you've always been mad about the daft idiot, but you need to let him make the decision.'

'I know.' Lottie said doubtfully.

'Say it like you mean it.' Pip grinned. 'Now help me fill these water buckets, then we can have a coffee and you can tell me what needs doing before the Fayre next week.'

Lottie picked up the hose and tried not to look at Tabatha, who was dressed in the shortest shorts that she'd ever seen, pumps and a vest top that exposed more skin that it covered. Pip grinned.

'Hard to believe this time last year she was goth girl and head to toe in black, isn't it? Must be the sun.'

Lottie, who had a fair idea that this was more to do with the fact that Tab lusted after Rory than the weather, frowned. She'd always trusted Rory around other women – she'd had to. She knew he was a complete flirt, and she knew he had more groupies than a lot of rock stars, but it had never seemed to matter. But she'd nearly jumped Mick, so what if…?

'He's scared of her.' Pip pointed at the hose. 'You need to turn that on.'

'I need to go.'

'You'll do no such thing.' Elizabeth let Mick settle her into the car. 'And where would you go?' She waited until he'd closed the door and got into the driver's seat. 'You wouldn't want to let Charlotte down, would you?'

Mick sighed and shook his head as he looked at Elizabeth.

'She needs you. I'd be grateful if you'd stay.'

'I need her, but you wouldn't be so grateful if I took her.'

She chuckled. 'Now you know you don't mean that. You don't need anybody, Michael, it's just a lusty, unfulfilled fantasy. Now, tell me about Niamh.'

Mick had been surprised when Dominic had rung, asking if he would go and collect Elizabeth from hospital. 'Sorry to ask, but we're supposed to be in Lancaster and she'll play hell if we leave her hanging around. Take my car,' he'd tossed the keys in Mick's direction, 'she won't approve of you turning up in the Land Rover.'

He'd been less surprised when he got there, and it looked as if she'd planned it all along. So now he could add chauffeur to the list of jobs she'd assigned him, alongside Lottie- minder and gate-mender. He glanced back at Lady Stanthorpe and tried not to smile. She was so like Dominic, her son, so unlike Lottie her granddaughter. Who had a huge chunk of Billy in her genetic makeup. She was waiting for an answer, obviously on one of her fact-finding missions.

'We grew up together, then I guess Niamh decided she needed to spread her wings and escape.'

'Escape or make a point?'

'Generally better to hang around if you're trying to make a point, I find.'

'Not if nobody is listening. Very British thing to do – shout louder when you're not understood, total waste of effort, I find.

When did Dominic last have this car valeted?'

'I don't know, but it hasn't been put on my list yet, I don't think.'

Elizabeth smiled. 'It's very kind of you to collect me.'

'You're welcome.'

'She sounds a nice girl.'

'Oh?' Mick waited, sure that eventually Elizabeth would tell him how she knew about Niamh and why he'd been summonsed. He also knew it would be in her own time, no point in asking.

'She went to Amanda's searching for you, and so of course Dominic told me. I take it that Rory has not been back in my absence?'

'Not that I know of.'

'Sometimes we need distance before we can get closeness.'

'Hm.'

'But it's all to do with the timing, isn't it Michael? Right time, right place. Ah, here we are. I do hope Lottie has made sure the larder door has been fastened properly, Holmes and Bertie can be such buggers.' She waited for Mick to help her out of the car and pass her a stick. He helped her wordlessly up the steps, knowing she wouldn't ask. Amanda met them at the door, which meant she could have well gone and collected Elizabeth in his place.

'I think you might find that Rory would be more than happy to have you back at the cottage – after the Wedding Fayre, of course, I think Tabatha and her hormones are proving challenging for him.'

He handed the car keys over. 'You can manage?'

'Yes thank you, dear. Amanda will help me settle. And,' she paused, 'I would appreciate it if you could escort my granddaughter at her first event, I won't ask again.'

Mick nodded, not sure who was craziest, her for asking or him for saying yes. He'd always credited Elizabeth with having a full set of marbles and being remarkably insightful.

'A platonic friendship can be of great value to a girl in her position.' Which put him firmly in his place. 'Right,' he got the briefest of winks, which, as she turned away, he decided his delirious mind must have imagined, 'a G&T now, I think, Amanda. Why those hospitals restrict your alcohol intake I don't know – miserable enough places as it is.'

Chapter 27

Pip had showered, changed and grabbed a sandwich before deciding that she needed to find out more. Despite the fact that these days she wrote less and less for the magazines and newspapers, her journalistic instinct could not be denied – she needed facts.

Most of her time these day was spent working on the yard with Rory and doing her freelance promotional work, where she was happy to put her little black book of contacts to good use and give the Tippermere and Kitterly residents the type of coverage they deserved.

When Pip had first moved to Tippermere, those same residents had provided inspiration for many a headline, but as time went by she'd lost the urge to see her name in print. She'd also grown to love the inhabitants of the village and as her outsider's independence was diluted, so was her ability to write cutting or witty articles about them. She'd found that she wanted to be a part of the life, not an observer making money from it.

True, she did still write the occasional column when a new celebrity appeared in Kitterly Heath, and the local newspaper quite often asked for her slant on something (more likely they wanted it spicing up and the editor was looking for a scapegoat in case it backfired and he lost local support).

Pip's last big scoop had been Billy's wedding, which was something that was newsworthy and (coincidentally) had a massive fuzzy feel-good factor – he hadn't been Britain's favourite show jumper for nothing. The fact that Todd had arrived on the scene and spiced up proceedings, and photo opportunities, had been a massive bonus. Pip couldn't help but smile to herself, Todd was a man who certainly knew how to make an impressive entrance and he was still trying to make an entrance with her… Whatever Tippermere hadn't delivered on, one thing was for sure, it had certainly delivered on the men. Which brought her full circle back to Mick.

When she'd first moved to the countryside she'd imagined she'd be bored, with more than enough time on her hands, and had toyed with the idea of writing a scandalous novel. But life had not quite panned out as she'd expected, and her relationship with Mick had somehow meant that the whole project had got side-lined. Maybe she should just write him into a novel, kill him off and be done with it once and for all.

Pip pulled her helmet on and started up her scooter. All Todd was, was a nice distraction, despite Elizabeth's meddling. And once again, it was Elizabeth who held all the cards, had all the answers. God, she'd kill to be like that when she was old enough to draw a pension.

Although, did she know about Niamh? Surely that would be messing up the old bat's plans to install Mick as Lord of the Manor? She would have loved to have seen the mysterious ex-lover Niamh's arrival herself; now that could have been interesting.

Pip had been pretty sure (and she was damned sure Elizabeth had spotted it too) that Mick had been lusting after Lottie since the day he first set eyes on her. She had, she admitted to herself, been mildly besotted with Mick. Okay, totally besotted. But besotted was the word, not love. And at long last she'd accepted the truth of the matter.

313

She'd thought for a brief time that it had been love, and thought she'd got a fractured heart when they'd split up, because he'd wormed his way into her heart in a way no man had before. But after a few drinks, a girlie chat or two, and a few wise words from Elizabeth she knew she'd deceived herself. She'd wanted to be in love. Desperately. Wanted this turmoil of emotions to have a label. But logic (and she did like to reason things out) had told her that she'd felt sick, upset and lost because for the first time in what was probably her entire life, she'd let someone in. She'd bared herself (and not just by stripping her clothes off), because she was pretty sure he'd never settle for anything less. He was an all-or-nothing type of guy.

And Mick hadn't abused what she'd given. She was pretty sure he'd wanted it to work out just as much as she did. He'd been honest. But they'd both been kidding themselves. For her it was like first love – for him it was an attempt to avoid the fact that he lusted after Lottie. Or maybe he didn't, maybe he was still in love with Niamh, who'd dented his ego and walked away.

Whether her previous choice of beta men had been a conscious move was a psychological minefield she wasn't going to venture into, but Mick was alpha all the way. After a string of lovers who'd done things her way, it had been a revelation to be in a relationship where there were clear lines, a man who knew what he wanted, a man who could more than stand up to her. Which was why, she guessed, the animals all respected him too. No confusion, clear messages, what you saw was what you got.

Pip hardly noticed the familiar lanes as she drove along them; she was too preoccupied with thoughts about Mick, Todd and what Elizabeth was up to. The text message from Amanda had been cryptic. *'Mick brought E home. She's told him he has to be L's bridegroom! Does she know?! E knows about his visitor. Can you take over? I need to sort flowers and caterers.'* Which Pip translated as *'Help! She's got me running round pouring gin and I'm worn out.'*

The first person she saw when she pulled up outside Tipping House was Amanda, looking out of the window. The relief on her face was almost comical and cheered Pip up. She didn't mind Elizabeth and her domineering manner, demands and mischief-making. She relished in it, and they shared the same sense of humour and nosiness (Elizabeth called it a desire for knowledge).

And she had some questions of her own.

'Thank you so, so much.' Amanda's stage whisper caused Elizabeth's eyebrows to rise, which Amanda saw and being so nice blushed furiously. 'It's just that Dominic fusses if I'm out too long.'

'That boy fusses over everything. Far too particular. I don't know where he gets it from. And pregnancy is a normal condition, Amanda. When I was carrying him I was still out hunting until I couldn't get in the saddle. Well,' she paused, remembering, 'the getting up was no problem, but damned difficult to get off the horse with a bump that size in the way. Had to ride side-saddle at the end. Never had any objections from his father, though.'

Pip laughed and said what Amanda was thinking. 'He probably didn't dare say anything.'

'Nonsense.'

'I'll go and finding your son, then, if that's okay?' Amanda looked from Elizabeth to Pip.

'Run along, dear, Philippa will give me an update, and I can tell she wants to talk to me. She's got that look on her face.'

Pip, who thought she'd got no such thing, shook her head and saw Amanda to the door.

'I'm sorry, I've got to rush, it's just—'

'No problem.' Pip grinned and gave her a hug. 'She's right, I have got something on my mind, and it involves interrogation. She's up to something.'

'Again.'

'Exactly, and I want to know what. I'm sure she thinks she knows what she's doing, but I'm not so convinced this time and I really don't want her dropping one of her surprises in the middle of the Wedding Fayre launch.'

'You don't think she's planning something?'

'I just know she is. Devious old trout.'

Amanda grinned. 'I sometimes wonder how she could possibly be Dominic's mother. I mean he's so sweet and organised and he likes to plan everything to within a millimetre of its life.' She paused. 'And he hates to upset anybody. That's why it took so long for him to say he wanted to marry me, you know.'

'I know. He's far too dutiful.'

'He's wonderful.'

The tap, tap of a stick carried clearly from the drawing room to the front door, and Pip grinned. 'I think I'm being summoned. See you later.'

Pip couldn't miss the fact, as she walked back into the room, that as Elizabeth shifted about in her seat she winced.

'Are you sure you should have come home so quickly?' It was too easy, Pip decided, because of her manner, to forget that Elizabeth was an old lady. And one who didn't respond well to sympathy and being wrapped in cotton wool.

'I wanted to be here for Charlotte. It's a lot to take on, you know. I remember what it was like when my mother died.'

Which made it even scarier, Elizabeth reminiscing.

'One day I was a little girl, the next I was running an estate. And my father was completely doolally – hopeless. He'd go out shooting in the middle of the night, stark naked, apart from his boots, and scare the game-keepers.'

Pip couldn't help but smile.

'I was always afraid the dogs would take a bite at the dangling parts of his anatomy, Labradors are always hungry, you know. And they followed him everywhere, even to the bathroom. Worst incident was when the old fool decided we were being invaded, was taking pot shots at everybody from the back terrace. The staff were being scattered in all directions before the farm manager managed to outflank him, put his bowler on, lit a cigar and pretended he was Churchill. Told him they'd surrendered and tea was served. Did the trick.' She paused and took a drink. 'The staff did adore papa. Life was quite boring once he'd gone. But anyway, enough of that, I have to be here for Charlotte, the only excuse to miss it would be if I was nailed in my coffin, and don't,' she gave Pip a look, 'think that will be anytime soon, young lady.'

'I wouldn't dare. I've missed you, you know.'

'You shouldn't be missing an old lady, you should be out having the wits scared out of you. You can't appreciate security until you've tasted fear, just as,' she took another drink, 'you shouldn't think about settling with one man until you've tasted real passion.' She fixed Pip with one of her eagle-eyed stares, a smile playing at the corners of her mouth. 'Should you?'

'And you shouldn't settle down until you've explored Australia with a beach bum?'

'He has a very nice bum from what I've seen, although a terrible seat when he's on a horse.'

'So,' Pip tried to deflect the attention away from her, and from Todd and his posterior, 'you are coming on Saturday, then, for the big event?'

'I wouldn't miss it for the world, Philippa.' Elizabeth had the slightest hint of a smile tugging at her mouth, and Pip gave her an assessing look. 'I wouldn't miss seeing my only granddaughter in her wedding dress.'

'It's not her wedding dress, as you know. And Dominic and Amanda might be presenting you with another granddaughter soon.'

Elizabeth smiled and didn't comment.

'What are you up to?'

'Me? Whatever makes you think I am up to anything? Honestly, you young people these days.'

'I know you well enough.'

'Well, I hope that you will do something with this stick of mine so it looks less of a geriatric aid and more of a fashion

317

statement, then. Shooting sticks are one thing, but these hospital-issue monstrosities are quite another.' She waved the stick in the air in disgust.

'I'm sure Mick can find you something more rustic, have you heard about him?'

'What about the boy? Come here Holmes, Bertie. I'm sure these dogs get fatter if I'm away.'

'That he's going.'

'Back to Ireland? Nonsense, he won't go back there. Not if that girl has any say in it, anyway.'

'So you do know about Niamh.'

'Of course I do.' Of course she did. How could Pip have ever, for one moment, thought she wouldn't? 'I've offered her a job here.'

'Niamh? You've offered Niamh a job?' Pip rolled her eyes and felt like hitting Elizabeth over the head with the much-abhorred stick.

'On certain conditions, of course.'

'Of course. And when exactly did you meet her?'

'I haven't. One doesn't have to do these things in person. It's a surprise for Dominic.'

'A surprise?' What on earth kind of surprised involved an ex-lover of Mick's, who'd broken (she was pretty sure) the man's heart, run off to the States, and then somehow ended up in Cheshire?

'You can't do that, what about Mick?'

'The girl was homesick. You youngsters these days have no real sense of adventure. In my day we'd be off at the drop of a hat, given the opportunity. I was in India on my own when I was twelve—'

'I'm sure you were. But she isn't twelve. Elizabeth, how come you've even heard of Niamh, let alone managed to discover she wants a job – and what about Mick?'

'I had someone talk to Michael's parents just after he came here. You don't imagine I'd let just anybody look after my grand-daughter, do you?'

She wouldn't bang her head on the wall, she wouldn't. 'How

could I ever imagine that? Elizabeth, he's just a friend of Rory's.'

Elizabeth made a noise that lay somewhere between a snorting horse and a bark. 'And he was riding out with Charlotte. I know exactly what can happen after a hard day in the field, young lady. Men can be very unchivalrous, and young girls can end up getting over- excited. That man has a very nice manner. Alexandra ran after more than one Irishman with a smooth tongue and strong physique. Such a melodious tone and poetic words. They always know how to woo.'

'That's what you call it, is it, strong physique? And you do know you're talking about *my* ex-boyfriend.'

'He was never really your type, Philippa, as you know, and I've noticed you're looking much happier now. But I couldn't possibly have entertained the idea of him staying in the courtyard unless I knew more about him.'

'But it was you who invited him.'

'I certainly did, once I knew his background. And now I'm inviting his friend.'

'I don't think they're friends now.'

'Oh, really?' Pip didn't like the sound of that. 'Well, in my experience, distance definitely does not make the heart grow fonder. Total tosh, that saying. Dreamed up by some poetic fool. Let's see what a few close encounters can do, shall we?'

'But Elizabeth,' Pip sighed, this was a meddle too far, 'she broke his heart.'

'I know,' Elizabeth tapped her stick gently on the floor. 'And he broke hers. She's desperate to see him again, and I think she's very brave to try, don't you?' She didn't wait for an answer, but her tone was soft. 'They deserve another chance, Philippa, but a man like Michael is never going to make it easy. He can't hide behind his fanciful notions about Charlotte forever. She's his smokescreen, a protective layer around his heart. Very sensible to plight your troth to the one girl you know will never say yes, isn't it?'

'I don't think anybody has been plighting anything.'

'In his head he has, and effectively shut every other woman out. But,' she paused, and fixed Pip with a stare, 'Niamh only has a job on the condition that Michael is happy for her to stay. She has a roof over her head until the Wedding Fayre and it's up to her to find out if they have a chance of mending bridges or not. It's not my job to interfere in their lives.'

Pip grinned and shook her head. Only Elizabeth could call that 'not interfering'.

'Now, enough of this talk. Help me up, dear.' Elizabeth struggled to perch on the edge of the chair. 'Darned old bones.'

'I think you should stay where you are for a bit. At least I know where to find you then.'

'Exercise. Can't be sat here seizing up.'

'Exercise within reason, Elizabeth. Please, just rest for a few hours. And what about Lottie?'

'What about Charlotte? Pass me that box, dear. I got Amanda to bring it down while she was here. It's my necklace. You need to help me with the clasp. Such a fiddly thing. I was thinking about wearing it on Saturday, if you don't think it's too over-the-top?'

Pip sighed. 'Lottie? You invited Mick here to look after her, I thought you...'

'Were match-making?' Elizabeth finally stopped fussing and chuckled. 'Is that what you thought? Oh don't be ridiculous. As if I would do such a thing. Oh no, no Michael wouldn't suit this role at all, dear, what were you thinking?'

'I wasn't thinking, it was you.'

'He's a nice young man, he brought you out of yourself and showed you that you can care, but he has always held a torch to young Charlotte. I saw the look on his face when she was out riding. I used to love it when I caught a young man looking at me like that. So exciting, makes one feel all hot and bothered. But that nonsense needed to run its course now. I wanted it out of their systems and forgotten. One doesn't want infatuations getting in the way in a few years' time when her marriage is stale and she's looking for adventure. That's the time she needs to concentrate on her husband.'

'But she hasn't got one.'

'She will have.'

'You're a crafty old goat.'

'And you're a very cheeky young lady. Now, what about this necklace?'

'Gorgeous. Sam will faint with envy.' Pip peered a bit more closely. 'Those diamonds, they aren't real ones, are they?' She did a quick mental calculations of how many lifetimes of her salary it would take to buy something like that.

'Well, of course they aren't, dear. It's my hip that's given way, not my common sense.'

'Oh.' She didn't know if she was disappointed or relieved.

'I will get the real ones out on Saturday. Now, I want you to do some fact-finding for me. That girl is staying in Kitterly Heath, you need to go and talk to her.'

Chapter 28

'Open your eyes.'

Lottie opened them, then opened them a bit wider. Then spun around to check that it was actually the front door of Tipping House that she'd been led through, and not some copycat film set that was actually all chipboard and props.

'Bloody hell.' She took a hasty step back when she saw the state of the worn floorboards. She knew she'd asked for them to be cleaned, but they'd been polished and waxed until they were a totally different colour, and you could hardly spot the woodworm holes at all. 'I should take my boots off.'

Samantha's hearty laugh echoed into the large space, almost drowning out Amanda's much more restrained one. 'Don't be daft, babe. But, isn't it amazing?'

She kicked them off anyway, and squinted at the panelling, which danced with reflective sunlight. It had never, ever looked like that. But, then again, she could never remember the grand staircase having a stunning red carpet like that either. Lottie suddenly thought about Harry, who was currently locked in the boot room. Oh God, what if he peed on it? There was another couple of days to go and he still hadn't the strongest bladder. How did one cover stains like that on a new carpet? She was much more used to dealing with moth-eaten, hair-covered rugs that made disguise easy.

322

'Elizabeth insisted on the carpet, she said it was obligatory for events, and we've got sheeting to cover the carpet until Saturday morning.' Said Amanda, who'd spotted the line of her gaze and correctly identified the worried look. 'Now, are you ready to hear Elizabeth's bit?'

'Do I need to sit down?' Since returning from hospital, Elizabeth had not been an easy patient. With her mobility limited she'd resorted to summoning Lottie and Amanda at what felt like hourly intervals for an update report. So, for the sake of their sanity the two girls had decided to put her in charge of organising the 'bride's arrival'.

It had worked like a charm as far as being left in peace went, but left Lottie with a whole new worry. Elizabeth had gone too quiet, which suggested it had been her intention all along to have control of this aspect of the day, and she had something up her sleeve.

Lottie crossed her fingers behind her back and wondered if it would have been safer to have disconnected the bell and worn earplugs. 'Right, then, let's hear it.'

'Okay,' Amanda checked her tablet, 'so, Rory will have the horse in the courtyard for you, and you'll ride—'

'Rory?'

'Well she said everybody will be expecting to see him.' Amanda looked apologetic. 'He is a star, and all the girls adore him, and Elizabeth was quite firm about wanting you on a horse, like your mother.'

'He's so cute.' Sam sighed. 'And those tight, white trousers.'

'Breeches.' Lottie corrected automatically, presuming she was talking about Rory on both counts, and not the horse. 'But I don't think he wants…' After the last argument they'd had, she really didn't think he wanted to ever set foot in the place again.

'He can't not be here. Elizabeth told me that if we had any trouble then she'd talk to him. And frankly it had to be Rory or Billy?'

'Christ, not my dad.' Lottie looked horrified. 'I just knew it was too good to be true, Gran saying she wouldn't interfere.' Amanda tried not to smile. The old lady had been quite specific about what to do if there were any objections to her last-minute plans.

Amanda had always been slightly in awe of Elizabeth, but she hadn't realised quite how much control the woman had – even when she declared absolutely no interest in anything. Despite handing over control of the event to Lottie, herself, Pip and Sam, Amanda was starting to suspect that the whole event had, in fact, been Elizabeth's idea, as was every last detail of what was happening.

'But I asked Mick. I thought Mick was going to do it?' She looked at Pip for confirmation.

Pip shrugged. 'I'll check, but it looks like Elizabeth has a change of plan.'

'So I don't even get to pick my own pretend groom now? Remind me never, ever again to let Gran have a say in how things are done.'

'She said she was concerned that as everybody knows you and Rory are an item, it'll look weird. And she does have a point. I mean, all the gossip will be about who Mick is, not about the venue, and you know what he's like, he won't be happy if reporters start to quiz him.'

'He won't?' Sam looked confused.

'He won't.' Pip was firm. 'And Mick did say he'd be your best man, not your groom, didn't he?'

'How do you know that?' Lottie looked at her with suspicion.

'Elizabeth told me.' Lottie groaned. 'Oh, come on, Lottie, you know she doesn't miss a trick. It'll be fine, trust us.' She linked her arm through Lottie's. 'Listen to the whole plan and then see what you think.'

'The whole plan?' There was more? Lottie's stomach sank further, if that was possible.

Sam was frowning, trying to work it out. 'And whoever it is will be in tight white breeches?'

'Definitely.'

Amanda decided to crack on. 'We will greet everybody in the courtyard—'

'Where Rory will be waiting with the horse?' She bit the inside of her cheek and carried on worrying. What if he refused to be there?

'Where Rory will be waiting. And you will arrive in the old Rolls, Lottie.'

Lottie was momentarily distracted from her worries about her groom. She was sure real brides never had this problem with stand-ins at the last minute. 'The one that the bank manager told me had to be sold?'

Amanda looked worried. 'You've not done, have you? Sold it?'

'Gran told me she'd misplaced it.' Lottie frowned. 'Said she'd got a horrible feeling that it had ended up in the lake after a hunt ball.'

'So that's what you told the bank?'

'I didn't think he looked like he believed me.'

'Well it's been rescued and miraculously dried out.' Pip's tone was dry.

'Ah isn't that fab? Her Ladyship is just so clever.'

'You don't have to call her Your Ladyship, Sam. And she's far too clever.'

'And,' Amanda tried to keep things on track, because she knew she'd need a wee soon. She might have gone past the sickness stage now, but this baby had found a new way to cause her discomfort, which seemed to involve prodding her bladder. 'And Rory will arrive on the horse.'

Lottie looked doubtful. 'But has anybody actually asked him yet? I really need to—'

'I have, he's cool about it. I told you he missed you.'

'But he doesn't miss this place.' Lottie who had been overjoyed at the beautiful, if slightly alien, appearance of the entrance hall now had a sinking feeling in her stomach. 'He told me, Pip.'

'We'll double-check, okay? But he was cool about it, as long as he's not actually involved in the getting-married bit.'

'So he's not my groom?' Now she was really confused.

'Shh. Listen to the rest.'

'And,' Amanda checked the list on her tablet and clenched her thigh muscles, not that her thighs naturally fitted together these days, or her muscles operated properly, 'we will have a little ceremony, to show people what a wedding could be like.' She glanced up, but Lottie, who was still wondering if she'd be stood up by Rory, just nodded. 'We've got details of the,' she paused, 'love-nest above the stables—'

'Love-nest?' Pip laughed.

'So romantic isn't it, babe, and it is like a little nest up there.'

Pip raised an eyebrow in Amanda's direction, which she tried to ignore as she just knew she'd laugh, which could release the floodgates.

'It's in the brochure, like you said, Lottie, with some fab pictures, but people can go and have a peep if they want. Then you and Rory will ride—'

'Ride? In a wedding dress?'

'In front of him, like in the picture of your parents. That is possible, isn't it?' Amanda frowned. 'Elizabeth said—'

Lottie and Pip both groaned.

Amanda backtracked. 'Well, she gave me that photograph of their wedding and said how she'd just love to see you like that.'

'I can't wait.' Sam gave a little squeal. 'Then you're going to walk up the red carpet we've got for these steps, and everybody will be waiting here for the bubbly. Isn't it glam? I told Davey I wanted to get married here, but he said two ceremonies is enough for anybody. So I said can't we have a wedding for Scruffy? I mean, I could get him a doggy tux.'

Amanda, who had been doing her best to juggle her tablet and cross her legs, giggled and knew she was in trouble. 'Crumbs, hang on. I really have to go to the loo.' And she bolted towards the large downstairs facility that she had last seen when they'd been showing Lottie her wedding dress.

'Aww, she's so sweet, and so ladylike about it.' Sam stroked her own stomach, which Lottie couldn't imagine being anything but super-flat. 'It must be wonderful.'

Pip raised her eyebrows. 'Puking for weeks, then having that replaced by the risk of wetting yourself if you sneeze?'

'You're funny.' Sam grinned, unperturbed. 'You're so lucky, Mandy.' She gave Amanda a hug as she re-emerged from the washroom and Amanda grinned, too relieved to notice the 'Mandy'.

'Lucky I made it in time. I feel like an incontinent old woman. Okay, so now to the big event. Mick will meet you here at the door.'

'Mick will?'

Pip grinned. 'This is the other part of her plan.'

'Yes, isn't that what you wanted? I thought, Elizabeth said—'

'Well, yes, but,' But whatever Lottie had been about to say was lost as Amanda pushed the large old doors open. If Lottie had been amazed at the way the entrance hall had been transformed, the Great Hall was staggering. She was so used to seeing it as it had always been, in all its shabby and worn glory, that she hadn't stopped to wonder about what it might have looked like when it was first built and furnished – when Tipping House really was grand with a capital 'G', and fit for all the Lords and Ladies that danced there.

She'd supervised all the early work and then left it in Amanda's capable hands to ensure that all the necessary tasks were carried out.

'Wow, it's beautiful.'

'Oh my God, look at those chandelier things. They look amazing now they're all cleaned up, don't they?' Lottie looked to where Sam was pointing and couldn't do anything more than nod.

'And the pre-ticket sales already cover all the bills.' Amanda smiled with satisfaction. 'I told you people were keen, partly because of all the wonderful press coverage Pip has arranged.'

'I did have to stretch the truth a bit.' Pip shrugged, not at all bothered. 'I hinted at a real wedding, and a few film stars and premiership footballers.'

'That's not a lie, babe.'

'Well, the wedding bit is. And I did kind of suggest we'd be announcing the first celebrity booking.'

'Have we got one?' Lottie looked alarmed. Doing this was one thing, but actual bookings?

'I'm working on it.' Pip winked. 'I have a shortlist.'

Whatever Lottie had originally imagined, it had been surpassed. The old drapes had been replaced by ones that looked just as old, but were minus the holes and frayed edges, the pictures had been restored to a former glory that Lottie had never seen before and the panelling had been polished until it glowed in the afternoon sunlight. 'Now, you're not going to let Rory and the boys have an impromptu jump-off like they did at your father's wedding, are you?'

'Crikey, no.'

'I was kidding.' Amanda smiled, serene and beautifully pregnant and calm (now she'd emptied her bladder).

Lottie, whose head space had been invaded by images of galloping horses, leftovers of the smelly kind on the red carpet and hoof marks the length of the ballroom floor, tried to shake the thought, but it just wouldn't let go.

'We'll keep the flowers and cake as a surprise, unless you want to see them? I've got the florist due at eight in the morning, the caterers booked…' Lottie wondered what her mother would think of all this. She'd ridden her pony through these rooms when she was a child – wild and happy. Would she approve of making money from her childhood home? '…and somebody will be here to do your hair and makeup… Lottie are you okay?'

'I'm fine. It's just so, so sorted. So,' she knew she sounded lame, 'real.'

'It is, and it will be wonderful. Here's your copy of the schedule, so you know what's happening.'

'Wow, isn't it fab? Amazing.' Sam clapped her hands and took her copy. 'You will die when you see the dress I've got, although

I won't upstage you, of course, babe.'

'Sure.' Lottie had bigger worries on her mind. Like Rory and Mick.

'It plunges right down at the back, and it's got this slit right up to my knickers, not that I can wear any, but I need to be able to dance, don't I? And Davey's got a new tux. He looks gorg with his tan. All the boys do – so fit and horny since they came back.'

'How do you know they're all horny?' Pip raised an eyebrow, knowing that Sam would be all too keen to give any extra details that might be required.

'Well, all the girls I've talked to—'

'Too much information.' Amanda grimaced and put the hand that wasn't holding her paperwork over one ear.

'Ah, bless. I bet you're not getting it the same in your condition, are you?'

She blushed.

'I suppose that is one downside, but you can make up for it after, can't you? You will get a nanny, won't you, babe? Cos I don't know what Davey would say if he had to share my boobs in the middle of the night, especially if we'd not been, you know, for ages.' Sam looked as if she was seriously considering this new complication for the first time, and Amanda busied herself with her list.

'Come on.' Pip tugged at Lottie's arm. 'Let's leave this pair to talking about shagging and go and work out how we're actually going to get some.'

***

'I really should hate her,' Pip, who had opted for leading Black Gold in hand, alongside Lottie, who had the wide-eyed Badger, was beginning to wonder if she'd made a mistake when both horses decided on a competition to see who could get through the gateway first. 'Aren't you supposed to lead youngsters out with something steady – not an airhead like Gold?'

'She's much steadier than she used to be.' Lottie hardly seemed to notice the fact that she'd nearly been squashed against the gatepost. 'She's much quieter these days. Mick said he thinks it's this place. Not just because she's in foal.'

Pip didn't comment on the fact that she'd heard a lot of Mick's opinions lately.

'I think it's because he's here too, all the horses like him.'

'And the people.'

Lottie gave a sideways look, under long lashes. 'Sorry, would you rather we didn't talk about him?'

'No, it's fine. I'm honestly over him. Once I thought about it properly, it was fine. But you don't think you're getting too…'

'Too what?' Lottie stopped abruptly and both horses tossed their heads in the air, sensing danger ahead. Pip cursed as Gold stamped on her foot for good measure.

'Too attached? I know he's really helping you, but what if he goes?'

'Why, where's he going?'

'I'm not saying he is, but what I was saying at the start, about knowing I should hate her, well, I was talking about Niamh.'

'Oh.' Lottie started walking again and both horses set off after her. Pip, being towed in their wake, jogged a few steps so that she was level.

'She's still here, staying in Kitterly Heath. And well – well I think she fancies Mick still.'

'Mm, so do I.'

'And what if, you know he still…?'

Lottie stopped again, but this time Pip was ready and dodged the stamping hooves. 'He's only helping me, I've not been sleeping with him or anything.' She glanced at Pip, as though expecting her to challenge it. 'Gran offered him the flat, not me.'

'But you like having him there? And he likes you.'

Lottie sighed. 'He did kiss me.' She saw the look on Pip's face, but she needed to be totally honest. 'It was after you finished, and it was only a quick kiss. I mean it wasn't a proper snog or anything,' she paused, then added for good measure, 'and we had all our clothes on. Both of us did. And there weren't tongues involved.' She set off again at a stomp, and Pip hoped nobody was watching their weird stop-start procession. 'I don't fancy him or anything. Well, I do fancy him a bit because he is hot, isn't he?' She didn't wait for an answer, 'but it's not like being with Rory.' She'd started to despair of ever working things out with Rory. It wasn't the same these days – it was almost like he'd stopped wanting to have fun with her because he thought she might suddenly insist he move back to Tipping House.

'He had a fit on me the other day. I completely forgot he was going to an event. He was so angry.' She frowned, there were so many entries in the diary, sometimes it was easy to miss the odd one. Except she had a horrible feeling that Rory's event hadn't even been written in the diary. 'He rang me at five in the morning cos I wasn't there to plait up, then went ballistic when I said I couldn't go. He said,' her insides shrivelled a bit even as she said it, 'that if I wasn't so obsessed with this damned pile of the past then I'd remember him once in a while.' And he'd asked her where the girl he'd loved had gone. 'He says he's lost the old Lottie.'

'Aww Lottie, I'm sorry. But he doesn't mean it. He does miss you. He'll get used to the fact that things have to change.'

Lottie wasn't so sure. 'He does mean it. I think I'm just going to be like a younger version of Gran, and I'll just gradually turn into her, on my own with the dogs.'

Pip laughed, and Lottie smiled despite herself. 'You will never be like Elizabeth. But, I did just want to warn you about Niamh. She seems nice.'

'I suppose Mick wouldn't go out with somebody who wasn't nice.' She raised an eyebrow, 'Don't you mind about Niamh?'

Pip shrugged. 'Honestly? No. No, I really don't.' She grinned. 'I really don't. Did you know Elizabeth has offered her a job?'

'What kind of a job?'

'As a companion.'

'But I look after Gran, and you do, and Amanda.'

'She said she doesn't want to turn into one of those old people who are an encumbrance. And she also said that as Niamh has experience as a nanny she'd be ideal to help Dom and Amanda out.'

'Do they know?' Lottie raised an eyebrow.

'Nope, of course they don't. It's one of Elizabeth's surprise gifts that you don't know about until it's too late to say no. She's probably already given her a key to their front door at Folly Lake Manor and instructions on how to bring up a baby the old-fashioned way.' Pip grinned. 'She'll be there to greet them at the door with the nappy-rash cream in her hand the day it's born.'

'Maybe Mick won't want to be my best man now.'

'I'm not sure he knows about Elizabeth asking Niamh to stay yet.'

'Oh. But even so.'

'He will, he promised,' she smiled,' and he promised Elizabeth, and Rory promised to do his bit as well. Elizabeth probably knew it was a step too far to expect Rory to do everything, so you get two men for the price of one. It'll be fine. Which is more than I'm going to be if your horse stands on my foot one more time.'

Lottie laughed and stroked Badger's long nose. 'Badger loves Gold. He's going to be surrogate daddy to her foal, aren't you sweetie?' Badger whinnied and tossed his head up and down, his long baby forelock covering one eye. 'Silly sod, you can't see. Here.' She reached up to push the hair out of his eyes. The shadow of her arm crossed the one eye he could see out of and Badger spooked.

Lottie ducked as he half-reared, his dangling forelegs just missing her head, then he staggered backwards, unbalanced, until he collided with the solid bulk of Black Gold.

Caught unawares, Gold shot forwards, knocking Pip over, her hoof catching in the dangling reins. The leatherwork wrapped around her leg, the mare staggered forwards, stumbled on a rut in the track that had baked concrete-hard over the hot summer, and went down with a heavy thud onto her knees.

For a second Lottie froze, then dashed forward, expecting the horse to be struggling to her feet before she got there. But she didn't, she lay winded, and didn't make a sound as the dark trickle of blood pooled in the dirt.

***

'Go and check Badger is okay, he's a baby.'

Lottie hesitated, and Mick looked up, his dark gaze meeting hers. 'Go on, I'll look after her.'

Surrounded by dangerous thrashing hooves Lottie was fine. But faced with the motionless Black Gold she'd panicked. Pip had picked herself up and gone after Badger, who, realising he wasn't about to be eaten, had trotted a short distance then put his head down to eat grass.

Thoughts of broken legs filled her head, followed swiftly by nightmares of the horse going into shock and losing her foal. Lottie tugged her mobile phone out of her pocket and frantically called Rory, whose cheerful voicemail message made her heart sink. She tried again and again, getting more and more desperate as she sat on the hard ground by Gold, who looked at her listlessly. He had to pick up, he had to answer. He had to help. But he didn't.

'Ring Mick.' Pip's instruction broke through her frantic dialling. So she had. He'd picked up on the second ring and was there within minutes, his calm voice drying up Lottie's silly tears and his gentle urging stirring the mare to her feet.

Pip had gone ahead with Badger, who didn't look as shamefaced as he should have done, and the sorry trio of Lottie, Mick and

Gold limped slowly behind back to the yard.

By the time Lottie had checked over Badger and Pip as instructed, Mick had slipped the bridle from the unresisting Gold and replaced it with a head collar. He was murmuring softly to her all the time as he gently ran the water from a hose over her knees, his other hand stroking with long, steady sweeps down her neck, over her shoulder.

'I'd call the vet if I was you, treas. She's made a mess of this knee, but that'll mend. She's just a bit more out of sorts than she should be.'

'Oh God, you don't think she's going to...'

He glanced up. 'I'm sure she'll be fine, but I'd get them to pop by to be certain.'

'Oh no, I'll never forgive myself if,' she could feel her lower lip wobbling, the tears threatening to brim over again.

'Come here, you daft woman.' And she did, letting him put one arm around her shoulder as he held the hose in the other, resting her head on his warm broad chest, and hoping to hell that her horse was going to be okay.

Neither of them saw Rory, who stood in the archway for a moment, then slowly turned and went back the way he'd come.

Chapter 29

'Oh, sugar, it must be that pizza I had last night.' Lottie wailed as Sam did her best to pull the material over Lottie's hips.

'Well, we can't put it over your head now you're made up, babe, it'll make a right mess. Wriggle.'

'You could always grease her up.'

Sam giggled. 'You are so bad, Pip.'

'Or we could put a tea towel over her head, then pull the dress down.'

'Will you stop talking about me as though I'm not here?' The thought of them both heaving to get the dress over her head and possibly leaving her trussed up like a mummy, filled her with more dread than the idea of it splitting as they tried to drag it upwards.

'It'll smudge her. Oo look, it's okay! I didn't pull the zip down properly – it's got at least another inch.' Sam gave a tug and the dress, as well as Lottie, seemed to give a huge sigh of relief.

'And we all know how much difference an inch can make, don't we?'

'Every millimetre counts.' Sam was laughing so much her hands were shaking.

'Oh God, I wish Amanda was here to control you two. Where is she?' Lottie looked around, hoping that she was there somewhere, hiding in a corner.

'She's helping Elizabeth.'

'Oh.' She was tempted to ask why Pip or Sam couldn't go and help her gran, but that would have sounded mean. 'Will you two please stop laughing and do me up, or I think I'm going to pop out of this bra. Whoever came up with the idea of balancing your boobs like this?'

'I think they're supposed to be in at least up to the nipples.'

Before Lottie could stop her, Sam was around the front and hiking up the cups of the bra. 'There, that's better, don't they look nice? Although if you'd had them done you wouldn't need the bra, babe.' And with that she pulled the dress the rest of the way over Lottie's hips, leaving her gazing down at her boobs and wondering if she really should consider taking Sam's advice.

'Arms up. There you go, babe. Gorgeous.'

Lottie was so relieved she had actually fitted in the dress, she was ready to do anything anybody told her, except she did have one worry on her mind. 'What if I need the loo?'

'We'll hitch it up for you, babe.'

'No, you won't.' She took an experimental step, just to check that the seams wouldn't split if she moved. 'How the hell do I get on a horse?'

'Helicopter?' Pip got a glare. 'I'm sure you'll get plenty of offers of help, don't worry about it. If your mum did it, then so can you.' Lottie squashed down the thought that she probably weighed at least a stone (or two) more than her slim and pretty mother had. 'Right, let's sort the crown jewels.'

The 'crown jewels', much to Sam's disappointment, were fairly toned down and tasteful. She was, Elizabeth had told Sam firmly, saving the best for herself and Lottie was wearing what all Stanthorpe brides had worn, no more and no less. Which satisfied Sam, as her Ladyship was the absolute expert in these matters.

'Bloody hell, love, you've scrubbed up well. Let's have a look at you.' Billy, who had marched into the room without knocking, propelled his daughter nearer to the window and then gave her a

336

once-over like she'd seen him do to a prize show jumper.

'Dad, you can't just…'

His lips were compressed into a straight line as he looked, then looked again. And if Lottie hadn't known him better, she'd have thought he was about to come over all emotional. When he did speak, his voice was as gruff as ever, but it was what she called his 'happy gruff', as opposed to his 'grumpy gruff'. 'Your mum would be so proud, Lots. You look gorgeous. She was a real stunner, and you take after her.' He gave her an impulsive hug and kissed her on the end of her nose. 'Although, of course, you've got my good looks as well. Looked the most beautiful ever on her wedding day, she did.'

'Dad, you do know it's not *actually* my wedding?'

'Of course I do, love. Mind you, when I told you to practise everything I didn't mean to go to this extent.' He gave a loud laugh, the sentimental moment passed. 'And I definitely don't want you going around rehearsing wedding nights.'

'Dad!'

'Oh good heavens.' Amanda flew in, looking as immaculate and cool as ever, apart from her flushed cheeks and the fact that a tendril of hair had escaped from her Alice band. 'Your bouquet. What have they done with your flowers?'

'I'm sure they'll turn up,' said Lottie, wondering how she was supposed to balance on a horse in a slippery satin dress (particularly as she couldn't sit astride), and hold a bunch of flowers, which no doubt the horse would either try and eat or decide was a scary monster. Either way, it was probably better if they turned up later rather than sooner. 'I can pick them up in the entrance hall, can't I?'

'Oh no, no, they have to be in the pictures. And where's the photographer from *Cheshire Life*? I just promised them an advance shot of you dressing,' she shot a look at Billy, who she'd only just noticed, 'without any men, in your bedroom, before you left. You'll have to wait outside, but don't go, Lottie. Please don't move.'

Sam giggled. 'A shot of you actually dressing would have been more fun – when we were trying to get the zip up.'

'And shoving your boobs into place.'

Billy turned puce and took a backwards step. 'I'll wait outside, shall I?' He didn't have that much choice as Amanda swept him out in front of her, her mobile to her ear, as she tried to track down the missing flowers and photographer.

The photographer had, it turned out, been side-tracked by a demanding Elizabeth, who mistaking him (or more likely not) for a member of the catering staff, had sent him in search of a large gin and tonic, or preferably a bottle, if he could smuggle one out from under Dominic's nose. The man had done his duty admirably, unaware that the bottle he'd been given had been doctored and diluted down to half-strength by Dom, who knew his mother only too well. He arrived slightly breathless, after Amanda had shoo'd him from Lady Stanthorpe's room and sent him running down the corridor to Lottie's, but fairly sure that he'd be granted access to all kinds of places that the other members of the press wouldn't get to.

Skidding to a halt outside the room, with his camera clutched to his chest, he smiled a hello to Billy, then paused, 'I know you, don't I?'

Billy was used to anonymity when he was out of his jodhpurs and horseless and toyed with the idea of saying he was the butler, until Sam poked her head out of the door and blew him a kiss. 'She's decent now, and we've stopped talking about boobs. Oh, hi. Are you here to take the piccies? You haven't got the flowers have you?'

He looked nonplussed, and Billy shrugged. 'Only my camera, love. I do know you,' his attention was back on Billy, 'Hang on, don't tell me. Film, no, starlet story? No, hang on, hang on, it's coming,' he suddenly grinned, 'Bonko Billy! You're the show jumper who shagged all four nations after the Olympics, kudos.'

'Will you shut up about that?' Lottie's wail carried clearly across the room to them. The picture of Billy naked (apart from the gold medal around his neck) in a Jacuzzi with three female show jumpers had haunted her through her teenage years, and she'd really hoped it had disappeared when she'd hit her twenties. 'That was years ago, and it was three bloody nations, you don't need to exaggerate.'

'Father of the bride.' Billy grinned, trying not to look too pleased with himself.

'And I'm not a bride. Stop calling me that.'

The photographer, by now beginning to enjoy himself, winked at Billy, then peered past Sam to get a good look at Charlotte. 'You're looking a damned good imitation of the blushing beauty.'

'Oh God, I think I need to go to the bathroom.'

'I feel another bare Brinkley shot coming on.'

Lottie glared at him. 'You are supposed to be working for the *Cheshire Life* not some, some…'

'Tabloid?' Sam supplied helpfully.

'Taste is my middle name.' He tapped the side of his rather bulbous nose.

'More like tosser,' muttered Pip into her fast-emptying champagne glass, before giving him her best professional stare, which he positively wilted under. 'Rosie will have a lot to answer for if you're not as good as she said.'

'Don't judge a book by its cover, love.'

'Well, I was actually. That coffee-table book that you've been flogging to every rich and not-so-famous person you've snapped.'

'Here, here.' Lottie was relieved that Amanda reappeared to break up the tetchy discussion, clutching a large bouquet of cream lilies. 'Ten minute, then you need to be off.' She pushed what looked to be half a florist's shop window display in Lottie's direction.

'But I think I need the loo.'

'You'll be fine, it's nerves.'

'Use the bottle in the Rolls, after you've drunk the bubbly, of course.' Sam giggled.

'I can't pee in a bottle.'

'Course you can, babe, nobody will see under that dress.'

'Photographs.' Amanda frowned. 'Pip, sort the photos, please? I really need to keep an eye on Elizabeth or she'll be heading to the stables on her own, and I really don't think cobbles and fractured hips are compatible.'

Standing still was not something Lottie had a particular aptitude for. Nor was smiling in an innocent, but coquettish, way – with a bunch of flowers in her hands and the afternoon sun glancing off the gleaming tresses of hair, so that she looked like an oil painting of one of her not-so-distant ancestors.

Pip read the look of increasing desperation in her big eyes. 'Can't we just go for the modern, carefree look?'

'Old Lady E said aristocratic and restrained, with a dash of spirit.'

'The only dash of spirit she'd be bothered about is gin. Lottie isn't some ancient relic! Does she look like she's tied up in a corset?'

The photographer grinned. 'I'm not bothered about staged stuff like that, poppet,' Pip glared at the endearment, so he redirected his attention to Lottie, 'just make sure you look my way when I shout your name, love. Right, let's get this show on the road shall we? Tracking down booze for the old bird has made me thirsty. Nice to see you again, mate,' he clapped Billy on the arm, 'and dressed, too – hardly recognised you.'

Pip stared as he ambled off, laughing. 'Hilarious.' Then she glanced up at the sound of a large sniff. Sam was dabbing at the corner of her eye with one finger.

'Aww sorry, babe, but she just looks so gorgeous, and it's so lovely. Aww don't you love a wedding?' She sniffed again. 'Oh, I'm just so happy for you.' Then blew her nose loudly on what, Lottie hoped, was a tissue and not the hem of her dress.

Lottie, who was feeling less romantic by the second and more and more worried that neither Rory nor Mick would be there to help her out, hitched up her skirts and shoved her bouquet in Billy's direction. 'Well, it isn't a wedding and even if it was, isn't it rather a lot of fuss? I think I'd rather just elope, to be honest.' She was beginning to see why Rory, in his panic that he might actually have proposed, had taken the open-window option. She was quite tempted herself, except it would be impossible in this dress, and it wasn't a real wedding. It was to save Tipping House for the future generations she'd probably never have.

'Your grandmother would kill you,' Billy, who had been watching without comment, passed her the flowers back, 'or more likely she'd kill me. Come on, love, everybody will be waiting for your grand entrance.'

'I haven't been in this car for years.' Lottie wriggled about on the leather seat and accepted the glass of bubbly that the chauffeur (who looked suspiciously like one of Elizabeth's gardeners) handed her. 'I really thought Gran had got rid of it.'

'She hides things. Paranoid that the bank will insist she hands them over. Do you mind if we take a bit of a detour, love, just want to check that Tigs didn't put the stallion in with any of the mares again? That woman's going to be the death of me – got a brain like a sieve.'

'Didn't Amanda say we had to drive around the estate and then go in the front gate and down the drive so everybody can see the grand entrance?'

'We will come in the main gate – we'll just go via Folly Lake. Take us ten minutes tops,' he checked his watch, 'but we need to get a move on.'

By the time they'd taken the back gate out of the estate, passed the front gate and were on the way to the Equestrian Centre, Lottie had all but forgotten Amanda's strict timetable as she finished her second drink and was hunting the cabinet for a bag of much-needed peanuts.

'Bad news, I'm afraid, folks.'

She glanced up as the car slowed to a halt and the gardener took off his chauffeur's cap and scratched the top of his balding head. 'Think we're out of petrol.'

'Petrol?' Lottie looked at him blankly.

'Fuel. Did none of you girls think to fill her up?'

'Us girls?' Lottie stared. 'Isn't it your job if you're the driver? You washed it, didn't you? Oh cripes! Amanda will kill us if we're late.' She looked around for her ever-present mobile phone, only to remember that she hadn't been able to work out where to put it. The only safe place seemed to be down her cleavage, but then she'd been worried about what would have happened if it had rung at any point. Vibrating boobs would have been bad enough, but fumbling between them to fish it out would have been worse.

She looked at Billy. 'You'll have to call Amanda or Gran.'

'Can't love, no phone.'

'But you always have your phone.' And he did, he was worse than her. He'd even been known to take a call in the middle of a show-jumping round once, and the steward had gone puce and tried to disqualify him, until Billy pointed out that there wasn't a rule that said calls couldn't be taken by riders – then given him the V's before taking first prize.

'It was confiscated.'

'Why?'

'Aren't we wasting time here, love? It's your wedding and all, but I think there's fashionably late and there's a point where, if you're not careful, the guests will be too pissed to recognise you.'

'I can't walk in these shoes, I just can't! I'll have to take them off.'

'I've got a phone if you want to borrow it?' The gardener-cum-chauffeur waved his own mobile in the air and Lottie made a grab for it, then hesitated – one finger poised over the keys.

'Who shall I call?'

'Dom. He'll huff and puff and mutter like a girl, but he's probably the safest bet. And I know he managed to sneak his mobile in.'

Lottie put the number in doubtfully. 'Uncle Dom?'

He didn't huff or puff. He sighed, checked exactly where they were and said 'leave it with me'.

Lottie had another drink and wondered if it would be like this if she was getting married for real.

Billy put his hands in his pockets, stood in the middle of the road and gazed up it impatiently.

The gardener whistled tunelessly and fiddled with the knobs and switches on the dashboard.

And the sound of hoof beats glancing off hard tarmac echoed up the quiet country lane.

'Now, don't you look a pretty picture?'

'Oh, Mick, you're a star.' Lottie beamed, then frowned. 'But you've got horses, I'm in a dress.'

'It was Elizabeth's idea.' Mick gave a crooked smile and handed the reins of the horse he'd been leading to Billy, who gave a loud guffaw.

'I bet it bloody was. So much for the idea that Dom would keep it quiet.'

'You can't keep anything quiet from Gran.'

Lottie looked at the horses glumly.

'Never a truer word said, treas. Come on, let your dad give you a boost up here – room for two.'

'Two?'

'I promise I won't hold you too tight.'

'But I can't.'

'You could stand on the car bonnet.' The gardener, who'd been watching with interest, chipped in. 'Piece of piss to get on from there, if you'll, er, pardon the expression, Miss.'

'Stand on the bonnet?' Lottie stared at him, and before she knew what was happening, Billy had grabbed her.

'Feet up. Come on girl.' She did as she was told and he tossed her up in much the same way he'd have thrown a bale of hay onto a stack, which wasn't good news at all when you were dressed like she was. The gardener, pleased that he'd been helpful, crossed his

343

arms and decided this was much better than dead-heading roses.

'Dad!' She wobbled and he caught her with a laugh, just as she was sure she was about to slide across to the other side of the car and end up in the hedge.

Lottie caught her breath and tried to be the lady-like bride they all expected. But standing on a car bonnet, in four-inch heels and a wedding dress was so not how life was supposed to be. Nor was having three men looking at her with smiles on their faces.

'Oh, just get on with it, please.' She tossed the bouquet, which she'd been hanging onto up to that point, purely because she'd forgotten she had it, into the field.

Billy raised an eyebrow.

'What? I can't carry those as well, can I?'

'You need to turn around, face the other way.' Mick had his hand on her waist, his horse motionless in front of her. Then the warmth of his arm was around her and she was nestled firmly against his hard thighs before she had time to complain.

'Christ, that's uncomfortable.' She wriggled, then froze when he gave her a warning look and she felt an unexpected area of extra hardness against her leg.

'I'd sit still if I was you, treas.' The soft words were just for her, and the look in his eye made her look away guiltily.

'This has to be one of her daftest ideas yet.' Billy, satisfied that she was secure, threw the reins over his horse's head and vaulted into the saddle.

Daft idea or not, it was, Lottie decided, actually quite nice, being perched in front of Mick. Now she was avoiding his look and trying to forget his words, and his bodily parts. She just hoped nobody saw them, because they just had to look like the weirdest wedding party Tippermere had ever seen.

Well, she was enjoying it, apart from the fact that if she as much as twitched she was afraid she'd slither out of Mick's grasp and slide to the ground, because whoever had decided satin was a good choice for a dress was mad. And Amanda would kill her if she arrived with added grass stains.

Billy, who had commandeered the gardener's phone and had refused to give it back after Lottie had called for reinforcements, was now busy closing a sale on a horse, which he said he might as well do now as leave until tomorrow. Lottie reckoned he actually was so used to riding and phoning that he'd forgotten how to ride with two hands free. Mick didn't say anything, just kept one hand firmly around her waist to make sure she didn't slip off and the other on his reins. She was so relieved when they turned in through the large gateposts that she didn't immediately see the welcoming committee, which consisted of several photographers and a few journalists, notepads in hand.

'Hey up, Billy, still got all your clothes on, mate?'

Mick raised an eyebrow.

'Don't ask.' Sighed Lottie, as Billy waved the V's in the air behind them, effectively ruining what the photographer had judged a prize snap of the wedding party. He swore good-naturedly, calling Billy an unsavoury name that Lottie hoped wouldn't be repeated in front of her gran.

'Are you sure this is what Gran had in mind?' She hissed at Mick as his horse skittered as a flashgun went off inches from its face and he had to tighten his grip.

'Steady, boy. Who knows with Lady E?'

'I think I'm going to slide off.'

'No you're not. I've got you.'

'Are there supposed to be this many people here?' As they approached the house the crowd had grown alarmingly, and she couldn't see a single familiar face. Well, not familiar as in somebody she knew properly, more familiar as in faces she'd seen on TV or in magazines. It was all getting a bit surreal. Any second now she'd wake up to find water dripping through the roof onto her face.

She glanced up as Mick's fingers tightened to hold her more securely, but he didn't look particularly bothered. 'Rent-a-crowd. Must be expecting somebody important.' He winked. 'Saw them all before I set off, darling, and they've all been tramping through our little love-nest,' Lottie stared fixedly at the horse's mane as the heat rushed to her face, 'went down a treat. Here we go, then, hold tight.'

Lottie did, gripping his arm as he turned the horse in through the archway that led to the courtyard. It was like a close-up firework display, and she was pretty sure that was illegal, as they emerged on the other side. She looked aghast at the sea of faces, and heard a blur of clapping hands, not to mention the blinding flash as a battery of shots went off.

The horse must have been as shocked as she was, because it stopped dead, then took a step backwards, luckily it was straight into Billy's mount, which had seen it all before and stood rock solid.

'Shall I let go, then?' The Irish burr was soft in her ear, his breath warm against her neck.

'Don't you bloody dare.'

'Where've you been? If you'd been with anybody but your Dad I'd have thought you'd been sneaking in a quickie. You were supposed to just drive around the estate, weren't you?'

Lottie didn't immediately answer Pip, because she was too busy staring, open-mouthed at the collection of guests, which had been neatly assembled on all sides of the courtyard.

'Bloody hell, where did they all come from? There's hundreds of people.' She swung around to check just how many hundreds, and Mick swore as she pressed against parts of him he was trying to ignore.

'Not exactly hundreds.' Pip looked smug.

'Hundreds.' Lottie swung around the other way and looked in awe. It was the type of crowd you'd expect in Westminster Abbey, not Tipping House.

'Will you sit still? Or you'll be ending up in the fountain.' The horse pawed at the cobbles, unsure of which way to go next.

'Amanda has a list of contacts even longer than mine. She's ace

346

at this, and she's been handing out glossy brochures like they've gone out of fashion. Elizabeth has been acting like she's the Queen Mother at a garden party, which is probably why she sent Mick with the horses so she could have her moment of glory without interference.'

'Probably.' Billy's tone was dry.

'Jolly good, you're back.' Amanda glided up in her normal effortless fashion, which Lottie had to admire given that she now had quite a baby bump. 'Running out of petrol was not on the schedule.' She gave Billy a gentle look designed to make him feel guilty, and it worked. 'But it's all worked out well, hasn't it? They've got some lovely photos. I think now if we can just have Lottie on the horse on her own. Is that safe?' She looked worriedly from Lottie, to Mick, then at Billy and Pip, hoping, no doubt, that somebody would say it was out of the question. She'd had enough trouble herself actually sitting astride on a horse, and it had scared her witless when it had moved, so that the idea of somebody sitting in a dress, side- saddle, was totally out of her comfort zone and idea of what was actually possible.

'Sure it is. Hang onto the horse's head.' Amanda took one look at the head in question and visibly flinched, which left Pip to take a hold of the reins as Mick swung smoothly to the ground and had his steadying hand back on Lottie before she had a chance to complain, or slide off her perch. 'Here.' He lifted her onto the centre of the saddle, which felt amazingly more secure, then his hand was on her ankle as he guided her foot to the stirrup. 'It'll help you balance.'

'Er, yes, er.' That touch had felt as intimate as if he'd run his hand up the inside of her naked thigh, which was pretty much what was on Lottie's mind.

'And if you stand at the side and hold the horse, Mick, I think that's what they want. Is it Pip? And where are your flowers? You must have flowers.'

Mick stood and wished he'd never promised Elizabeth that he'd be there today. But 'no' was not a word Lady Stanthorpe recognised, and he'd known it would have been futile complaining. And, if he was honest with himself, a large part of him wanted to do it, but it was torture.

He smiled as the photographers instructed, looked up at her as they told him and it made his heart hammer. She'd never looked so unbelievable. The wild glint in her eye, her hair tumbling down her back, and only the way she was chewing on her lip between shots betrayed the fact that she was nervous. Then she grinned – the fun-loving Lottie he knew. It was there for a split second, and he didn't even need to turn his head to know why. She'd spotted Rory, appearing on the other side of the yard.

Then the grin had gone – gone in like the sun. Extinguished, which was roughly how he felt. His stomach lurched, just as his groin tightened painfully. The horse fretted as he tightened his grip on the reins. He took a deep breath, relaxed his hold, looked up ahead and met the eye of Elizabeth. A small smile playing on her lips as she gave a little nod of her head in his direction. But it wasn't Elizabeth who held his attention, it was the girl next to her. Niamh. It had been so good once – they'd been good, until he'd refused to be told what to do. And she'd refused to wait. He shook his head slowly.

'I can't.'

'Sorry?' Lottie's soft voice made him realise he'd said it out loud.

'I can't stand here much longer, treas.'

'Me neither. Just how many photos do they need?'

'I think maybe a few with the bride's father?' He'd addressed the comment to the crowd, and a roar of approval went up. Everybody loved Billy.

Mick glanced up at Lottie as he swapped places with Billy. 'I'll put this horse away, darling. I'll catch you later.'

'But aren't you?' She frowned as he patted her leg.

'I've things to sort,' and the look Elizabeth gave him as he led the horse past her was, he felt, an acknowledgment that he'd been relieved of duty.

By the time all the photographs had been taken, Rory had disappeared from sight and Lottie was feeling distinctly fed up with being the centre of attention. Her bum hurt from the strange position on the saddle, and there was a pain in her chest that had settled there the moment she'd realised that Rory wasn't going to join in. It was Mick, reliable, dependable Mick who had been on the horse with her. Not Rory, the man she'd given her heart to so many years ago – the man who wanted nothing to do with her future life. Unless, just maybe, he'd turn up now, ride to the house with her?

And her face ached from smiling. Maybe, she thought, that was why Botox was popular. If it could keep your face fixed permanently in a certain position that had to be a bonus, didn't it?

And she was hungry. Her stomach was making noises. She shifted uncomfortably in the saddle as the guests were led out of the courtyard by Amanda and what seemed like an army of organisers and nearly fell off the horse. 'Bugger, can I get off now?' She'd have given anything to be able to search the stables, find Rory, sort things out. But it wasn't an option. For the first time she could ever remember, though, she was dying to get off a horse.

'No.' Pip laughed. 'Have you not read your spreadsheet? You've got to ride over to the main entrance of the house, then be led up the steps by your bevy of young men.'

'Oh hell fire, I forgot that bit.'

'What time's dinner, love?' Billy glanced at his watch.

'Soon. Once the bride has waltzed down the red carpet.'

Lottie groaned. 'You are kidding? If a bride did this for real there'd be no consummating anything for weeks. Have you any idea how uncomfortable it is on this horse? Crumbs.' She put a hand on the pommel of the saddle and tried to relieve the pressure. 'And where's Mick gone to?'

Pip shrugged. 'Not a clue.'

'And I thought Rory was supposed to be doing this with me?' She didn't miss the worried look on Pip's face. 'He promised. What's the matter? Where is he? I saw him in the yard, then...'

'I don't know, Tab spotted him throwing his boots at the wall and she was going to talk to him, but he was being weird. That was her word not mine. I think he scared her. Muttered something about how he'd forgotten something, then he put his boots back on, said horses were more bloody fun and rode out of the back, she said.'

'Rode off? So he doesn't even want to do a fake wedding with me? I told you he didn't! I knew he didn't want to be involved.' The hollow feeling that had lingered in the pit of her stomach after she'd spotted him leave the courtyard spread.

'Lottie, stop it.' Pip gave her a stern look, panicked that the bride of the day was going to dissolve into a sad pool at her feet.

'Look, girls, it's none of my business but I'm bloody starving and I'm sure everybody else is, so come on.' Billy urged the horse forward a step and Lottie nearly fell off.

'Dad, stop.'

'No, he's right.' Pip nodded. 'We're running late as it is. You and Billy go, and I'll find Rory.'

'But what are you supposed to be doing?'

'I'm supposed to be helping with crowd control, but it's more fun watching you trying to ride in a posh frock.'

'Funny. They do all know it's impossible and pretty stupid to arrive at a wedding on a horse?'

'It's for show.' Pip shrugged. 'Fairy-tale romance and all that crap. Right, come on Billy, let's deliver the blushing bride to her guests.'

Which was roughly how Lottie felt, like she was being delivered. Like some gift to the gods, a sacrifice on the altar of love. Except now it seemed as if she'd been abandoned by the groom as well as the best man.

'Well, there's no room for my big arse up there as well as hers, so I'll walk, if you don't mind.'

'I don't mind at all,' was Pip's response, 'and I'm sure Lottie doesn't, not that you should be calling her arse big.'

'My left cheek's gone numb.' Lottie decided the most secure way of sitting was completely side-on, clutching the pommel in one hand and the cantle in the other. Which might not look particularly romantic or ladylike, but gave her a better than even chance of staying on, she reckoned. Which she did, until they covered the short distance from the courtyard to the entrance of Tipping House.

'I have never been so glad to get off a horse in my life.' Lottie slithered to the ground and was capably caught by Tom, who looked very pleased with himself.

'I've been dreaming about this for years.' He grinned, took advantage of the situation and gave her a sloppy kiss on the cheek. He'd had what could only be termed a crush on Lottie when he'd first arrived in Tippermere. And despite telling himself it had to be a mid-life crisis and she was too young for him, and he'd be better off with somebody like Pip (who'd dragged him off to bed and giving him a night he'd still not been able to blot out of his mind) the desire had been real enough and kept him awake far more nights than it should have. And had amused his teenage daughter no end.

Now, though, it seemed to have sadly matured into a more fatherly affection, which was good for his blood supply, which now stayed where he needed it instead of heading into his pants. 'You look absolutely stunning.' He was generally happy to look, not touch. 'He's a lucky man.'

'He's the invisible man. I lost Rory and my flowers along the way, oh and the car. You're looking pretty good, too, you know.' And he was. These days she rarely saw Tom, and when she did he was in jeans and a big old worn t-shirt. But today there was no missing the fact that he'd been a top model in his day. He smiled and the warmth flooded his face. Tom was nice, dependable and Lottie sometimes had pangs for a similar type of man to fall in love with. At least Tom wouldn't have forgotten something and rushed off when he was due at his reception. But she really wanted a man who could ride, obviously, and was a bit more wild, and liked a dare, and…

'Penny for them?'

'I wonder if I'll ever get married, you know, for real?'

'Of course you will, beautiful Charlotte.' He took her hand and linked it through his arm, and brushed his floppy fringe back with his finger. 'Love and marriage go together, and all that.'

'But I only had the horse, not the carriage.'

'Good to be halfway there, then.'

She would have quite liked to have had a think about that one, but Tom was already keen to get going.

'Tabatha, get your arse over here and get this horse back to the stables like a good girl.' Her father's bellow echoed behind them as they walked up to the steps, the red carpet. And she really did feel as though she was a sacrifice. This was it. This was the start of a new future for Tipping House and for her. If it all worked out.

'Ready?'

Tom squeezed her hand.

'Ready.' She would have loved, more than anything, to have had Rory at her side, Rory walking with her. But he wasn't, and she'd do it on her own. She had to.

Chapter 30

Getting not-married wasn't so bad after all, Lottie concluded, as she was lifted aloft by four Premiership football players.

She giggled as they put her down and she wobbled against Sam. 'You look so gorg, babe.' There was another tear in Sam's eye as she handed her a glass of bubbly, then pulled her in close for a hug. 'It's amazing, isn't it?' She waved a hand that encompassed pretty much everything and Lottie's eyes widened as Sam's boobs threatened to break free from the sheath dress that was losing the battle to keep her covered.

Sam saw the look and giggled. 'I've got loads of tit tape on, don't worry, babe. Do you think they look bigger?' She leaned in and for a moment Lottie thought she was supposed to be giving them a close up, then realised that Sam wanted to whisper. Unfortunately the stage whisper carried alarmingly well and Lottie was pretty sure everybody within a thirty-foot radius heard.

'Well...'

'I wasn't going to tell anybody yet, but we're having a baby.'

'Oh wow. That's brilliant.' Lottie was genuinely happy for her friend, whose broodiness had grown at a faster rate than Amanda's stomach. Exactly what kind of a mother she'd make was going to be something to be seen. Sam was as warm-hearted and generous as they came, but this baby would be bling and designer from birth.

'Me and Davey,' Sam added, in case there were any doubts, 'and I think my boobs are already getting bigger. Does it happen that quickly?' She put a hand under, which boosted them further, and Lottie moved back hastily.

'I think you'll have to ask Amanda. I only know about horses and dogs and I'm sure they're different.'

'Oh she's here. Mandy! Mandy!' Sam waved vigorously, putting the tape to the test, 'isn't it all fab? You're so clever, babe, you and Lottie, putting it all together.'

'We all did it, and Lottie had the most brilliant idea in the world.' Amanda winked at Lottie, 'And the most wonderful place in the world. We, girls, are a wonderful team.'

'Aren't we just? Better than Davey and his football lads. And you're the best friends I've ever had, and I'm just so, so happy. Guess what, babe? I'm not supposed to tell anybody yet, but I'm having a little baby. Isn't it fab?' She clapped her hands. 'Our children can do everything together.' She hugged Amanda, who was too polite to say anything, but Lottie was pretty sure she looked queasy. 'It's so exciting, they can be playmates, isn't that great? Should my boobs be getting bigger already? Oo look, Lady Stanthorpe is waving.' She waved back enthusiastically. 'Should I curtsy when I meet her? I never know.'

'No, you shouldn't. Come on, she wants us over there.'

'Me too? Oh my God, my mum will be made up if she sees piccies of me with a real Lady in *Tatler* or one of those posh mags.'

Lottie gave Sam a quick nudge in the ribs when she really did look on the point of making a curtsy.

'We are having a photograph taken of you, Dominic and I, apparently, Charlotte. Three generations.' Elizabeth thrust her stick in Sam's direction, determined not to appear an old lady. Then looked more closely. 'I hope you're not cold, dear. You need to wrap up in this place.'

Sam grinned, totally unaware that it was her uncovered chest, and the length of leg on display that had caused the comment, not a concern for her welfare. 'I'm fine, thank you Ma'am.' And did a bob.

'Sam, don't.' Lottie rolled her eyes and Dom raised an eyebrow and coughed. 'Can Sam be in the pic as well, you know David Simcock's wife?' The photographer from the *Tatler* looked confused. The one standing next to him, from a gossip magazine, did a thumbs- up and looked thrilled.

By the time the last of the photographs had been taken and they were allowed to sit down to eat, Lottie was dying to kick off her shoes, and she would have done if Elizabeth hadn't caught her in the act and given her a look.

'But my feet are killing me.'

'In my day that was the least of your worries. I do wonder if we should have sent you to finishing school.' Lottie, who could think of nothing worse than learning how to walk with a book on her head (how much use was that as a life skill?), and being taught how to lay a table properly just smiled politely. 'Young Amanda has already taken provisional bookings for the next six months. I always said she'd make Dominic a splendid wife, didn't I?' Lottie nodded, it was easier to agree than debate the matter. 'I do hope somebody has brought the Rolls back and parked it at the front as I instructed.'

'You don't seem very cross about that.' Lottie glanced up from her starter. 'Gran,' she put the spoon down and frowned, 'you knew we'd run out of petrol, didn't you?'

'I never told you to have a jolly ride around Tippermere.'

'You knew Dad would.'

'Nonsense. Eat up and keep smiling, Charlotte, everybody is watching.'

Lottie fixed a smile to her face, which was quite hard when she was trying to eat soup and work out what Elizabeth was up to, and talk through her teeth.

'Did you have a nice ride?'

'Wonderful. Gran, I—'

'So difficult to sit like that on an animal. Damned good job they got rid of side saddle. He's a very helpful young man, Michael, isn't he? Sit up straight dear, don't slouch. It so unladylike, not attractive at all and you will look absolutely terrible in the photographs. I think him and that girl of his will make a splendid couple. And keep your head up or your double chins will show.'

'I haven't got—'

'Everybody over twenty has if they don't sit properly.'

'Is it true you've offered her a job, and it's you that invited her here?'

'It is, as long as Michael is happy, well somebody had to sort him out, didn't they? Who is that, over there?' She picked up her stick and waved it imperiously in the direction of one of the guests, nearly knocking the cut glass off the table. 'That young man, dapper chap.'

'I don't know.' Lottie squinted. 'Wasn't he in that James Bond film?'

'That's the one. You may introduce me later. He looks interesting.'

'But I don't know him.'

'Nonsense. Why on earth would he be here if we didn't know him.' Lottie groaned inwardly. 'And who is that with your father?'

'It's Tiggy, of course.'

'Victoria? Is it? Good heavens, I'd forgotten what she looked like when she dressed properly and put some make-up on.' Elizabeth fished her glasses out and peered over the top of them.

Lottie sighed with relief when, with the food finished, Pip appeared and pulled up a chair between them. 'This is going quite well, isn't it? You are up for a first-dance thing aren't you, Lots? They'll be ready soon.'

'But I haven't got a man.'

***

356

Mick had found the whole wedding occasion a step too far, particularly bearing in mind he'd been coerced into agreeing that the girl he'd been lusting after for months could spend a fair part of the afternoon, in a wedding dress, between his thighs. Bouncing against his groin.

Much as he wanted to honour his promise to help and support Charlotte, who he was so fond of, it was torture. Sweet, sweet torture. It was wrong to run, but it seemed so much worse to stay and be tempted by someone who he was sure would never be his.

He'd finally admitted defeat and fled when the afternoon had been topped off by the appearance of Niamh, the girl who had broken his heart and kicked his libido into touch in the not-so-distant past.

Mick much preferred, he decided, the company of animals and he had been about to calm his temper and his frustrations with a vigorous session of grooming when Dom had arrived unexpectedly, with a bottle of whiskey and a word or two of advice. 'Elizabeth brought Niamh here,' he handed a glass to Mick, 'she thinks you need to talk. And for all her faults, she's normally right.'

'Ah. And she sent you here to tell me?'

'No. I just didn't want you to get the wrong idea and think Niamh was hounding you. I'm used to my mother's games and manipulation, and I do know she always does it with our best interests at heart. Just say the word and she'll send her away just as smartly. But,' he topped up the glasses, 'she wants you to look after Charlotte. You will take her to the ball, so to speak?'

'I've never met a family like yours.' Mick gave a short laugh and knocked back the drink.

'Duty and family, it's what we do. Damned bugger at times, but it has its advantages knowing why you're here.' Dom shrugged and stood up, brushing imaginary flecks of dirt from his jacket and straightening it. 'I'm needed at the house.'

Duty and family. Mick laughed inwardly. Lottie and he really were planets apart. If she'd been born an Irish colleen, life would be different. But she hadn't. And Niamh had. And running away wasn't an option. He put the empty glass down, shut the tack-room door and, with a last glance around to check all the stable doors were secure, he headed up for a shower and a duty he didn't have to serve.

'You're here.' Lottie, who had started to feel mild panic about the dreaded first dance, couldn't believe her luck when she spotted Mick. She'd been more convinced by the second that she was going to have to dance with either her father, her Uncle Dom or Tom, all of whom were fine, except not quite what she, or the magazine editors had had in mind when it came to romance.

'I thought you'd abandoned me.' She smiled at him with the openness he loved, and flung her arms around him with the affection he wasn't quite as keen on. He extricated himself carefully.

'Now how could I do that to you?'

She straightened his bowtie, and he put a hand over hers awkwardly. Being here was one thing; intimacy was another.

'It's sure to be a good craic. How could I miss it? And how could a man leave such a beautiful bride on her own?'

Lottie was looking at him through those big eyes, a worried half-smile on her lips. 'You're not going to leave, are you? I thought you felt at home here. You said you love it here.' White teeth worried at her bottom lip.

'I do love it.' He wanted to tell her to stop, to kiss her instead. 'It's a wonderful place.'

'I'm not sure Rory does.'

'It'll grow on him, pet. Give him time.'

'But you are going to hang around?'

'Oh you can't get rid of me that easily.' He dropped a kiss on her head, and knew what he had to do, what he'd been avoiding. 'But I need to sort things out with Niamh.'

'I know you do. Does she mind you being here with me?' She looked around worriedly, but there was no sign of Niamh, although

Lottie really wouldn't have put it past Elizabeth to have her hidden behind the panelling, ready to spring out and declare her feelings.

'I don't know, I didn't ask. But your wise old gran made it quite clear to me that I had to talk to her.' He gave a crooked grin. 'And she's right.'

'Do you still love her?' Now there was the rub, the question in his mind he'd been determined to ignore.

'Elizabeth?'

'You know what I mean.' She thumped his chest.

'I need to find out and say goodbye properly if that's the way it's meant to be.'

'But you're not going to leave Tippermere are you? I'd miss you if you went back to Ireland.'

'I'm not going anywhere right now, I seem to need permission from your gran.' He gave a wry smile. 'I did think it might be for the best, but she seems to have other plans. And she's very proud of you and your plans too.'

'But I didn't—'

'You did. If you didn't love this place so much you wouldn't have come up with the perfect plan, and that, treas, is why Elizabeth entrusted it to you. You belong here, Lottie, it's a part of you.'

'So things are working out how you wanted?' Dom sat down next to Elizabeth and watched as Mick and Lottie talked, two dark heads close together. He wasn't the only person watching so closely, he was sure of that. 'Did you really want him here today?'

'He's quite beautiful, isn't he? Has that wild edge, like a stallion that's about to take off. I can quite understand the attraction. If I was a young girl myself, but sadly... Can you find me that damned stick please Dominic? I think it's nearly time I retired.'

'I've been saying that for years.'

'I mean to my room for the night, as you well know.'

'And you'll be happy with events like this taking place every other weekend?'

'It won't be every other weekend, dear boy, I'll make sure of that. Amanda has done an excellent job with the diary to ensure things are kept at a reasonable level, and I expect her to carry on doing it and supporting Charlotte when my grandchild arrives. The nanny will help.'

'And what if we don't want a nanny?' Dom's tone was mild.

'Why would you not? Anyway I've already appointed one, call it a gift.'

'Oh, mother, you're a gem.' He tried to keep a straight face and failed. 'What if we'd ended up with a Samantha-plan involving man auctions and celebrities? Would you have been so pleased? Or a Pip pop concert in the grounds once a year?'

'That was never going to happen. Philippa was joking and you know it. It was just a case of encouraging them to make their silly suggestions and I knew it would push Charlotte into taking the reins up and devising something appropriate. She loves this place, Dominic.'

'I know.'

'And I knew she wouldn't let me down.' She patted his knee. 'And I knew that once you'd chatted to her it would clear her mind, remind her of what's important. You're a good boy, dear, very logical.'

'And what about him?' Dom nodded at Mick, who was gazing at his niece.

'Oh, he has other things on his mind now. He's confused, but he'll do the right thing. And Charlotte likes him. He will be handy to have around. A nice stabilising influence.'

'Did you have one of those when you were younger, then, mother?'

'A stabilising influence? Oh yes.' A small smile twitched at the corner of her mouth. 'He was always there for your father, and he was always there for me. Very young and dashing he was, too. I did love him a little.' She fixed her son with a stare. 'And a little bit of love is a very powerful thing, but it should never be confused with something that will endure.'

'Now is that a fact, Elizabeth?' Pip plonked herself down on a chair next to Elizabeth.

'It is indeed, Philippa. As you already know. Now, where's that Rod chap?'

'Todd.' Pip corrected her automatically.

'Well?'

'He caught an early flight.' She paused. 'Back to Australia.'

Elizabeth waited.

'It'll be touch and go whether he gets there in time.'

'For his brother? I'm so sorry, Philippa.'

'I don't think they were that close, but he'd promised to go back with news and he'd wanted so much to be able to.'

'And he didn't find anything out?'

'Nope.' Pip took a swallow of wine. 'Tiggy was right. Her Will is only interested in himself. He couldn't tell us anything, couldn't even remember who Todd's mum was. Just another pretty admirer.'

'And you didn't want to go with him?'

'I had to be here for Lottie, didn't I? She's my best friend.'

'But you've told Charlotte that you are off to Australia?'

Pip grinned. 'Bossy boots. I hadn't fully decided yet.' But after today, she knew she had to. The news that Sam was pregnant had, if anything, made her mind up. Elizabeth was right, she needed to do something. Life here was changing, and she was stuck in a rut that wasn't a good fit. And she wanted to be there to support Todd. She'd told him she'd look at flights first thing tomorrow. They had unfinished business.

'I think you have decided, dear. I will miss you, but I know you'll be back.'

'I'll Skype you.'

'My eyes are too tired for that nonsense. You can telephone, and then when you've cleared your head, you can come back and tell us about it.'

'You're incredibly bossy, you know.'

'And you, young lady, have stopped doing all the things that matter. You need to get back to basics and then start poking around in people's lives again. You were a good journalist.'

Pip rolled her eyes. 'What if I don't want to poke around in people's lives any more?'

Elizabeth chuckled. 'Oh I'm sure you'll find you will. It's your basic instinct, dear. Now go and tell that conductor chap that we will be needing some music. He can warm up or whatever he needs to do.'

'Now?'

'Well, we don't want to be here all night, do we?'

***

With a carefully selected catering company and a wine merchant who was used to supplying some of the best-stocked cellars in the country, the guests had been wined and dined to perfection. Amanda had handed out every brochure she'd had printed, had filled her diary with enough bookings to mollify the bank manager and was now relieved that all that remained was the dancing and firework display.

'Not too tired, darling?' She looked up from her tablet to see Dominic, looking as immaculate and debonair as ever, watching her. 'I think mother is up to something. She's demanding the music now.'

'Your mother is always up to something.' She kissed his cheek and let him wrap his arms around her. 'It's gone well, hasn't it?'

'Wonderful, but I don't want you to overdo things.' He patted her stomach. 'Have you heard about her present?'

'Niamh? Oh yes, I've heard. I think everybody in Tippermere has. A stranger in the village is big news.' She smiled. 'She seems nice. Elizabeth sent Pip over to interrogate her and then Pip filled me in.'

'You can say no, you know.'

'We can see how things work out, and she can help Elizabeth out for now. Your mother's not as mobile as she likes people to think. She's getting older, you know.'

'I know.' He grimaced. It was something he was trying hard not to dwell on.

Amanda covered his hand with hers. 'Stop worrying, she'll be fine. Lottie's proved she can do it, hasn't she? I think she'll take good care of Tipping House and that will take an enormous load off Elizabeth's shoulders.'

'She will take excellent care of the place.' He rested his chin on her head. 'She's got quite assertive hasn't she? Mother said it would be the making of her.'

'And your mother always knows best.' Amanda smiled. 'But we don't know for definite that Niamh will stay, do we?'

'I suspect she could be here for a while, judging from the state of Mick when I caught him in the tack room earlier. Ah,' he paused, 'I think I hear music. Can I tempt you to dance, Mrs Stanthorpe?'

'That sounds delightful, Mr Stanthorpe.' Amanda's smile broadened. 'I do love you, you know. Do we have to let Mick and Lottie do the first dance?'

'I think she needs company.'

'I think she's about to get it, Dominic.'

He followed his wife's line of sight and let out a sigh of relief. 'Well I haven't a clue how Mother orchestrated that.'

Amanda smiled and hugged her husband. 'Maybe she didn't.'

Lottie was worried. Dancing wasn't her forte. Dancing on the table after a few bottles of wine at the hunt ball was one thing; smooching in a dark corner with a tipsy Rory was also perfectly within her capabilities. But on a dance floor, pressed against Mick and with most of the Kitterly Heath superstars and every Cheshire photographer that was worth his salt lining up his lens on them was quite another. There was a fairly good chance that she'd trip over the hem of her dress, or stand on Mick's toes, or just make a complete idiot of herself. She needed another drink, but the band was warming up and her gran had fixed her with the type of look that said there was no escape.

'Hell.'

'You'll be fine.' Mick took both her hands. 'They're all too pissed to care what you do.'

'I will, I will.' If she said it enough times she would be. 'I will, oh God.' Her hands flew to her mouth and every eye that had been fixed on her swivelled towards the door.

It wasn't God, but it felt as good as. It was Rory, striding into the room as though he owned it. And he had never, in his entire life (or the bit Lottie had known him for, which was most of it) looked more dashing or sexy. He was dressed for riding, in his best leather competition boots, perfect off-white breeches, his best dark jacket with tails (which Lottie noted was spotless) and a top hat, but he looked so incredibly dashing she couldn't get the words out to tell him. And he was striding across the red carpet, aiming straight for her. And for once he didn't have Tilly with him.

'You've got to listen.' She had a feeling that everybody else in the room was going to as well. But it was so nice to see him she didn't care. 'I've been a complete numbskull, I know, don't say anything.' She hadn't been about to, nor had anyone else by the look on their faces. Only the photographers had moved, edging closer like hounds to the kill. 'I love you, I can't not love you and I want you, need you. Oh, God I need you, Lottie.'

There was a loud crash as a photographer, who was perched on a ladder, leant too far forward and the whole thing toppled over, just missing a reporter, who was texting Rory's words as fast as she could to her editor. 'I was a stupid twat, I should have been there the other day but I'd lost my mobile. I didn't even bloody know about Black Gold until you were back in the yard with her.

I am so sorry, really, really sorry.'

'I know. I know you love all the horses.'

'I love you, Lots, not the horses. I want to be there for you when you need me.' He paused. 'Well I do love the horses as well, but you're the hottest girl I've ever known, even though you can be bloody annoying at times and you have the most opinionated and interfering family in the world.'

'I heard that young man.' Elizabeth, even with a walking stick, had not lost her ability to creep closer undetected.

'And you can't marry him.' He glared at Mick.

'I wasn't going to.'

'But you were with him when I finally got your message, you were—' He suddenly realised that the crowd were hanging on every word, and moved to ear level so he could whisper. 'Making out with him when I got to the stables.'

'I was not making out with anybody.' Lottie forgot to lower her own voice.

'And you came riding in with him today.'

'Only because the Roller ran out of petrol, and we didn't want Gran to know, but I think she already did.' She shot a sideways look at Elizabeth, alarmed at just how close she'd got. 'And you were supposed to take over, but you buggered off.'

'So you're not shagging him?'

'Rory.'

'And you definitely haven't married him?'

'It's pretend, I told you, it's,' she glared at Elizabeth, who was now almost on top of them, 'Gran stop listening.'

'Lottie, stop. Right.' Rory took a breath. 'Will you marry me, Charlotte Alexandra Elizabeth Brinkley? And live with me in the courtyard, because it's all we need, a small pad where I can't lose all my stuff, or you, and we've got the horses, and dogs.'

'Aww the love-nest, isn't that the most romantic thing you've ever heard?' Sam wrapped her arms round her Davey and looked up at him.

Lottie stared. Then whispered. 'But it's not a real wedding, you know.'

'I know.' He went down on one knee. 'Lottie, you're amazing.' Held her hand tightly, his gaze fixed on her face. 'Everything you've done, organising all of this, it's incredible. You're not just my funny, sexy girl, you're an astonishing woman. You will make a wonderful Lady Stanthorpe. God, I am just so proud of you.' Lottie couldn't remember the last time he'd said so many words to her, or the last time he'd made her feel like crying happy tears. 'I know I've been a complete prat, but marry me, please, this time I mean it. Let me help you do this. Please? I've thought it out, and I'll sort a proper wedding, with a vicar involved, and all your mad family, if that's what you want. Although, if I'm truthful, I'd rather elope.'

'Oh, me too.'

'Please, I adore you, Lottie, I'll look after you, help you, I promise, even if we're broke with a leaky ceiling.'

'I don't think we will be, broke that is. This was going awfully well, until now.' She looked round, half expecting to find the guests had abandoned them. But they hadn't.

'Is that a yes?' He stood up, suddenly unsure. 'Because I am actually asking this time, I mean it was a bit of a mistake last time, if I'm honest.'

'Thank heavens we've finally got that out of the way and I can retire. Dominic, help me to the stairs, if you will, and let me have a quick word with Philippa.' Elizabeth tapped her stick on the ground, but Lottie didn't hear it.

'You really want me, Rory?'

'I really want you, Lottie.'

'Even though I'm not as much fun these days and very bossy?'

He moved in, his mouth close to her ear. 'I think I might like you to show me just how bossy you can be actually.' And as he stepped back, the dirty grin was just for her. 'What do you say?'

'Oh, please.' And with a squeal Lottie covered the remaining ground between them and leapt into his arms, and, as he hadn't quite got his balance, it sent them tumbling to the red carpet. Which was how the glossiest magazines in the country got to reveal to the world that under this particular bride's dress, there was indeed something blue.

Acknowledgements

A huge thank you to my editor, Charlotte Ledger, who inspired me to write about Tippermere in the first place, then helped me make Country Affairs the book that it is.

Turn the page for more scandalous antics in Tippermere
with an exclusive extract from the first book in the series,

Stable Mates

Chapter 1

'I think he's dead.'

Rory Steel had been enjoying, in his semi-conscious state, a particularly gratifying dream, in which he was just about to clear the last cross-country hurdle that stood between him and the gallop down the home straight, when his mobile had started to buzz like an irritated hornet inches from his ear. He'd picked it up automatically, horse suspended mid-leap.

'Shit, you're kidding.' The horse dissolved, along with his dream of a perfect round, as he sat bolt upright. Something he instantly regretted as a sledgehammer came into contact with his skull and church bells started ringing in his ears. 'Fucking hell.' As he sank back on to a soft pillow, clutching his throbbing head, Rory briefly wondered if the caller had been making a pronouncement of his own demise, then decided that was rubbish. It hurt too much.

And he could see faint outlines in the dark that surrounded him, and surely death was a total blackout? He prodded his temples experimentally and decided his head probably wasn't about to disintegrate in a bloody mess. But, where the hell was he?

From somewhere in the general direction of his feet came an indignant disembodied voice, which meant he hadn't flung the phone far. Now all he had to do was find it, without causing himself grievous bodily harm.

Rory put an exploratory hand out and came into contact with skin; soft, warm skin that definitely wasn't his own. And it all came flooding back with clarity. He was in a horsebox, crammed into the bulkhead bed, with a tin roof only a foot or so above him. Which explained the ringing in his ears. And he was with Lottie.

'Bugger off.' She pushed his hand away, her voice groggy with sleep.

'I was trying to find the light switch.'

'Not heard it called that before.'

The phone was squawking, more desperate by the second, from its mystery location.

'What's that funny noise?' The words came out on a yawn as Lottie stretched, groaning as her foot came into contact with the wall.

'My mobile.'

'Well bloody answer it.' She rolled over and buried her head under the pillow, and his hand shifted to the dip in her waist before drifting down to her hip. He liked Lottie's hips.

'Proper child-bearing hips these.' His fingers tightened, in sympathy with other parts of his body.

'Huh, you mean big.' She didn't sound as drowsy now, as she swatted at his hand again and shifted onto her back. 'And don't you dare go back to playing with my boobs. Answer the phone.'

'I can't find the bloody thing in the dark, can I?' He groped further down her body, which earned him a slap, and finally his fingers closed around the lump of hard plastic, just as Lottie flicked the light on. She was shaking her head at him.

'You're hopeless.'

'And you're just so fuckable.' He blew her a kiss and stared openly at her naked body. He'd missed a lot of things about Lottie while she'd been gone, but that glorious body had been his first thought when he'd heard she was heading back.

In fact, Lottie's uninhibited nakedness had probably been what he had fallen in love with in the first place. Sometimes he found it hard to believe that he'd found someone even more disorganised than he was, and he'd found her need to flee the country even more incomprehensible. But when it came to bed and her body, her complete lack of hang-ups made her irresistible.

'Who is that? Who's there?' The voice in his ear had moved on from hysterics to a mix of suspicion and brittle annoyance and he half wished he'd prolonged his 'find the phone' game. Who knew what it might have led to?

'It's me of course, who the hell do you think it is? Who's that?'

'There is a chance, darling…' Lottie straddled him, which was no mean feat given the headspace, and his cock hardened in anticipation. He could ditch the phone right now, straight out of the window. She reached forward, those perfect breasts bobbing against him; he could already taste her kiss. Except he couldn't. She'd grabbed the phone and was waggling it in front of his face.

'Hang on, that isn't my bloody phone.'

'Exactly.' She giggled and fell sideways.

'Hello? Hello? You're not—'

'Pip.' Rory stared at the bright-pink phone in disgust. 'Hell, I'd forgotten I'd ended up with bloody Pip's phone again. Why the fuck does she keep walking off with my mobile?' Pip was lovely, Pip was totally, one hundred per cent organised when it came to work and a shambling mess when it came to everything else. And this was the third time in a week she'd picked up his mobile by mistake and walked off with it. Which left him with hers.

'Why don't you keep it in your pocket, like everyone else?' Lottie was regarding him through big green eyes, her head cradled in her hand. Mussed-up hair in a tangle round her face. A very kissable face, and he just knew that mouth would taste of sex. He leaned forward, just as she put a hand out to his chest. 'Rory, you're on the phone, remember?'

He sighed. 'I'd rather be on you.'

'Shush,' she giggled, 'she can hear you.' He made a move to chuck the phone back down the bed, but she grabbed it from him before he had chance.

'Hello?'

He trailed a finger over her slightly rounded stomach and was rewarded with a slap. 'Stop it.'

'I can't. You're irresistible, especially when you're cross.'

'You're not Pip, either.' He could hear the voice, sharp, on the other end of the line.

'Nope. It's Lottie. Pip has got Rory's mobile, her number—'

'I know what the number is, thank you.'

'Hey, is that Amanda? Hello? Amanda?' Lottie dropped the phone on his chest and flopped back. 'Well thanks to you too. She's bloody hung up on me.'

'I'm hung up on you.' He stroked a finger down one of the forbidden breasts, over the peak of a nipple. 'So, fancy a bit of mounting practice?'

'What time is it?'

Rory sighed and held his wrist up so she could see his watch. 'I really don't know why you haven't got a watch.'

'I lose them, or drop them in water buckets. And they leave tan lines.' She stretched perfectly bronzed, unmarked arms out in front of her and squinted again at his watch. 'You do know your class starts in an hour?'

Oh yeah, that was what he was doing shacked up in the crummiest horsebox that Billy Brinkley owned. With the man's daughter. They'd got to the showground and hit the whiskey and an uncomfortable, cramped bed with the long-legged shapely Charlotte had, in his drunken haze, seemed a far better bet than the comfort of the hotel that the horse's owner had booked for him half a mile up the road.

'And Flashy needs a good half-hour work-in unless you want to exit over the judge's car like she did last time.'

'Well you'd better shift your arse, hadn't you gorgeous?' He gave the bum he quite fancied fondling a shove with his foot. 'I can't exit anywhere with you in the way.'

Three minutes later the horsebox door was open and Rory Steel stood in nothing more than breeches and boots, surveying the showground. There was an early-morning spring nip in the air that did nothing to clear his head, nor did the sight of already gleaming horses being walked out.

His two least-favourite aspects of the world of eventing he competed in were dressage and small events like this. Unfortunately, Flash didn't approve of dressage either, so he'd been forced to take the sensible route and bring her to a smaller dressage competition. The other competitors would hate him because they knew who he was and considered it jolly bad form to compete at a lower level. And he'd hate every minute because there was a good chance the stroppy little mare would play up like the prima donna she was and make him look a prize dick.

Hot Flash had been named well, though as far as he was concerned it was more like Hot Flush; she was as temperamental as a menopausal woman. Not that he'd known that many, but the image of his mum at fifty stuck in his mind. She'd developed a temper worse than his dad's had ever been. Which was going some.

'Are you going to just stand there showing the world your abs or let me get past so I can get her ready?'

'I'd rather have just lain there, actually.' He ran his fingers through his hair and could swear his head was literally throbbing. 'Christ, was that whiskey you were plying me with last night bootleggers' stuff?'

'Probably. You know me, anything to get you into bed.' She grinned, which made her even more shaggable, and he couldn't resist kissing those full lips, sliding his hand round onto her firm bum so he could pull her closer.

Lottie wriggled her way past him. 'Are you going to ride dressed like that? Try distraction techniques so no one notices what a crap test you've done? I can see the headlines now,' she waved her hands in the air 'Rory Steel, the fearless eventer, beaten by a bunch of Cheshire WAGs.'

'Piss off.' His foot missed her bum by inches as she jumped down the steps laughing. It beat him how she managed to get up so bright-eyed and bushy-tailed when they'd spent the evening getting slaughtered and the night getting shagged.

***

It wasn't until Lottie was grooming the laid-back Flash that she remembered the phone call. If Pip had been calling first thing in the morning, it wouldn't have seemed strange. Pip had been shadowing Rory's every move lately. But it was Amanda. And that was just weird. Pip did horses, didn't think anything of getting up before the birds had started tweeting to get a horse ready for a show. But Amanda was a lady of leisure; well at least that's how the rest of Tippermere saw her. Marcus made the millions and his beautiful wife spent them. His extravagance had been to buy Folly Lake Equestrian Centre and sponsor one or two of the riders who frequented it, but his lovely wife had zero interest in the centre, the horses or even the riders, which was a constant source of amazement to Lottie. If she'd been married to the slightly portly and very bossy Marcus, she'd have felt entitled to eye up every single fit horseman at close quarters as a consolation prize, but the only time she'd ever spotted Amanda down at the stables was when she'd been searching out her errant husband – who had no qualms about mentally undressing every groom and female rider on the yard. Lottie reckoned he was totally shameless; he'd have shagged anything with a pulse, even the podgy dishevelled Tiggy or the bad-tempered Fliss.

Maybe Amanda was frigid. But she didn't seem like that; she'd been a bit of a laugh at the parties they'd held in Folly Lake Manor, or Follyfoot funny farm as Rory and his mates often referred to it. To them it was a majestic home for misfits. To others, like Billy, her father, it was a necessary evil in the village.

Either way, Marcus and Amanda were regarded with amused

suspicion by some, and as generous benefactors by others. But everyone agreed they threw a bloody good party.

Maybe, Lottie thought, Amanda had married Marcus for his money, and he'd married her for her looks and that was it. A shiver ran down her spine as Flash nibbled at her collar.

'Now you are going to behave for Rory, aren't you?' She knew how much he hated events like this, but Flash desperately needed some smaller venues to persuade her that dressage arenas weren't inhabited by lions. The mare was a dream in the stable, and had a jump as big and brave as her heart on the cross-country course, with flicking heels that respected the flimsy show jumps, but in the vast emptiness of the dressage arena she was like a firecracker about to go off. Lottie knew how she felt. It was like being dropped on a fashion runway in uncomfortable shoes and being told not to trip up, not that she knew much about fashion shows, but she imagined it was the same. Hushed silence, everyone watching and an acre of space poised to make a fool of you.

But in the few three-day events Rory had entered her, the cricket score of the dressage section had meant any hope of being on the leader board was doomed, even when the fiery, fearless chestnut jumped out of her skin in the other two phases of the competition.

Lottie dropped the white pad and elegant black saddle onto the mare's iridescent back just as an out-of-tune whistle announced Rory's arrival.

'Some of those plaits look like a poodle's topknot.'

'You're very lucky you didn't have to do them yourself, mate.' She bent down to tighten the girth and took the time to admire his toned thighs on her way back up. 'I'm only here because there wasn't anything else to do, and if I'd stayed on dad's yard for another five minutes I'd have screamed and hightailed it back to Barcelona.'

'Why go all the way to Spain when I'm here?' His lazy gaze drifted over her body as the soft drawl made its way straight between her thighs. Charlotte loved Rory for many reasons: his sense of humour, easy-going nature, fit-toned body, but most of all because he didn't mean a word he said. No expectations. Just fun. Which was exactly what, she'd decided she needed after leaving her shit of a boyfriend on a Spanish beach and heading reluctantly back to Cheshire, because she had nowhere else to go. When Lottie had left Tippermere one of the reasons (and there had been several) had been Rory and his complete inability to take anything, including relationships, seriously. But now she was back she'd concluded that it was actually a bonus.

'Because it's sunny there and no one gives a damn about Billy bloody Brinkley, and,' she paused in her list of some of the other reasons as she got to the crux of the matter, 'there aren't any horses.' Which was, she told herself, why she'd run first of all to Australia, then somehow ended up in Barcelona after hooking up with an adventurer who had itchier feet than she had. Todd.

It was slightly ironic that in the search for a soul mate who didn't want to be tied down or committed to anyone or anything, she'd managed to end up with a serial adulterer who also happened to be a bigamist. Spreading it around was bad enough, but the arrival of a platoon of police armed to the teeth, on the beach of all places, had been the ultimate in humiliation. It wasn't like she'd even had her best bikini on. Todd the hunter could, as far as she was concerned, go screw himself. Which might be the only option left if he got deported from Spain and stuck in the slammer.

'How boring.' Rory grinned and ran a large, capable hand through his messy curls before checking the girth. 'What the fuck do you do then, apart from drink?' He didn't wait for an answer. 'Now, do I risk working her in and scaring all the other riders out of the warm-up area, or shall I just enter at A?'

Knowing Rory as she did, she guessed it was probably a rhetorical question, but answered it anyway. 'And exit three seconds later?' She patted the docile Flash, who was looking like a tired donkey. 'I suppose it might give you a chance of getting in the top twenty if you manage to scare all the others off.' She worked on keeping a thoughtful face, but one glance of the sexily frustrated look Rory shot at her tickled her somewhere deep down and brought a grin to her face. It was hard to stay serious with him around; you either laughed with him, or, as he was so funny when he got angry, you had to laugh at him. 'I don't know what your problem is, call yourself a horseman, you could put a baby on her.' She gave the mare a dig in the ribs as the horse was now resting a leg, and leaning half a ton of horseflesh against her. 'Come on you old nag, let's go bust some balls.'

'That's what I'm worried about, busting mine.' Rory gave the mare a hearty slap on the rump as they walked out of the stall past him and flicked some shavings out of the long tail. 'Call yourself a groom.'

'No, I don't actually. Remind me not to come to your rescue again you ungrateful sod.'

Lottie watched as he buttoned up his jacket and straightened the cravat. He was the type of man she couldn't resist coming to the rescue of. One flash of that wicked grin and she came running like a bloody lapdog, well like his army of terriers. Which reminded her... 'Are the dogs okay in the back of the lorry?'

'They were trying to dig a hole in the floor when I left them, hope the floorboards are more solid than the rest of that rust bucket.'

'At least that rust bucket,' Lottie tried to look haughty and was pretty sure she'd failed, 'is one up on your posh purple passion wagon, which wouldn't even start.' The wagon was nothing like the lorry that had been gifted to Rory by one of his rich owners, who liked only the best for their darling horse. But it was the only thing Billy would lend her. This one didn't have shiny livery, full kitchen area, shower and double bed. It had space for three horses at the back, a narrow tack room with just enough room to swing a very small cat in the middle, and an 'almost' double bed squashed above the cab.

'I suppose well used and dirty,' he winked at her, 'but in full working order is better than immaculate and good-looking but can't rise to the occasion.'

She followed his line of sight straight to the upright and correct figure of her uncle, Dominic Stanthorpe. Dressage rider extraordinaire, or so a certain gushing woman's mag had once labelled him. 'Are you having a go at Uncle Dom again? And how do you know he can't rise to the occasion?' She raised an eyebrow, then held up a hand as he opened his mouth to answer. 'No, on second thoughts, don't go there. I don't want to know what the latest trailer-trash gossip is. I *like* Uncle Dom.'

'You like everyone, darling. Which is why you call so many shits your friends.'

'And are you one of those many shits?' She checked Flash's bridle as she spoke, straightening the bit, running a finger along the curb, trying not to be concerned whether he answered or not. 'Maybe you should try her in a hackamore?'

'Maybe I should put my name on the suicide watch.' His tone was dry. 'And no, Charlott-ie,' his firm, dry lips came down lightly over hers, 'I try not to shit on my own doorstep.' He pulled down the stirrup leathers and Flash, who'd gone back to resting a leg, nearly fell over as he landed lightly in the saddle.

Lottie grinned as they staggered sideways. 'Never seen a half pass performed half-mounted before. Can you do them when you're in the saddle too?'

'Smart-arse.' Rory gave her the finger and straightened his hat. 'Maybe you should let the dogs out; might be a good distraction.'

She smiled and dropped a kiss on the mare's velvet soft nose, breathing in the horsey smell. 'Try and stay in the ring this time darling.' Flash snorted in response, not a good sign, her nostrils flaring until she could see the pink lining.

'What the fuck is he doing here in this backwater, anyway?' Rory was still staring suspiciously over in Dom's direction.

Lottie shrugged. 'Gran probably told him, so he could keep an eye on us.'

380

'Oh great, so we trek all the way out here where nobody can witness my death and Elizabeth goes and spreads the word to the whole county. I wondered why it was so bloody busy.'

'You're exaggerating, about the whole county and about your death. Stop being such a prima donna.'

***

Rory and Flash were early in the running, which was a bonus as the patch of grass set aside for warming up was quiet. If they were jumping, it didn't matter how many other horses were around, Flash had the poles to concentrate on and everything else faded into insignificance. Given an obstacle-free area, though, and the horse seemed to think someone was waiting to plan a surprise, suspicion traced its way through every muscle in her body and anything from another horse to a spectator's hat was guaranteed to wind her up.

However much she teased him, Lottie knew Rory was a good rider, and so did he. He was strong from eventing, a sport not for the faint-hearted or weak-bodied, but his muscle tone was long and lean rather than the short, compact build that her show-jumping father sported. And he didn't seek to dominate, which was a saving grace when it came to a horse like Flash. He sat quietly, confidently, long legs wrapped around her – holding her in a safe embrace. When Flash spooked, he didn't react, his body going with her, his hands giving but firm.

Lottie's gaze was locked onto him. She couldn't help but watch him. He might not portray quite the picture of elegance and control that Dom did, but it was almost like he was part of the horse. His body adapted, flowed in response, shifting like he had to do during the wild cross-country rollercoaster of twists and turns, ups and downs. She flicked her gaze from Rory to Dom and back again, so different and yet so the same. And yeah, Dom was so controlled, so distant almost, in contrast to the fiery ball of energy that was Rory, that she could see why each regarded the other with suspicion.

To Dom, Rory was a wild child with no respect for his own safety, and no style. The latter probably being the most injurious to his fine sensibilities. He distrusted the man's apparent casual attitude to women, was wary of his easy sense of humour and cavalier approach to life. And to Rory, Dom was too prim and proper, totally unbending and most likely gay, which was quite an accomplishment given his parentage and upbringing.

Lottie grinned as Flash fly-bucked and Rory did a good imitation of a rodeo rider, waving one arm in the air. She could almost feel the waves of disapproval emanating from Dom on the other side of the area. But whatever they said, she was pretty sure they admired each other in some weird, indefinable way.

The judge's car horn went and Lottie checked the running order. She signalled at Rory, next in, and saw Flash's ears flicker in what could have been warning or anticipation.

Enter at C, working trot was the official first line of the dressage test. The fact that Flash entered was in fact a bonus, but there was nothing that suggested 'working' and only a smattering of 'trot' in what followed. She danced in a zigzag combination that involved trot, canter and an amazingly good pirouette. Lottie could have sworn Rory closed his eyes briefly as he silently willed the horse down the centre line.

The next few instructions on the test would have been a mystery to even an experienced onlooker. The ten-metre circle resembled a broken egg and the extended trot, which should have been a thing of controlled beauty, would have been brilliant put to music – the type of music that is played as background to firework displays. Lottie realised she was humming the 1812 Overture in time to the fly bucks and heel kicks, whilst Rory sat strangely calm on top of Flash, resigned to his fate, as if he was hacking out the quiet nag she'd appeared in the stable. They really excelled when they came to the flying change, for a moment they seemed suspended in the air as Flash decided whether to paddle desperately in an attempt to fly into hyperspace, or give up and come back to terra firma.

Lottie covered her eyes and peered through her fingers, half expecting them to come crashing down in a heap of tangled legs, and then, miraculously, as the mare's hooves hit the ground, she seemed to calm down. Maybe it was because she'd had that sensation of jumping, and it had switched her mad chestnut brain on to automatic, but something happened. She flew through the next few movements, finished the test with the kind of perfection that instilled silent awe, and then carried on flying – straight out of the ring, narrowly missing the judge's car and scattering the onlookers who'd come for a quiet day out to watch the horse world's answer to ballet.

Rory grinned and dropped the reins as the steward jumped out of the way, clipboard flying straight at the judge's secretary whose hat went one way and cup of coffee the other, splashing a passing great dane, who, with a yelp of surprise, headed off in the opposite direction, towing his surprised teenage owner, baseball cap askew, with him.

Lottie started giggling, then glanced up to find Dom had ridden over and was in front of her, staring disapprovingly down his elegant long nose. Even his horse looked like it took a dim view of the situation. 'That man really doesn't do the dressage world any favours at all.' He gave an exaggerated sigh. 'Airs above the ground aren't normally performed at this level, which even a numbskull eventer like Rory should know.' He tutted, the horse gave a discreet snort. She tried to keep the laughter in, she really did, but it hurt. Her ribs hurt, her eyes started streaming and suddenly she couldn't help herself anymore. She let it all out, howling with laughter until she was doubled up and could hardly breathe.

She paused, aware that Dom and his mount were still standing motionless in front of her. Tiny equine hooves oiled and polished so she could see a whisper of her reflection in them. She took a calming breath and wiped the tears away with the back of her hand. 'He's not that bad, and you know it.'

Dom shook his head slowly. 'I think you better go and catch them, don't you?'

'They'll be at the horsebox; Flash always heads for home when she's upset.' She blew her nose, which helped a little at calming the hysterics that had been bubbling around in her chest. 'Christ, I hope she hasn't actually headed for the main gate, she might really want to get home this time.'

Dom raised an eyebrow even further.

'Kidding. Honest. They'll be fine. Oh, good luck.'

'Thank you, Charlotte.' She half expected him to add, 'but there is no luck involved', but he didn't. He just nodded, although she could have sworn there was a glimmer of a smile chasing across his perfect features as he nudged his horse into a walk. 'Oh, Charlie,' he turned in the saddle, almost as an afterthought. 'Don't let him break your heart, will you? Men like him are never worth it, believe me.' Then he gathered his reins and trotted back across the arena.

'No heart left to break, Uncle Dom.'

***

Flash was, as Lottie had expected, by the horsebox when she got there; tied to a piece of twine and tugging lazily at a hay net, happy as an old-age pensioner on a day trip to Brighton.

Rory was sitting on the ramp, smoking a cigarette. His jacket had been discarded beside him, the cravat on top of it, his dark curls damp and flattened from the hat. He grinned. 'What kept you?'

'Couldn't keep up.' She sank down beside him, took a draw on his cigarette and handed it back. 'I'm not one hundred per cent sure, but I'd say you were probably eliminated.'

'I don't believe in doing things by halves.'

'Nope. Balls still intact then?'

'I might have to check on that one, unless you want to do it for me?'

'It's a bit public here.'

'True.' He took another long draw on the cigarette, blew a smoke ring. 'I'd sell that horse if she wasn't such a bloody good jumper.'

'Maybe next time you should warm her up in the show-jumping ring?'

'Hmm.' He stood up, ground out the cigarette butt with his boot and picked up his jacket.

'Or maybe you should just use her as a showjumper?'

'And let some idiot like your dad get his heavy-handed mitts on her?'

'Or maybe you should ask Dom to have a look at her?'

He gave her a look, which she guessed equated to something like, when hell freezes over. Then paused. 'You can, if you want.' Which was the closest he was going to get to a yes. He liked the horse, she knew he did. She could be the best on his yard, if she'd do even an average test. And she would be wasted just doing show-jumping. Cross-country was her forte. And the way she'd flown today, even Lottie could see she had paces to die for. Though 'to die for' probably weren't the right words to use where she was concerned.

'You want to check out these balls, then?'

She grinned. 'Could do, I'm good at medical things like that.'

'Right, you sort out the Menopausal Madonna and I'll give the dogs a run before we head back for a full inspection.'

He stepped off the ramp, then held out a hand and hauled her to her feet.

'Yes sir, Mr Bossy Boots.'

'Do as you're told for once.'

'Hey, don't forget this.' She picked up the bright-pink mobile phone, which he'd dropped on the ramp next to his packet of fags. 'You never said, what was Amanda calling about this morning?'

Rory dropped the phone into his pocket, his brow wrinkled as he tried to remember and she fought the impulse to stroke the lines away. 'Oh, she said he was dead.' He stared into the distance, still deep in thought. 'I presume she was talking about Marcus.'

'Marcus, dead?'

He shrugged, threw open the door of the box and stood back as the three terriers tumbled out.

'She said Marcus was dead?'

'Dunno, don't worry about it, I probably misheard. Be back in a bit, darling. Come on gang.' And he whistled the dogs up and headed off, surrounded by a whirlwind of brown and white yappiness, leaving a gobsmacked Lottie staring after him, mouth open.